Stefan Mohamed is an author, poet, occasional journalist and full-time geek. He graduated from Kingston University in 2010 with a first class degree in creative writing and film studies, and later that year won the inaugural Sony Reader Award, a category of the Dylan Thomas Prize, for his first novel *Bitter Sixteen*. He lives in Bristol, where he works as a general purpose editorial node, writing stories and performing poetry in his spare time.

# ACE OF SPIDERS

STEFAN MOHAMED

# ACE OF SPIDERS

SALT

CROMER

PUBLISHED BY SALT PUBLISHING 2016

2 4 6 8 10 9 7 5 3 1

First published in Great Britain in 2016 by
Salt Publishing Ltd
12 Norwich Road, Cromer, Norfolk NR27 0AX United Kingdom

www.saltpublishing.com

Salt Publishing Limited Reg. No. 5293401

A CIP catalogue record for this book is available from the British Library

ISBN 978 1 78463 067 6 (Paperback edition)
ISBN 978 1 78463 068 3 (Electronic edition)

Typeset in Neacademia by Salt Publishing

Printed and bound in Great Britain by Clays Ltd, St Ives plc

*For anyone who read the first book and thought*
*"ooh I wonder what happens next"*

# ACE OF SPIDERS

# PART ONE

# Chapter One

So if I'd had my way, this would be the 'previously' montage:

A frenetic and stylishly edited sequence set to some propulsive piece of rock or techno or drum and bass, showing me flying between buildings, swooping into dark alleys, kicking down doors, psychically grabbing would-be muggers, murderers, loan sharks, internet spammers and multifarious other potential evildoers and hurling them into walls, saving distressed damsels (and whatever the bloke versions of damsels are), engaging in spectacular fights on rain-lashed rooftops, chucking a few cars about (maybe at a giant monster) and generally being utterly superheroic, black coat flapping behind me in the wind, always leaving the scene of the awesomeness without giving my name. Maybe interspersed with a few headlines, done in that old-school spinning front page style.

*Who is London's new dark avenger?*

*Police baffled by plummeting crime rate!*

*'He's an absolute dream,' says smitten young damsel, 'what a shame he already has a brilliant girlfriend whom he loves, and even if he didn't, he would never take advantage of someone he'd just rescued, what an absolute bona fide legendary hero type!'*

*'I totes agree,' says smitten young boy damsel.*

And so on. Also, at some point, a shot of me walking away from a massive explosion. In slow motion.

In actual fact (record scratch), it was more like this:

Me foiling a bag-snatcher by psychically tripping them up

from across the road, because crime generally doesn't tend to happen in obvious places and it's hard to patrol a city the size of London when you're: a) just one person, and b) unable to fly around with impunity because of all the CCTV cameras. This latter fun fact was duly impressed upon me as soon as I arrived back at Connor and Sharon's house, fresh from my very first dawn flight.

Eddie (because of course he was there first thing in the morning): 'What if someone saw you? Took pictures? We agreed to keep a *low profile*! Blah blah Angel Group! Blah blah responsibility! Blah blah blah! Blah! And also blah!'

Me (trying not to sound petulant): 'But blah blah powers! Blah blah *actual* responsibility! Blah blah saving people! Blah blah helping the helpless! Blah blah *my city*! And stuff!

Eddie (trying not to totally lose his rag): 'Blah blah understandable! But blah blah dangerous! Blah blah irresponsible! Blah blah that's what the police and the justice system are there for anyway!'

Me (sounding really petulant now): 'Blah blah everything I just said again! Also *who cares?*

Oddly, this wasn't as effective a resting of my case as it seemed in my head, so I had to content myself with wandering around the city, vainly looking for crime to fight or any disasters that might be occurring. Spoiler alert – it didn't really work. In fact, the main thing I got out of it – apart from the exercise, I suppose – was a general depressed feeling, because poking your nose, however stealthily, into strangers' business mainly serves to illustrate how crap humans can be.

But did I give up? 'No!' he declared, with his hands heroically on his hips.

Well . . . not really. I might have buggered off early from a few potential scuffles, purely because the individuals involved

4

seemed like such terrible people that working out which of them needed helping felt like a waste of time.

Not very superheroic, I hear you say.

Well . . . try it yourself sometime. See how far *you* get. Also, bear in mind that on the couple of occasions when I did try to intervene directly in a conflict and break it up, I was told in no uncertain terms to mind my own effing business and sling my hook sharpish, and ended up having to creatively negotiate my way out of a beating. It was a good test, I suppose, knowing I could have decorated the walls with these fools without lifting a finger and then literally flown away, and instead opting *not* to do those things, but it rarely left me feeling satisfied.

Again, I hear you say, not very superheroic. Surely it's not about satisfaction, or a job well done? It's about helping people. Doing the right thing. Upstanding moral whatevers.

Well . . . yeah. And . . . shut up.

So there you go. I'd fully expected to spend my time living in some sort of badass superhero story, hurtling between adventures, a blur of power and selflessness zipping from burning building to bank heist to hostage situation. What I ended up with was more along the lines of a cynical, this-is-modern-London cinéma vérité documentary with footage from an aggressively good-natured indie romance spliced in.

This romantic aspect made for a much more enjoyable focus, so now the desaturated theoretical superheroics fade into brightly lit scenes of niceness. I'd spent a lot of my first London summer – when I wasn't recovering from my encounters with child-eating monsters and mysterious corporations – missing Kloe, as her parents had conveniently decided that a very long impromptu family holiday would be a capital idea. We both knew that this was their passive-aggressive, highly roundabout way of ensuring that she didn't spend any time with me, but they ended up regretting it when she spent the whole holiday sulking and chatting with me on the internet. Kloe is a luminous ray of sunshine in human form, a genuine supernova of joy and love and enthusiasm, but boy, when she decides to sulk, winter comes early. Like, now is the nuclear winter of our discontent.

As a fairly prolific sulker from way back, I respect that.

My second London summer, which was fading to autumn as the opening credits roll on this new tale, was a different matter. Kloe had spent a *lot* of time working on her parents, wearing them down, and after a couple of hideously awkward dinners that had tested my acting-like-a-regular-human-being skills to their absolute limit, they had finally relented, and we'd been able to spend pretty much the whole summer together. We'd gone to a music festival in Wales, explored London, gone to gigs, watched films, got drunk (which it turns out I'm not very good at), started having sex (which it turns out is bloody brilliant and also none of your damn business), all the good stuff that one does. The rest of the time I'd worked at 110th Street, read a lot of comics, systematically listened my way through Skank's extensive music collection, recorded a series of relatively popular 'stop-motion' YouTube videos in which I psychically re-enacted scenes from films and TV series with action figures, and generally, if I'm honest, had a pretty sweet time of it.

The itch hadn't gone away, though. The feeling that there was more to be done, a bigger, stranger, scarier, more exciting world to explore. People to save, and also fight. So despite my misgivings about the general attitude of London's populace, and the futility of wandering around looking for trouble, I did it anyway. 'Cos that's what the hero does.

At least, I told myself that's why I was doing it.

Roll opening credits.


'Big Issue, pal?'

I jumped, having left my ninja cat reflexes at home, and took off my headphones. I was pretty sure I'd heard him right, even over the screech of Tom Morello's guitar, and the red and white *Big Issue* uniform was another clue, but I said 'Sorry?' anyway because that's what my mouth had decided was happening. The guy wore thick glasses that looked to have been Sellotaped together more than once, and had a masticated bush of ginger hair, and his grin exposed a load of gaps with a few teeth here and there to break up the monotony. The teeth themselves looked like old, chewed-up Werther's Originals. '*Big Issue*? Top of the range reading material for the discerning pedestrian. And it's my last one, which means I can bugger off home.'

I smiled. 'Yeah, sure.' I bought it and the dude thanked me and went off whistling. I rolled the magazine up, tucked it away in my coat and resumed walking. It was late September, a week after I'd turned eighteen, and I was in Peckham on what I optimistically called my evening patrol, trying to lose myself in the labyrinth of fried chicken outlets, betting shops and bus stops, to be a shadow, an invisible element rippling through the urban sprawl. Either the *Big Issue* guy had super-developed senses, or I wasn't doing a very good job. I tried to do a patrol most nights, and luckily this month had been markedly cooler after the heat of the summer, which meant that I could wear a coat and keep my hood up. Much better uniform. Plus it's tricky to hide your identity when you're just wearing shorts and a T-shirt.

As I walked, I did my best Sherlock Holmes impression, sizing up the people I passed, projecting (i.e. inventing) backstories for them, trying to work out where they'd come from, where they might be going and, most importantly, whether they might be about to start some trouble that might require a spot of righteous smacking down. Was that bearded man in the duffel coat on his way to purchase a shit-ton of heroin from some dodgy Russians? Might the deal turn sour? Might someone need to swoop in and whip away their AK-47s, flip their car over and tie them all up, leaving them in a neatly-wrapped package for the police with a note gaffer-taped to one of their foreheads simply signed 'A Friend'? Maybe, but it was academic because the bearded man in the duffel coat was going in the other direction and I didn't fancy turning around and following him.

If it seems as though my heart wasn't quite in this, that's because it wasn't.

Part of that was undoubtedly because I'd been given a tantalising taste of a genuinely deeper, darker, weirder world, which had then stubbornly refused to reveal any more of itself. No more monsters, and nothing to indicate that the Angel Group had any interest in me whatsoever.

Not that that diminished my interest in them. I'd bought myself a pretty flash laptop, and one of my new favourite hobbies was researching weird stuff on the internet. Turns out there's a lot of it about, although frustratingly little of it pertained to my new ultimate foe, or uneasy potential ally, or whatever the hell they were. The company kept a very smart, very vague, very corporate website, with no lists of key personnel or anything that might be construed as useful – even their 'about us' section was written in such densely coded business wonk speak that you'd need a PhD in advanced hypereconomics to work out if they even provided a service that you needed. The most helpful words were 'brokering', 'investment' and 'compliance'.

*What were you expecting, to be fair? Menu tabs for 'monster research', 'superhero research', 'evil plots' and 'ultimate shadowy purpose'?*

Maybe not. But the name was definitely out there, in the real world (i.e. not the internet). I'd been surprised to hear it coming from somebody who hadn't been involved in the craziness at the Kulich Gallery, although having talked to the guy for a bit he did seem like the type to know this stuff.

8

*Flashback sound effect.*

His name was Damien. He was an older guy, approaching thirty or possibly beyond, heavily dreadlocked, clad from head to ankle (he was barefoot, obviously) in hemp and beads and existing in a permanent fug of weed smoke. I'd met him at Bubble Hill, the festival Kloe and I had been to during the summer. He was a friend of a friend of a friend's dealer, or something, and he and I had ended up talking extensively, sitting around a fire with various colourful casualties while Kloe was off dancing with Lynsey. Damien was a veritable repository of conspiracy theories, everything from 'the moon landing' (his implied inverted commas) to chemical sky-engineering, and most of it had been pretty entertaining, until he'd casually mentioned the Angel Group. My ears had immediately pricked up, and he'd noticed. Stoned but still sharp. 'You've heard of them?'

'Yeah,' I said. 'Vaguely. Just another corporation, I thought.'

Damien laughed. His laugh was like someone chewing a cork mat. 'No such thing, bro. Goddamn corporations will be the ruin of this little world of ours . . . and the Angel Group's one of the worst.'

'How come?'

'They got *ties*,' said Damien. 'I mean, it's all connected once you get to the top – businessmen, politicians, religious leaders, doesn't matter what country they're from. At the top of the tower, where the money's free-flowing and endless, even if they're supposed to be at war, even if *officially* they are, even if the papers are reporting battleships trading bullets, even if their disciples are blowing themselves up in crowded market places, the guys at the top are all just chatting away, seeing who they can screw over to make each other richer.'

It made some kind of paranoid sense. Plus, I'd once split

9

open the head of a child-eating creature shaped like a mutated man and a pair of multi-mouthed spidery black hell-beasts had popped out to greet me. Something like that tends to redefine your perception of what's ridiculous and what isn't.

'But the Angel Group's got fingers in *all* those pies,' Damien continued. I had a feeling he'd practised this routine. 'Every one. Cyber espionage, big oil contracts, elections, geo-engineering, they've always got a representative sitting at the back, taking notes.'

'You're saying they're pulling the strings? Secretly? *Everywhere?*'

'Something like that,' said Damien. 'Plus, you've heard about all the weird shit that goes on, right? *X-Files*-y stuff? Extrasensory perception, kids with powers. *Monsters?*'

'Heard a bit,' I said, uncomfortable but also kind of enjoying knowing far more than I was letting on.

'*That's* where they live,' said Damien. 'The way we figure it, they keep someone at every big meeting in the world, to keep up with what's going on, and they've got people implanted in every government, every military organisation. Means they can come and go as they please. Do worse things. Stranger things. More evil and messed-up things.'

'Like what?'

'If I knew anything specific, they'd have killed me by now,' grinned Damien. Through the flames, against the sky, he looked vaguely demonic. 'Although I've heard whispers about black sites where they test out experimental torture techniques. Imagine Gitmo reimagined by H.P Lovecraft.'

*Sounds like fun.*

*Also, I wish I'd thought of that phrase.*

He'd recommended a blog to me, called Weird, Sister. It was run by some anonymous conspiracy theorists, and counted among its scoops an exhaustive and, as far as I could see, accurate timeline of the movements of Smiley Joe – minus being axed in the head by yours truly – and fairly detailed reports of what sounded like empowered people: a couple in the UK, some in America, one or two in Europe and the Middle East. I wasn't sure what to make of those.

I wasn't sure what to make of any of it.

Freeze frame on Damien's creepy grin, then smash cut back to the present.

A man emerged from a chicken shop yelling into a phone. 'You'd better not be telling me this bruv! You know this ain't what I want to hear!' I slowed down, pretending to peruse the menu in the window, but the guy was in a taxi and away before I could hear any more of his conversation. I made a face that suggested I'd decided I didn't fancy chicken after all, for the benefit of anyone who might be watching – *no-one's watching, kid, literally no-one cares* – and headed onward.

It may sound facepalmingly obvious, but things felt so different here compared with things up town, where I'd been patrolling last night, that it might as well have been another city altogether. It was, effectively. Up there, it was all smooth, creaseless suits and severe hair cuts, slimline specimens with shiny black briefcases muttering into hands-free devices, like NPCs in some cyberpunk RPG, albeit one with the punk aspects heavily dialled down. As though if you stopped to talk to them, you would get one of three possible responses: 'Leave me alone, I'm late for a venture capitalist roundtable'; '100100010101110001'; or '. . .'. Up there, the buildings were clean and anonymous, the cameras gleamed and the polluted air somehow managed to smell more expensive than the polluted air down here. It was kind of a trip to wander around amongst all that weird, characterless opulence, but I couldn't help but think that the only way I'd foil any evildoing in that part of town was to wander into random buildings and threaten people into divulging exactly how much tax they weren't paying.

Maybe at some point I'd give that a go.

I'd already tried various different tactics during my year of attempted superhero-ing. By far the most moody and dramatic was lurking on the roofs of buildings, hood up, scanning the streets below, listening, but that was also arguably the least effective (in relative terms – none of my methods were effective) because I didn't have super-hearing or super-sight. Hanging around waiting for police sirens, meanwhile, was a good idea on paper, but have you ever tried following a speeding police car on foot? On a couple of occasions I'd tried to follow them via the rooftops, moderating my brief bursts of flight so they seemed more like parkour than anything supernatural, but even when I managed to follow the police all the way to the scene of the crime I'd been confronted with a truth that, in hindsight, should have been obvious – if the police were there, my presence was basically redundant.

I kept walking, eyes darting from person to person. A girl in a red hoody: I imagined us duelling psychically, cars rolling, lampposts bending, shop windows shattering with the force of our mental blows. An old man with two heavy bags of shopping: I imagined him pulling off his face, revealing it to be a dastardly, highly convincing flesh mask, reaching into his shopping bags, revealing them to be full of guns, and firing at me and being oh-so-surprised to find that I had *goddamn superpowers*. A trio of teenaged boys listening to something grimy through an inadequate phone speaker, leering at passing women and spitting on the pavement: I imagined beating them up, just because they were obviously massive wankers.

Before I knew it I was standing at the edge of an estate, scarred tower blocks looming over me, eyeing this interloper with suspicious, hooded eyes. Dying street lamps buzzed feebly as I stood there and debated whether or not to enter.

*Sod it.*

I went in, striding purposefully. Suddenly my ghostly shadow act seemed pointless. I wanted to be noticed.

*Come on.*

*Come at me.*

*Someone come at me.*

The place was oppressive, dripping with sadness, potential gone mouldy. I couldn't work out what I was feeling. On the one hand I was itching for something, some kind of trouble, a battle, a fire, anything. On the other, I felt sorry for anyone who had to live here. Not because there was anything shameful in it, just because it was so *depressing*. The tiny flats, packed so tightly into ugly, charmless buildings. The grubby windows and grim stairwells. Even the graffiti seemed weirdly defeated. A few people passed me: a woman with some shopping, head bowed, a young man nodding moodily along to whatever was in his headphones, a man in a big coat and a woolly hat, trudging exhaustedly. None made eye contact. I considered approaching a group of kids who were sitting around a minirig, blaring out some hip-hop and sharing a joint, but what was I going to do? Demand to know where their dealer lived? Ask if anyone had a knife on them? Tell them to go and do their homework? Ask how it felt when everyone, even someone like me who liked to think of themselves as reasonable and decent, automatically assumed that they were doing something dodgy?

I kept walking, my confrontational pose shrinking away until I was just another faceless figure, head down, hands pocketed. The longer I spent in there, the more ashamed I felt of my reason for being there, and eventually I thought *balls to this* and headed home, stopping on the way to grab a milkshake.

Connor was already in bed when I got back, but Sharon was

awake, drinking tea and reading at the kitchen table. She smiled tiredly. 'Hello, young man. How's the world?'

'Still there.'

'Good to know. Tea?'

'No thanks, I won't sleep if I have caffeine now. Whatchya reading?'

'Sociology. As you do.'

'As you do.'

Sharon looked at me for slightly too long, and I shifted uncomfortably. 'What?'

'You didn't get into any trouble, did you?'

'I wish.'

'I'm serious.'

*Me too.* 'No,' I said. 'No trouble. Just wandered around. No flying. No fighting. No nothing.'

'Please don't go looking for it,' said Sharon. 'If it finds you, that's one thing . . .'

'I'm not looking for it,' I shamelessly lied. 'You don't need to worry.'

Sharon nodded, although she obviously knew. 'Good. I do worry . . . but so does Eddie. And then he nags. Everyone.'

*Yeah.* 'I know,' I said, offering what I hoped was a charming and reassuring smile. 'I'm always careful, anyway. *Nos dda.*'

She laughed. 'Good night in Welsh to you too.'

I sat at the window in my room, staring out at the dark garden, brooding. I thought about Tara. It was her birthday in a few weeks and I needed to pick an appropriately awesome present. Turns out that I'm not that brilliant at coming up with gift ideas for eleven-year-old girls. I pictured her as I'd first seen her, on our first meeting, blonde curls and red pyjamas, so calm and curious, even though she'd been kidnapped by the worst thing in the world. I remembered us sitting together, waiting for Smiley Joe to come, and her face when she unknowingly saved me from a fatal bullet wound. My daughter, whom my future self had somehow brought back through time. To save her.

But from what, I had no idea. Not the faintest clue, not an inkling of how it all fitted together. All I knew was that she was mine, mine and Kloe's. I pictured Kloe, a hundred miles away in Sixth Form in Wales, and my stomach did another lurch. This one hurt, although it was a good hurt, in a way. It was kind of nice to wallow in it, to wax self-indulgently poetical, and for a long moment I daydreamed myself away, imagining her face spelled out in snow, running water, icicles dangling delicately from frozen rose petals. I pictured her in flaming autumn leaves, in a clear sky, in layers of spilled ink. If I imagined hard enough I could almost feel her kisses . . . but I could never keep it up (quiet at the back) for long. Even though it was all occurring in my own mind, it made me feel embarrassed, as though someone were peeping in, spying on my private, silly little romantic brain videos and laughing, and I tossed the dream aside and adopted the pensive frown of the moody superhero.

*You're too meta for your own good, kiddo.*

I thought about my parents. They'd divorced in the time I'd been away, which had seemed like the best outcome for all concerned, and my dad was apparently living several miles away with the woman who used to occasionally clean our house. I found this blackly amusing, as she wasn't exactly a fountain of charisma, and the idea of my dad having the energy or patience for courting was faintly ludicrous. I felt bad for my mum, though. I hoped she could find someone else. I knew that Kloe went to see her from time to time, that they got on well, and every now and then I gave her a ring, just to keep in touch, but it wasn't my life any more. Kloe had friends and school and stuff up there, and I had . . . what I had here. My friends and my powers, and Jack's sense of futile frustration.

I wanted to fly. I wanted to bathe in the air, roll on the

thermals like a peregrine falcon, do backstroke thousands of feet above the ground. I wanted to swoop and dive. I wanted to use London, use its geography, its buildings, as a playground. Jump off the Shard with 'Baker Street' playing on my mp3 player, then pull up into flight just as The Best Saxophone Riff Ever™ came in. Or walk down the street with my black coat flapping in the wind, listening to 'Wake Up' by Rage Against The Machine, then take off, *Matrix*-style, just as the main riff dropped. COME ONNN.

I just wanted to be *out there*, doing things. Investigating crimes, kicking down doors, throwing bad guys through windows, making threats, combing the streets for evildoers. I wanted to be by Eddie's side while he did his hard-man thing. Considering that I'd already been involved with plenty of unpleasant violence, I was practically itching for some more. And failing that, I wanted to be in Blue Harvest tapping my feet to some good jazz, or high above the streets, keeping a watchful eye, or just shooting the shit with a talking beagle. I didn't want to be sitting inside thinking about all the things that I wanted.

I lazily floated a few of the twigs that had collected on the back lawn, made them spin around one another and snapped them one by one, scattering the debris to the wind. I thought about doing some drawing, but couldn't be bothered. I thought about reading, but didn't fancy it. After a while I just went to bed, stewing quietly in the dark.

If only I'd known that somebody was going to try to kill me a week and a half later. That would have cheered me right up.

# Chapter Two

I T WAS A Thursday. We were about ten days into October
and the weather had taken a perversely warm, cheerful turn,
and I spent my lunch break sitting by the river, eating a burrito
and finishing the latest *Saga* trade paperback. It was a carefree
day, a light-on-your-feet day, which was ironic considering what
was going to happen.

Back at the shop, systems were operating within normal
parameters. Skank, my bushy-bearded Zen geek boss – who also
did a pretty good line in heavy weaponry, a fact that nobody
seemed particularly inclined to talk about – was at war with
a number of online forums, so barely spoke except to say 'yes
please' or 'no thanks' when offered coffee. Connor was currently
splitting his time between 110th Street and various labouring
jobs around the city, where his super-strength was apparently
coming in pretty useful. At least, according to Sharon. Connor
and I seemed to have forgotten how to have extended conversations lately. It was troubling, but I didn't really know how to
address it, so I did what any self-respecting eighteen-year-old
would do and totally ignored it.

And while I was a little bit jealous that he was using his
powers for something useful – and making some half-decent
dollar into the bargain – this did mean that I was often able
to declare myself *de facto* king of the shop, which was a good
feeling.

Being in charge this afternoon involved sitting by the register, reading, drinking coffee and bantering with Nailah. She was

about twenty-five and possibly Nigerian, and had first come in to the shop at the beginning of the year. Now she was a regular, popping in at least once a fortnight to peruse the weirder, more out-there indie comics that few other shops stocked, and to chat. Well, chat or wind Skank up, something that she did with an effortless skill that was beautiful to behold. He was indisposed today, though, so we were talking about music. 'The Beatles are overrated,' said Nailah. 'Discuss.'

'No.'

'No? No we're not discussing it?'

'No, they're not overrated. Here endeth the discussion.'

'Correct answer.'

'Obvz.'

'I only brought it up because my friend dropped it on me the other day.' She rolled her eyes and tossed her intricately braided hair. 'We were chatting about punk, which led to other talk of old guitar men, and then suddenly, out of nowhere, boom. "The Beatles are overrated, you know". I'm pretty sure he was just saying it to get a rise out of me.'

'Did it work?'

'Obviously,' she said. 'You can't expect to spout heresy like that unchallenged. And I'm not even their biggest fan. I mean, there's a lot of their music that I love, but they're fairly far down my list of people I'd listen to day to day. Stevie, Aretha, Dusty, MJ, pretty much everything that happened in the Nineties. That's my bread and butter. But you can't claim to have an interest, knowledge or passion for the history of western popular music and just handwave the Beatles' contribution away like it's nothing. History is history and facts are facts, whether you like them or not. Do you concur?'

'We are in concurment.'

'So I took great pleasure in explaining exactly how wrong he was. And eventually it came out that he'd only ever listened to one of their albums all the way through. The compilation with all the number ones on it. And he might have been made to sing 'Yellow Submarine' at school.' She shook her head, drumming her fingers on the counter. They were festooned with rings and it made a perilously loud noise, and I saw Skank twitch out of the corner of my eye.

'Ludicrous,' I said. 'So did you school him?'

'Oh, I schooled him,' said Nailah. 'I school-of-rocked him. Probably didn't convince him, but I definitely made him wish he'd never brought it up in the first place. I was about to take him track-by-track through their undisputed best album, which is obviously *Revolver*—'

'*The Beatles*,' interjected Skank, not taking his eyes from his computer screen. 'Popularly known as the White Album.'

'Really?' asked Nailah. 'White Album? *Best*?'

Skank didn't answer.

'Yeah,' I said, feeling emboldened, 'really, Skank? Best? Not "your personal, subjective favourite"?'

'Remember who pays you.'

'Yeah, Nailah,' I said, without missing a beat. '*Obviously* the White Album is their best.'

'Thank you,' said Skank.

'Or maybe *Abbey Road*.'

'This conversation can serve no purpose any more,' said Skank. 'Please talk about something else, I need to concentrate.'

Nailah shot me a sly look, and we talked quietly about less contentious matters, like government surveillance, until closing time rolled around. She paid for her comics and left and I grabbed my headphones. 'See you tomorrow, Skank,' I said. 'Good luck on the forums.'

'The war rages on.'

Deciding not to head home immediately, I wandered into town listening to Jimi Hendrix. I wasn't on a mission.

I had no agenda. It was just a perfect afternoon for wandering. In fact, I got so utterly absorbed in walking and vibing with my music that I might well have been shot in the head had a passer-by not screamed at the sight of a gun. Being an ultra-attuned, hyper-aware superpowered sort, I managed to spin around just in time to think my assailant's gun away. Unfortunately, the psychic move was sloppy, so I also sent my headphones plunging off the pedestrian bridge that we were on, taking a brief echo of 'Voodoo Chile (Slight Return)' with them.

Said assailant was a tall dark-haired guy in a suit. Nasty eyes, nastier mouth, skinny but in that wiry way that suggested he could still deal out some swift pain. Before I could say or do anything he came at me, wielding a wickedly sharp knife that seemed to have been ejected from his sleeve. I thought that weapon away too, my heart earthquaking in my chest, and in hindsight I kind of have to admire the conviction of the guy's next move, which was to charge at me and send us both straight over the edge of the bridge towards several lanes of fast-moving traffic.

So there I was, falling through the air. My brain had one of those long moments where everything seemed to slow to less than a tenth of the speed of reality, as it attempted to make sense of the situation in which I had found myself. It failed. Maybe it was because the situation was completely unprecedented. Or maybe it was simply because it's hard to form a coherent thought when you're plunging backwards off a bridge. To be fair to my brain, though, it did manage one coherent, albeit unfinished, thought.

*My headphones . . .*

The drop was at least twenty feet, possibly more, and my brain was screaming *fly*, but it was all I could do to stop my new mortal enemy from crushing my windpipe with his long fingers.

I had just about enough concentration left over to slightly slow our descent.

THUD.

*Ow.*

*Very* slightly.

I landed on my back on the roof of a double-decker bus and bounced, my assailant flying head-over-heels towards the other end of the vehicle. I was half-winded but forced myself to jump up and we faced each other, his face grim and set, mine a mess of pissed-off confusion. The bus was moving at about twenty miles per hour, which isn't that fast if you're inside it or watching it from a vantage point of elsewhere, but if you're standing on the roof it's fairish quick. I could see people from other cars watching us at the periphery of my vision, and hoped that I could take care of this guy before the police arrived, which they surely would. They only ever seemed to be on hand when I could really do without them. 'Who are you?' I said, pulling up my hood. Might as well attempt to maintain anonymity.

The guy stayed silent, his hand rattlesnaking into his pocket and withdrawing another knife. *All right, Knifey McLoadsofknives.* He lunged, and I stepped wobbily around him and ripped the blade from his grasp with my mind, tossing it away into the traffic. At the last minute I realised that it might slash somebody's tyres and I caught it again and flung it towards the Thames, which was flowing dark green and murky a little way to my left. Now the guy aimed a kick at my head and I jumped backwards, landing right at the front of the vehicle, arms flailing. *Balance, balance.* I created a tentacle of mental energy, coiled and sprung it like a whip, wrapping it around his ankles and flipping him onto his back. He wasted no time, righting himself quickly and coming at me with a flurry of kicks and punches.

*This isn't getting either of us anywhere, just fly away!*

*I'm not running away.*

21

*I didn't say run away, I said—*

I threw a punch of my own, which was stupid, because punching is not my thing. He caught the blow with embarrassing ease, performed some kind of martial arts move and twirled me around so that he was behind me with both of my arms locked in an agonising grip. Two more seconds and he was going to break them.

*Remember, dirty is allowed.*

I stamped on his foot as hard as I could and his grip lessened for a second, giving me a window to wriggle free and slam my head back, straight into his face. The crack sounded break-y - *good* - and I pivoted on the spot and kicked him clumsily but efficiently in the chin. He wobbled but immediately came at me again, his face contorted scarily with rage.

*Now fly, you plank!*

OK.

I jumped off the bus and flew over to the next lane, alighting gracelessly on a lorry, trying to make it look more like a leap than flight, for the benefit of the million or so CCTV lenses and phone cameras that were no doubt trained on us. We faced each other from our respective vehicles and his face was so full of fury that I really wished I knew what I'd done to piss him off so much.

*Apart from break his nose?*

*Well, he did attack me before that.*

Then he did something that was more than a bit stupid. He stepped back, tensed himself up, ran and jumped the gap between the two vehicles, crashing into the side of the lorry, barely managing to keep his grip and avoid falling into the road. It was a big gap to jump and I suddenly wondered whether he was empowered. It didn't seem likely - why wouldn't he have used his powers while we were fighting? The fact that he hadn't quite made it, and was now flailing around trying to pull

22

himself up onto the lorry, also suggested that maybe he wasn't supernaturally-endowed. *Just really good at jumping, then.* I stood there stupidly, looking down at him, trying to think of what to do.

*Stamp on his hands! Stamp on his hands, you knob!*

*But he could die.*

*No, really?*

*He might not die . . .*

*He probably will.*

*And I don't kill people.*

*He'd quite happily kill you. He probably will in a minute if you don't do something.*

It was tempting. More tempting than I wanted to admit to myself. This joker had just attacked me out of nowhere, pulled a gun and two knives and thrown me into the traffic, and I had no idea who he was.

*Stamp on his hands.*

*No. Better idea.*

*Better?*

*Well. Not worse, maybe.*

I kicked off from the lorry and shot up, grabbing the guy's ankles with my mind and heading away from the road and over the trees with him held in place beneath me, suspended upside-down. When we were over the river, I stopped and looked down at him. 'All right. Enough pissing around. Who are you?'

He didn't answer, choosing to struggle impotently instead. 'Do you work for the Angel Group?'

The look in his eyes told me nothing. 'Why were you trying to kill me?'

No answer.

'I'll drop you in the river.'

He actually smiled at that. 'I can *swim*.'

*Fair play. Not the most threatening of threats anyway. Also, hey, he can talk.*

'All right,' I said. 'I'll hold your head under until your face turns blue and your brain seizes up and then I'll let you float away, and the coast guard can retrieve your waterlogged corpse.'

For a moment his eyes narrowed, as if he wasn't sure whether I was bluffing, but he could read me, I could tell, and he simply shook his head with an amused smile. *Balls.* 'Fine,' I said. 'I'll carry you to the sewage works and you can claw your way out of a billion tons of other people's shit and piss, how about that?'

The nauseated look on his face was very entertaining, but I could tell he wasn't going to give me anything. I couldn't decide what to do. I definitely couldn't kill him, but I couldn't just let him go, either. I was tempted to follow through on my sewage works threat but I knew that in the long run, despite being a laugh, it probably wouldn't help. What the . . .

*Give Eddie a call.*

I took out my phone, making a concerted effort not to think about all the people who were probably watching and snapping away with their own phones, and dialled my cousin's number. 'Hello?' he said.

'It's me.'

'Stanly? How's it going, what are you—'

'Some bloke just tried to kill me.'

'What? Are you—'

'I'm fine.' I knew it was rude to interrupt, but I needed to get this over with. Plus I had hardly any credit left. According to Kloe, I was the last person in the universe to still be on Pay-As-You-Go. 'I'm currently dangling him upside-down over the Thames. He's not talking, and I'm not really sure what to do with him.'

'Um . . .' A second of muffled conversation. Then: 'Connor

24

says take him to the shop. We'll meet you there. I'll call Skank and let him know.'

'OK. Cheers.' I hung up. A quick set of mental calculations. 110th Street wasn't that far, but I couldn't just parade this guy around while I looked for a taxi. That meant flying, very high, during the day, which was something I absolutely, positively, almost never did.

*But . . . desperate times and all that . . .*

I looked up, tightened my psychic grip on my would-be killer and jetted skyward as fast as I could, riding the familiar rush of oxygen, cold electrical shivers spidering down my spine. To his credit, the guy wasn't screaming.

*He obviously knows who you are, what you can do.*

*Yeah, but being dangled upside-down hundreds of feet above the ground, unsure of whether you're going to plummet to your doom or not? I'd probably be screaming.*

*Well, we've learned a lot about ourselves during this whole fiasco haven't we, Captain I-Would-Totally-Be-Dead-Right-Now-If-It-Wasn't-For-Blind-Luck?*

*Damn you, Hendrix.*

I stopped for a second to take in the view. The city looked small but huge at the same time, miles of skyscrapers and homes and railway lines and snaking, intricate roads. I could see the Gherkin, the Shard, St Paul's, the breathing green expanse of Hyde Park. Cars and people going about their tiny, insignificant business. I allowed myself a moment of breathless appreciation, because there should always be time for that, before motoring in the direction of 110th Street with my passenger squirming beneath me.

# Chapter Three

I STAYED HIGH for the duration of the flight, then shot groundward. I was aiming to land as quickly as possible and ended up overdoing it slightly, hurtling into the shop's junk-strewn backyard and landing bumpily, keeping the guy suspended in space – above me at this point, as I didn't want to pancake him before we'd had a chance to question him. I managed to regain my balance and spun my murderous passenger around several times, very fast, before dumping him head-first into a dustbin. His legs flailed comically as he attempted to right himself, failed spectacularly and collapsed on his side with a clatter and a moan.

Skank emerged from the shop, looking unpeturbed, which was a specialty of his. 'Stanly,' he said, as though we hadn't seen each other for a couple of days.

'Skank. How's it going?'

'Same as always.'

'That bad, huh?'

That got a slight smile. 'Not as bad as you, by the sounds of things.'

'Not been a great evening so far,' I said, nodding towards the dude in the bin. 'Bit of a ball-ache, actually. This clown just tried to kill me.'

'Is that right?' Skank inspected the undignified pile of man and bin with mild interest, as though I regularly brought assassins round for tea and interrogations, pursed his lips thoughtfully for a second, then reached behind his back and pulled a gun from the waistband of his shorts. He drew back the hammer with a lack of menace that still managed to be pretty menacing, and spoke quietly. 'Could you go and unlock the cellar while I keep an eye on your wee pal?'

'Sure thang.' I entered the maze of science fiction and fantasy paraphernalia, observed quizzically by cardboard cut-outs of Buffy, Judge Dredd, Imperial stormtroopers and characters from *Adventure Time*, retrieved the keys from their brass hook and unlocked the cellar door. I called to Skank to let him know it was open and headed down into the bowels of the shop. Heated by an ancient, ill-tempered boiler that grumbled like a snoozing troll, the space – Skank called it his office, I called it his lair – was a chaotic jumble of rare, framed posters, shelves of ring binders in which he kept important paperwork and other business gubbins, and random bits and pieces: old broken action figures, boxes of variousness, piles of newspapers and magazines tied up with yellowed string. A desk in the middle of the room, with two black swivel chairs on either side of it, held an old typewriter, a pile of paper, a *South Park* ashtray, a coffee-stained Boba Fett mug and a tin with a cartoon of Bob Marley on it. *Wonder what's in there.* Another table held a pair of half-dissected record decks, a pile of tools and several stacks of records. The place smelled of coffee, old smoke and old stuff.

Skank appeared a few moments later. He had tied the guy's hands and feet together and was making light work of dragging him down the stairs, and when he got to the bottom he threw him unceremoniously into a chair and set about tying him to it with garden twine. I was starting to feel uneasy. I'd only ever seen Skank the eccentric proprietor, the guy who argued with customers who thought that the 1998 American *Godzilla* could be considered an official Godzilla film, who was often stoned beyond the capacity for human communication at nine in the morning, and harboured what seemed to me to be an unreasonable dislike of Sylvester McCoy's Doctor (or 'that question-mark-wearing buffoon'). Now, standing in front of my bound attacker with a gun in his hand, he was giving me uncomfortable *Pulp Fiction* vibes. 'Has he said anything?'

'Nothing,' I said. 'Apart from telling me that he can swim.'

Skank nodded. 'Fair enough. We'll skip the waterboarding then.' He pulled up one of the swivel chairs, sat in it and started to roll a cigarette. 'You might as well sit down. Eddie and Connor will be here before long.'

After nearly fifteen minutes of horrifically awkward silence, I heard Eddie and Connor arrive upstairs. They came straight down to the cellar, clearly worried but also definitely ready for any necessary carnage. It made my stomach flip, remembering the last time I'd seen them like that. Eddie came over and looked me up and down, one hand on my shoulder. 'Jesus, Stanly! Are you all right?'

I smiled brightly. 'I'm fine. I took care of him.'

'What happened?'

I didn't answer at first. I was looking at Connor. His entire body was tensed, and he had a look in his eyes that I'd seen before, a cool, steely resolve. 'Got any more guns, Skank?' he asked, in his measured Irish tone. *Hello to you too.*

Skank nodded.

'Cool. Hopefully won't need them, but where? Just in case?'

'In my other black box.'

'Other? Is that the night-black one, or the jet-black one?'

'The *Back in Black* one.'

'Where's that?'

'It's where the Bernard Black one used to be.'

Connor nodded. 'OK, I'm with you.'

'What happened, Stanly?' asked Eddie.

'Um,' I said. 'Well, I was just out walking. Ended up on some pedestrian bridge in the middle of town, and suddenly this guy appears from behind me and pulls a gun. Someone screams so I get out of the way, just in time because suddenly, boom, he fires. I managed to knock it out of his hands and we fought, and then he pulled out a knife, which I also managed to get rid of, and then he grabs me and we go right over the edge of the bridge. Landed on a bus.'

Three sets of eyebrows raised simultaneously and a chuckle found its way up my throat despite my valiant attempts to keep it down. 'Anyway, yeah, we kept fighting, on top of this moving bus, until I managed to get the better of him. I flew him over to the river, threatened him a bit, got nowhere, rang you. Brought him here.' I shrugged. 'And . . . there you go.'

'You did all that in broad daylight?' said Eddie.

'No, I asked the murderous assassin if we could wait until it got dark, and he said yes, and we waited until it got dark, and then I did it, and then it got light again for some reason.'

'Haha, my aching LOLs.'

'Well, you said it in that disapproving way,' I said. 'Your "we can't let the rest of the world know what we can do, for the good of whatever" voice.' I could see he wasn't a fan of this comment, or the peevish high-pitched tone I adopted when doing an impression of him, but I wasn't feeling particularly delicate. 'The dude tried to kill me! I was improvising! It's not like I used my powers to pop down to B&Q and pick up some plywood and a roll of PTFE.'

Eddie's brow furrowed. 'What the hell is PTFE?'

'Polytetrafluoroethylene tape,' said Skank. 'Or Plumber's Tape For Everything.'

'Oh.'

'Ahem,' said Connor. 'Coming rocketing back to this guy we've tied to a chair? You couldn't get anything out of him?'

'Nothing,' said Skank.

29

'OK. How d'you reckon we approach this?'

Skank looked from Connor to Eddie to me. 'Good cop, bad cop, idealistic rookie cop who can fly, morally ambiguous cop with beard.'

'Cheers. Helpful.'

Skank shrugged. 'Asking him politely would be my suggestion. Then improvise based on how cooperative he decides to be.'

'Fair.' Connor walked forwards. 'All right, mate. Who are you? And who sent you to kill Stanly?'

The guy, who had been listening to all of this with an expression halfway between amusement and contempt, remained silent.

'Who are you?' growled Eddie. 'Who do you work for?'

No response.

'I don't think he's going to tell us anything,' said Skank. He put his gun on the floor, pulled his chair forward and leaned in towards the guy. 'Do you watch *Doctor Who?*' he said, conversationally.

The guy looked taken aback. 'Uh . . . what?'

'*Doctor Who.* TV show. Wacky guy in a blue box, travelling in time and space.'

'Yeah, I know what it is.'

'Good,' said Skank, with a chuckle. 'Thought maybe you'd been living under a rock!'

Now the guy actually laughed nervously.

'So do you watch it?' said Skank.

'When I was a kid I did, yeah.'

'Who was your favourite? I always liked Tom Baker.'

'Yeah, probably him,' agreed the guy.

'Good choice.' I glanced at Eddie and Connor, but they didn't seem phased by what was happening. *Am I the only one hearing what's being said?*

30

'Not a fan of the new ones,' the guy continued. 'Too manic.'

'Fair assessment,' said Skank. His voice was perfectly measured and calm. 'You watch much TV these days?'

The guy shrugged. 'A little. I like *NCIS.*'

'Ah. Not a fan of that, to be honest. Generally not one for procedurals or case-of-the-weeks. I like my arcs. How about *Buffy*? You ever watch that?'

'No.'

'Fair enough. How come?'

'Just not my kind of thing.'

'Each to their own, I suppose. I think it's brilliant. Part of me wishes it was still on, even though intellectually I know that it would probably have deteriorated to the point of unwatchability by now.' Skank smiled ruefully. 'What about comedies? *Simpsons*? *Louie*? *The Big Bang Theory*, insofar as that can be described as a comedy?'

'I like *The Simpsons.*'

'Well, who doesn't like *The Simpsons*?' Skank smiled. 'Even if it definitely *has* deteriorated. At least you didn't say *The Big Bang Theory*. I might have had to kill you.' He laughed.

The guy laughed too. 'But you brought it up!'

'Trick question.' Skank winked. 'Do you have a favourite *Simpsons* episode?'

'Too many of them really, aren't there?'

'Yeah, good point. Favourite character? Got to be Homer, right?'

'Absolutely!' The guy seemed completely comfortable now. I was baffled, but I'd started to enjoy it. Even Eddie and Connor looked amused. *This guy tried to murder you earlier on, and now he's discussing* The Simpsons *like we're all good mates.*

Skank grinned. 'Obviously. Homer all the way. Goes without saying. So, what's your name?'

'Masters. Scott Masters.'

'Why were you trying to kill Stanly?'

'I was contracted by a man named Morter Smith.'

'Do you have a number for him?'

'No, he contacts me.'

'Does he work for a particular group? Government?'

'I don't know, he never said and I never asked. He paid well.'

'And you don't have any idea why he wants Stanly dead?'

'No. I just do the job.'

'He told you about Stanly's abilities though? What he can do?'

Masters nodded. I was gobsmacked. Eddie and Connor were staring intently at the suddenly chatty assassin. 'So this guy knows about Stanly's powers,' said Skank. 'Did he mention anybody else? Anything about the Angel Group?'

'I've never heard of the Angel Group,' said Masters. 'And he didn't mention anyone else. I work freelance, he contacted me with a name and a description and sent me off to do my work.'

'That's it?'

'Yeah, that's it.' There was a brief silence, then Masters blinked once. Part of me expected him to come to and start raging at having let his guard down, but instead he just . . . stared. His face, his eyes, everything had gone completely blank. 'Hello?' said Skank. 'You all right there, buddy?'

'I . . . ' said Masters. 'Who are you? Who . . . who am I? What am I doing here?'

There was a general exchange of nonplussed looks. 'You just told us who you are,' said Connor. 'Scott Masters. You tried to kill Stanly here.'

Masters looked utterly, painfully confused. 'What? Scott who? Stanly . . . who tried to kill . . . I don't know what the hell's going on . . .' He started to struggle, pulling at his bonds as if he'd only just realised he was tied up, taking in his surroundings with sharp, panicked twitches of his head. 'Why am I tied up? Who the hell *are* you?'

'OK, this is weird,' I said.

'Nice try, mate,' said Connor. 'But you're going to have to do better than—'

'Wait,' said Skank. He was staring at the wriggling, desperate man through narrowed eyes, brow furrowing. 'I think he's telling the truth.'

'What?' asked Eddie. 'So he just suddenly, randomly developed amnesia? Like that's a thing that happens?'

'I didn't say it was random.'

'But—'

'He's telling the truth,' Skank said again, not taking his eyes off Masters. 'I promise you.'

'Well how the hell did that happen?' asked Connor.

'Some kind of failsafe, I imagine,' said Skank. 'A trigger.'

'Who the hell *are you?*' yelled Masters. He was rocking back and forth on his chair, threatening to tip himself over, and Skank threw a hefty punch that immediately knocked him unconscious.

'Wow,' said Eddie. 'I . . . didn't think that actually worked in real life.'

'You have to hit them really hard,' said Skank. 'In the right place. And even then it's fifty-fifty.' He stared at the silent hitman, frowning and blowing on the hand he'd used to punch him.

'What did you mean by "trigger"?' said Connor. 'Like a . . . brain chip?'

'More like behavioural conditioning, I'd imagine,' said Skank. 'A command implanted in the mind of the assassin, presumably intended to kick in *before* he could give anything away. I imagine someone's going to get fired for that blunder.'

'An assassin with a self-wiping brain?' I said. 'That's . . . mental.' *Literally.*

'I point you in the direction of your ability to fly,' said Skank. 'In fact, he might even have been empowered. Maybe they found a way to turn his power against him, in the event that he was caught . . . although it seems likely that he would have used his powers against you if he had them. I don't know, this is all conjecture . . . but I'm certain that he wasn't lying.' He shook his head and breathed deeply. 'I could do with a sandwich. I'll be back.' He tucked his gun into his shorts and pulled his T-shirt over it, and headed upstairs.

'Right,' I said. 'So. I'm not sure which "what the hell" to address first.'

'You and me both, kiddo,' said Eddie.

'How did Skank *do* that?'

'We think it might be his power,' said Eddie. 'Well . . . we're not sure, exactly. He's never brought it up, and you know what Skank's like. If he doesn't bring something up, it's probably pointless asking. We're guessing it's some kind of psychological power. He draws people out, makes them feel completely comfortable, as though they can share anything. Catches them off-guard. Did you see how he kept constant eye contact? I don't know how the hell it works, but when it does . . .'

'OK,' I said. 'So what do we do now? I mean . . . someone we don't even know is taking out hits on me. Is that on top of the other mysterious group we've fallen foul of?'

'I don't know.' Eddie sat down and rubbed his eyes.

'Seems strange that the Angel Group would decide to strike now,' said Connor. 'It's been more than a year since we heard from them. And we know they had at least one dangerous empowered in their employ.'

'Pretty sure I killed him,' said Eddie, which gave me pause.

It had come up a few times in conversation, the likelihood that Eddie had killed Leon that morning at the Kulich, but he'd always changed the subject. He obviously regretted it, even though he had been defending us, but right now he stated it as though it was nothing.

*Do you get used to the idea?*

'Stands to reason they'd have more, though,' said Connor. 'So why send a standard hitman? Apart from the memory-wiping thing, of course.'

'Maybe they think I'm a standard target,' I said. That thought annoyed me, and not quite in the way that you'd probably expect.

'I'll get on to some of my contacts,' said Eddie. 'Skank can too. In the meantime, you two should head back to your place.'

'What?' I said. 'Um . . . no thanks. I'd quite like to find out why some wanker I've never met wants to kill me, if it's all the same to you. Plus, I don't want to put Connor and Sharon in danger. What if he sends someone else? To the house, or something?'

'He'd better not,' said Connor. 'I've had enough of arseholes busting into my house.'

'I'm sure that won't happen,' said Eddie, 'but even if it does, you guys will be ready, right?'

'Oh yeah. I've got a few bits and bobs saved up for a rainy day.' Connor didn't sound thrilled by the idea. Although, I guess, why would he? 'Also these,' he said, holding up his fists.

*Plus, your girlfriend's kind of a terrifying badass when necessary.*

'Good,' said Eddie. 'And Stanly, I can feel you itching to say that you can take any bad guys who come knocking, and I believe you, but the best way for you to stay safe, for now, is to stay out of sight. Please. I promised your parents I'd look after you. I'm all responsible and stuff.'

35

'Yeah, well I have responsibilities too,' I said, feebly. 'To . . . like . . . the city.' I knew exactly what Eddie thought of my entirely ineffectual crime-fighting mission, but still. It was the principle of the thing. 'And to Kloe and Tara, obviously . . .' *OK, neither of them have any idea about your future family craziness, so that probably sounded like a mega weird thing to say.*

'Tara has her own family,' said Eddie. 'She's not your responsibility.'

*Oh, if only he knew.* I wanted to argue but there was no point. Eddie was wearing his 'just don't bother' face, and who's got time to push against that immovable object? I sighed and nodded. 'Fine. I'll go home and hide.'

'What are you going to do with him?' Connor nodded at Masters, who was still sparko.

'I'm sure Skank and I will think of something,' said Eddie. He looked at me, then back at the hitman, then sighed. 'Well. I'm sure Skank will think of something.'

It was a very British autumn evening, hazy and slightly warm with an edgy tingle, winter reminding us that it wasn't as far away as we'd like to think. The sun was low, the remains of its light spread delicately over the horizon, and I was sitting at my bedroom window once again, watching the city and the distant fug. The tree at the bottom of the garden was starting to shed its leaves, which had recently become trimmed with orange, yellow and deep red, and I could hear birds, and the rustle of branches as they murmured impenetrably to one another. A squirrel performed an acrobatic leap from one branch to another, landing with absolute grace. It was utterly tranquil, the perfect cliché of a perfect evening. And somewhere out there was someone who wanted me dead.

It was all so weird. I'd always known that something like this would happen, sooner or later. Our encounter with Pandora, Lucius and their henchmen had to have been a prelude to something. There was no way that that was *it*. It was impossible. Maybe in the world I'd lived in before I'd turned sixteen, but I didn't live there any more.

The timing, though . . . like Connor had said, it had been over a year since the battle at the Jonathan Kulich Gallery. They'd not been particularly forthcoming with details of their true agenda, although I felt like 'something bad' wasn't beyond the realms of possibility. At any rate, there had been absolutely no sign of trouble in the intervening months.

*And now there is Morter Smith.*

I wondered who the hell he was. Who he was working for, why he wanted me dead. Was he connected to the Angel Group? I wasn't sure whether I wanted him to be or not. It would tie up a bit better if he was, but the appearance of a third party did make things a lot more interesting. And God, it was about time things became more interesting.

Surely I hadn't done enough to irritate any third parties, though?

'Stanly! Dinner's ready!' Good old Sharon. We'd arrived home and explained the situation, and while she was obviously concerned, her solution was to be calm and reassuring, and act normal, and have a nice dinner. It was great . . . although it also made me feel much worse about potentially bringing trouble to her door. Connor, to be fair, had been friendlier to me than he had been for a while. Not that he'd been *un*friendly lately, just not friendly, if that makes sense. But he'd asked me if I was OK, and said we'd sort it all out.

*So even if he was secretly thinking he wished I didn't live in his house any more, at least he didn't say it out loud.*

*That's something.*

'Stanly!' Sharon called again. 'Come for dinner or it's to the cupboard under the stairs with you!'

'Sorry,' I called. 'I'll be right there.'

I stood up and inhaled the air again. Something wicked was definitely this way coming. I just hoped that it had nothing to do with Tara, because as my supreme klutziness this afternoon had showed, I was not prepared for a fight, let alone a war.

Not yet, at any rate.

*I miss Daryl.*

# Chapter Four

WHEN I WENT down for breakfast the next morning, I wasn't surprised to find Eddie there. Nor was I surprised that he looked annoyed, or that he had his laptop open, along with two of the day's papers, ready to show me various photos, videos and other references to my encounter with Masters. I wasn't even particularly surprised that the general consensus had it down as a staged stunt, using wires and special effects and a hidden hot-air balloon – viral marketing for a new TV series, or possibly just a piece of performance art.

What did sort of surprise me was how little inclination I felt to take any of Eddie's crap this morning. So when he banged his fist on the table in response to my nonchalant dismissal of the pictures and video footage and demanded to know why I was being so glib, I snapped. 'God, Eddie, what do you want me to say? Do you want me to apologise for defending myself? How exactly would you have played the whole thing?'

'That's not the point—'

'What *is* the point, then?' I was very aware of Connor and Sharon hanging back in the hall, trying to make it look and sound like they weren't there. 'Please do enlighten me, as I'm clearly far too dense or immature or maybe both to pick up on such a subtle—'

'*Everything* is in there!' Eddie yelled. 'The fight on the bridge, the fight on the bus – you neglected to mention the fact that you jumped on to a truck from the moving bus – and then you dangling this guy over the river and flying off! It's all there!'

'Do you get a good look at my face in any of those videos?'

'No, but—'

'Do any of them lead back to us?'

'I don't—'

'And have *any* of the papers or sites ventured anywhere near the truth?'

'Stanly, that's not the—'

'*Christ*, Eddie!' Now it was my turn to slam a fist down, except when I did it Eddie's pile of newspapers flew off the table, along with his laptop, and the fridge door burst open, spilling milk all over the kitchen floor. Sharon immediately stepped in, catching the laptop with her mind before it could smash. Eddie seemed too stunned to do anything. Connor strode past Sharon, one hand raised. 'Stanly,' he said. 'That is *enough*. All right? Calm down. Right now.'

I breathed deeply, avoiding eye contact. *He's right. Calm down.* 'Sorry,' I said, as levelly as I could. 'It's just . . . I don't know what you want from me, Eddie. And attacking me, and constantly saying "that's not the point", and not actually *telling* me what the point is . . .' I looked at him, expecting rage, but he just looked crestfallen. 'Someone tried to kill me. I defended myself, using the skills I had available - I don't have super-strength, remember? I'm not dead. No-one's kicking the door down. Seems like the whole thing's worked out about as well as it could have.'

'I agree,' said Sharon, softly, placing Eddie's computer back on the table. As she did so, I saw a wet cloth leap from the sink to the floor, cleaning up the milk like something from a Disney film. The fridge door closed itself quietly.

'I'm sorry,' said Eddie. 'I didn't mean to . . . attack you. That's not what I . . . I just . . . I worry.'

'Yeah,' I said. 'I know you worry. If there's one thing I'm painfully aware of, it's that you worry.'

40

'Stanly,' began Sharon.

'It's fine, Sharon,' said Eddie.

'But I'm not a child,' I said. As usual, saying 'I'm not a child', or anything to that effect, made me feel about as childish as I'd ever felt. Irony's kind of a dick sometimes, eh? 'I *do* understand how things work. I know what's at stake. I know you . . . I know you feel responsible. But waiting down here with a pile of papers and a computer, giving me a bollocking like I'm some disobedient eight-year-old who had a fight at school . . .'

'We need to keep out of sight,' said Eddie, 'that's all. There's so much we don't know. I want to keep us all off the Angel Group's radar. Off *anyone's* radar.'

'A plan I'm also very down with,' said Connor.

Eddie nodded. 'And this sort of thing . . .'

'How many times?' I said, starting to feel the anger bubble up again. '*He tried to*—'

'We know,' said Sharon, stepping in. 'Stanly, we know.' She looked at Eddie. 'I think the point's been made, yes?'

Eddie nodded.

'I'm going to work, anyway,' I said. 'I'm going to be late.'

'Oh no.' My cousin moved to block me as I headed for the door. 'You're under house arrest until further notice.'

'You've *got* to be f—'

'We had this discussion last night,' said Eddie.

'Um, no *we* didn't,' I said. 'We didn't have anything remotely resembling a discussion, actually. *You* sent *me* home. Unless you're talking about a conversation *you* had with Connor and Sharon from which I was excluded?' *Ooh, go get 'em small whiny tiger.*

'No, but . . .'

'Did you get anything from Masters, anyway?'

'We didn't,' said Eddie. 'His amnesia act pretty much saw

41

to that. And nobody I spoke to could tell me anything about Morter Smith.'

'So basically, we're none the wiser,' I said. 'So I should be able to go to work.'

'The shop's not even open today,' said Eddie. 'Skank . . .' He turned to Connor. 'He wants us to meet him in town.'

Connor nodded.

'Great,' I said. 'So what do I do while you guys are off playing detectives?'

'Stay in,' said Eddie. 'Watch TV. Play Scrabble. Just don't leave the house. Please.'

I deployed my most petulant eye-roll. Playing the moody teen seemed a better option than doing what I wanted to do, which was call Eddie loads of names, psychically shove him aside and fly out the front door.

'Sorry, Stanly,' said Eddie. To be fair, he sounded as though he meant it. 'And I'm sorry I got angry.'

'Yeah, me too.' *Not really actually, fingers crossed behind my back, \*raspberry\*.*

*Nice. Real mature there, sport.*

'And I'm sorry about making you stay in,' said Eddie. 'I know you want to be out there doing the thing. We will bring you in, of course we will. I just want to wait until we know a bit more about what we're dealing with.'

'Do you not remember me rescuing Tara from Smiley Joe?' I asked. 'Or chasing Pandora through that trippy dimension slide-show thing? I came out of those intact and I did it all by myself.'

'I don't doubt your skills,' said Eddie. His voice sounded genuine, but both he and Connor suddenly had a look in their eyes. I knew what they were seeing in their heads. Me, whaling on the horrific black beast that had emerged from Smiley Joe's head, pulverising it, smashing it against the ground long after it had died. *Jesus. You lose your temper one time.*

*And you don't even kill a person.*

*Wow. Not a cool thought to have.*

Eddie put his hand on my shoulder. 'But you can't fight if you don't know what you're fighting.'

He had me there. I nodded. 'Fine. Go and do the thing. I'll be an indoor pet.'

'Does the indoor pet want eggs?' said Sharon.

'Eggs?' I waved at Eddie. 'Cool, fine, bye, I'm good here.'

'Egg delivery,' said Sharon, floating a pair of poached eggs on to my toast.

'Thanks.' I sprinkled salt and pepper on them and started to eat. 'Flying eggs are best eggs.'

'You're welcome.' She sat down opposite me and poured herself a cup of coffee. Sharon was one of the most beautiful people I'd ever seen. She had long, silky blonde hair and cosmic blue eyes, and an aura somewhere between endlessly comforting earth mother and reluctant warrior woman. As well as her telekinesis, which was a good deal more precise than mine, she had a way of reading people, of sensing their lies and uncovering their real emotions, no matter how well-hidden they were.

Not that anyone would have needed such skills to work out my mood at that precise moment. I might as well have been starring in an off-Broadway revival of *Stanly Is Really Fucking Pissed Off Right Now!*. 'I'm sorry about before,' I said. 'The fridge and stuff. It's embarrassing.'

'It's OK,' said Sharon. 'Although it has been a long time since I've seen you lose control. I half thought we might have to separate you two.'

'Eddie would bounce me round the kitchen,' I said, although it wasn't necessarily what I thought.

'Not *my* kitchen, he wouldn't,' said Sharon. 'I'd bounce *both* of you around it before I let that happen.'

'Without even lifting a finger.'

'Well, one must keep one's nails clean.'

'I really thought I was past that,' I said. 'Random power bursts. But sometimes . . .'

'Sometimes tempers get lost,' said Sharon. 'Happens to everyone.'

'Not to you.'

'Yes it does.' She smiled. 'And it's OK. Most people have it in them to cause damage when they lose their tempers. The problem is, that danger is massively increased for us. So we have to be careful.'

'I know,' I said. 'I try . . . I *will* try. Harder. No, actually, I won't try. Do or do not, innit.' Thinking of Yoda made me think of Daryl, which dramatically increased the levels of woe-is-me in my bloodstream, and I sighed. 'I'm sorry about the arguing, too. Seems to be happening more and more these days.'

'You're pushing your boundaries,' said Sharon. 'And Eddie is both intractable *and* a massive old woman. Albeit one trapped in a young masculine warrior's body. There are bound to be some sparks.'

'What does Connor think about it?'

'He longs for a quiet life,' said Sharon, fondly.

'Yeah, I get that impression.'

'Meaning?'

I had a feeling she knew, but I just shook my head. 'Doesn't matter. Look, I just . . . it's all frustrating.'

'I know,' said Sharon. 'And I sympathise, I really do. You're smart, and you're powerful, and you want to be in charge of your life, not hanging around while other people sort things out for you. I understand. But you need to put yourself in his shoes.'

'He doesn't exactly go out of his way to put himself in *my* shoes.'

44

Sharon shrugged. 'What else can I say? I already said "intractable", didn't I? How about "stubborn"?'

'How about *you* try and put me in his shoes?' I said. ''Cos generally I'm too busy wanting to slap him for treating me like a child to really empathise with his point of view.'

'It's complicated,' she sighed. 'He feels responsible for you.'

'He *isn't*, though. *I'm* responsible for me.'

'That's not the way he sees it,' said Sharon. 'I remember when I first met him. He was still so angry about how he left things with your parents. He felt so guilty. This . . . I think he sees it as giving them something back for being so difficult, looking after you. Plus the fact that he cares about you and couldn't bear to see you get hurt.' She smiled. 'But I can see how it could become a drag. He shouldn't have come down on you the way he did. He just . . . doesn't know how to deal with these feelings. They're still very new for him. Sometimes his wires get crossed, or steam comes out of the wrong valve. Mix a few more metaphors in there for me, maybe it'll make sense.'

That made me laugh. 'Yeah. Well. It just . . . I died, and I came back from it. You'd think that would earn me a sliver of respect.' *To be fair, it was a nine-year-old girl who brought you back, it was nothing to do with you, really.*

*Shut up.*

'I think it earns you more than a sliver of guilt and over-protectiveness from Eddie,' said Sharon. 'He didn't show it when you told him, but he was furious with himself. He kept saying: "he died and I should have been there". That's why he might seem like even more of a nagging old baggage now than he did before.'

'Sounds like someone needs to prune his guilt hedge,' I said, finishing off my eggs.

Sharon raised an eyebrow.

'You asked for another metaphor. You didn't specify a good one.'

'I'm not even sure that *was* a metaphor.'

'Oh God, what*evz*. Step away from the semantics with your hands in the air, or I'll take a load of apostrophes and put them in the wrong places.'

Sharon made a big pantomime of clawing at her eyes. 'I'm afraid you'd be out on your ear if you tried that, boyo.'

I smiled. 'Nice to hear a bit of Welsh lingo creeping in. We'll have you pronouncing double Ls and CHs next.'

Sharon laughed. 'I'm afraid that speaking Welsh is one superpower I'll probably never master.'

'*Sbwriel.*'

'Eh?'

'It means "rubbish".'

'Ah.' She waved her hand. 'Pfft. It's a silly language anyway.'

'Watch it. That's the language of my fathers.'

'Your fathers can have it.'

'*Ddoniol iawn.*'

'Beg pardon?'

'It means "very funny",' I said. 'Anyway. Speaking of speaking Welsh, I'm going to go and ring Kloe.'

'Won't she be in college?'

'She has a free morning on Fridays. And I know she'll be dying to hear about my brand new death warrant.'

'Stanly? Break it to her gently, OK?'

'Oh I will.'


'You *what*?'

For some reason – possibly because, for a generally intelligent person, I can occasionally be astronomically dense – I'd expected Kloe to be calm about the whole thing. It was only after she'd shrieked 'you *what*' down the phone at a nerve-shredding volume that I realised exactly what it was that I was telling her. 'Um,' I said. It was about the best I could do.

'A *hitman*? Why? Who was it? Someone wants to *kill* you? *Who* wants to kill you? *Why* do they want to kill you?'

'I don't know. Some guy called Smith put him up to it.'

'Smith? Smith who? What's going *on*, Stanly?'

Too many very similar questions to which I had no answers. 'Kloe, I honestly have no idea what's going on. I'm under house arrest at the moment. Eddie and Connor and Skank are looking into it. They're going to let me know when they find anything out.'

'So you're just sat at home waiting for someone else to come and *kill you*?' She sounded close to hysterics. I had to make something up to calm her down. It had been a monumentally stupid idea to tell her, it's just that I'd really wanted to hear the sound of her voice, and when she'd asked what was new I couldn't very well lie to her.

*Except that you're going to lie now.*

*Oh shut up.*

'Don't worry,' I said, lamely. 'Eddie and Connor will find out what's happening, and until then I'm perfectly safe here. I've got my powers, remember? Plus, nobody knows where I live.'

'Didn't those Angel people break in that one time to kidnap Tara?'

*Bollocks.* 'Um . . . well, yeah, they did, but that was different. We were all out at the time except for Daryl, and he was kind of in league with them anyway.' *Unfair.* 'There was no-one with powers.'

'What about Sharon? She was there.'

*Bollocks bollocks.* 'Yeah, but . . . well, yeah. Exactly. And she did a pretty damn good job of holding them off. She properly messed that one guy up. And that was just by herself. And she wasn't prepared. So with a couple of us, if we're all prepared,

47

there shouldn't be any trouble. Plus, nobody's going to try anything in the middle of the day, are they?'

'You said that hitman attacked you in the middle of the day.'

*Bollocks shit piss.* 'Plus Eddie and Connor will be back later,' I said, skipping over that one entirely, 'and they've got powers *and* guns, and I've got my powers as well, remember.'

'You said that already.'

'Just wanted to make sure you didn't forget. I'm not helpless. And I fought that Masters guy off single-handedly yesterday. You can watch the footage online if you want.'

'What?'

*Shitting bollocks pissing crap, why am I suddenly the worst person ever at talking.* 'Yeah, um . . . there might have been a few cameras.'

Eventually, by some miracle, I managed to calm her down. She even said she'd check out one of the videos later, although she said I should expect another shrieking phone call, just in case she couldn't handle it. 'I'm sure you can,' I said. 'You're a tough—'

'Oh no you don't, boy. Do not try to disarm me with sweet talk. I am allowed to freak out about someone wanting to murder my boyfriend.'

*Fair point, well made.* 'OK,' I said. 'I promise not to do that *if* you promise to—'

'And *don't* make me promise not to worry, like that's a thing anyone can ever promise.'

'OK. I promise. But you *do* have to promise me one thing.'

'What?'

'Don't share the video on Facebook.'

A pause, then she laughed. 'Fine. Good.' *OK. Think you just about managed to salvage proceedings.* 'I just wish you were here,' she said. 'Why do you stay down there? Where all that stuff happens? Assassinations and monsters and stuff?'

'It beats wasting away in Tref-y-Celwyn.'

'I suppose. Hold on . . . does that mean that I'm wasting away in Llangoroth? Is wasting away in Llangoroth better than wasting away in Tref-y-Celwyn?'

'By a *mile*. Llangoroth has *way* more pubs than Tref-y-Celwyn. And the recycling centre's loads bigger. I don't know if ours even does cardboard.'

She laughed. 'I've actually been looking at universities in London.'

'Really? Despite all the assassinations and monsters and stuff?'

'Well, that's your stuff. I'd be doing other stuff.'

'Are they any good?'

'I got a few brochures. They all look good, and there are loads of wicked courses. I'm a bit torn at the moment. Plus there's the whole being-in-debt-for-the-rest-of-my-life thing to consider. But I guess my children can pay it off after I'm dead.'

That made me think of Tara, and I felt momentarily dizzy, as I generally did when my temporally confusing familial situation came up. 'When do you need to decide?' I asked, managing a pretty good approximation of a normal tone.

'Needs to be sorted out by February, I think.'

'Well, what have you looked at?' I seemed to have managed to get her off the topic of assassinations and monsters and stuff, which was good, and we spent about half an hour talking about various things, conspicuously avoiding any potentially sore subjects. It was lovely, although I felt guilty when she talked about university, about the healthy, normal, wicked things she wanted to do. At some point things were going to get really messy, and we'd have to take our newborn daughter and travel back in time. And deep down I knew that in some way, however tangentially, it was going to be my fault.

'Sorry,' she said, after a while. 'I've got to go and meet Lynsey.'

'Blonde Lynsey?'

'No, the other Lynsey who we know.'

'Haha. Ha.'

'So I'll speak to you over the weekend sometime?'

'Yup. Take care.'

'You too. Stay out of trouble. *Please.*'

'Oh, you know me.'

'Yeah. I do.'

There was a brief pause, pregnant with things better left unsaid. 'Love you,' she said, softly.

'Love you too.'

'Don't say "too". It sounds like you're just saying it 'cos I said it.'

'Sorry.'

'I'm sorry too.'

I laughed. 'You're welcome. Bye.'

'Hello.' Click.


'How did it go?' asked Sharon when I returned to the kitchen.

'Note to self,' I said. 'In future, do not appraise girlfriend of assassination attempts.'

'I could have told you that.'

'Then why didn't you?'

'I thought you wanted to deal with things yourself?' Her eyes glowed with mischief. 'And actually, having said all that, it's good that you told Kloe. It's not fair to keep things from her.'

'Hmm.'

'So, anyway. What was it like jumping from a moving bus to a moving truck?'

'It was brilliant,' I said. 'I had a lovely time, and I hope to do it again very soon.'

'Please don't,' said Sharon. 'Now I believe you have some washing to do?'

I rolled my eyes. 'Yes, *Mother*.'

'Don't ever call me that.'

'Sorry, *Grandma*.'

'That's Eddie.'

'Oh yeah.'

I did washing and tidied my room and half-heartedly surfed the internet, but I felt too restless to concentrate on anything properly. It's weird how you can find pretty much anything on the internet, but if you're not in the mood it might as well just be a holding page that leads to nowhere. I didn't have any new books to read or films to watch, and there was nothing on TV. Sharon had some paperwork to deal with so I ended up meandering around the house, fidgeting from sofa to chair to chair, sitting for a while staring into space, then moving on again. After about an hour and a half of this I felt a *sod it* spark in my brain, and I went downstairs and grabbed my coat from its hook. Sharon looked through from the kitchen. 'Stanly. Eddie said for you to stay in.'

'I'm going nuts in here!' I said. 'I need to be out doing stuff. I need to find out who wants to kill me! And I need to buy Tara a present.'

'Stanly . . .' Sharon stood up and came through. 'I understand. Honestly, I do. But the safest thing for you to do is to stay in.'

'But I'm *bored*!' I said, adopting the whining tone of a petulant seven-year-old girl from New York.

Sharon smiled. 'All right. Let's do something, then.'

'Something?' I wasn't really in the mood for our usual games, which included psychic DIY (more fun than it sounds), psychic Lego (exactly as fun as it sounds), psychic chess (the novelty wears off surprisingly fast) and psychic high or low (fun even though Sharon always won).

'Something different.' She beckoned, and I followed her back to the kitchen. She grabbed a packet of self-raising flour from the cupboard, turned and faced me. 'Dexterity practice. And imagination practice. I'll throw some flour into the air. See what you can do with it.' She raised a finger. 'But if any of it goes on the floor, *you* have to clean it up.'

'OK.' *Could be a laugh, I guess.*

Sharon reached into the bag and pulled out a small handful of flour. 'Ready?'

'Hold on.' My mind felt blunt, and I spent a few seconds with my eyes closed, sharpening, focusing, visualising what I would do, how it would feel. 'All right,' I said, opening my eyes. 'Shoot.'

She threw the flour into the air and I concentrated. The small mass that she had kept enclosed in her hand expanded, coming apart into thousands of dusty white particles, and I stopped them all, leaving a cloud frozen in space between us. I didn't miss a molecule. 'Good,' said Sharon. 'Now what can you do with it?'

*Keep concentrating.* I kept my gaze focused on the floating mass of powder and let my mind extend and wrap around it, feeling every part. Slowly and delicately, as if manipulating a tower of glass shards, I pulled the cloud apart and re-arranged the flour into the shape of a question mark. Sharon smiled, but didn't speak. *Good. No distractions.* I let the question mark hover in the air for a moment, tore it apart and formed a circle.

*Now for the tricky part.* I took a second to *feel* my brain inside my head, to stay completely aware of the tool that I was using for this operation, before slowly splitting the psychic action in half so that one invisible force was holding the suspended circle of flour in place, leaving another free to play. I used this second force to grab an apple from the fruit bowl on the table, throw it through the centre of the circle, catch it and bring it back through. After repeating this a couple of times I moved the flour downwards so that it was hanging around the apple like a ring around a planet, and slowly I started to rotate the two, one clockwise and the other anticlockwise. I could feel a slight strain on my brain, as it wasn't used to controlling separate movements at the same time with such delicacy, but I maintained my concentration for about a minute before pulling the ring apart and assembling the flour into a small ball, which I dropped back in the bag.

*Finishing touch?*

I slid open a drawer and withdrew a knife, and started to peel the apple in mid-air, unable to resist a cocky grin. Sharon laughed. When it was fully peeled I deposited the long ring of apple peel in the compost bin, dropped the knife in the sink, drew the apple into my waiting hand and took a bite. My mind relaxed and I felt a little light-headed, the way you do if you stand up too fast, but it passed quickly. 'That was really good,' said Sharon. 'How did it feel?'

'Not easy, exactly, but . . . OK?' I crossed the room to the table and sat down, rotating the apple on the palm of my hand. 'It's usually big single movements, not lots of little precise ones. Even when we play with the Lego, I'm usually just concentrating on one piece at a time. It's tricky . . . but I can do it.'

'And how's the flying?' Her tongue may well have been in her cheek, considering yesterday's escapades, but I didn't rise to any bait.

'Fine,' I said. 'Getting better, actually. Manoeuvring is a piece of cake these days. And my acceleration's improved.'

'Great. That's great.' We both laughed. 'I've got to sort the rest of this paperwork,' said Sharon. 'All this admin we've been getting lately is nightmarish. Give me a giant evil worm to battle any day of the week.'

My ears pricked up at this. Sharon rarely mentioned her encounter with the Worm, her formative experience of London's monstrous underside, and when she did it was with a quiet, haunted air. She seemed pretty casual about it now.

*Maybe she's getting over it.*

*That's good. That means you get over it.*

I asked Sharon if I could borrow a book, and after fifteen minutes perusing her extensive library I settled on *The Time Traveller's Wife*. As soon as I'd read a few chapters I realised that it was probably not the best thing to be reading when you were feeling alone and frustrated and missing your girlfriend, but it was so good that I had to carry on. It kept me absorbed for the better part of the day, although I immediately dropped it when I heard Connor and Eddie return from their mission. 'Anything?' I asked.

'Nothing,' said Eddie. 'With a side order of sweet FA, and a jack shit chaser.'

'Some people had heard the name Morter Smith,' said Connor, 'but we couldn't get any information about him.'

'Which makes us think that he's a major player,' said Eddie, 'and not someone you want to come face to face with.'

'Please,' I said. 'What kind of name is Morter anyway? Do you think he has brothers called Bayonette and Assault Rifle?'

'It's Morter with an E, apparently,' said Connor. 'The explosive kind is with an A.'

'Is it?' asked Eddie. 'I thought it was always spelled with an E.'

Connor shook his head.

'Well,' said Eddie. 'You learn something new every day, eh?'

'Except for anything useful about my would-be arch-nemesis person,' I said.

'Sorry,' said Connor. 'Thing is, Eddie might have slightly overstated our underworld connections. A few minor-level shady characters, that's about it. This Smith is on the top rung, and people are either too scared to spill, or too far below to actually know anything about him. That's what's worrying.'

'So what now?'

'Stay in,' said Eddie. 'Out of the line of fire. There's no point in trying any other avenues today. We'll see if Skank calls, but unless he does we're going to leave it alone for now.' For once, I decided not to argue.

I spent the rest of the day pacing, reading, and half-composing letters to Kloe. I never send letters, but sometimes it's quite cleansing to write down thoughts. Darkness fell, and then it was dinner time, and then the house shut itself off. Maddeningly calm, maddeningly tidy. Nothing being done.

*And there's nothing you* can *do,* I thought as I lay on my bed, still fully clothed. *Nobody you can ask for information.* I hated this helpless feeling. At the mercy of an invisible man, waiting around for him to make his next move, or for a non-existent source to give us some useless information. *See above, re: nothing.*

*Well. There's something.*

*I shouldn't.*

*It's been ages, though.*

*But if I get caught . . .*

*Sod it.*

I got up and floated out into the garden, psychically closing the window behind me and touching down silently on the grass. I looked up at the sky. Took a deep glug of cool air. Closed my eyes.

Smiled.

Flying is the easiest, most beautiful thing. I simply sprang up from the ground, gravity went *oh, OK then, well, see you later I guess* and I kept going, quickly gaining speed, up past the buildings, up into the clear space beyond the fumes and fog and sirens and cars, up into my own world, so fast that even if someone had seen me, they'd never have registered that it was a person.

*Except if they saw one of the videos, which statistically literally everyone in the world has now seen.*

*Except who cares.*

Right now? Not me, not by any stretch of the imagination. I reached out to touch the moon, laughed like a child, turned and flew, stardust on my shoulders. Below me the city creaked and undulated, a mosaic of blinking lights and black shapes with great flowing grey canyons between them, and a plane roared overhead. I wondered if anybody saw me. *Doubtful.*

*And again, a hearty 'who cares'.*

I flew on, past the highest spires in the city, over St Paul's, garlanded by pillars and great concrete rings, until the sprawl started to fade, replaced by rolling shadowy hills and uneven fields. I had so much energy that I couldn't even begin to worry about distance. I just flew, casting a brief Peter Pan shadow on sheds and barns, over villages made of paper and chalk and tiny farmhouses that glowed like gingerbread dwellings.

*Speed of sound.*

I chuckled.

*Speed of light, mate.*

I zoomed past a wind farm, its sails turning slowly and benevolently in the wind. A train snaked through the hills and I matched its course for a little while before letting it chunter on, and in the sudden fresh quiet I heard the bleating of animals and felt a sudden pang. *That's what home sounds like.*

*Theoretically, I could get there.*

*If I really wanted to go I would have done it by now.*

*Kloe is there.*

*Shut up and fly.*

56

The smells of grass and silage and the odd car, and plumes of smoke rising from painted chimneys. A glistening river winding around the countryside like tears down an old man's face, a grass-bearded face with gnarled tree trunk skin and frozen sap for eyes. I shed a few tears of my own but they dripped into my smile and were absorbed. Not even the distance between Kloe and me could spoil the sheer ecstasy of flight, and now, balancing every molecule in my body and brain, I turned a loop-the-loop, spiralled downwards and pulled up inches from the ground, so close that I could feel the long grass brushing my chin. I shot back up towards the moon, briefly taking my own breath away with the movement, my stomach lurching as though I were riding a plunging rollercoaster, and laughed that child's laugh again.

*How far is the sea?*

*I wonder.*

Another burst of energy and I was roaring through the sky, parting reality with my hands and face, streamlined, a human bird preying on moonlight. I flew for at least an hour, stopping only for brief, playful indulgences, until I could see a distant, shimmering carpet through two grey-white teeth of cliff. I slowed down, and only now did I begin to realise how tired I was. I must have flown over a hundred miles, but I didn't care. I touched down on the very edge of the cliff and stared.

The ocean at midnight. Vast, darkest blue, rippling like half-formed glass, shards of moon dancing on the foamy tips of the waves, cast like boomerangs from the orb in the sky. It was white now, away from the city, pure and haloed with silver, and the sea rushed gently, whispering to itself, one more instrument in the lunar-conducted symphony of wind and whalesong, the throbbing bass drum in my chest keeping bittersweet time. I was pretty sure there were no whales nearby, but I could still hear them.

I wasn't sure how long I sat there, or how many tears fell, or how many times I wished that Kloe was sitting next to me watching this melancholy supernova. I didn't want to know. It was almost perfection.

And almost is pretty good, to be fair.

*Time is flying.*

*Something we both have in common.*

*Ha.*

I don't remember flying home. I don't remember smells or sounds, or the shape of the countryside, or the taste and touch of the air. All I remember is being transferred softly and tenderly from the cool, sensual kiss of the sea to the warmth of my own bed, guided by the welcoming lights of peaceful dreams, all thoughts of enemies and anger and loneliness temporarily silenced. A chance of serenity.

I walked through the graveyard with murder tingling in my fingertips. Infinite tombstones loomed, some brand new, some crumbling and overgrown with creepers, their mourners either uncaring, forgetful or deceased themselves. Some were so huge that they ended beyond the sky. I didn't recognise any names, and I counted that as a good thing. The sky itself was full of dead light, a few stars, an elderly moon. It was cold, but there was a kind of heat on the breeze, nothing to do with the weather, more a sense of something coming, a promise. I couldn't put my finger on it. Somewhere among the tombstones, something moved. A mass, human but not, a temporary mouth flickering in its great head. I knew who that was. I saw him regularly.

Tonight, though, he was keeping his distance.

'She's finally asleep.' Kloe was kneeling next to a cradle full of blankets, a tiny shape breathing regularly underneath. I smiled and knelt down next to her, put my arm around her slender shoulders.

'Well done. She's been pretty restless lately.'

Kloe nodded. 'I wonder why.'

'It's the weather.'

'Probably.' Kloe looked up at me, and although she was smiling her eyes were wet. 'What's going to happen when they take her?'

'No-one's going to take her.' I pulled her into an embrace. 'She's ours, and I will protect her and you forever.'

'You might not be around forever.'

'You'll never be alone. I promise.' It was a real promise, but Kloe laughed.

'You should give me more credit,' she said.

'I should.'

She shrugged and turned away. The regular, fragile breathing had stopped. I pulled the blankets aside but the cradle was empty, and Kloe was wandering off into the mist. The cradle was sitting on a plot of soil with a fresh, blank tombstone at the end, and I started digging and clawing at the ground, screaming silently, but every time I ripped away a chunk, fresh bloodied dirt oozed into its place. My own tears seemed to be hardening the earth, and when I looked up at the tombstone again I saw letters beginning to appear. The first hadn't quite formed, but I knew what it was going to be, it was—

no—

*no—*

NO—

'NO!'

I woke up, of course, hot and sweaty and anxious and breathing hard and heavy, my heart pumping with such brutality that it shook my chest. My skin tingled and my fingers trembled, and it took nearly a minute for the panic to subside, lying there, willing myself into calmness. *Slow down. Quiet. Still. A dream like any other. Over-active worry gland, plus trauma, plus your own particularly messed-up imagination, plus deep sleep. Nothing to worry about.*

Eventually my breathing became regular and I was no longer aware of my heartbeat, but despite the cold outside I felt weak with heat. I stared at the ceiling for hours, afraid to close my eyes again, trying not to think about the worst possible things, wishing I wasn't alone.

*So much for serenity.*

# Chapter Five

I SLEPT UNTIL almost one the next day and woke feeling uneasy; an odd mixture of groggy and wired.

Showering didn't help, and when I went downstairs there was nobody there, just a note from Sharon saying she'd be back from work around four. I slumped down at the table and made coffee and cereal with my mind, amusing myself by marching the caffetiere and the Bran Flakes box around on the counter as though possessed.

*Simple things.*

Bored of rattling around sulking, I decided to make the most of having the house to myself and plugged my laptop into the sound system in the living room. While Skank was a big fan of vinyl, his digital collection was also fearsome, and I'd been regularly, greedily raiding it for new and peculiar delights. My own musical experience had been pretty much exclusively confined to stuff with guitars, but I'd now discovered that I really liked weird noises.

I closed the curtains, cranked up some Aphex Twin and went a bit nuts with my powers, standing on the ceiling, rearranging the furniture, juggling pictures and books. After a while I decided to go all out and turn the whole room upside-down, *The Twits*-style, moving the chairs, sofa, rugs, lamps and hi-fi up to the ceiling, an inverted mirror image of the room it had been. I sat on the upside-down sofa, positioned my laptop and snapped a picture, which I then sent to Eddie's phone with a message saying *this is what happens when you make me stay at home*. He replied with a smiley face, and although I usually found emoticons and text speak unreasonably irritating, today it was quite nice.

I replaced the furniture in its usual formation (after hoovering some of those hard to reach corners), made some coffee and decided to try a bit of internet detective work. After all, I had multiple worlds at my fingertips. Neither Connor nor Eddie had really embraced this oh-so-new-except-it's-really-not frontier, and although Skank had probably already done some electronic investigating for them I figured it was worth a try. I'd familiarised myself with a number of strange blogs in the last year or so, not just Weird, Sister. Maybe there'd be something out there.

Morter Smith, unsurprisingly, yielded no useful search results. In fact, there were no recorded instances whatsoever of Morter being used as a first name. A surname, here and there, although it wasn't common.

*Worth a shot.*

I dug around a few blogs and forums, seeing if there was anything Angel Group-related, and found a couple of discussions of my new viral video showcase. People seemed overwhelmingly unimpressed with the special effects, which gave me a chuckle, but when I logged on to Weird, Sister I found a detailed post analysing the video next to what seemed to be a picture of me flying across the city at night, probably back when I'd first named myself London's resident superhero. They were taking it seriously. Luckily my face wasn't visible, but still . . . someone was watching.

*I have a doubleplusbad feeling about this.*

'Stanly?' I jumped. Sharon's voice. 'I'm home!'

'Hi!' I hurriedly logged off and headed downstairs. She was making coffee, looking tired but smiley in her pale blue scrubs. 'Long shift?' I asked.

'Long but fairly tedious, which was actually a nice change of pace. How's your day been?'

'Fine. Quite nice to be alone, actually.'

'You haven't been,' said Sharon. 'Eddie's been watching the house all day.'

'You *what*?'

'He's gone now.' Sharon smiled at my indignant face. 'Figured you'd want a bit of space, but he was pretty insistent about not leaving you alone to be possibly murdered.' She was feigning lightness, but I knew she was bothered by the possibility and it took the wind out of my frustrated sails. We sat and had coffee, and after allowing the companionable silence to stretch out a bit I decided to ask a question that I'd never felt able to ask before. 'Sharon . . . what was the Worm like?'

Her hand stopped mid-way to her mouth, and her cup shook a little. 'Sorry,' I said. 'I know it was . . . bad. I just . . .'

'It's OK.' She put the cup down very carefully. 'I can talk about it. I just prefer not to, generally. That's all.'

'You don't have to—'

'No, really, it's fine.' She sipped her coffee, as though steeling herself. 'We're all monster-killers here.' The grim smile accompanying her words chilled me. It wasn't an expression you should ever have to see on the face of someone you care about. *I've seen stuff*, it said. *And all you can do is get on with it.* 'Well,' she said, 'like I told you before, I was sixteen . . . no, actually, seventeen at that point. Just. And Freeman . . .' She stopped again. I knew why. Mr Freeman had appeared out of nowhere one day when I was first in London and kept re-appearing at random convenient points, giving me lectures and coded information, hardly any of which ended up being of any use to me. He kept alluding to the future, to my power, and I'd eventually learned that he was a veteran liar, a professional manipulator of impressionable minds who singled out people with powers

– like Sharon, Connor and Eddie – and fooled them into doing his dirty work. Finally, when he'd brought us before the Angel Group for a singularly confusing confrontation, I'd seen him shot dead in cold blood on his boss's orders. I could see him with perfect clarity now, lying on the polished floor, oozing life. I can't pretend to have liked him, but he hadn't deserved that.

'Anyway,' said Sharon. 'I'd heard stories about some creature living in the sewers, attacking people. *Eating* them. Obviously I didn't believe it, not until Freeman told me it was true . . . and I don't even know why I believed him. It's not like he was particularly likeable or trustworthy. I was naïve, I suppose. He told me that I had a duty to use my powers for good, and that if I killed this monster I would be under some kind of protection. That's exactly what he said to Connor and Eddie too, and I'm pretty sure it was a lie . . . although we are still here, so . . .' She shrugged. 'Anyway. I didn't know any of that at the time, so down I went. Down a manhole, down a ladder, into the darkness. The smell was so disgusting I almost threw up immediately. I managed to force myself to get used to it, though. Had to. I just remember walking and thinking *what the hell am I doing down here, I don't know the first thing about fighting, I barely even understand my powers.* I knew that I could do things, but I'd . . . I'd had problems. So I'd been taking as much rubbish as I could get my hands on, thinking I could suppress the power. I never took drugs again after that trip down the sewer, incidentally.' She smiled the rueful smile of an ex-wild child, and took a sip of coffee. 'So I was walking, and suddenly I felt this force, this . . . alien presence. Completely impenetrable. And a second later there was this horrible scream. Like metal being scraped along metal. I almost fainted on the spot. And then it appeared.'

I had been waiting for this. 'It was huge,' Sharon said. 'Fat. And so long I couldn't see its tail. Not that I was looking that way, all I was thinking about was its face.' She shuddered. 'Massive and flat, all mouth, with a million teeth. Have you ever seen a picture of a lamprey's mouth?'

'Yes.' *Like the black things in Smiley Joe's head.*

*Maybe they're related.*

'Like that,' said Sharon. 'Just the most horrible . . . and there was blood on its teeth. I think that was what gave me courage, weirdly. I remember feeling anger, beneath the fear. Enough to grab hold of, turn into action. And then it came at me.' She was getting into the swing of the story now, gesticulating as she spun the yarn. 'I managed to flatten myself against the wall so it went past me and then I just stopped thinking, and I grabbed one of its horrible slimy scales and pulled myself up onto its back. Don't even know how, it's not like I was strong . . . I've often wondered if maybe I was subconsciously channelling my telekinesis, using it to make myself stronger. I think that's what Eddie and Connor do. Anyway, I was about an inch from the ceiling, and it was rocketing along, like being on top of a living train. I didn't have a plan, so I started to crawl along towards the head. I just kept thinking *no more blood for you, no more blood for you.*' She stopped for breath. 'So I got to its head and found its eyes. Small and black and glassy . . . they were nearly the scariest feature. And that was when I knew that there was nothing in this thing's mind that I could understand, it was just a monster. That . . . made me hate it even more.' She looked almost regretful now. 'Not a particularly healthy thought process. But useful if you're going to kill something.'

'So what did you do?'

'Jammed both thumbs into its eye sockets,' said Sharon. She turned slightly pale at the memory, and I tried to get my head round it. It was virtually impossible to reconcile this ethereal, gentle person with the image I had of a telepathic Buffy riding on the back of a giant worm. 'It was *so* disgusting,' she continued, 'you can't even imagine, there was purple gunk pouring everywhere, and it went all over me, but I held on and I shut my eyes and I . . . I kind of entered it with my mind. Maybe instinct kicked in, but . . . I just tried to shut out all of the fear and noise and become one with it. I don't know how long it took, I just remember suddenly feeling like I knew every molecule of its body, and that gave me an advantage. I could see its heart, and I used my telekinesis to burst it. Just . . . pop it open.' She smiled grimly. 'Anyway, the thing stopped dead and I flew off it and landed in the sewage, which really *did* make me throw up, and when I turned around it was just lying there, dead. Goop pouring out of its mouth. So I vomited until there was nothing left, like you would, then got out of the sewers and ran. And then vomited some more. Needed to wash every square inch of my body for a good few hours. And I burned my clothes.' She sat back, looking slightly dazed. 'And that's it.'

'Crikey.' My respect for Sharon, which was already pretty stratospheric, shot up into another galaxy. 'And Freeman?'

'Didn't see him again until that night at the Kulich.'

I nodded. 'Sorry about the walk down memory sewer. I'm a sucker for monsters and ultraviolence.'

'That's fine. It felt good to talk about it, actually.' She smiled, but there was something in her eyes, something I couldn't place. Something like disappointment. 'Speaking of showers, I'm going to head for one now,' she said. 'Do you have plans for the rest of the day?'

'I was going to stay in the house. Followed by a bit of light staying in the house, then maybe stay in the house for a bit, just as a little change of pace, before plunging headlong into some serious house staying-in.'

'How did we survive around here before you and your wit.'

'I have no idea.'

Sharon was halfway down the corridor when I called after her. 'Sharon?'

'Yes?'

'You know you said that you once used your powers at the hospital?'

She looked at the floor. 'Yes.'

'Don't you ever want to . . . do more of that? Use them to help people?'

Sharon looked as though she was struggling with the response. Finally, she nodded. 'I do. Often. But . . . it's not as simple as that.'

*Isn't it?* 'I suppose.'

'I was thinking about it the other day, though, actually,' said Sharon. 'About what it might be like if powers were out in the open. If there were more of us, if it was common knowledge.'

'What do you think it would be like?'

'Absolute bloody chaos,' she said, without hesitation. 'Although it could be incredible for things like medical science . . . actually, weirdly, I ended up thinking more about the media response. How 24-hour news and the blogosphere and the think-piece mafia would react. Which also led me towards absolute bloody chaos . . . and then I ended up thinking about an article I might write.'

'Really?' I had no idea that Sharon was the article-writing type. 'What about?'

'The psychological implications of people's powers,' said Sharon. 'Specifically what individual powers say about their owners. Which might touch on the internalisation of gender roles, for example.'

*Um . . .* 'Hamnu?'

'I assume that means you don't understand what I'm on about.'

'Yarp.'

'Well,' said Sharon, 'take what I said about Eddie and Connor. They're clearly empowered, but they don't have telekinesis, do they? Not like you and me. They're both abnormally tough. Strong, fast, massively increased endurance. Traditionally masculine traits. I certainly don't have super-strength. Neither do you, do you?'

'No. I can take a punch, but . . .' *But what? You thought you were some sort of hard nut? Like, naturally?*

*Well . . . yeah, kinda . . .*

*This makes a lot more sense, to be fair.*

*Wow. Took a while for that penny to drop.*

*Better late than never, I suppose.*

'So why is that?' said Sharon. 'Why don't we have super-strength? And why do we have the powers we have? Maybe my . . . empathy thing, or whatever it is, is the result of internalising what society thinks a woman should be. Compassionate, empathetic. Passive.'

'But what about telekinesis?' I said. 'That's kind of the opposite of passive, isn't it, in a way? Maybe that's you pushing *against* internalised roles of whatever.'

Sharon laughed. 'Maybe. Or maybe it's a manifestation of . . . healing? Creation? That's quite feminine, isn't it? I suppose men are the ones who build stuff, traditionally . . . but you're also traditionally the ones who blow stuff up . . . maybe it's to do with control? Men are generally in control, in terms of society and power structures . . . so it could be me pushing against my perceived role, wanting to be more in control, have agency . . .' She shook her head. 'As you can see, I haven't got very far through my sociology book.'

'Don't worry,' I said, 'compared to me, you're a professor of it. So . . . you think we *choose* our powers, then? Based on who we are? How we think?'

'Not exactly. Not consciously. But I've often thought about

why we're all different. And I wonder if maybe, *sub*consciously, there is a part of us that chooses.'

'Like you said, though, I'm not super-strong. Or super-empathetic. So what does my telekinesis mean?'

'That you're in touch with your feminine side?' Sharon smiled. 'I'm not sure.'

'And flying?'

'Again, I don't know. Although you seem to be the only one who can do it.' She shrugged. 'Could all be nonsense. Probably is.'

'Maybe we're busting free of the stereotypes that society has forced us into,' I said. 'And Eddie and Connor are still . . . shackled. Or something.'

'Shackled, eh?'

'I don't know gender studies.'

'Me neither. Ask me about it again when I write the article.' She winked and went upstairs, and I stayed at the table. Intriguing thoughts about powers turned pretty swiftly to brooding thoughts about powers, and how to waste them, and once again I found myself wishing that Daryl was there. I hadn't seen him in over a year.

*Good*, said an unnecessarily spiteful voice somewhere in my head.

It wasn't good, though. Not at all.

The weekend dragged on with no news. Eddie went AWOL, as he often did, and Connor was reluctant to discuss anything, and although I managed to distract myself with a few documentaries – one, about black bears, was particularly interesting - by the time Monday rolled around I was really starting to get to grips with the phrase 'stir crazy'.

At least I had something to do that day, even if it was somewhat bittersweet.

'Hello?'

'Hi Jackie, it's Stanly. How are you?'

'Oh hello, Stanly! I'm very well thank you, how are you?'

'Oh, you know. Not too bad. I was wondering if I could speak to Tara?'

'Of course. Just a moment.'

Crackling, voices, and then Tara: 'Hi Stanly!'

'Happy birthday, you gigantic eleven-year-old. How's things?' Even though I had what I supposed was a pretty good reason, I felt guilty because I hadn't got her a present. Not even a card. *I'm a lousy not-yet-dad.*

*Extenuating circumstances, she'll understand.*

*Don't you* dare *tell her about Morter Smith, dickhead.*

*What do you think I am? A dickhead?*

'Great! I got some new clothes and a bag and some jewellery and some music, and I have to go to school today, but I'm having some friends around after school.'

'That sounds wicked. What music did you get?'

'You wouldn't have heard of it.'

'Ouch. I'm that old already? Try me.'

She giggled and said some names. I hadn't heard of any of them. 'Oh yeah,' I said. 'Those guys. I was into them for a while but then they got popular and now I don't like them.'

She giggled again. It was a good sound. 'When are you coming over?'

I hung my head a little. 'I'm sorry, I can't.'

'Why?'

'I . . .' *Don't lie.* 'I have some very important things to deal with. Really important. You know I'm not exaggerating when I say important stuff.'

'Are you in trouble again?' *Astute kid. Also, she sounds reproachful, rather than worried. Got to love that.*

'No. Well . . . a little. But it's nothing for you to worry

about. I'm so sorry I can't come and see you. I will as soon as I can.'

'Am I in trouble again?'

'No! No. You're the birthday girl, and you're going to have a fantastic day and everyone's going to spoil you absolutely rotten, and you're going to become this horrible pampered big-headed heinous—'

'I *am not*—'

'—*heinous* preening princess, and then as soon as I'm done with all my rubbish I'm going to come round with a massive present and make things even worse. OK?'

'That was a pretty long sentence.'

'Good, eh? Nine out of ten?'

'Seven out of ten.'

'Well, thank you *very* much.'

Another giggle. 'You're welcome.'

She made me laugh as well, which was good. I was glad I wasn't on the receiving end of an eleven-year-old's guilt trip. I remembered laying those on my parents when I was younger. Not that Tara had any clue about the real nature of our relationship. 'OK buddy. I've—'

'Don't call me buddy, it sounds *weird*.'

'OK pal.'

'*Ugh*, not *pal*, either.'

'OK sport. I—'

'*Stop calling me things!*'

'OK . . . OK. I've got to go now. You have an unreasonably wicked day, and if anyone doesn't treat you like you're the centre of the universe, you let me know and I'll give 'em a good going over.'

'Thank you, I will. Take care of yourself.' She said it so solemnly that I almost pissed myself laughing. 'You too, kiddo—'

'*No.*'

'OK, no more names. See ya soon. Happy birthday.'

'Thanks. Bye.'

Click.

I spent the rest of the week under house arrest, and it was the longest week of my entire life. Connor brought back various care packages from the shop courtesy of Skank, containing the new trade paperbacks for Ms. Marvel, Rat Queens and the like, but I devoured them too fast and kept ending up with what felt like more free time than before.

So I tried to be productive, practising with my powers as much as possible, attempting to meditate while levitating (although it's kind of tricky to meditate when your brain is screaming THIS LOOKS SO COOL RIGHT NOW) and lifting as many objects as possible, but even with superpowers I was still limited by what was in the house. All I could think about was being *out there*, using my powers in the real world. I'd gone from feeling woefully underprepared and un-practised last week to feeling pretty much unstoppable now, and while part of me knew that I should be cautious, and that this fearless feeling was no better an indication of my actual preparedness than drunken bravado would have been, the rest of me ended up dragging that part off to the toilets and flushing its head in the bowl until it shut up.

Finally, on Friday night, I cornered Eddie before he could even step through the front door. 'This is ridiculous.'

'I know—'

'I can't stay in this house any longer.'

'I *know*, but—'

'No, no *but*, if you make me stay I'm going to just fly out the window.'

'Stanly!' said Eddie. I could see that he was trying to keep cool, but I was not in the mood for it. 'How about letting me in the house before giving me the Spanish Inquisition?'

'Inquisitions ask things,' I said. 'I'm telling you things.' But I stepped aside anyway, and we went into the kitchen.

'I'm sorry about keeping you cooped up,' said Eddie. 'I know how frustrating it must have been.'

'Not sure you do, to be honest.'

'Fair enough. But we've still not been able to find anything. Skank's got some much dodgier connections than us, and he's heard nothing, although he says he's trying some new leads. We can't exactly go to the police . . .'

'And I can't exactly stay in this house forever.'

'Hear hear,' said Connor, a little more emphatically than I felt was necessary.

'Connor,' said Sharon.

'He's got a point, though,' said Connor. 'Don't get me wrong Stanly, obviously you're . . . this is your home, for now, and having you is a pleasure. But some space really wouldn't go amiss.'

'Jesus,' I said, although I already knew that the forthcoming sentence should probably remain unsaid. 'Really sorry that the threat of my assassination has been such an inconvenience for you.'

'OK, now you can keep *that* tone to yourself—'

'Guys,' said Eddie. He had this way sometimes, a certain inflection, that positively compelled you to shut up. It worked on me, but more importantly it worked on Connor, and a part of me, I'm ashamed to say, felt gleeful. *Yeah, shut up,* it said. *My cousin's talking.*

*How about* you *shut up, brain? Put yourself in Connor's shoes. You wouldn't want you hanging around all day every day.*

'I know that this is trying for everyone,' said Eddie. 'I really do. And Connor, Sharon, I know that when I first asked if Stanly could stay, you did me a favour.'

'It's nothing to do with favours,' said Sharon. 'Stanly needed help. And we all need to stick together.'

'Obviously,' said Connor. He was having trouble sounding like he meant it, though. I said nothing.

'There is something going on,' said Eddie. 'Something bad. Stanly is in danger, and it is a more real, more *present* danger than any of the theoretical danger I was babbling on about when he first arrived in London. So until we know something, he needs to stay here, inside. Safe. And we need to keep trying to find out what's going on.'

'How, though?' said Connor. 'Like you said, you and I have exhausted our connections.'

'Skank's still looking into it,' said Eddie. 'You know him and rabbit holes.'

'Rabbit holes don't necessarily lead anywhere useful.'

'*Anyway,*' said Eddie, doing his voice again. 'Like I said. I appreciate that it's hard. So tonight I am getting the beers in, we are ordering a take-away, and we are going to have a nice evening like normal people who don't have mysterious figures trying to kill their friend. OK?'

'OK,' said Sharon. 'Excellent. I wasn't feeling particularly enthusiastic about cooking anyway. Connor?'

Connor nodded. 'Sounds good.' This time he actually sounded pretty genuine.

'Stanly?' said Eddie.

'Awesome,' I said. *Now that's how you pretend to be genuinely enthusiastic about something, Connor.*

*Shut up, brain. Stop being a dick.*

*YOU'RE a dick.*

'So,' I said, sitting back, full of Thai food and beer. 'How's Hannah?'

As predicted, Eddie underwent an instant metamorphosis from commanding, slightly-tortured-with-a-side-of-joviality adult in charge to awkward teenager. 'Fine,' he muttered.

I glanced at Sharon and Connor. Sharon was making a valiant effort to remain composed, but I could see mischief in Connor's eyes, the same frequency of cheekiness that I was feeling right now, like complementary protons or a science metaphor that actually makes sense. It was nice to know we still had that. 'Is that where you've been disappearing lately, pal?' he said, a pantomime of innocence.

'Don't see how it's anyone's business,' said Eddie.

'Yeah, Connor,' I said. 'Can't you see that Eddie minds you minding his beeswax?'

'Enough, tiny silly boys,' said Sharon. 'Leave poor Eddie alone.'

Eddie offered a 'yeah, leave me alone or I'll pulverise the pair of you' grunt, but I knew he appreciated it, behind it all. Hannah had had a pretty rough time the last couple of years, what with her place being brutally shot up. Her brother was in prison now. But she and Eddie had unofficially rekindled things, so that was good.

Not that he could talk about it like a normal human being, of course.

*Glad for him, though.*

It was a nice evening, although I excused myself earlier than I might have under normal circumstances. I knew they all cared, that they were trying to keep me safe, but even with all the food and the booze and the happy chatter, I couldn't fight the frustration. I was starting to hate the house, the same walls and rooms every single day, meandering around.

Later I sat on my bed, waiting to hear the front door open and close, signalling Eddie leaving. Not long after that, Connor and Sharon headed to bed.

I was halfway towards the open window when my phone started vibrating. It was Skank.

*Weird.*

'Hello?' I said, keeping my voice low.

'Stanly. Skank.'

'Hi. How's it going?'

'It's going. How's protective custody?'

'Also going. On and on and on and on.'

'Yes . . . Stanly, I had an interesting conversation with Nailah today.'

'Han vs Indy again?'

Skank laughed. 'No, nothing so contentious . . . she was asking after you. Wondering where you'd been. At first I thought that maybe she was . . . that she was interested . . . well, you know.'

'OK . . .'

'But I eventually ascertained that she wanted to talk with you about . . . something else. Something related to your situation.'

'Morter Smith?' *That doesn't make sense.*

'No, not that situation . . . the general situation.'

'Skank, no offence but can you stop being so cagey?'

'You never know who's listening.'

'Fine,' I said. 'Do you mean about powers and stuff?'

Skank sighed. 'Yes.'

'She knows about me?'

'That's the impression I got, yes.'

'How?'

'She didn't say. She just said that she had some important information, and she wanted to speak with you face to face. She asked if I could set up a meeting.'

'What did you say?'

'I said I'd see what I could do.'

I nodded. 'OK.' Excitement was bubbling in my gut. Finally,

*something.* God, anything would be better than the nothing my life seemed to have become. 'So . . . what do you think? Should I meet her?'

'I think that it might be worth a try,' said Skank. 'There is risk, of course. We can't be sure that she's not somehow working with your enemy, whoever that is. But we could meet quite privately and safely at the shop. I would prefer to sit in.'

'Of course.'

'It is somewhat awkward,' said Skank. 'I feel as though I'd rather not tell Connor or Eddie or Sharon at the moment. Nailah was very clear about wanting to speak to you, and you alone. I think we might be able to swing my presence, but anybody else . . .'

'Fine,' I said. 'We'll tell them when we feel the time is right.'

'Yes . . .' Skank sounded reluctant, but at this point I was beyond caring. I *needed* this.

'How about tomorrow evening?' I said. 'Half eleven-ish, at the shop?'

'All right. I'll confirm by text. Meet us downstairs. I'll leave the front door open.'

'Great. Thanks Skank. See you tomorrow.'

'Yes. Bye.'

'Bye.'

I tossed my phone on the bed and levitated up to the ceiling, rolling around in the air, silently whooping. Finally, something to do. Something to think about. I decided not to push my luck and stayed in. I was so wired though, tingling with anticipation, far too buzzing to go to sleep, so I eventually decided to try meditating. I lit one of the scented candles that Kloe had left behind after her last visit, sat cross-legged in the air above my bed and closed my eyes. *Calm. Calm. Breathe in, breathe out.*

*In.*

*Out.*

*Calm.*

*A still and silent ocean.*

*Washes of breeze.*

*Silence.*

*Death threat.*

*No. Shh. Silence.*

*Death threat. Morter Smith. Nailah. Angel Group.*

*I said shut up.*

*Death threat, Morter Smith, Nailah, Angel Group, Eddie, Kloe, South Park, cake—*

I SAID SHUT UP.

STILL AND SILENT BLOODY OCEAN, YOU BLOODY CRETIN.

WASHES OF BLOODY SILENT LOVELY BLOODY QUIET BLOODY BREEZE.

STUPID BLOODY STUPID SHIT BRAIN.

SHUT UP SHUT UP SHUT UP SHUT UP.

I opened my eyes, floated down to my bed – *bugger that for a laugh* – and read old Charlie Brooker columns until around three in the morning, when sleep finally engulfed me. And when I woke up, there was a text waiting for me from Skank.

*Tonight is on*, it said.

*Groovy*, said my brain.

# Chapter Six

IN THE GRAND pantheon of days that dragged, this one could have stood shoulder to shoulder with the very draggiest, head held high. I forced myself to read, although I took in little, and when evening eventually came I was lying on my bed, digesting sausage and mash and staring at the same page of *Consider Phlebas* that I'd been looking at for the last hour. Sharon had gone to get an early night, and Connor would probably stay up for a little while. I was usually the last one left awake anyway, which was handy. I have that night gene.

I popped downstairs at half ten to get a glass of water and found Connor yawning over the paper. 'I'm going to sleep,' I said, feeling like a traitor. 'Kippered.'

'Presuming that's rural Welsh slang for tired?'

'*Ydw.*'

He nodded. 'I'll be heading that way too shortly.' He glanced at the clock. 'Not too hardcore these days, are we?'

'Old age catching up.' For a second I thought about asking him whether everything was OK, whether I'd done something, why he seemed so distant lately, but the moment passed, or perhaps I hadn't ever really intended to say anything. Either way, I just smiled. ''Night.'

''Night.'

I shut my bedroom door, drank half of the water and sat watching the clock, listening. I heard Connor come upstairs a few minutes later, heard the bathroom door groan, toilet flushing, teeth brushing, then his and Sharon's bedroom door. I waited a little longer, just to be safe, then donned my coat, steeling myself.

*This has to be a trap.*

*But Nailah seems so . . .*

*It's too much of a coincidence though, surely? Death threat, then this?*

*Maybe Skank was right, maybe it* is *a come-on?*

*Oh don't flatter yourself. She's way older than you. Plus why would she want to meet at 110th Street? With Skank? Would he be there in a chaperone capacity or what? Also, let's face it punk, you're not exactly Ryan Gosling.*

*Plus, Kloe.*

*Not that I even—*

*THIS THOUGHT PROCESS IS RIDICULOUS. CEASE AND DESIST, AND GO OUTSIDE.*

Sometimes I honestly wondered how I was able to maintain even the tiniest semblance of control over my psychic powers, with such an uncooperative brain.

The night was like a cold shower and I slipped into it gratefully. It was a bit of a way to the shop and I considered flying, but that felt like tempting fate. Plus, if it was a trap, they'd expect that. Pedestrian transport.

*Train.*

My gratitude for my freedom didn't last long. Usually I felt confident moving around in London, secure that I knew the place, that nobody would try to tangle with me, and that I could take them if they did. Now I felt paranoid, edgy, hyper-aware of everybody else I saw, my eyes darting to the source of any sudden movement as I was propelled through glow-streaked tunnels by unfriendly currents.

What if this really *was* a trap?

I got to the shop in one piece. The door was unlocked and

I slipped inside, turning the deadlock behind me, and moved as quietly as I could towards the stairs. I could hear Skank and Nailah's voices quite clearly – *aww, they started without me* – but when I realised what they were talking about, I had to stifle a laugh.

'You are missing the point,' said Skank. '*Again*.'

'What do you mean, "again"?' said Nailah. 'When did I last miss the point?'

'You know when.'

'Oh, that. Look, I *maintain* that Han's sneakiness would give him the edge.'

'*Wrong*. He *prefers a straight fight to all this sneaking around*—'

'But is *willing* to shoot first, *willing* to hide under the floors, *willing* to—'

'Indiana Jones represents *pure aggression and endurance*, which—'

'Oh God, it's just cavemen vs astronauts again—'

'*Of course cavemen*—'

'Look, can we maybe not do this again, please? And also maybe come back to how I somehow missed your point? Could it have been because the logic was so obtuse and wrong-dimensional that MC Escher would be like "nah mate"? How am I missing this point?'

There was a pause, and I could almost see Skank taking a very deep breath. It was always amusing when my otherwise supernaturally placid boss lost his rag, but I rarely saw anyone take as much pure pleasure in goading him as Nailah seemed to. I knew I should go down and announce my presence, but this was too much fun. 'You are missing the point,' Skank continued, 'that I am  very clearly making. I am *not* saying that Abrams made a bad film. At least not until the second one. It's not a *great* film, by any stretch of the imagination, but it's fast-paced, exciting, brainless fun. What I'm *saying* is that aside from the superficial nostalgia bait of the characters and setting, it has about as much in common with *Star Trek*, the true *essence* of *Star Trek*, as *Battlestar Galactica*, i.e none. *The Motion Picture—*'

*OK, enough eavesdropping. Best make an entrance before genuine physical violence erupts.* I started walking down the stairs, calling, 'Yo. Hope I'm not interrupting anything important.'

They were in a small room adjacent to the one where we'd interrogated Masters, which Skank had kitted out with a green sofa, an armchair, a massive flat-screen television, a Blu-Ray player, several games consoles and a top-of-the-range sound system. He was sitting on a beanbag rolling a joint and Nailah was on the sofa puffing on an e-cigarette. Skank looked at me with an expression that said *why did you leave me with her for so long.* Nailah smiled, friendly but guarded. 'No, nothing important,' she said. 'Usual banter.'

'*Banter*,' said Skank. 'But not as we know it . . .'

'So,' said Nailah. 'Where have *you* been recently? Holiday?'

'House arrest,' I said. 'Someone wants to kill me.'

She nodded. 'Figured it might be something like that. The guy on the bus?'

My spine went cold. 'What?'

'Nasty guy? You fought him on a bus? And a truck? That's the guy who's trying to kill you?'

I stared at her, and she rolled her eyes. 'I know it's you in the video.'

'Really.' I sat down on the arm of the chair. 'Why do you say that?'

'Because it couldn't more obviously be you?' said Nailah. 'That's why I'm here. You've got powers.'

I glanced at Skank, who shrugged almost imperceptibly. He

seemed to have regained his composure. *Trust him to lose his rag over a conversation about* Star Trek, *and be utterly un-phased by this.*

*Un-phasered, more like!*

*Yeah, good one.*

'All right,' I said. 'Yeah. It's me. And I do have powers.'

Nailah nodded. 'And Skank? You know about all this business?'

'I do,' said Skank, sticking his joint.

'OK,' said Nailah. 'Cool. We're on the same page, then.'

'Not exactly,' I said. 'What this about, Nailah? You're not Angel Group, I hope.'

'Course not, although if I was you I would have asked me that *before* admitting being a superpowered type.'

'Thanks. I'll remember that next time. You know about the Group, though? The *real* Group?'

She nodded.

'How much?'

'Usual. Behind the scenes, string pullers. Dodgy experiments. Political corruption.'

'And how do you know about me?'

'You heard of Weird, Sister?'

'Yeah.'

'That's me,' she said, with a crafty smile.

'*You* run Weird, Sister?'

'Yep. Well. Co-run, with a conspiracy nut who I'd probably have gently let go if he hadn't done me so many insane tech-related favours. I'm more legwork than admin anyway.' She mock-bowed. 'London's self-proclaimed number-one anonymous investigative supernatural blogger at your service. Style of thing.'

'Pretty long title.'

'I have very long business cards.'

'I thought you said you were anonymous?'

'Never said they had my name on them.'

'Pretty crap business cards if they don't have your name on them.'

'I also never said they were any good.'

'Is Nailah even your real name, anyway?'

'Has anyone ever genuinely made the choice to spell Stanly the way you spell it?'

'Do you even *like* the Beatles?'

Skank coughed politely. 'As much as I love fast-paced screwball comedy-style back and forth . . .'

'Sorry,' I said. 'So how *did* you work out it was me? In the video?'

'Did you miss the "investigative" bit? I did some detective work. Plus, like I said, obvious. Had some other pictures of you too, and various whisperings. You killed Smiley Joe, didn't you?'

'I might maybe have helped,' I said. 'You left all this off your site. Why?'

''Cos I think there's more important stuff happening than getting scoops on private individuals,' said Nailah. 'Like making alliances. And I think that you're in danger.'

'Tell me something I don't know,' I said. 'Like who Morter Smith is, maybe?'

'Never heard of him,' said Nailah. 'Weird name.'

'I know, right? He's the one who wants me dead, apparently. Hence the cloak'n'daggery.'

She nodded. 'Fair 'nuff . . . well, I'm sorry to hear about the price on your head, if that's what it is, but when I say *you* are in danger, I mean superpowered types in general. And by extension, possibly everyone else.'

'Scoop many "superpowered types" then, do you?'

'I've found some,' said Nailah. 'But I'm not making stories out of them.'

'You hosted those videos, though,' said Skank. 'On your site. Compared them with another picture of Stanly.'

'That wasn't me,' said Nailah. 'Well . . . I took that other picture, yeah. But it was Damien, the guy who conjures the ones and zeroes, he put that stuff up, without asking me. I actually made him take it down.'

'Hold on,' I said. 'Damien? Captain Conspiracy, hippie, dreadlocks, stoner?'

Nailah frowned. 'Yeah?'

*Small. Goddamn. World.* 'I know him,' I said. 'Well. Met him, at a festival. Friend of a friend of a friend or something.'

'Woah,' said Nailah, her eyes widening. 'That's . . . I mean, that couldn't possibly be a coincidence? Perhaps this is all connected? Maybe it's *meant* to happen? Like destiny? Or perhaps it was all engineered by someone . . .'

'Really?'

Another eye roll. 'No, not really. Look . . . you might think this sounds ridiculous, considering the website I work for, but I've never been much for conspiracies. Even if things seem weird, generally there's going to be a mundane explanation, and usually a depressing one, 'cos that's the world. I never really thought that there were evil government agencies or sinister corporations lurking out there. Well, no more sinister than regular corporations, anyway. I just figured it was run-of-the-mill people, some stupid, some clever, some greedy. Then I started hearing about superpowered types, and monsters, and I did some digging, which led to deeper digging . . . so . . .'

'OK,' I said. 'Fair enough. You got a glimpse of the weird world within the world. But what's this *about*? What's this danger?'

'There should be a lot more of you out there,' said Nailah. 'Enhanced people, or powered individuals, or special folk, or whatever you call yourselves.'

85

'We tend to say "empowered",' I said.

She looked amused. 'Cool. And also kinda naff.'

*She's not wrong.*

*And also . . . when did we collectively decide to adopt Angel Group nomenclature?*

'Anyway,' Nailah continued, 'I think the Angel Group has snapped most of the others up. Honestly, they should have got *you* by now. They're incredibly powerful, incredibly well-connected, and no offence, but you're not exactly sly. I mean, not to downplay my detective skills or anything, but if I could find you then they definitely could. So either you're working with them already, or—'

'I'm *not* working with them.'

'-*or* they're saving you up for something.' Amused turned to grim. 'Something . . .'

'Bad.'

'It makes sense,' said Skank.

'Yeah?' I said.

'Well,' said Skank, 'think about the empowered that you've met, that you know. Apart from the Angel Group's lackey, what's his name . . .'

'Leon.'

'Yes. Apart from him, there's you, there's your cousin, who's from the same tiny little middle-of-nowhere Twin Peaks-without-the-fun-stuff town as you, and there's Connor and Sharon, a couple who knew each other well before they met Eddie. I'm no statistics man, but the likelihood of you all being the only empowered out there is slim.' He lit his joint and smoked thoughtfully. 'I've thought about this before. It's always bothered me, and I think Nailah could well be right. Maybe they are saving you all up for something.'

'We might just be staying under their radar,' I said, not feeling particularly inclined to elaborate on our history with the company, not until I was a little more sure about the implications of this conversation. I knew I didn't sound very convincing, and Nailah's expression and tone confirmed it.

'Yeah,' she said. 'Maybe. Look . . . did you notice how hardly any mainstream press outlets picked up on that video of you fighting on the bus? Maybe two of them gave it one dismissive paragraph, tucked away on page 94, and they all ran with it as some kind of viral thing, a stunt, but they weren't even impressed by that. Like, "is that the best you can do now, the special effects aren't even that convincing, yadda yadda yadda".'

'You think that the Angel Group is muzzling the press?'

'I think that a corporation doing literal evil would probably be stupid not to,' said Nailah.

'Then why have they left *you* alone?' I asked. 'You and all the other weirdo blogs that suggested it was someone with powers?'

"Cos the percentage of people who take us seriously is barely a drop in the ocean,' said Nailah, as if I were an idiot. 'We're not a threat. In fact, I'd say leaving us alone actually strengthens *their* case. Makes us look more like a bunch of tinfoil-hatted crackpots smoking super-strength skunk and burbling about chemtrails and the Illuminati. Which, to be fair, is what a lot of my contacts do on their evenings off. And during the day. But if it's not in the broadsheets or the red tops, people *en masse* don't want to know, even now.'

'Maybe,' I said. 'But maybe they don't consider *us* a threat, either.'

'Maybe they don't,' said Nailah. 'But I'd say you're more of a threat than a bunch of keyboard warriors tearing forums apart arguing over whether 9/11 was perpetrated by superpowered CIA sleeper agents.'

'Are you serious? That's a thing?'

'I know,' said Nailah. 'Telekinesis can't melt steel beams,

right?' She started to smile, then frowned. 'Although, actually
. . . *can* it?'

'Honestly, I have no idea.'

'Fair enough.' She nodded at Skank. 'You don't have powers,
then, Freaks and Geeks?'

Skank shook his head. 'No. I just roll the joints and sign
the cheques.'

*Interesting. Pretty sure that's at least half a lie.* 'Look,' I said.
'I appreciate you telling me all this stuff. And it's cool that
you're being responsible about your reporting now. But I don't
know what you—'

'There's another one out there,' said Nailah. 'Superpowered
type. Or empowered, or whatever the word is.'

I frowned. 'What? Who? Where?'

'Her name's Lauren Stone. She lives in London. Hiding.
Probably from the Angel Group.'

'Not hiding very well,' I said, 'if you managed to find her.'

'I didn't just *find* her,' said Nailah. 'Not like . . . she wasn't
standing in her front garden levitating things. I have sources. I
investigate stuff. Look, it doesn't matter how I found her. What
matters is that she's out there, and from what I can tell she's
alone . . . but she hasn't always been.'

'Meaning?'

'There were two,' said Nailah. 'Her and her friend. Up until
about a year ago.'

'You've been keeping tabs for that long?'

'Longer,' said Nailah. 'On and off. There's a whole network
of us. We share information, keep our ears to the ground.'

'Oracle?' said Skank.

Nailah frowned. 'Yeah. How do you—'

'Other people know things too,' said Skank.

'Um, what's Oracle?' I said.

'Network of deep web forums,' said Skank. 'Constantly

shifting, moving around. They share bizarre information with one another. I've been looking into them recently, trying to find more information about Morter Smith and the Angel Group.'

'Right,' I said. *More on that story later.* 'So Nailah, again . . . why are you telling us this?'

'Seems like you superpowered types should probably stick together,' said Nailah. 'Especially if I'm right, and the Angel Group has been snapping you up for something sinister.'

'You don't *know* the Angel Group took this other person, though?'

'Look,' said Nailah, 'I get that you're not leaping to trust me. But I'm not running some half-arsed Facebook page. I vet my sources, I double, triple, quadruple check every bit of information. And based on everything I've heard, it sounds like Lauren's friend was taken.'

'But they didn't take Lauren? Why?'

She shrugged.

'Right,' I said. 'OK. So . . . what, you want me to bring this Lauren into the fold, even though there isn't really a fold? And rescue her friend from wherever she's supposedly being held?'

'I think that would be a good thing to do, yes.'

'You *do* realise that having superpowers doesn't automatically make me a resourceful private detective slash secret agent slash commando person, don't you?' I said. 'They don't just conveniently make everything easier to do.'

Another shrug.

'Fine,' I said. 'Whatever. But . . . look, I'm still confused. What's in it for you?' I was pretty sure I did trust her, but I felt as though it made sense not to go all in on being super-best-friends club immediately.

'I want to be a part of what's happening,' said Nailah. 'All the weirdness? Monsters, superpowers, government conspiracies, evil corporations? It's *real*. It's happening. And I don't think it's going to stay hidden for long. I want to be involved.'

'Basically,' I said, 'when it all blows up, you want a scoop.'

'Well, yeah,' said Nailah. 'I'd be lying if I said that wasn't part of it. I'd be pretty happy to be the first journalist to print an official interview with a superpowered type.'

'Empowered.'

'I've decided I prefer my phrase,' she said. 'OK . . . look, I'm giving you this information, and promising not to report on any more of this stuff until . . . I don't know, until things are more certain. And Damien and the rest of Weird, Sister will stay quiet too. Just . . . keep me in the loop, OK?'

I nodded.

'Here's Lauren's address.' Nailah handed me a piece of paper. 'You should find her. Before they do.'

I nodded and pocketed it.

'It's got my number on the back too. We should stay in touch. Drop me a text or something so I know how to get hold of you. If I hear anything else, I'll pass it on.' Nailah checked her phone. 'Ah. I've got to be somewhere.' She stood up.

'You're going? Thought you'd want me to show off my superpowers or something.'

Nailah raised one eyebrow. 'What an offer.' There was something in her voice, and my eyes doubled in size of their own accord.

'What?' I said. 'No! I didn't mean—'

'Relax, dickhead.' She rolled her eyes. *Girl does a lot of that.* 'That was a joke.'

'I didn't—'

'You're painfully obvious.' She smiled. 'Although you looked panicked rather than smug, so I'll let you off.'

Skank actually stifled a snigger, and I stood up, struggling to regain my composure. 'Right. Anyway. So . . . yeah. Next time, or something.'

'Next time,' said Nailah. 'Or something. Anyway, I've seen the video. Pretty cool, admittedly. And maybe we'll have time for your origin story at some point.'

'Young Welsh lad with superpowers flees his quiet rural town for the bright lights and violence of London, and is taken in by the kindly proprietor of a comic store,' said Skank. 'It's the classic immigrant story, essentially. Like Superman. Or Paddington Bear.'

Nailah laughed. 'Great. I'm sure you'll make a fascinating interviewee. I'll be in touch. See y'all later.'

'See you,' I said.

Skank nodded and got up to let her out, passing me the rest of the joint as he did so. I sat on the sofa and held it, too preoccupied with my thoughts to even consider smoking any. When Skank returned, I passed it back. 'What do you think?'

'I think I should probably tell Connor, Sharon and Eddie that you sneaked out of the house for a clandestine meeting,' said Skank.

'You Lando.'

He smiled. 'I won't, though. I know Eddie wants to keep you safe. They all do. And I hate going behind my friends' backs. They've done more for me than . . . well. They've done a lot. But personally, I think this is your battle. The rest of them clearly want nothing to do with it, and I respect that, but I also respect your desire to be involved. It's unfair for you to be out of the loop. And although it may be extremely unsafe, I think that by the time a superpowered kid turns eighteen, he's earned the right to unfasten his seatbelt and fly through the windscreen into the real world.' He shrugged. 'And the whole thing intrigues me. So if that makes me a Lando . . . so be it. Pass the Colt 45.'

'Cool,' I said. 'So if I go and find this Lauren, you won't rat me out?'

'I won't,' said Skank. 'Although I'd suggest you don't go tonight. I doubt that it's a trap – Nailah seems trustworthy to me, and I like to think I'm a pretty good judge of such things. But it might be best not to rush in, regardless.'

'Yeah. No news on your front?'

'Nothing about your death threat, I'm afraid,' said Skank. 'Although I have met some quite interesting new people in the last week or so. I haven't told Eddie or the others about them yet, but they may well have information about the Angel Group.'

'Anything to do with this Oracle thing?'

'Maybe.'

'Why haven't you told us about them already? Or about Oracle, for that matter?'

'When it became relevant, I was going to,' said Skank. 'And these new people are especially secretive. Some might say paranoid.'

'Are they empowered?'

'I don't believe so. Just . . . aware. And well-equipped.'

'Fair enough.'

'I'm going to organise introductions soon,' said Skank, 'but I thought it would be a good idea if everyone met at the same time. You, Eddie, Connor, Sharon, these new folks. Maybe this Lauren, if she's interested.'

'I understand.'

'As soon as I get anything concrete about Morter Smith or his plans, you'll be the first to know,' said Skank.

'Thanks.' We sat in silence for a moment, and then I said something that I hadn't been planning to say. 'What are you up to now?'

A tiny wrinkle of surprise registered on Skank's face. 'Not

much,' he said. 'You're welcome to hang out, if you want. We could watch something.'

*Bizarre, but a better proposition than doing bugger all.* 'Yeah, that'd be cool. Feels like I've been stuck inside for months. Just being in a different room is great.'

Skank nodded. 'Do you smoke?'

'Um . . . I have done.'

'Fair enough.'

'By the way,' I said. 'What did you do with Scott Masters?'

'Handed him over to some people,' said Skank. 'He was no threat to anyone.' There was a finality to his tone, so I left it. 'What do you fancy watching?' he asked.

'I honestly don't mind.'

'Some Buffy, perhaps?'

'Good shout.'

'Season?'

'Um . . . what's your favourite?'

'Depends what day it is.'

'Well, we could each pick a couple of our favourite episodes, or something like that.'

'All right.'

So for the next few hours I sat with my oddball urban bushman millionaire boss smoking very potent spliffs, drinking tea and watching *Buffy the Vampire Slayer*. Every now and then we would exchange a few words about a particular character or line or plot arc, but mostly it was silence, broken by the occasional laugh. The last time I'd got stoned I'd ended up taking a talking beagle home with me. This was different. It was normal. It was nice, actually. Eventually, however, I had to try and stand up, and the ceiling rushed down at me, the floor lurching upward to meet it. *Woah.* 'Cheers,' I said, in a slow croak. My mind was full of fumes. 'And um . . . yeah. Cheers.'

'You're quite welcome,' said Skank. 'How are you going to get home?'

'Fly,' I said, jokingly. Then I remembered that I actually could fly, and laughed like a twat for about thirty seconds. Skank chuckled drily, which was his version of hysterical laughter. 'Fly,' I said again, and left.

The journey back was intense, and not a little wobbly. I kept getting distracted by oddly-shaped clouds, or the way the moonlight hung in a certain way, or the way that building down there looked slightly like a . . . like a thing.

*Like a what?*

*Oh for gawwwd's sake.*

When I finally managed to float back into my bedroom I banged my head on the window frame and tumbled in, barely managing to avoid knocking my desk over. I bit my lip to avoid swearing loudly and thought the window shut, then climbed out of my clothes, fell into bed and quietly span out.

*Remember the murder threat?*

*No.*

*And the new empowered person?*

*Nope.*

*And all the other stuff?*

*Noooooooooooooooooope . . .*

# Chapter Seven

I WOKE UP at twelve the next day, body full of wet sand, brain a mess of tangled fuzz, throat arid. The light wandering in through a gap in the curtains was far, *far* too bright, and I sat up and groggily thought an instruction towards them. But rather than closing the curtains, my careless thought ripped one straight off the rail, flooding the room with light. 'Bollocks,' I said. Or at least, a vaguely 'bollocks'-shaped grunt struggled out of my mouth. I thought the curtain back up, but replacing it properly required a level of dexterity that I simply didn't possess right at that moment, so I crudely bodged it and sat there with the word 'monged' floating above my head in thick green bubble writing.

Sharon poked her head around the door. 'Afternoon teenager,' she said. 'Mind if I come in?' Even through my haziness, I could tell something was up.

*She knows.*

'Yeah,' I said, sitting up. Sharon came in and sat down at the end of the bed. She raised an eyebrow and sniffed demonstratively. 'Something smells herbal.'

'Um,' I said. 'I kind of . . . well, I had some stuff that was . . . leftover, and it was kind of, and I couldn't sleep. So I was just . . . I wasn't smoking inside. I was on the window sill. Outside the window. And . . .'

Sharon waved her hand. 'OK, this is pretty torturous, so let's not, shall we?'

My eyes dropped, ashamed. 'Sorry.'

'I don't mind about the weed, you idiot,' said Sharon. 'You're eighteen, and it's not exactly crack. And I'm not your mother. What matters is you sneaking out without telling us.'

'I know. I just . . .'

'I understand,' said Sharon. 'You know I do. But we've talked about this before. You sneaking out, using your powers. Not only is it dangerous, especially now, but . . . Stanly, we were happy to take you in, give you a place to stay, help you set yourself up. We love having you here.' *Maybe you do.* 'But you have to respect our rules. We're not your family, but you live under our roof.' The quiet, matter-of-fact disappointment in her tone made me squirm inside.

'Sorry,' I said, ineffectually.

'I won't ask where you went,' said Sharon. 'I think I can probably guess, anyway, based on the smell. I didn't tell Connor, and I won't be telling Eddie. I don't think either of them would be as understanding as me.'

'Thanks.'

'Look,' said Sharon, 'I know you want to be out there, getting involved. But the fact is, Connor and I want no part of whatever the Angel Group might or might not be doing. We don't want to get involved in anything dangerous. We don't want to be fighting any more monsters. That chaos last year was quite enough. We've made a very conscious decision to steer clear of it.'

It had been on the tip of my tongue to mention Lauren, but after she said that, I realised that it would be both a bad idea and pointless. So I just nodded, staying penitent. 'I know.'

'OK.' Sharon smiled. 'Just about to have a last tea before I head to work. Double shift today, yay. Cuppa?'

'Definitely.'

'Thought so. I know stoners have a very close relationship

with tea.' She winked and left the room, adding, 'Don't forget to fix the curtain properly.'

'I will,' I said. 'I mean . . . I won't. Forget.' I sat and tried to force my head to be clearer. I needed to work out what I was going to do. I needed to think things through very logically, and come up with the best possible plan.

I also needed tea. A lot.

*Tea first. Then plan.*

It was Sunday and 110th Street was closed, so Connor was home. I felt like it would be a good idea to keep out of his way, so I stayed upstairs and tried to think about what the hell to do. Typical. Something meaty had finally happened, several things in fact, and I felt entirely out of my depth. I wished I could ask Eddie. Maybe I could . . .

But I couldn't. Because he would have been cross and he would have nagged.

And none of them wanted anything to do with this kind of crap.

*So plan, kid. Plan solo.*

It seemed to make sense to go and find Lauren, speak to her, find out what – if anything – she knew. Maybe do a bit of probing about this friend of hers. The idea of having a new superpowered friend was appealing, while the idea that there was someone, maybe loads of people, who might need rescuing . . . well. I'm not going to lie, the thought of busting into whatever theoretical prison was holding my empowered brethren and setting them free . . . it wasn't a terrible notion.

No. I gave myself a mental slap. *People. People trapped, held against their will. That is a terrible notion. This isn't a game.*

*Need to think clearly, remember? Logically.*

So. Logic. Somebody wanted to kill me, someone who was very probably affiliated with the Angel Group. The fact that

97

they hadn't tried again was odd – *perhaps it was a test, hopefully I passed I guess* – but I had to assume that they were watching me. In which case, I could end up leading them straight to Lauren. Which would be bad.

*Why, though? So long as neither of us use our powers they'll just think I'm visiting a friend.*

It wasn't that simple, though.

Eventually I got tired of running around in circles, and called Nailah. 'Hello?'

'Hi. It's Stanly.'

'Ah, Junior Birdman.'

'You what?'

Nailah laughed. 'OK, excuse me while I high-five myself for out-obscure-pop-culture reference-ing you.'

'Consider yourself excused. Can you talk?'

'Yeah. Wha' gwan?'

'I'm not totally sure what to do.' I filled her in on my tangle of circular thoughts, and she listened in silence. 'So,' I finished, 'as someone who's fairly high profile in terms of the maybe-bad-guys' radar, seems like maybe I'm not the best person to go and bring the person we want to keep safe into the open.'

'That was a fairly dreadful sentence. But yeah, I guess you've got a point. Maybe I should go then.'

'Would you?'

'Yeah. I mean, I'm not on anyone's radar. And I was thinking about going myself before . . . just thought it might be better coming from you.'

'Give her my number,' I said. 'Tell her everything about me, whatever's necessary. But make it very clear that, if she wants, she has friends. Allies.'

'Will do. And I'll report back. Got a load of stuff to do this afternoon but I'll head over there this evening. Wait to hear from me, OK?'

'Thanks, Nailah.'

'No problemo. Laters.'

I hung up and my brain, being what it was, immediately felt guilty and pathetic for not going myself. Intellectually I knew it made sense – I was a target, and it was utterly counterintuitive to go to someone who we thought might be in danger with the intention of making her less in danger, and potentially make her more in danger in the process. *Another cracking sentence there, sport.* But still . . .

By the time darkness fell I still hadn't heard anything, and I was starting to worry. What if something had happened? Maybe I *should* go? I decided that whatever happened, I would head out that night, either to go and find Lauren or just to go out and stretch my legs and work off some of this tension. But then I started to feel bad about sneaking out behind Connor and Sharon's backs, and a couple of times I was *this* close (holds up thumb and forefinger so they're almost touching) to telling Connor and asking him to come with me . . . but no. I had to keep reminding myself that they didn't want to be involved.

*And anyway, you're the one Morter Smith wants to kill.*

*You've got every right to be going out and investigating.*

*Yeah, every right to betray your friends' trust.*

There was a whole other side to this as well: Tara. At some point in the future, Kloe and I would have a child, and the danger from the Angel Group, or whoever else, would be so great that I would find a way to bring her back in time, to keep her safe. It was incredible, ridiculous, more ridiculous than any of the other ridiculous stuff I'd experienced, but I *knew* it was true. If Pandora hadn't convinced me, Oliver and Jacqueline would have. And even if *they* hadn't . . . I knew. Tara and Kloe and I were connected. I couldn't have found and rescued Tara by accident. I couldn't have found Kloe in a city of over eight million people, in the right park, at the right minute, on the right afternoon. Maybe it was my powers, subconsciously guiding me. Whatever. I didn't care. But we *were* connected. And if that kind of trouble was on the horizon, trouble so terrible that we would need to travel in time to escape it, I was going to need all the superpowered allies I could get, reluctant or otherwise.

*And if I have to move out and find somewhere else to live . . . so be it.*

Finally Connor went to bed, and I sat in my room and stewed. *Wait to hear from me,* Nailah had said. It was pretty late now, and going to Lauren's myself was starting to seem silly. If I hadn't heard from Nailah, it was for a good reason.

As if on cue, my phone bleeped. It was a text from Nailah. *Went to see her,* it said. *She didn't want to know. Told me to leave. New plan?*

Damn.

Now what?

I texted Nailah back: *I'll go myself.* Her response was quick: *Do you think that's a good idea?*

I didn't bother answering.

Out the window again.

I liked to think that I knew London well, insofar as anyone can know such a mind-bogglingly big city, but the area that I needed to go to was pretty foreign territory. I racked my brains, trying to remember the route I'd less than meticulously planned out earlier on. A bus and two Tubes, and after that I could probably walk.

I felt totally different tonight. Whereas last night the city had seemed full of strangers, now I felt on top of it. It was as if little videogame-style menus were appearing above the heads of anyone who might have been a threat, detailing their weaknesses. I was on a mission. I was *doing* something, finally, after what felt like forever. I transferred from one train to the other, surrounded by heat and cold, fabric, people's breath and words, phrases from posters and billboards and timetables bleeding together, forming cryptic haikus. City code.

I narrowly caught my last train, which was almost empty, apart from an old woman sitting at the other end of the compartment. She was completely wrapped up in coats and headscarves but wore no gloves, and her fingers were almost skeletal, and her expressionless face was a mass of wrinkles. I couldn't even see her eyes because they were too sunken, too dark. She barely moved, although she was definitely breathing. I didn't relish spending an entire train journey with a living corpse so I tried to disappear into my brain. I was getting good at it. So good, in fact, that I almost missed my stop.

The moon flickered, a pale pensive sliver in the deep night. Time was getting on, and I was feeling slightly less safe. Something about that old lady, and the way the lights had dimmed to a seedy dullness. Like harbingers. People hurried as though they were frightened, eyes stared distrustfully from under hoods, grim men observed me balefully from doorways, arms crossed over broad chests, and the wind played desultory street games with old kebab debris. I love my city, but sometimes it finds it hard to love me back. Or maybe it could sense that something was afoot and was picking up on my anxiety, the way a pet does.

I vaguely knew where I was going now. I passed a club, the walls and air around it reverberating with the sound of heavy techno beats, and imagined people dancing, pulsating, cells in a brand-new, temporary organism. I liked the poetry of that, although I was pretty sure I'd loathe it if I were actually in there. Too much noise, too much sweat. *And why are people raving on a Sunday night anyway? Does nobody work Mondays anymore?*

*Directions, remember directions.*

I pulled out my A-Z and studied it. *Focusing might help,*

*less wandering in a daze if you please.* I managed to work out exactly where I was, and that I needed to go down the dark alley to my left. Oddly, it felt safer than the street, and I emerged at the other end facing an empty road and a hunched-over heap of tower block beyond, most of its windows darkened.

*Not far now—*

A howling roar like a planet exploding, and something tore its way out of the ground behind me, showering the street with shards of broken tarmac. I swivelled around and looked up, and *up*, straight into the face of a heavily-muscled dog. It was the size of a small elephant and a bright electrical blue, and as it shook itself free of the wreckage it opened its mouth and howled again, showing far too many teeth. Faintly ridiculously, I struck something that could have been a fighting stance, my brain and heart and muscles all bellowing different instructions at me. *Trap! Run! Fight! Fly away! Psychically tear a lamppost out of the ground and beat it to death! Phone Eddie!*

No time. It lunged and I dived to my left, the dog's jaws snapping shut with a sound like grinding steel. I got to my feet, trying to win back my equilibrium, keeping my eyes fixed on the monstrous canine. I wasn't even aware of any people around me, there had to be some, surely, and cars, and were they watching? I couldn't . . . this thing—

*—stop thinking and jump out of the way—*

—I dived to the side again, and this time I felt its stinking, molten breath as it came at me. My brain was flashing through possible strategies at lightspeed, but none seemed workable. I could fly out of its reach, but—

*—jump out of the WAY—*

—I jumped backwards, right into the road, and heard a car spin to a halt, and a crash, and an alarm . . . and screaming. Lots of screaming, in fact. The dog raised its head and howled at the sky, melting my skin, and when the noise subsided the immense beast looked down at me, straight into my eyes, and I stared back into its own shark-like orbs. I knew that if I looked for much longer I would be hypnotised and it would devour me.

*I can't die now. Tara needs me. Kloe needs me. So many things to—*

*MOVE then, you berk!*

The dog snarled and lunged again but I was already ten feet in the air, fifteen, twenty. It passed underneath me, spun and jumped, snapping and bellowing. *How can something that big be so graceful?*

*Ooh, yeah, let's think about that LATER IF WE'RE NOT DEAD.*

I was hanging in the air out of reach, trying to think, but—

—*it's jumping*—

—I flipped over backwards, feeling friction and smelling its breath as its jaws smashed together inches from my head, and flew without looking, slamming into the side of a building. *Winded, ouch, ouch, ouch.* I slid down a few feet, unable to keep altitude because of the pain, and now the dog leapt towards me, all four of its feet leaving the ground. I spun clumsily out of its way and it crashed against the building, denting the concrete with the force of its jump and raining glass and ruined brickwork down on the street. It snarled and swiped at me with one of its paws and *just* caught me in the back, knocking me down. I hit the ground, rolled instinctively and jumped to my feet, diving forwards and flying between its legs, but it adjusted too fast, whirling around on the balls of its feet and snapping behind me again, countering my dodges so fast that I couldn't possibly think of an attack. I darted up again, turned in the air; it was coming towards me again, soaring up, and I rolled over its head and for one hellish second our eyes locked again. Nothing there . . .

I heard Sharon's voice in my head: *That was when I knew that there was nothing in this thing's mind that I could understand, it was just a monster . . .*

*Eyes!*

*Take out its eyes!*

I couldn't possibly get close enough to its face to do that . . . but there was another way. I headed back groundward, landed roughly and sprinted towards the alley from which I'd just come, towards the hole in the ground that the monster had created. It was pounding behind me, roaring, and I jumped, flew, planted both feet on a wall and backflipped, back over the beast, and as I turned in the air I concentrated on its eyes with my mind. *Burst. Burst. BURST! BURSTBURSTBURST—*

They exploded, just as a huge paw scored a direct hit on my back. I felt sharpness too, lost control and hit the ground, all of the wind I had managed to regain knocked out of me for a second time. I was cut and bruised now – although if the angle had been different its claws would probably have ripped straight through me – and I rolled over on my back and looked up at the beast. It was screaming, a sound that was, amazingly, worse than its howls, dark blood pouring from its ruined eyes, but still it turned and faced me and I knew it was sniffing me out, and I couldn't do anything. *Move!*

*I can't.*

*MOVE!*

I turned to fly . . . but something made me stop. Chancing a look back, I saw that the giant beast was shaking and staggering, trying to fight off a small blur of white and brown that was rushing around and around its neck and head, tearing out chunks of bloody flesh and tufts of blue fur and spitting them away. The dog was moaning and roaring in agony, snapping at the tiny blob of energy that was killing it, blood and torn fur flying, and eventually, with a final low moan and a shuddering spasm that racked its entire ruined body, it collapsed into the road and lay still. I glanced around. There were people everywhere now, staring, some standing in shock, some running away, a few unconscious. I could hear screams too. None of the cars were moving.

Turning back to the dead dog, I saw something small and white trotting down the great corpse like it was a familiar hill, a place for strolling. It stepped onto the pavement, looked up at me and cocked its head, inviting me to speak.

'What . . . the . . . fuck?' I said.

Daryl winked. 'You were expecting somebody else?'

# Chapter Eight

I BLINKED SEVERAL times. *Giant dead dog / small talking dog (beagle) who used to be my best friend / people watching (screaming, sirens?) / small dog killed big dog / can't form coherent . . .*

'We'd better skedaddle, chief,' said Daryl, in a low voice. 'Police and all that. Just follow me, walk naturally, and maybe don't talk to me for a minute.'

I nodded dumbly and followed him across the street. A group of people parted hurriedly to let us through, and I made brief eye contact with a kid about my age wearing a heavy green coat. Weirdly, he was the only person who didn't seem utterly flabbergasted by what had happened. I didn't like the look he gave me, but I must have been in shock because I immediately forgot about him and followed Daryl on autopilot, up a street, down a street, across a road, right turn, along an alley choked with rubbish, a steel-tinted puddle reflecting the moon, another right turn past boxes and walls daubed with illegible graffiti, an empty spray can lying discarded in a nest of old newspaper. I tried to think but couldn't so I just followed the dog, remembering our last conversation.

Daryl: "Where do we stand?"

Me: "Unless you get some new information that I might need, we stand a long way apart."

*What the* hell *is going on?*

Daryl slowed down, glancing up and down the alley. 'Good. Probably OK to stop for a minute. Catch your breath.'

Now I realised that I was gasping. Panic? *Probably a delayed reaction to the enraged elephant-sized dog that almost killed me to death.* I closed my eyes, gripped my body's reins and tried to bring my breathing under control, willing my hands to stop shaking. Daryl waited quietly until I was able to open my eyes.

'OK,' I said. 'What the *shit* was that?'

'Monster.' He was always like that, so to-the-point. No messing about.

'It was after me?'

'Maybe,' said Daryl. 'It could just be another one random-ly finding its way up . . . but it's a funny coincidence, you walking over that particular spot just as a monster dog the size of Belgium decides to pop up for a snack. And it was bigger than any I've ever seen. Well . . . pretty much.'

'So who could have sent it?' *I'm sounding pretty calm now. Fair dos to me.* 'And what do you mean, "pretty much"?'

'I did have a life before you, kid,' the dog smiled. 'And as far as who sent it . . . search me. I honestly don't know who would be able to summon a beast like that, let alone control it. If *anyone* could. Maybe your powers attracted it? There is a weird connection between these monsters and empowered people. You probably noticed that when you fought Smiley Joe.'

I had. 'I suppose . . .'

'So until I see evidence to the contrary,' said Daryl, 'I'd probably go with coincidence. Or a six-pack of bad luck. What were you doing out here, anyway?'

'I'm looking for someone.'

'Looking?' said Daryl. 'Found someone you have, I would say, hmmm?' His Yoda accent had improved. I laughed weakly. 'Right.'

'Sorry. You were saying.'

'Looking,' I said. 'Yeah. For a girl. Woman. Another empowered, name of Lauren. That's all I've got, name and address.' I took out the piece of paper with Lauren's address and showed it to Daryl. It felt like a minor victory that I still had it.

'Who gave you the address?' asked Daryl. He was scrutinising me with his quiet beagle eyes, all business. I don't know how I could talk to him so normally, considering the history we had behind us, and the slightly insane manner of our reunion. Maybe I was still in shock. I think I probably was. My foot kept twitching, and I was speaking in a dull monotone. 'A friend,' I said. 'Kind of. Blogger. Investigates weird stuff, people with powers, monsters. She worked out who I am. Came to me with the name.'

'Hmm. You trust her?'

'I guess,' I said. 'At least . . . I did. I didn't have any reason not to.'

'Until le chien gargantuan.'

I shifted uncomfortably on the spot. 'It doesn't . . . I didn't tell her my route. And . . .'

*She said that Lauren said no . . . she must have known I'd go instead . . .*

*Maybe . . .*

'I'm sure she couldn't have,' I said, although I was surprised how *unsure* I sounded. 'She wouldn't . . . Jesus, I haven't got a clue.'

'Maybe someone fed her the info,' said Daryl. 'Hoped that it would somehow get back to you or Eddie or Connor and that you'd fall into the trap.'

'She was reluctant to tell us how she found Lauren,' I said. 'But she . . . no. She's on the level, I'm sure she is. We—'

'Stanly,' said Daryl, 'I have a feeling that things are about to take a pretty extreme detour up shit creek. And we've got fans instead of paddles.'

'Fans?'

''Cos, you know. Shit hitting the fan. And being up shit creek with no paddle.' Daryl shook his head. 'What I'm trying to say is that shit's getting real, and I need you to think at Defcon 1. Don't trust what you think you know.' That almost made me laugh, because if I couldn't even pick up on the fan/paddle joke, it seemed unlikely that I was going to be much use at thinking, generally.

'Should I trust you, then?' I said, staring him in the face.

Daryl nodded. 'Yes. Now, either someone sent Old Bluer after you, which, hey, let's not rule it out entirely, or London's monster problem is getting worse, which, hey, also not fantastic news. We're going to need to be careful. Personally I'd advise not going back to Sharon and Connor's just yet, in case.'

'In case?'

'If someone *did* set up this mutant Crufts routine, they'll most probably be watching the house. If you come back in one piece they might move to whatever their plan B is. Based on plan A, I'd file plan B away under "eminently skippable". If you don't come back, they'll hopefully assume you've been taken out, and that'll buy us more time.'

'What if they move in on Connor and Sharon and Eddie now that I'm gone?'

'They can take care of themselves,' said Daryl.

'They're my friends . . . my *family*,' I said, charging the word with as much venom as I could muster. Anger felt better than numb with an edge of panic. 'I'm not going to abandon them to be chewed up by hellhounds or whatever else is prowling around this city. I'm not going to hide.'

*You were perfectly happy to go against their wishes and sneak off. You've even started thinking about where else you could live.*

*Shut up, brain. Being righteously angry right now please, thanks.*

'Stanly,' said Daryl. 'I understand how you must be feeling . . .'

'Oh, really?'

'Yes. And I'm asking you to bury it, Romeo. It's a particularly misshapen chaos but you have to understand that I intend to *keep you alive*. And in order to do that, I need you to trust me. There are a lot of issues between us, I get that, and we'll address them when we have the time. Until then, I'm afraid you're going to have to lump it, boss.'

I didn't answer for a moment. I *wanted* to trust him. If I'm honest, I wanted to forget everything that had gone wrong between us. I didn't even want to talk about it. I wanted my friend back.

But he was right about one thing: I needed to think at Defcon 1. 'How did you find me?' I asked.

'What do you mean?'

'I mean what I said. Seems a helluva coincidence, you being on hand to rescue me.'

'You're telling me,' said Daryl. 'I was . . . nearby.'

'Once more with me feeling more convinced.'

Daryl laughed ruefully. 'OK. I was looking for you, actually.'

'Yeah? Why?'

'Well I saw those swish new promo vids that you filmed,' said Daryl. 'I thought they were pretty cool and that you must be on to something big, wondered if there might be a slice for a roguishly handsome four-legged fella.'

I couldn't help it; I cracked up. So did he. It felt better than anger. 'So you were following me,' I said. 'Covertly.'

'When you put it like that, it sounds so unethical.'

'It *is* what you were doing, though?'

'Ish.'

'You could have jumped in a bit earlier, in that case.'

'I said *ish*,' said Daryl. 'I was staying pretty far back. Didn't want to risk you seeing me yet.'

'All right . . . well, we'll get to the ethics of that later.'

I paused for a second. 'OK, it's later. Don't follow me covertly.'

'Yes, boss,' said Daryl. 'Imagine me saluting.'

'Right,' I said, 'now we're going to carry on, and we're going to find this girl Lauren.'

'Let me see the address again,' said Daryl. I showed him, and he nodded. 'Cool. My inner DavNav tells me—'

'DavNav?'

'Just go with it. It tells me that we're nearby, but I think we should take a roundabout route. In case we're being followed. Sound like a plan?'

'Plan-shaped.'

I pulled my hood up and we started to walk. 'So what have you been *doing* for a year?' I said. 'Wandering around killing monsters? Are you Daryl, rogue demon hunter, now?'

'What's a rogue demon?' We laughed, and Daryl shook his head. 'Not really. Left London for a while. Drifted, not at all sure of what the hell to do. Then I decided to come back.'

'Why?'

'Because I knew you'd be screwed on an epic scale without me, obviously.'

I laughed. 'Yeah, whatever.' It felt good to laugh with him again, it felt *right*, but I had too many questions to just coast on happy feelings. 'Who's Morter Smith?'

'Morter Smith?' Daryl looked surprised. 'He's Angel Group. I don't know him personally, we never crossed paths . . . why?'

'He wants to kill me, apparently. He sent the assassin after me. The guy on the bus.' I filled Daryl in on what little we knew about Masters, and what even littler we knew about Smith.

'Jesus,' he said.

'Yeah, it's weird. For a year there's been nothing, then suddenly out of nowhere there's this guy Morter Smith and he's taking out a contract on me.'

Daryl shook his head. 'Weird indeed.'

'A bit.' My breath was coming in hot clouds, the cold night like bitter silk around me.

'Suggests to me that maybe someone *did* send that dog after you,' said Daryl. 'Someone like Smith.'

A *d'oh* the size of a small asteroid pancaked me in the face. 'Jesus. Have I always been incredibly dense?'

'You have your moments.'

'It's just, you'd think that during a discussion of someone possibly wanting to kill me with a giant monster, a name might have immediately occurred, i.e. the name of a person who I definitely know wants to kill me, who has actually already tried once.'

'Hey, don't beat yourself up about it. Sometimes humans are incredibly stupid.'

My phone rang. Someone seemed to have tampered with the volume and made it roughly fifty billion times louder than usual, and we both jumped. Daryl laughed. 'Wow. Check us out. Baddest of the bad.'

I looked at the screen. 'It's Nailah. Girl who gave me the tip. Should I answer?'

Daryl attempted a shrug.

'Sod it.' I answered. 'Hello?'

'Stanly, it's Nailah.'

'Hi Nailah, what—'

'I'm guessing you're on your way to Lauren's?'

'Yeah. How—'

'Don't go tonight, OK? Don't go.'

'What? Why?'

'You're being followed. The Angel Group is all over that business with the dog, and they've got eyes on you. You'll lead them straight to her.'

'How the hell do you *know*—'

'Sorry, gotta go. I'll call again when I can. But the Angel Group doesn't know about Lauren, and as discussed, I really don't think it's a great idea to lead them straight to her, do you?'

'No, but—'

'Gotta go, sorry.' She hung up, and I looked down at Daryl.

'Curious?' he asked, his head on one side.

'As a fox,' I said. 'A fox who's just been made Professor of Curious at Oxford University, and is also starting to get pretty pissed off about being kept in the dark. We can't go to Lauren's, is the upshot of that. So . . . screw it, the Angel Group knows where we live anyway. Might as well go home . . .'

'Have a nice cold pint and wait for all this to blow over?'

'Yep,' I said. 'Or at least, get some rest and try to come up with a plan tomorrow.'

Daryl nodded. 'OK . . . well . . . I guess I can find somewhere to—'

'Don't be thick, you're coming home with me.' We stared at each other for the duration of an awkward pause. 'OK,' I said. 'Imagine that I phrased that in an old-friend-helping-out-an-old-friend way, rather than a pushy-guy-propositioning-a-woman-in-a-bar-way.'

'Cool.' We walked on, and after a brief and very loud silence Daryl spoke again. 'So. How've you been?'

A pause. 'Fine, thanks.' Another pause. 'You?'

'Not bad.'

More silence. 'Daryl,' I said.

'Stanly.'

'You know monsters?'

'I do.'

'Where do they come from?'

'Underground. As far as I can tell.'

'Ah. Anywhere in particular underground?'

'Wish I knew, boss.'

'OK.' Pause. 'Daryl?'

'Stanly.'

'You know Tara?'

'I do.'

'She's my daughter. From the future.'

Daryl put his head on one side. 'Your daughter from the future.'

'Yeah. Apparently future me brought her back in time to protect her from some great danger.'

Daryl moved his head back to its usual angle. A pause. 'Fair play,' he said. Another pause. 'Remind me to remind you to check the lottery numbers before you bring her back.'

About a mile from home, my phone rang again. I took it out, fully expecting to see Nailah's number again . . . but this time it was a name.

Sharon.

The bottom fell out of my stomach. 'Uh-oh.'

'What?' asked Daryl.

'I think the technical term is "busted".' I took a deep breath and answered the call. 'Hello?'

'Where are you?' Her voice was so cold. It made my stomach twist.

'I'm nearly home. Sharon—'

'We'll see you soon then. You might as well come in through the front door.'

'OK, see you . . .' But she was already gone. I looked at Daryl. 'You might want to reconsider coming back with me. This isn't going to be much fun.'

'I'll stick with you, if that's all right,' said Daryl. 'Hey, maybe my incredible oozing charm will help to smooth things over.'

'Chance would be a fine thing.'

The last part of the walk felt like a death march. Incredibly, I'd pretty much forgotten about the giant monster dog that had tried to kill me. I felt like this was going to be worse. We walked up the path in solemn silence, and my key was inches from the door when it opened. Connor was standing there wearing a vest, pyjama trousers, fluffy werewolf slippers and an expression that could have meant anything. 'Hi,' I said.

He nodded, and glanced down at the beagle. No surprise registered on his face. 'Daryl.'

'Hey Connor,' said Daryl, breezily. 'Long time no see. How are things?'

'Been better,' said Connor. He looked at me. 'Where'd you find him?'

'Out and about,' I said. 'He helped me with something . . . can he come in?'

'I guess so,' said Connor. 'If we're all forgetting about that massive betrayal that happened.'

'Don't worry,' said Daryl. 'I can stay out here, or go somewhere else, or something . . .'

Connor shook his head and rolled his eyes. 'Get in here, both of you.'

We walked past, down the hall to the kitchen. Sharon was sitting at the table in her dressing gown, staring at an untouched cup of tea. Everything bright about her seemed to have dimmed, her blue eyes had frosted over. 'Sharon,' I said.

'Sit down, Stanly,' she said, softly. I did. Connor was standing by the door with his arms folded. Sharon looked down at Daryl. 'Daryl. This is a surprise.'

'Hi Sharon,' said Daryl, remaining admirably cheerful. 'It's good to see you. How are you?'

'Not terribly great, I'm afraid,' said Sharon. She turned back to me. 'The police were just here.'

I frowned. 'The police? Why? What did they want?'

'They *said* they were police, at any rate,' said Sharon. 'They were plain clothes. Unmarked car.'

'Angel Group,' said Daryl.

'Very possibly,' said Sharon. 'They wanted to know where Mr Freeman is.'

My frown became a black hole that swallowed my entire face and regurgitated it as a Dali-esque melted clock version of itself. 'Mr Freeman? As in . . .'

'As in Mr Freeman,' said Sharon. 'He's alive, apparently.'

Talk about a sledgehammer to the brain. 'How the . . . what? What the . . . how is . . .' I trailed off, unable to correctly construct the remainder of the question.

'That was our reaction,' said Sharon. 'These people seemed convinced that we . . . and more specifically *you* . . . know where he is.'

I looked at Daryl. 'Did you—'

Daryl shook his head vigorously. 'Not a clue, chief, I swear.'

'How could he be alive?'

'I don't know,' said the dog. 'Seriously. It's . . . I mean, I wouldn't put it past him, he's the slipperiest, most unpredictable, conniving sonofabitch I've ever met. Worked with him for years, never knew anything beyond what he wanted to tell me . . .'

'Could he be empowered?' I said.

Daryl shook his head. 'No. Definitely not. I'd have known.'

'*Anyway*,' said Sharon, bringing us abruptly to attention. 'They wanted to speak with you. I said that you were fast asleep upstairs, more of which later, and that I was not going to wake you up for this. Then Connor told them in no uncertain terms what would happen if they tried to come in without a warrant.'

I chanced a look in Connor's direction. Still, his face betrayed nothing.

'Their parting words were quite interesting,' said Sharon. 'They suggested I ask you where you'd been tonight, and said that they would be back.'

*Balls.*

'Where were you?' she asked.

*Wow. Have I ever had a telling-off from my actual mum that felt this bad?*

I explained as quickly as possible. Nailah's information, going to find Lauren. I decided to leave Skank's name out of it. *No need to overcomplicate things.* The monster dog won me a few points, with Sharon's old warm concern returning. Even Connor's inscrutable mask fell briefly, and we transferred to the living room to see if there was anything on the news. Not a great deal, as it turned out. No reporters were allowed within a hundred feet of the site, which had already been closed off and surrounded by police and what looked like military trucks, and the body itself was enclosed within a huge white fabric dome. There were biohazard symbols everywhere. The official story seemed to be that something had escaped from an animal testing facility. Mercifully, my name didn't come up. 'Seems fishy,' said Daryl. 'There were plenty of witnesses.'

'Let's just count ourselves lucky,' said Sharon. 'You particularly, Stanly. I wouldn't want to be the one to break *that* extra bit of good news to Eddie.'

*Eddie.*

*Oh my furious Christ.*

*Please can he never be told anything ever.*

'I'm sorry,' I said, fighting the urge to act the penitent child, to stare at my shoes and mumble, hoping for mercy. It had been my decision to make. They were perfectly within their rights to be angry with me. If tonight was the night that they decided to kick me out of their house, then that was what would happen. But I'd decided to go, and I was going to stand up and take whatever came at me as a result.

'I just can't believe that after our conversation *this morning*, you'd go straight out again,' said Sharon.

'I needed to go,' I said. 'I have to . . . I have to be involved. I'm sorry, I know what I said to you, I know that I broke your rules. I'm *sorry*. But I couldn't not go. I couldn't not get involved. And I didn't tell you about it because I knew you didn't want to be—'

It takes a lot of strength to knock a heavy wooden door off its hinges, and it makes a loud noise. Sharon, Daryl and I all jumped, our eyes flying to the living room door, which was now in the hall on its side. Connor had his back to us. His fists were clenched. He was shaking.

Nobody said anything forever.

'You didn't tell us because you knew we didn't want to be involved,' said Connor, finally. It didn't seem physically possible for his voice to have gone so low, so deep. It rippled at the edges. '*Really.*'

'Really,' I said, my voice a plaintive, kittenish mew in comparison.

Connor nodded slowly. He picked up the door and leaned it against the wall, and turned to me. 'Well the problem with that, Stanly, is that not telling us about something doesn't actually mean not getting us involved.' He looked like not going completely mental was taking an unreasonable amount of energy. I'd never felt so scared of someone wearing fluffy slippers. '*Not* doing something would actually be a better option. Because now *we've* got people knocking on *our* door, demanding to talk to *you*. People who know we're lying to them.'

*They might have come anyway*, I thought. It didn't seem like a thought worth vocalising, though.

'Don't get me wrong,' said Connor. 'I had a pretty wild youth. I spent a lot of years pissing a lot of people off, going my own way because I felt like I had to. But if I'd ever thought, for a *minute*, that I was putting people in danger, or dragging them into any kind of trouble, I'd have got the hell out. And I would respect the wishes, and the *rules*, of the people who were kind enough to take me in.'

The words stung. Actually, they burned. But I stood up and I looked him in the eye, and I spoke quietly, and as firmly as I could manage. 'I'm sorry,' I said. 'I really am. And I'm grateful, so grateful, for everything you guys have done for me. I'll leave. I'll go now.'

'Stanly,' said Sharon. 'We're not . . . it's not that . . .'

'I think it is,' I said. 'Isn't it, Connor?'

His sudden talkativeness seemed to have abated. He just breathed deeply and turned away, crossing his arms.

'Things are happening,' I said. 'Bad things. I feel like it's going to get a lot worse. And I'm going to be involved, whether I like it or not.' *Bit disingenuous.*

*Shut up.*

'So I'll go,' I said. 'And you guys won't have to be anywhere near it.'

'Why do you have to be involved?' asked Connor, his back still turned. 'Why do you *have* to?'

*Because my school careers adviser basically told me to be a superhero?* 'Because I do,' I said, rubbishly. 'Because I've got these powers, and I'm in this world.'

Connor threw up his hands and stalked off to the kitchen. I looked at Sharon. 'I'm sorry,' I said. 'I'll—'

'Shut up,' said Sharon. 'Just . . . wait here. Don't you dare go anywhere.' She got up and followed Connor through to the kitchen, and I sat on the sofa next to Daryl.

'Wow,' said the dog. 'Next time, we should just let the giant monster dog eat us. I think that would have been more fun.'

'I know, right?'

I'd not expected to hear Connor and Sharon's conversation, but somehow I'd underestimated how pissed-off Connor was, because seconds later I heard him yelling. 'I can't believe I'm bloody *hearing* this!'

*Oh God.*

'Connor,' said Sharon. 'I know this is not what you want to hear. But if things really are about to get bad, we can't just let him—'

'We *talked about this,*' said Connor. 'We *swore* that after all that shit, we would *never* get involved with the Angel Group, with monsters, with fighting, with *any of it*. You know what happens when we get involved with this stuff? I come home and I find you bleeding on the floor.'

'I remember what happened, Connor!'

'So why the hell would you want to get back into that?'

'Because if bad things are going to happen, maybe we *do* have a responsibility to help! We're *stronger*, Connor, stronger than other people! We have powers, and we've seen things, and we've done things! Maybe—'

'What, just because that little idiot has a superhero complex, suddenly we're all contractually obliged to follow him into battle? We *don't* have a responsibility, Sharon! Just because we randomly ended up with these powers, and just because we're *still* babysitting that kid long after he should have struck out on his own, it does *not* mean—'

'Look,' muttered Daryl, 'I enjoy a massive domestic blow-out and an apocalyptic rain of burning home truths as much as the next beagle, but I reckon I should probably be out trying to find Freeman. If he really *is* alive . . .'

'Yeah,' I said, trying not to show quite how much Connor's words were cutting me. 'Cool. Go. I'll . . . I don't know what I'll do. Wait here, I guess. If you find anything, just look for me in the usual places.'

Daryl nodded. 'Rightio, chief. Good luck.'

'You too. And thanks. For rescuing me. And stuff.'

'Any time. Laters.'

He left, and I'd never felt so lonely. I'd also never heard Connor and Sharon row before, not properly, although I don't think they'd had much practice as the ferocity was mercifully short-lived. Connor eventually stomped off upstairs – he didn't return to the living room, which suited me fine – and Sharon came back in, her cheeks red. I sat awkwardly, wondering what the proper etiquette was. A sympathetic look? A hug? More apologies?

*Waiting in silence is probably your best bet.*

'Sorry about that,' said Sharon, after a minute. 'Some things that needed to be said, I suppose. Or shouted.' She looked over at the living room door. It lifted up from its lean, and she started to repair it with her brain.

'You don't have to apologise,' I said. 'I do. I'm . . . I really am sorry.'

'I know you are.' The door swung quietly closed, good as new, and Sharon looked at me. The frost had thawed. 'I don't know what's going to happen,' she said. 'But I'm not letting you run off into the night. For now, this is still your home and you'll sleep here.'

'OK,' I said. 'Thank you.'

'Hopefully we can at least discuss things tomorrow. Rather than, you know. Shouting and smashing doors.'

'That was pretty . . . major,' I said. 'I've never seen him like that.'

'It's been a while.'

It seemed like the right moment, if there was such a thing, to voice a thought I'd been trying to ignore. 'Sharon . . . have you been reading me lately?'

'No,' she said, immediately. *Too immediately.*

'Really?'

'I've told you before,' said Sharon. 'I don't like to read people

I trust. Even if I'm suspicious of something.' She stood up. 'And if I *had* been reading you lately, I'd have known that you'd been lying to us, and doing things behind our backs. But I've not said anything about it. Which would suggest very complicated feelings about who's right and who's wrong . . . if either of those things even mean anything. So no. I think it would be easier if I hadn't read you. Or . . . less complicated, anyway. Goodnight. Love you, you infuriating boy.'

'You too. 'Night.' I sat up in the living room for a long time, trying to process everything that had happened. It didn't work, so I brushed my teeth, headed to bed and braced myself for some supremely messed-up dreams. No such dreams materialised, though.

Mostly because I didn't really sleep.

# Chapter Nine

I HEARD CONNOR leave early in the morning. I wondered if he was going to see Eddie. God, did I ever *not* have the energy for a confrontation with Eddie.

*S'gonna happen, though.*

A little while later Sharon knocked on my door, and came and sat on the edge of my bed. 'How's it going?' I asked.

She laughed tiredly. 'Not brilliant.'

'Where's Connor?'

'He just said he needed to go out.' She rubbed her eyes.

'Have you told Eddie? About yesterday?'

'Connor tried to call him this morning but he didn't answer.'

I sat up, frowning. 'Should we be worried?'

'I doubt it,' said Sharon. 'He does vanish off the map from time to time. And even if something did happen, you know he can handle himself.'

'And he'd come straight here.'

She nodded.

'So,' I said. 'Where . . . what next? I mean . . .'

'I don't know,' said Sharon. 'Connor is angry, obviously. He wants nothing to do with any of this. But I really don't see how we can just bury our heads in the sand and ignore whatever's coming, and it definitely seems as though *something* is coming. So I think questions about your long-term accommodation plans are best left until later. We need to find out what's happening, and deal with it if we have to. Then we can discuss things.'

'Do you want me to leave?'

She sighed. 'Of *course* I don't want you to leave, you idiot. Apart from anything, even with Connor working two jobs, paying the rent isn't getting any easier.' She smiled slyly, and I felt immeasurably better. 'So that's it,' I said. 'You just want me around to make up the rent. I should have known.'

'Watch it,' said Sharon. 'Just because I'm joking around doesn't mean you can. I'm still angry, and when I say that we'll discuss things we are *definitely* going to discuss things.'

'Sorry. And . . . honestly? Connor wants me gone, doesn't he?'

'I don't know,' she said. 'We'll have to see. This is my home too.' She looked at her watch. 'I need to get ready and go to the hospital. What are you going to do today?'

'Daryl went to see if he can track down Freeman,' I said. 'If he *is* alive, I'm willing to bet that he knows what's going on, and I have a few questions for him.'

'You should tell Eddie.'

'If we hear from him. But if not, I'm going.'

'I know you are,' said Sharon. 'But please be *careful*. And let me know what's happening.'

'I will.'

It was another long day. Connor didn't return. There was no word from Eddie. I dozed a little in the afternoon, waking up feeling groggy and discombobulated, and checked the news every now and then. No further developments surrounding my battle with the giant dog, although speculation was rife that there was more to the story than the authorities were letting on. I was surprised that there was no footage of the battle whatsoever: no CCTV, not even phone footage. Something about that smelled dodgy.

I heard nothing from Nailah either. Darkness arrived, and I

was about ready to spontaneously combust from stir craziness when my phone rang.

'Found him,' said Daryl. 'He *is* alive.'

'Sonofabitch. Where?'

Daryl told me he was calling from a phone box about a mile from where we'd fought the monster dog, and that Freeman was nearby. I noted the address, deciding not to bother asking exactly how the hell Daryl was managing to operate a payphone, and ordered him to wait for me.

I was going to enjoy this.

Eddie tried to phone me a couple of times on my way, and I made myself ignore him. I was relieved that he'd resurfaced, but now was not the time for a bollocking that would probably register on the Richter scale. I'd meet Daryl, go and interrogate Freeman, and then call my cousin back with actual news. Maybe it would soften him up.

*Yeah, keep telling yourself that, squirt.*

I found Daryl and he led me off towards a decrepit-looking block of flats, where our newly reincarnated friend was reportedly hanging his hat. 'How'd you find him?' I asked.

'Still have the odd source kicking around,' said Daryl.

'Is it like the Twilight Barking?'

'The what?'

'From 101 *Dalmatians*. Do you have, like, a network of dogs who pass information back and forth around the country?'

'Are you being serious?'

'Maybe?'

'You think I talk to dogs? Normal dogs?'

'I don't know . . .' To be honest, I'd never actually thought about it. 'Do you not speak dog?'

'Dogs don't *speak*,' said the dog. 'They don't have language.'

'But if you barked at a dog . . . it would know what you were on about?'

'If I barked aggressively at another dog,' said Daryl, in the manner of a tired supply teacher fielding deliberately stupid questions from uncooperative pupils, 'it would know I was being aggressive. If I barked vaguely neutrally and then started running, it would probably be able to work out that I wanted it to follow me. And if I wandered up and sniffed its arse, unsolicited, in the middle of a crowded park, then it would know that it was business time. But a) I wouldn't do any of those things, and b) no, I don't "speak dog".'

'Jesus. Touchy. So when you said sources . . .'

'I meant humans,' said Daryl. 'People who talk. Plus good ol' fashioned nose work, of course.' He sniffed demonstratively.

'You'll have to tell me how you got so good at tracking some time. And fighting.'

'Long story, sport.'

'I love stories.'

'I know.'

We stole round the back of the flats and Daryl nosed open a rotten-looking door. He trotted on ahead and I followed, thinking about the hundreds of things I wanted to say to Mr Freeman, to do to him. We were in a dim, grimy corridor, the floor so filthy that it was impossible to tell where the dirt and chewing gum ended and the carpet fibre began. My phone buzzed again and I could almost see Eddie's furious face looming out of the screen. I flicked it on to silent.

'He's in Number 19,' said Daryl. 'Two floors up.'

The lift was one of those old-style ones with a concertina grate that you had to swing back, completing the film-noir atmosphere. Daryl jumped up on his hind legs to press one of the buttons, and with a moaning, slightly off-putting crunch of mistreated gears, the lift started to pull itself agonisingly up towards our destination. 'Shoulda taken the goddamn stairs,' said Daryl, affecting a gumshoe accent.

'Word.'

After about five years the lift ground to a halt and I swung the grate aside with my mind. Number 19 was right at the end of another musty corridor, by an open window through which I could hear sirens. London was on high alert; the people we'd passed had seemed extra nervy, there were police cars everywhere, and helicopters were chugging menacingly above.

I stood outside Freeman's door for a second, breathing deeply. *This is going to be weird.*

*Weirder than clandestine meetings with supernatural bloggers?*

*Weirder than an assassin coming after you in broad daylight?*

*Weirder than nearly being eaten by a giant blue dog?*

*Weird in a slightly different way, then.*

I knocked. Silence . . . then quiet movement from inside, and a voice. 'Who's there?' I knew that oily voice so well, but there was a note of panic in it now that was entirely foreign, and not a little disconcerting.

'Here to appraise your furniture,' piped up Daryl. 'Also, have you accepted our Lord Jesus Christ as your personal saviour?' I stifled a snigger.

There was a pregnant pause before Mr Freeman spoke again. 'Ah. I was wondering how long it would take for you to track me down. Are you alone?'

'Aren't we all?'

A low, hissing laugh and the sound of a bolt sliding back, and I was face to face with Mr Freeman, dead man un-deaded. His expression was so priceless that I stupidly wished I had a camera with me. 'Stanly . . .'

'Evening Freeman,' I said, grinning in a slightly unstable way, just to freak him out a bit more. 'How's tricks?' I moved to come in and he stumbled backwards down his hall, nearly falling to the ground. Anxiety – and possibly gin – rolled off the man in waves. 'Please,' he said, as I advanced. 'Don't—'

'Shh.' I flexed my mind and held him where he was as Daryl closed the door behind us. I felt in control for the first time in God knows how long, and it felt good. 'Now,' I said. 'I don't know how you're back on the mortal coil and I'm not particularly bothered right at the moment. I want to know stuff. If you don't tell me the stuff I want to know, I'm going to hurt you.' I let that sink in. 'A lot,' I added.

*Hmm. Maybe that last bit was unnecessary.*

'You're not going to hurt me,' Mr Freeman said, uncertainly. 'You're–' He stopped, unable to speak, because I was psychically constricting his windpipe, just enough to stop him from talking, although he could still breathe. I raised a hand, levitating him a few feet above the ground, and stared into his eyes, which were wide and full of the realisation that I was no longer a naïve sixteen-year-old who would do what he was told and jump through hoops. I relaxed the pressure on his windpipe and regarded him. He looked different. The guy had always been pale, but now he was almost ghostly, and much skinnier, with none of the presence that he'd had when I'd known him before. His eyes were forests of shadows and his grey suit was crumpled, the shirt creased, the tie loose. 'You've let yourself go.' I moved him through a doorway on my left, into a sad little living room with a small TV, a coffee table and two armchairs, and held him in the middle of the room. 'Right. First things first. How are you alive? I've decided I actually am bothered about that.'

'I have,' he choked, 'a slight advantage over most people when it comes to dying.'

'What?' I said. 'Nine lives?'

'Four, actually,' he said. 'This is my third, hence my rather less than healthy appearance. I was actually quite strapping when I was first alive.'

'Really.'

'I'm not going to go into the explanation,' said Mr Freeman. 'It's rather a twisted origin story, and one best saved for a later date. If both of us survive the coming madness, I'd be happy to relate it to you over a cup of coffee or a stiff Scotch—'

'That would be lovely,' I said. 'Now tell me how you're actually alive, because I'm not a *retard*, OK?'

'Stanly,' said Daryl. 'Not very PC.'

'I've *definitely* heard you use that word in that way before.'

'Yeah, and I don't anymore because it's not OK. It's called learning and growing.'

'Fine. I'll never say it again.'

'Thanks.'

Freeman choked out a laugh. 'Oh, you two are priceless . . .'

'Quiet, you,' I said. 'How are you *actually* alive?'

'All right,' he said. 'I'll admit, I was lying about having four lives. Just a bit of a fun, trying to lighten the mood—'

I squeezed a little harder. 'Having fun now?'

'If you must know,' said Freeman, with some difficulty, 'it was your little girl.'

I frowned. 'What?'

'Tara,' said Freeman. 'She brought me back to life. Just as she did you. She didn't mean to, of course, but—'

'You knew she was my daughter,' I said.

'Not at the time,' said Freeman. 'I found out later. All I know is that one minute I was dead, the next I was getting to my feet, fatal chest wound very much *in absentio*.'

'Well,' I said. 'Fancy that. Good girl, Tara, I guess. Right, well now we've got that out of the way, I'd like you to tell me some more stuff. Starting with why the Angel

Group came to *my* door demanding to know where you are, then followed by everything you know about what's going on.'

Freeman shook his head defiantly. 'This is not the way things are supposed to go. You're not*gaarrgh*–' I flipped him roughly around and moved him over to the window, which I opened with my brain. Slowly, I began to slide him through, face first, inch by inch.

'I'm going to drop you out of the window,' I said. 'You probably won't enjoy it.' I relaxed my grip on his windpipe and he gasped. 'And Tara's pretty far away. I doubt she'll be able to inadvertently save your worthless hide this time.' I could sense that Daryl wasn't entirely comfortable with the bad cop routine I was working. To be honest, I was a little surprised myself at how easily it was coming.

*Gotta be done, though.*

*I think.*

'What d'you reckon?' I said. 'Going to co-operate? Or is that about all we've got time for from Mr Freeman?' *What am I saying? What am I doing?*

*God, shut up. I'm not actually going to drop him.*

The anxiety in his slack face had graduated to full blown fear. He was trembling. 'Stanly,' he said, 'if you kill me, you'll be crossing a line. It will change you. Forever.'

'From what I've been hearing,' I said, 'lines and suchlike are the least of my worries.'

He was beaten. I'd broken his power, and now he was just a pathetic man with no chips left to play. 'Fine,' he said, almost in a whisper. 'I'll co-operate.'

'Good.' I brought him back from the window and placed him gently in a chair. 'Right. Now. I'm guessing you heard about the blue dog the size of a truck that appeared yesterday.'

Freeman nodded.

'It tore its way up out of the ground. Right underneath me. We fought.'

'It was one of the biggest I've ever seen,' said Daryl. 'Remember Prague? Bigger than that.'

*Prague? What the hell happened in Prague?*

*I really need to hear this long story sometime.*

'My God.' Freeman stroked his chin. It was interesting seeing intrigue and anxiety co-existing on the same face. 'That means that the walls between this world and theirs have weakened considerably. Dangerously.'

'Theirs?' I said. '"They" being . . . ?'

'The monsters,' said Daryl. 'They're from another world?'

'Of course,' said Freeman, as though Daryl were several stops past dense. 'Where did you think they came from? Monster Island?'

'Well, I did ask you about . . . hmm . . . about *several thousand times*, but in case you've forgotten, you've always been pretty good at never, ever answering questions properly.'

'Why are they here?' I said. 'How have the walls been weakened?'

'The Angel Group,' said Freeman.

'What? How? Is that why they're looking for you? What do you know?'

'Stanly,' said Daryl, a new note in his voice. 'There's something wrong.'

'What?' I snapped, too harshly. *God's sake, we're finally getting somewhere . . .*

'I don't know,' the dog said, standing up from where he'd been sitting. 'I can just . . . there's something. Out there . . .'

I turned towards the window, just as the grenade sailed through it. *SHIT.* I blasted it back through the window with my mind, spun and flew through to the kitchen, psychically dragging Daryl and Mr Freeman after me, along with one of the armchairs to act as a barricade. The explosion came a second later, deafening, shaking the whole building and filling the living room with fire. Glass broke, walls and furniture were demolished and hot rubble hailed down on us.

I stumbled to my feet, dazed, ears ringing, vision blurring, gagging on smoke. What remained of the living room was a mess of fire and debris, unrecognisable, and where there had once been a wall and a window there was now a gaping hole into the cold city night. *Smith. Son of a—*

'They're here for me,' choked Freeman, his voice muffled by the ringing in my head. He clawed at my chest imploringly, his eyes wide with terror. 'Please help me, Stanly! *Please*! I will tell you everything you need to know, I will help you as much as is humanly possible, I swear, but *please* don't let them take me! You have no idea what they'll do to me!'

It wasn't a difficult decision to make. 'All right,' I said. 'Who is it? The Angel Group? Morter Smith?'

'Yes! I—'

'Freeman!' yelled a voice, amplified by a megaphone. 'Stanly Bird! We have orders to take you out! Don't bother resisting!'

'Oh God,' said Freeman.

'Shut it,' I said. 'And come with me.' I headed down the hall, hopping over burning detritus, thought the door open before I got to it and stepped out into the main corridor. *All clear.* I ran past the elevator to the stairs, Freeman and Daryl in tow, and psychically pushed the button for the ground floor, hoping it might work as a distraction if there was anybody waiting for us downstairs.

Turned out that there was. As we emerged in the lobby I saw four men entering, clad in black body armour and weird, vaguely insectoid helmets with blank face masks, machine guns at the ready. They looked like what I imagined SWAT teams might look like in ten years. Mr Freeman drew a revolver but I got in before him, knocking the four guys back through the main doors with a wave of brain energy. *No killing if at all possible.* 'Back door,' said Daryl.

We ran, shouts and machine gun fire echoing behind us, through the back door and out into a side alley. I made a quick calculation. 'Can't fly yet. We need to get clear . . . in case they have snipers or something . . .' *Plan forming . . . possibly an excellent plan . . . going to be hard, though . . .*

*Excellent? Try MENTAL.*

*Why don't you try MENTAL?*

'Stay as close to me as you can.' I shoved a massive rubbish skip in front of the door to barricade it and headed out towards the main street, ignoring Daryl's protests. Another calculation. There were more solders with guns out here, and lots of parked cars. *So far so good.* Concentrating all of my adrenaline, anger and other spare emotions into one action, I picked up four cars and brought them hurtling towards me, flipping three on their ends and forming a protective ring around my body, with the fourth on top as a roof. *That was easier than I thought it would be.* I moved one car to the side to create a door, and yelled back towards the alley. 'Come on!'

Freeman and Daryl dashed over to join me inside the ring of cars, and I shut the 'door' and began to move us down the street, taking care to keep the vehicular coat as tight around us as possible, with no gaps for stray projectiles. I could hear shots hammering against the outside of our makeshift armour and hoped that none of our attackers had automobile-piercing rounds in their guns. For good measure, I sent random waves of thought outward to help deflect the bullets. 'What the hell are you doing?' screamed Daryl.

'Improvising!' I yelled. *Also, sorry, I can't hear you over the sound of how AWESOME I'm being.*

*No, don't say that.*

'Improvising?' said the beagle. 'This is—'

'Shut up! I need to concentrate.' *I wish I could see where I'm going.* I risked stopping, turned and opened the suit of cars a crack, enough to see ten guys running towards us firing non-stop. I kept moving backwards as fast as possible and tried to tune out the sounds of screams and crashes and gunfire. 'Daryl,' I said, as calmly and clearly as I could manage, 'can you tell if anyone is firing from behind us, or are they all coming from the direction of the building?'

'I think they're all coming from that way.'

'OK. Let's hope you're right.' I closed my eyes and spent a whole second focusing. *These are my powers, this is my mind, this is what I've been waiting for, even if I didn't count on quite this many bullets. I can do anything with my brain if I want it enough.*

*Except maybe this.*

*Shut up.*

With a roar that at least felt like it helped, I psychically threw two of the cars towards our attackers, spinning them so as to catch as many bullets as possible. The cars crashed into the road and skidded, shedding sparks, and the gunmen all dived for cover. Some might have been hit, but I didn't have time to care. *Maim or be maimed.* Without wasting a second I grabbed two more cars and yanked them in to replace the two that we'd lost. *Hopefully all these people are insured.* 'Right,' I said. 'Now for the tricky bit.' I wrapped my concentration around myself, the cars, Mr Freeman and Daryl so that to all intents and purposes we were one object, braced my body and flew us straight up, gaining height as rapidly as possible. The sounds of fire and guns slipped away, and when I was quite sure that we were completely out of range of any pesky bullets – or nearby helicopters – I allowed us to stop, opening our suit of cars like a flower and re-arranging them as a platform on which to stand.

The three of us took a second to look around. We were suspended far, far above the ground, surrounded by curtains of midnight-blue sky studded with fiery white stars. Safety. Nobody said anything for what probably wasn't very long but felt like it. Daryl was the one who broke the silence. 'Christ on a bicycle,' he said. 'If there's such a thing as a Chosen One, I reckon you're probably it. Or at least on the reserve list. That was *ridiculous*.'

Mr Freeman seemed to have lost the power of speech. I didn't bother talking, I just sat down and crossed my legs and tried to control my breathing. I felt numb, drained. 'Stanly?' said Daryl. 'You OK, chief? What's the plan?'

*He's asking* me *what the plan is? I don't know! I don't know what's going on . . .*

*Did I really just do what I did?*

*I'm not built for this. It's too mad. This makes Blue Harvest look like . . . I don't even . . .*

*Connor and Sharon and Eddie were right, should have . . .*

*Oh God, Connor and Sharon . . . Eddie . . . what if they've been . . .*

*No, don't think about it . . . not yet, not until . . .*

*What if they go after Tara?*

*What if . . .*

*Keep it together, boyo. You've started so you'll finish.*

*Focus.*

'Stanly?'

I looked around at the beautiful, freezing night, letting the cold air and the moon give me energy, my skin hardening against the wind. Not the time to fall apart. In fact, possibly the worst time in the history of falling apart to fall apart. 'Freeman,' I said. 'Why are they after you?'

'Because they know that I've got all the information you need to turn their plans upside down and burn them to the ground,' said Freeman, his voice shaking. *Wow, he really hates them now.*

*Finally, something we have in common.*

'Oh,' said Daryl. 'Is that all?'

'I can get you inside,' said Freeman. 'Give you everything you need.'

'I thought they had connections everywhere,' I said. 'Surely I can't destroy them alone.'

'All the political strings in the world aren't going to help them if you really set your mind to taking them out,' said Freeman. 'They . . . they're not who they were when I worked for them. There's a man . . .'

'Smith.'

'Yes. How do you know about him?'

'He wants me dead too.'

Freeman nodded. 'Well. That certainly makes sense. For the last few years, Morter Smith has been slowly but surely taking control of the organisation's most secret, most *dangerous* operations, and from what I've been able to work out he has a plan that we really don't want to come to fruition.'

'This plan . . . that's why the dog got out? Why the . . . what did you say . . . why the walls between here and there are breaking down?'

'Exactly.'

I nodded. 'Fairish.' *Great Scott. This is heavy.*

'The Angel Group,' said Freeman, 'and Morter Smith in particular, do not have the good of mankind at heart. Not any more. You have never met a liar like Smith. In all my time with the Group, few ever worried me. Smith frightened me. He is a ruthless, back-stabbing, self-serving psychopath, and he has the most powerful organisation on Earth at his disposal. You, the other empowered, everyone in London, everyone in the *world* is in danger now.'

*Everyone in the* world?

*Holy balls.*

*Why am I trusting him?*

*Look at him. All his smugness is gone. He's terrified. He's not lying.*

*Plus, all those guys with machine guns and grenades.*

*Maybe . . .*

*Everyone . . .*

*Tara.*

*Kloe.*

'I have to get Tara out of London,' I said. 'If the Angel Group are making their move now, if they've decided that we're liabilities, then that means they might try to take her again. And that's not happening.' *Plus the fact that monsters are breaking loose.*

'Understood,' said Freeman.

'All right then. Where will you two go while I get her?'

'Don't worry about us,' said Daryl. 'Take us down, drop us somewhere quiet and go and get her. We'll start formulating some kind of plan while you're gone.'

'Are you sure?'

'Hey,' said Daryl. 'Just because you can throw cars around doesn't mean you're everybody's bloody saviour. I took care of that dog pretty sharpish.'

'True.' *Good. Almost a plan.*

I took us down to a scrap yard, a silent wasteland of old metal, dead cars and rusty shadows. 'How am I going to contact you when I get back?'

Mr Freeman pulled out a mobile phone. 'The boring way, I'm afraid.' We swapped numbers and for a moment I wanted to laugh. I was swapping phone numbers with someone who had almost got me killed, someone who I was ready to throw out of a window less than twenty minutes ago. *My life is not the same as most people's lives.* I gave him Eddie's number as well.

'Contact him and tell him what you've told me,' I said. 'I'm going to call him on my way to get Tara, but I won't have time to go into it all. He probably won't be too happy, which is the understatement of forever, but if you explain . . . he'll understand. Hopefully. Be prepared to maybe get punched in the face a couple of times.'

Freeman nodded. Half-grudgingly, I shook his hand. 'I'll be back soon.'

He nodded. 'Be careful.'

'You too.' *What am I saying?* I bent down and patted Daryl on the head. 'You be a good boy, now.'

'Screw you and the cars you rode in on. I ain't nobody's pettin' horse, fool.'

*OK. Let's-a-go.*

I took off, way past caring who saw me, and flew as fast as I could through the city, between skyscrapers and through underpasses and tunnels, dodging cars and pedestrians, a ghost in the chilled air. I thought my phone into my hand and called Eddie, and he picked up after one ring. 'Stanly? Where the *hell*—'

'I don't have time to talk,' I said. 'So please, listen. I'm taking Tara out of London. It's not safe.'

'What do you mean, not safe? Stanly—'

'It's not safe for her, or for any of us. You, Connor, Sharon, you all need to be ready. I was just nearly killed by the Angel Group. Soldiers with guns.'

'What the hell? Are you all right? How did—'

'I'm fine, Eddie, please, I don't have time to explain. Just get Connor and Sharon and Skank, warn them, get together in case you need to fight. I don't know how much longer your homes will be safe, find somewhere you can all hide. I'm getting Tara and taking her away. I'll be back as soon as possible. You need to tell Hannah and anyone else the Angel Group might go after, tell them to get out of town.'

I knew he was fighting with himself, wanting to tell me off and ask me questions and order me back, but his common sense prevailed. 'OK,' he said.

'Good. Thanks. I'll contact you as soon as I'm back.'

'All right.'

'Did . . . Connor told you everything I guess?'

'Yes.'

'I'm sorry, Eddie. But there's no time to discuss it now.'

'I know.'

'You should expect a call from Mr Freeman.'

'The arsehole *is* alive, then.'

'He is. He's alive, and he's in as much trouble with the Angel Group as we are. I know this is pretty screwed up, but we're going to need him. He should be calling you any time now.'

'Stanly—'

'I have to go. Take care of everyone.'

'*You* take care. You need to make it back in one piece so I can administer the arse-kicking of a lifetime.'

'Roger that.' I hung up, and immediately called Nailah and told her as quickly as I could what was going on. I said that she was going to have to try again with Lauren, explain that things were going to hell in a hand basket, get her on side. 'I'll be back soon,' I said. 'Just need to sort some things out. Tell everyone you know, everyone that you can trust anyway . . . the Angel Group are moving. The danger's real.'

'I will,' she said. 'Be careful.'

'You too.'

It was nearly midnight when I arrived at Tara's house. I knocked urgently on the door, and saw her foster father Oliver do a faintly comical double-take through the glass when he saw me. 'Stanly!' he exclaimed, hurriedly opening the door. 'What are you doing here this late?'

'I'm sorry, Oliver,' I said. 'I don't have time to explain, but I have to get Tara out of London.'

'What? I—'

'There's no time,' I insisted. 'Please, you have to trust me. She's my daughter, you know I'd do anything to keep her safe, and London just became extremely not safe. I have to take her away with me.'

Oliver stood still for a moment, then nodded and stood aside.

'She's asleep?' I asked, as I went in.

'Yes,' he said. 'I'll wake her and Jacqueline.'

'Get a sleeping bag,' I said, 'pack her some spare clothes, and wrap her up in the warmest ones she has. It's going to be cold.'

I waited downstairs in their living room, pacing, clenching and unclenching my fists. I took in the cosy bits and bobs, the family pictures, the tacky but comforting china figurines. I'd seen them so many times on visits. They were an integral part of the fabric of Tara's life, and now I couldn't promise when she'd see them again. *What the hell am I doing?* I stomped that thought down, stomped on its face. There was no time for anything resembling doubt. I just had to keep going.

A few minutes later Oliver and Jacqueline came downstairs with a sleepy Tara. She looked funny, bundled up in jumpers and extra trousers and socks and a coat. 'Stanly!' she cried, waking up a bit and running clumsily over to me like a little Eskimo. *Not so little anymore.* I hugged her. 'Tara,' I said, 'you remember I told you that there were bad things happening?'

She nodded.

'Well, we're going to have to leave London for a while. It's a bad place to be at the moment, and it'll be safer for you and me if we're as far away from it as possible.'

'Where are we going?'

There was only one place I could think of for now. 'First, we're going to go to my mum's. Then . . . we'll see.'

'I'm really tired. Do we have to go now?'

'Yes,' I said. 'I'm sorry, but we really do.'

She looked at her foster parents, their faces full of so much strength, but so much pain too. 'What about—'

'We'll be fine, darling,' said Jacqueline. 'You go with Stanly now.'

My little girl turned back to me, a mess of confusion, and nodded reluctantly. 'OK then. When are we coming back?'

'Soon,' I lied. 'Do you have a sleeping bag?'

'It's in the cupboard,' said Oliver.

'Also,' I said, trying to maintain an unnaturally cheerful tone, 'I seem to have left my gloves at home. You don't have any I could borrow, do you?'

He nodded, and fetched me some thick black gloves. 'Could I have a quick word?' he asked. 'In private?'

'Of course.' We went through to the kitchen and Oliver opened a small bronze box on the sideboard, one I'd never noticed before. He removed an envelope and handed it over. It had my name on it. The handwriting looked very familiar. 'What is this?' I asked.

'You left it with us,' said Oliver. 'The older you. When you first brought Tara. You said that one day you'd come bursting in, saying that you needed to take Tara out of London, and that when you did I was to give you this.'

'Thanks,' I said, slightly shaken. I opened it. It contained a letter, a key and a piece of paper with directions written on it, directions from Tref-y-Celwyn to . . . *to where?* I quickly unfolded the letter. The handwriting looked sort of like mine, but somehow different. As though my handwriting had aged. *Well, obviously. Nice one.* I forgave myself for having a stupid thought, there was a lot going on in my brain.

*Dear Stanly*

*I remember being very confused about all this. Don't worry, it does eventually make sense. Kind of. The directions below indicate a hidden spot not far from Tref-y-Celwyn, a safe haven that I've left for you. For me. One day you'll go back in time and you'll build it for the next version of yourself, and it goes on. You must take Kloe and Tara there as soon as possible because at this point in your time things are about to get really bad, and they need to be as elsewhere as possible. You can leave them there and rest assured that they'll be completely fine. I know, OK? You can trust every single syllable of this letter, because I know it all happens.*

*You'll need to stock up on supplies for the two of them. Enough for about a week and a half will do. And even though it's a faintly sinister-looking place in the middle of a substantially more sinister-looking place, it's absolutely safe.*

*I know it would be the sensible and most obvious thing to leave a detailed list of everything that happens next, so you could approach what's coming with more information. Like a walk-through for a computer game. Trust me again, there would be a hell of a lot more of a mess if I did that. So all I'm going to say is: be careful. And don't spend too much time thinking.*

*Take care of the girls. And take care of yourself. Please! I got through all this crap the first time, just about, so you can too.*

*See you soon.*

*Stanly*


*p.s. There may be a shimmer in the forest. Don't let it get inside your head.*

'Does it make sense?' asked Oliver.

*Absolutely not.*

'Yeah.' I quickly replaced the letter, directions and key in the envelope and tucked it in my pocket. 'It does. I . . . I should be going now.'

'If anything happens to Tara . . .'

'Nothing will,' I said. 'You have my word.' I shook his hand. 'It might be a good idea for you to get out of town as well. As far as you can.'

'Things are really bad, aren't they?' he said, looking so grave I could barely look him in the eye.

'They are.'

'We can go to my sister's,' said Oliver, although I felt like he was only saying it because I wanted to hear it.

We walked back through to the living room, where Tara was standing ready with Jacqueline. The goodbyes were tearful, painful to watch, and I stood off to one side, hating myself for dragging this little girl away from everything she knew, off to some uncertain future in a strange place. I hated the Angel Group for whatever they were doing, and I hated the phantom image of Morter Smith. *Too many things to hate.*

Finally, it was time to go. Tara was wrapped up as snugly as possible in her thick layers, and I zipped her into her sleeping bag and gathered her up in my arms, channelling some mental energy into the action as she was way too heavy for a scrawny specimen like me to carry. We went outside, and turned back for one last goodbye. 'Thank you,' I said. 'See you soon.' *Will you?*

I *will*, I thought, fiercely.

'Take care,' said Jacqueline. 'Fly safely.'

'Always,' I said, and took off into the sky, full as ever with

143

unknowable cosmic shapes. We flew, carried on the night breeze, over and out of the city, away across the patchwork countryside, following the snaking patterns of railway lines and the roll and swish of hills. For the first half an hour or so Tara asked questions and I answered her as best I could, but after a while she fell asleep and I flew us silently over the same rivers and houses and undulating green that I had seen . . . how long ago? A week? Less? Ridiculous.

*A lot can happen in a week.*

*A lot didn't happen in a week, a lot happened in about ninety minutes.*

*Yeah, OK then.*

I didn't sleep, of course, but I did shut down as much of my mind as possible to give it a break, allowing the remainder to take over, flying on instinct, autopilot. It steered us left and right when it needed to, kept us in the air, acknowledged the night birds and the half-formed creations of clouds, the lunar cut-outs skating through the black. It meant that I didn't have to think properly for a bit, which was good.

*Too many thoughts to think.*

# Chapter Ten

I WAS FULLY awake again by the time we reached Tref-y-Celwyn. The town seemed to shimmer into view, nestled sleepily in the crooked arms of the valley, and the strangest, most potent cocktail of feelings bubbled up in my stomach. I saw flashes of the night that I left, like a montage of painful film clips: fighting with Ben King, everyone's eyes on me as I hurled him through the air with my mind; mine and Kloe's first non-staged kiss, hugging each other in the rain; then off into the darkness, to this new life, this warped new screenplay, reels changing so abruptly that if I'd woken up the next day and found that it had all been a dream, I doubt I'd have been surprised.

Tara was still asleep as we touched down on my mum's patio, and I laid the little girl down as gently as possible on the wooden bench outside the house. There was a conservatory now. I wondered how long that had taken, whether it had been a joint decision before my dad left, or if Mum had just decided on a whim. *Focus, Stanly.* I rang the doorbell and waited, fiddling nervously with my hands. A light came on upstairs. My mum had always been a light sleeper. I heard her coming down the stairs, saw her come to the door and look through, bleary-eyed. When she realised that it was me the tiredness fled from her face and she hurriedly unlocked the door and ran out, and we collided in a fierce hug. 'Stanly,' she whispered. 'Oh my God . . .'

'I'm back,' I said, stupidly.

We hugged for a long time, and when we broke apart my

mum was smiling so widely I thought her face might crack. 'What are you doing here? I mean, how . . . if I'd known . . .'

'Last minute decision,' I said. 'Some crazy stuff occurring.' I picked Tara up again.

'Who's that?' my mum frowned.

'Tara,' I said. 'The little girl I told you about.'

'Oh . . . why is she here?'

'I'll tell you in a sec,' I said. 'First, let's get her inside. Freezing out here.' I carried Tara into the kitchen and set her down on the sofa by the Rayburn. Some of the furniture was new, and there were unfamiliar pictures on the walls.

Mum put the kettle on and we sat at the table. 'How are you?' she asked. 'You haven't phoned in ages . . .'

'A lot's been happening,' I said. 'An awful lot, in a disorientatingly short amount of time. But I'm OK, I think. How are you?'

'Oh, you know,' she said. 'All right. Things are going well at the moment. I haven't spoken to your father for a while.'

'Oh.' A bit of awkwardness, but I pushed it aside. 'Mum,' I said, 'London isn't safe for Tara any more. There are extremely bad people there, and maybe other things, and I can't risk them getting their hands on her. I had to bring her here.'

'Will they come after her?'

I shook my head, even though I wasn't at all sure about that. 'I don't think so. But I'm not leaving her here anyway, we just need to sleep the night. I'm going to go and get Kloe tomorrow, and then I'm taking the two of them to a safe place out of town.'

'Where?'

*I have absolutely no idea.* 'It's probably best that I don't say,' I said. 'Then if someone does come looking for her, you won't have to lie.' *I'm putting a lot on her. If they come here . . . . God. I hadn't even thought of that. What if they came and hurt my mum? What would I do then? Don't think*

146

*about that now. Too many things to think about. She'll be OK.*

*But for the record, what you would do is communicate to the Angel Group, in a very violent way, just how terrible an idea it was to come near your mother. Maybe with explosions.*

Mum put her hands over her face and shook her head. 'Stanly, what is going *on*? I don't understand! It's been over a year since you ran away. I haven't been able to tell anyone the real reason. I don't even *know* the real reason! You have . . . magical powers! Is that even it?'

Not really knowing what to say, I opted to make the tea, and we sat and drank it and I gave my mum as much information as it was safe to give. She had heard the news about some escaped animal in London, but it seemed that the Angel Group were still doing a pretty good job of suppressing the specifics, so I decided not to go into too much detail. I don't know how much she took in, but once the initial befuddlement wore off I saw her strength come through, the strength that she'd always had but hadn't always known how to show. I knew that she trusted me, despite everything that had happened. She was my mum. 'I'm going to put Tara to bed,' I said.

I carried her upstairs to my room. She was still sound asleep, breathing deeply and regularly, sighing softly every now and then. My bedroom was exactly the same, every poster, every piece of junk, every scrunched up bit of paper. The bed had been made, but apart from that it was the same. Everything in its right place. That was comforting, if weird. I put Tara down on the bed, and her eyes flickered open. 'Are we there?' she mumbled quietly.

'Yes,' I said. 'We're here. We're safe. You can sleep here, I'll be close by.'

She sat up, and started to extricate herself from her fifty or so jackets. 'OK.'

'Goodnight,' I said.

'I need to brush my teeth.'

That almost made me laugh. Good kid. I showed her to the bathroom and she brushed her teeth, then I took her back upstairs. ''Night.'

'Night,' she yawned.

'Sleep well.'

Mum was waiting at the bottom of the stairs and we went back into the kitchen to finish our tea and chatted about normal stuff. I asked her if she'd seen Kloe at all, and she smiled and nodded. 'She pops by regularly. She's such a lovely girl, Stanly.'

'I know,' I said. 'I've not done too badly, for a superpowered delinquent who didn't finish school.'

'Please, don't remind me,' said Mum. But she smiled, and I smiled, and we both laughed. Thank Christ for laughing. When it had subsided I stood up, suddenly overwhelmed by tiredness.

'I'm going to have to go to bed. I'm completely wiped.'

'OK. You can sleep in the spare room.'

She helped me make the bed up, stretching the sheet over the mattress as carefully as she always had, and insisted on giving me a duvet cover and pillow cases, asking if I needed a hot water bottle or another cup of tea. It made me realise how much I missed having a parent. Eddie and Connor and Sharon were amazing, but there's no real substitute.

I wondered what they were all doing. Eddie would blatantly have got in touch with Connor and Sharon by now. Would they have assembled? Had they talked to Mr Freeman? I didn't want to imagine how awkward and hostile their first meeting with him would be. I decided to turn my phone off and not think about it. I'd done all I could for now.

Plus, I didn't feel ready to speak to any of them. Particularly Eddie.

*Jesus. Evil corporations and soldiers and monsters, and you're worried about your cousin.*

'What time do you want me to wake you up in the morning?' Mum asked.

'Eight,' I said. 'No . . . nine.' I was thinking more about Tara than myself, she needed to have something resembling a decent night's sleep. 'If I get up at nine, I can wake Tara at half past. Or ten.'

'Stanly, what is it about this little girl?' My mum's arms were folded, and I knew she knew there was more going on than I was willing to divulge. 'Why is she your responsibility? What about her parents?'

'I can't explain,' I said. 'I'm sorry. I don't even know the full deal myself. I just know that she's special, and that I have to look after her.' For a moment I felt an almost overpowering urge to tell her the truth, to say that her grandchild was slumbering in my room, but I couldn't. It was impossible. 'I have to look after her,' I said again.

'All right,' said Mum. 'I believe you. It's all just so strange . . .' She laughed. 'But I suppose I should expect nothing less from my strange son.'

'Thanks for that.'

'You know what I mean.' She hugged me. 'I love you.'

'Love you too.'

Sitting on the edge of the bed, I unfolded the letter I'd left for myself, years ago. I was trying not to dwell on the tangled timeline. It messed with my head too much. I re-read the message several times, my frown growing progressively bigger with each read.

*There may be a shimmer in the forest. Don't let it get inside your head.*

I sat for a few minutes, marvelling at what a douchebag my future self must be. Why would I leave myself a cryptic clue, rather than an explanation of some kind? A shimmer in the forest? What the hell did that mean? I vowed to leave a forensically detailed forty-page manuscript with strategies and footnotes and high quality full-colour photographs and a bibliography when I got to the future. Or the past. Or wherever – *when*ever, said an irritating voice in my brain – the hell it would be when I arrived at where – *when*, insisted the voice, smugly – I was going to come back from.

*I really need to go to bed.*

I looked at the directions, which were followable, then re-read the letter one more time, shook my head and called myself a four-letter word. It was a word I'd once said in front of my mum when I was quite young, and immediately wished I hadn't.

Once in bed, even though I'd had a pretty awful night's sleep last night, I lay awake for a long time. *Why not just leave Tara here with Mum? Then Kloe can stay home too, she won't have to come with me and the daughter she shouldn't have yet. She won't have to hide.*

*I wouldn't have left myself that message if I could just leave Tara here.*

*That means people are going to come looking for her. And for Kloe.*

*If anything happens to Mum, or to anyone else, it's on you.*

*No it isn't. It's on them. I'm doing everything I can.*

*And surely I wouldn't have let myself put Mum in danger? If she needed to be kept safe as well, I'd have told myself.*

*I would have.*

The boy sitting sulking in his adopted room, desperate for action, seemed very far away. I spent at least an hour torturing myself over what would happen if anybody hurt my mother, my daughter or my girlfriend. I imagined my fiery revenge, the apocalyptic violence I would visit upon anyone who so much as thought about harming them, and I thought about monsters, and how long it would be before they all got out. Whether we could stop it. I tried not to imagine creatures worse than Smiley Joe, mightier and more furious than the blue dog, although of course the more I tried not to think about them the more they stampeded through my mind, and eventually I spiralled into a series of messy, twisted dreams, all black and white and bloodied, familiar faces crying in pain, the suggestion, the *promise*, of awful beings, giant and merciless . . .

And, for some reason, Daryl asking me over and over again where he left his trilby.

Stupid brain.

I woke up confused and scrunch-faced. Why was I in the spare room? Why was I not in my bed? It couldn't possibly be time for school. Too early. Not even light yet. I looked at the clock. Seven. Crap. Nearly time to get up. *Why am I in the spare room? And why is it my job to keep track of Daryl's stupid hat?*

Then of course it all came back, droplets of bright truth infiltrating the cracks in a dusty window pane. I was immediately wide awake and lay there for a while, working out my schedule. Make Mum a cup of tea. Shower. Breakfast. Sort myself out. Wake Tara, get her breakfasted and ready. Then off to get Kloe. I couldn't fly and get her.

*Ah. Now will Mum let me borrow her car?*

I'd noticed a new car outside when we'd arrived, a silver Ford Fiesta. She'd always wanted a little silver car. Her previous car was in London, parked near Eddie's, right where I'd left it. I'd borrowed . . . well, commandeered . . . no, I'd pretty much stolen it when I'd left, long ago, and unbelievably it had never cropped up in any of the conversations I'd had with my parents in the meantime. I half-remembered them saying something about getting a new one back before I'd pilfered it, although that might have been wishful thinking. I suppose that once they knew I was safe and well, they were willing to forgive and forget. Something told me the forgiving and forgetting came more from my mum than my dad.

*Although he was never a huge fan of the Polo, to be fair.*

*At least they had another car.*

*Shut up. FOCUS.*

*Ford Focus?*

*Ford Prefect . . .*

*SHUT. UP.*

I considered punching myself in the face for flying all the way to Wales when there was a perfectly serviceable vehicle available to me, but thought better of it, 'cos what are ya gonna do? Plus, there was a more important question afoot, namely: would Mum let me borrow her car, when I'd neglected to return the old one? She knew how important my mission was, she had at least some inkling of what was at stake. She was sensible, she knew I couldn't just fly myself, my girlfriend and an eleven-year-old around in broad daylight. I wondered for a second if she'd seen anything on the news about a flying boy in London, but figured she would have mentioned it if she had. And the likelihood of her coming across it online was slim; as far as I knew, she still thought the internet was something that happened to other people.

*Will she let me borrow the car?*

*Maybe if I promise to bring it back this time?*

It was nearly eight by the time I'd assembled my plan, and I made my mum a cup of tea before getting ready. She came down to the kitchen after I'd showered, and I broached the subject of the car. There was obvious reluctance, and a few pointed hints about the green Polo, even a mention of insurance that was so incongruous that I almost laughed. Eventually, after ruthlessly deploying my best pleading eyes and my fiercest wheedling, with a subtle but healthy undercurrent of implied guilt, she acquiesced, and we even managed to chat about normal things for ten minutes before a blonde girl in red pyjamas wandered into the kitchen, rubbing sleep from her eyes. 'Morning,' she smiled.

'Tara,' I said, 'this is my mum, Mary. Mum, this is Tara.'

My mum stood up and gave Tara a hug, and immediately the two of them loved each other. I wondered when Mum would first hold Tara as a baby, when she would bake her her first birthday cake. *Or if.* For almost a second I wanted to cry, seeing my mother and my daughter connect on such a basic, amazing level, but I bottled it fiercely and asked Mum to sort Tara some breakfast and explain what was going on while I acquainted myself with the new car.

Turns out that it's not like riding a bike. I stalled several times before I managed to actually start the damn thing properly, then the gears were different and the buttons were in the wrong places, and my clutch control was all over the shop. I spent a good half an hour driving very slowly up and down the road willing myself to re-learn everything. *Jesus, it's a miracle you managed to drive to London. You're rubbish, mate.*

As I pulled back into the driveway, switched off and locked the car and headed inside, it suddenly occurred to me that Kloe was going to be at Sixth Form. I couldn't just turn up there, could I? It would freak everybody out, it would mess Kloe about . . . I tried to call her but she'd switched off her phone. *Typical. Chicks, amiriiiiite?*

*That wasn't funny, brain. You are hereby sacked from funny with immediate effect.*

'So what are you going to do?' asked Mum. Tara was getting her things from upstairs. 'Just turn up at Sixth Form and grab her? What will everyone say?'

'I'm going to have to not worry about that,' I said. 'Kloe's too important.'

Tara came back in, smiling, chipper, innocent. So adaptable. It was incredible. 'Ready!' she said.

'Well done,' I said. 'Now—' I was interrupted by a tinny rendition of 'Seven Nation Army' by The White Stripes, and got my phone out eagerly, thinking it would be Kloe . . . but the name that came up on the little screen was Connor. *Balls.* I stared at it, half of me desperately wanting to answer, half of me convinced I shouldn't.

*Answer.*

*Don't answer.*

I answered. 'Connor,' I said, 'I can't talk right now. I'm safe, I know what I'm doing.'

'You know what you're doing, do you?' asked Sharon. 'Wow. And there I thought you were making it all up as you went along.'

*Oh God.* 'Sharon. I . . . I'm sorry. I—'

'I managed to wrestle the phone out of Connor's hands,' said Sharon. 'He was planning on giving you an earful, but I thought it might be more productive to find out exactly what the hell you think you're doing.'

'I can explain,' I said. 'I *will*. But right now I need to take Kloe and Tara to safety. Have you met up with Freeman?'

'Yes, which is a whole different kettle of what the hell. Stanly, people came to our house. *Again.*'

'Shit. Are you OK? You were ready for them, presumably?'

'Barely.'

'Well if I *hadn't* sneaked out, got into trouble and warned you, we'd have been completely unprepared . . .'

'Seriously? *That's* your defence?'

'OK,' I said. 'Fair enough. Sorry. Look, by all means bollock me later, but I'm doing the best I can with what little I've got. I will call you as soon as I can. Just stay safe.'

I heard a voice, probably Freeman's, suggesting that we didn't stay on the line much longer in case people were listening in, and Sharon said a few choice words that sounded pretty shocking coming out of her mouth. 'Fine,' she said. 'Talk later. Be careful, you idiot.'

'You too,' I said. 'And I'm sorry.'

'I know. Eddie sends a mixture of love and incandescent rage.'

'OK. Tell him I'm doing that smile I do when I know I'm in trouble but am hoping everyone will just forget about it.'

'Will do.' She hung up, and without missing a beat I turned to my mum and did the smile I do when I know I'm in trouble but am hoping that everyone will just forget about it. 'Right. Well. We'd best be off, then.'

It was a weird moment. I hugged Mum, saying I'd bring the car back as soon as possible, and Mum hugged Tara, and the two of us got in the car and drove off. 'Stanly,' said Tara. 'What's going on?'

I owed her something. 'Some evil people are operating in London,' I said, 'and some dangerous creatures. Something big and bad is going to go down, and you and Kloe need to be as far away from it as possible.'

'What about Oliver and Jacqueline? Will they be all right?'

'They'll be fine,' I said. 'They're getting out of London too. Could you look through Mum's CDs and see if there's anything good?'

A rummage. 'Um. Beatles. Radiohead.'

*Radiohead? That's a bit up-to-date for Mum.* She must have discovered them herself as well, because I hadn't been into them when I'd lived at home. 'Um,' I said. 'Which album?'

'*The Bends*. That's the one with 'Fake Plastic Trees' on, isn't it?'

'Yeah.' I'd been very impressed when I'd introduced Tara to

Radiohead and she'd immediately liked them – I'd only recently got my head round them, and it had taken me a while.

'That's my *favourite*,' said Tara. 'Some of the songs are too loud and angry, but that one's so good, can we have it?'

'Um,' I said again. 'Sorry . . . I love it as well . . . but I don't know if I can quite handle it right now.' I felt bad for refusing her request, but she understood.

'I know,' she said. 'You do have to kind of be in the mood for it. Like 'Hallelujah'.'

'Yeah,' I said. 'Which Beatles albums?'

'*Abbey Road*.' We looked at each other and smiled.

'*Abbey Road*,' I said. Tara put the CD on and we drove and sang, cheerful and tuneful, about toejam football and walrus gumboot and monkey finger. Neither of us had a clue what John Lennon had been on about, but we both knew all the words.

*She's definitely my daughter.*

I pulled in to a parking space opposite my high school, a little involuntary shiver passing through me as I took in the familiar grubby corners and old glass. The place looked an awful lot smaller, but it still brought a rush of jumbled memories: years of horrendous PE lessons, doodle-filled exercise books and confrontations in musty corridors, with Bunsen burners and board rubbers marching up and down in the background, singing the school song, which . . . why exactly could I remember that appalling dirge?

*This just keeps getting weirder.*

'OK.' I switched off the engine. 'I'll just be a minute. I'm going to lock you in.'

'OK,' said Tara. 'Can you leave the keys in so I can keep listening to the music?'

'Sure,' I said. 'Lock yourself in, then.' She nodded, and I got out and headed towards the Sixth Form, a small converted greenhouse attached to the school, thinking of the word *purpose*. No stopping, I couldn't afford to let my guts burst the way they were threatening to. It was going to be in and out. Talk to as few people as possible, answer no questions. Wham, bam, thank you ma'am, or something to that effect.

I entered the common room, feeling more like a new student who was late for their first day than a superhero here to dramatically rescue his girlfriend. There were sofas and chairs and a pool table and a small hi-fi system and a kettle, all incredibly cheap-looking, and several people hanging about, many of whom I recognised. Multiple jaws dropped when they saw me, and my eyes zeroed in on the people playing pool, specifically Ben King, who caught my eye, mis-cued and tore the green. I felt like somebody should have abruptly stopped playing a honky-tonk piano. Nobody seemed to have anything to say for a few seconds and I stood there like a complete lemon, all purpose forgotten. 'Um,' I said. 'Hi guys!' "*Hi guys*"? *Who the hell even* are *you?*

'What are you doing here?' hissed Ben. He dropped his cue and walked towards me, his body language full of fight. He obviously still bore a grudge. That wasn't terribly surprising, but as I watched him stride towards me, burdened with glorious purpose – *hey, I'm* the one with the glorious purpose, *dickwad* – I realised that I couldn't just not be arsed with him, I couldn't even be arsed to not be arsed with him. He wasn't going to feature in anything that was about to happen. He was barely an obstacle, a meaningless object taking up the space between me and what I'd come for, a deleted scene left to rot on the cutting room floor. I didn't even bother to answer him, I just punched him in the face and continued through the room, trying not to wince at the pain in my fist, leaving him to fall to the floor moaning. Nobody else came near me. Someone actually said, 'That was sick.'

I checked all the other rooms in the Sixth Form, ignoring

all questions, and finally found Kloe in the little library at the back of the building. Our eyes locked and she squealed, jumped up and ran at me, leaping into a hug. 'What are you *doing* here, you massive freak?' she said, delightedly. 'Best surprise *ever*!'

'Hey darlin',' I said. 'I'm sorry, but you've got to come with me.'

The smile fell, at least partly because *darlin'* was what I called her when I was saying something I knew she wouldn't like. 'Where?' she said.

*Don't say 'back to the future'. Inappropriate.* 'I'll explain on the way,' I said. 'There's no time right now. You just have to come with me. It's not safe for you.'

'But . . . why? Stanly, I can't just—'

'Kloe,' I said, fixing her with my gaze and holding her shoulders, 'you know I wouldn't be doing this if it weren't absolutely completely one hundred per cent kosher and important. Don't you?'

'Yes, but . . .'

'So *please* come with me.' I took her hand and led her out, back down the hall and into the common room, where someone I didn't know was tending to a bloody-nosed Ben. When he saw me leading Kloe out he launched himself at me, but I blocked him psychically and he tripped over, banging his head on the door. He tumbled back to the floor, cursing, and a couple of people laughed.

'You should probably just stop, Ben,' said one kid whose face I recognised, although I couldn't remember his name. Someone else yelled after Kloe, asking what the hell she was doing. She didn't know what the hell she was doing, or what the hell I was doing, and she didn't answer. I led her across the playground to the car, where Tara had climbed into the back, and we got in.

*Wham, bam, thank you ma'am, indeed.*

'Tara?' Kloe said. 'Um, hi. What are you . . . Stanly, what is she doing here? What are you *both* doing here? What's going *on?*'

'I'll explain on the way,' I said.

'On the way *where?* Give me *something*, a bloody *sentence* at least!'

'Um,' I said. 'Road trip?'

And we were gone.

# Chapter Eleven

IT TOOK ABOUT two minutes for Kloe to decide that she wasn't entirely satisfied with my explanation. 'Stanly,' she said, 'what the *hell* is going on? And why did you punch Ben?'

'Um,' I said. 'Kind of felt like it. Unfinished business?'

'What do you mean?'

'Well, he is sort of the reason I had to run away in the first place.'

Kloe nodded. 'OK, yeah, fair enough.'

'Plus he went for me. And I didn't really have time to talk him down from his angry ledge.'

'All right, fine. Now, where are we going?'

I explained as much as I could in as un-worrisome a manner as possible, and she seemed to take it quite well, although she got a bit quiet and reached for my hand. I held hers for a minute, but then I had to change gear and she didn't take my hand again. We drove for a while in silence, listening to *Abbey Road* for the second time, and I wondered what the atmosphere was like for Tara. It was certainly tense in the front. I was pretty sure that Kloe had accepted my reasons, but she was still palpably unhappy about them. I found myself flashing back to uncomfortable car journeys with my own parents, as we drove around getting more and more lost on non-descript ring roads, their voices steadily rising as I tried to bury my head in a *Goosebumps* Choose-Your-Own-Adventure book.

*Time really is a flat circle.*

Eventually we pulled into a service station. Kloe got out

without saying anything and headed towards a sign marked TOILETS, disappearing around a corner. I turned to Tara and smiled unconvincingly. 'Sorry, I should go and talk to her. Will you be OK here?'

Tara nodded. 'Lock yourself in again,' I said. 'I'll be as quick as I can. Do you want anything from the shop?' She shook her head.

I put some petrol in the car and got a few provisions. Kloe hadn't come back, so I walked around the side of the petrol station to the toilets. She was leaning against a wall with her arms folded, looking up at the sky. Her cheeks were scarlet. I didn't quite know what to say. Things had never been this tense between us before. 'Um,' I said. 'Are you OK?'

She shook her head. 'No.' She looked at me, then down at the floor. 'Yeah.' Then she unfolded her arms and ran her fingers through her hair. 'No, Stanly, I'm not bloody OK! You just turn up out of the blue, drag me out of sixth form, punch Ben in front of everybody! What the hell are they going to think? What are they going to say when I get back? What are my teachers going to think? My mum and dad? They're going to think you've kidnapped me or something! You talk about bad people, and monsters, and danger, and assassins trying to kill you, and what the hell does it all *mean*? It's your world! It's not mine! It's nothing to do with me!' I didn't know what to say, so I just stood there uselessly. She was staring at me, though, inviting a response, so I moved forwards to hug her, to run my hands up and down her arms and kiss her forehead like I always did, but she pulled away. 'No,' she said. 'Don't try to fob me off with a cuddle. Obviously I'm going to come with you. Obviously I trust you. But you owe me an *explanation*. A proper one. You *owe me that.*'

'I know,' I said. 'I know! I . . . you just, you need to know how important it is for me to keep you safe, for . . .'

'Oh, don't be so *patronising*,' said Kloe. 'You're my boyfriend and I love you and I know you love me, but you're not . . . *responsible* for me.'

'I am,' I said. 'When it comes to this stuff, I am.'

'*What stuff*? Tell me what's happening, right now. I'm not getting back in that car until you tell me *exactly* what's going on. And don't you dare leave anything out.'

*Come on, kid. 'Fess up.* 'OK,' I said, and broke it down in as much detail as I could, telling her about the blue dog, and Freeman, and the Angel Group's plan. I still left out the part about Tara being our daughter, and the twist in my gut told me that neglecting that aspect was *definitely* going to come back and bite me somewhere painful at some point, but right now I had to get her on side. Apart from needing her to agree to come . . . she was right. I owed her honesty.

So I was as honest as I could be.

'So that's it,' I said. 'That's what's happening. That's why I had to come. And why we have to go. Now.'

Kloe nodded. 'Fine.' She laughed, and only a little bitterly. 'You're lucky I'm really in love with you. Like, a lot. Otherwise I'd probably have told you to get to fuck by now.'

'Feel free,' I said, holding out my hand. 'Just do it on the way.'

It didn't take long to reach the village at the edge of the forest. I stopped the car outside a small supermarket to buy some more extensive supplies, then we set off again. Kloe had calmed down, and she and Tara had even hit upon a hilarious new game that involved relentlessly taking the piss out of me for being a huge drama queen and a pretty naff driver.

It wasn't exactly negative, as developments go.

We parked in a layby next to the forest, which definitely looked sinister. Dense and ragged, it let very little light in, even though it was a pretty bright day, and barely any sound out, just the odd rustle and squawk. Tara clearly didn't like it and Kloe seemed far from keen, although she put on a brave face. 'Seems nice enough,' she said, 'for a *Blair Witch* remake. Why are we here?'

'I'm just following directions,' I said.

'Whose?'

'Someone trustworthy. A friend with powers.' It wasn't exactly a lie.

Kloe raised her eyebrows. 'Would it be wrong of me to say that this whole thing's a bit . . . serial killer-ish?'

'Hopefully nobody will have to cut their own leg off to escape from some nightmarish trap,' said Tara, solemnly.

We both looked down at her. 'Um,' I said. 'What?'

'What kind of films do you think me and my friends watch when we have sleepovers?' asked Tara, rolling her eyes. 'Spoiler alert – not *My Little Pony.*'

Kloe and I looked at one another and cracked up. Trust a kid to defuse the tension.

*And where does an eleven-year-old learn the phrase 'spoiler alert'?*

*I'm so proud.*

We unloaded everything and I glanced over the directions. 'This way,' I said, leading them down the muddy, narrow country road until we found the entrance, a path bordered by thorn bushes. There was a wooden stake hammered into the ground with an exclamation mark engraved in it, just as was indicated on the piece of paper. Quite a nice touch, I thought. *Good skills, future me.* 'Here we are,' I said. 'Um. Well. In we go.'

The woods smelled wet and bracken-y and the floor, a fragrant carpet of dead leaves and damp bark, shifted underfoot. Kloe and Tara kept close to me. I hated the idea that I was going to leave them somewhere in the middle of this wood for over a week, and I anticipated a horrible, horrible goodbye, but I tried to put it out of my mind and concentrate on finding our safe haven. Every now and then there would be a little marker, which was reassuring. The trees were stern, ominous sentries, tall and unfriendly with rough trunks and no branches for climbing, and when they creaked it sounded like a warning. A few times the words *there may be a shimmer in the forest* came back to me, and I shivered and wondered what it meant, but nothing strange occurred, just a few woodland creatures scampering past. At one point a bird screeched and we all jumped and yelled in fright, but laughed it off. I half-expected laughter to sound scary and out-of-place, but it was actually light and soothing . . . until the echoes returned to us, distorted and mocking, as though the mirth had been filtered through something.

*Or as though it's not our laughter.*

*It's the forest, laughing at us.*

*God, shut up! You're supposed to be the hero. If you're pissing your boxers because of a slightly spooky forest, what chance does the world have?*

Thankfully Tara started a conversation about a lyric she half-remembered. 'It's got something to do with . . . um . . . a treehouse? And . . . the birds. Birds and bees. And maybe honey? That's all I can remember, it's been annoying me for ages.'

*Oh thank Christ for that.* Kloe and I joined in with the thinking, desperately racking our brains, even though the fragments of lyric meant absolutely nothing to me. 'I'm sure I know it,' said Kloe. 'It rings half a bell.'

'Half a bell?' repeated Tara. That made us all laugh.

'Maybe you can make a full bell between you,' I said, 'and then we can ring it.'

*Unutterably lame, but you're forgiven.*

The conversation lasted until we reached the very centre of the forest. It had taken us about three-quarters of an hour and we were all knackered, but the sight of our destination gave me a lift: a clearing, dominated by a big wooden cabin. It had a chimney and actual glass in the windows, and a log pile outside, and a door with a flower carved into it. Another nice touch. It looked cute and cosy, homely, safe in the heart of the woods. I took the key from my pocket and unlocked the door, and in we went. The place had electric light that ran off a generator – I'd thoughtfully left instructions for myself detailing how it worked – and nice furniture, even pictures on the walls. *Jesus. Did I actually build this?* It meant that at some point in my life I developed some kind of practical skill, which was a revelation. Electrician, builder, plumber, superhero. Blimey.

*You probably just thought everything into place, like telepathic Lego. You couldn't build a house of cards.*

It had a kitchen, a bathroom, a little living room with a sofa and a fireplace, and two adjoining bedrooms, one with a large bed, one with a slightly smaller one. There were a few books, which I didn't bother examining, and I'd left clothes for Kloe. *Obviously, because I knew she didn't have time to bring any.* I was starting to enjoy this a little bit, the way things were falling into place. Falling very slowly, and into a no less confusing place, but falling into place nonetheless.

We set ourselves up, putting food in cupboards – there was even a fridge – and then I built a fire, with quite a lot of help from Kloe, and we had tea and biscuits. I'd decided to stay with them tonight, just to get them settled in, and leave tomorrow morning. I managed to block off part of my brain so I wouldn't think about tomorrow; I wanted to have one nice, quiet day with my girlfriend and my daughter. We played stupid games like Consequences and noughts and crosses, and endless rounds of Cheat and Pontoon with the pack of cards that my future self had left us, and soon it was dark and I stoked up the fire, and we cooked and ate a meal together, and told jokes and played more games. It was almost wonderful. Actually, it *was* wonderful. Wonderful, but also painful, because I knew I was going to have to leave them here.

Tara went to bed at about nine because she was exhausted, and Kloe and I sat on the sofa in front of the fire staring into the crackling, writhing flames. I found it hard to believe that not twenty-four hours ago I had been psychically throwing cars around and dodging grenades, and that a day before *that* I'd nearly been eaten by a dog the size of an elephant. It didn't make sense. It was another world . . .

*You might have killed someone last night*, muttered a new voice in my head, cold and malevolent and unwelcome. *More than one person, even.*

I tried to justify it to myself. It had been them or me, and if I'd let them take me I wouldn't have been able to protect my family. It balanced out. It *had* to. They had attacked us with guns and explosives, they hadn't even tried to negotiate, to resolve things peacefully. Fight fire with fire and all that.

*Plus, Eddie and I are both maybe-murderers now.*

*Yay.*

Suddenly Kloe leaned over and kissed me, and all dark thoughts evaporated. Her lips were so soft and felt so good, and the heat between us started to rise, like mercury in a thermometer, rushing upwards. Neither of us said anything, we just got off the sofa and went next door to the larger bedroom.

Later, as we lay side-by-side, hot and cold and vulnerable, I kissed Kloe's neck and whispered, 'I love you.'

'I love you.' She kissed my shoulder, and my lips, and I felt her smile in the dark.

'What are you grinning at?' I asked.

'Nothing.'

*That was awesome.* There was a new voice in my head. It talked kind of like a frat boy. In fact, I was surprised it hadn't added the word *bro* on the end. *You'd better just be visiting, boyo. Got no need for dude-bros in my head.*

*Chill, bro. It was pretty awesome.*

*Yeah, fair enough bro.*

We lay in tranquil darkness for a while before drifting into sleep, and for the first time in what seemed like years my dreams were soft and full of light, and the memory of kisses, imprinted on my mind, kept the monsters at bay.

# Chapter Twelve

I WOKE TO waxy golden daylight beyond the window, and a feeling of perfect calmness. We'd fallen asleep in each other's arms but rolled in opposite directions during the night, and I sat up as quietly as I could and stared at her, peaceful, her breathing soft and rhythmic.

*Seriously hot.*

*Innit.*

I was just wondering at what point this would become creepy when she woke up, blinking sleepily. 'Morning,' I said.

'Morning,' she yawned. Then she gave me a suspicious look. 'Have you been watching me sleep?'

'Only for a few hours.'

'Weirdo.'

'*You're* a weirdo.' I kissed her and the kiss lingered, all rosy and light, and then I made to get out of bed but she stopped me, wrapping her arms around my chest from behind and leaning against my shoulder.

'Wilt thou be gone?' she said, affecting a voice somewhere between Olivia Hussey and William Shatner. 'It is not yet near day. It was the nightingale, and not the lark that pierced the fearful hollow of thine ear. Nightly she sings on yon pomegranate tree. Believe me love, it was the nightingale.'

How could she remember all her lines? It had been so long since we'd done *Romeo and Juliet*, that one night when everything had spun so spectacularly out of orbit. *What's the next line?*

*How about that? I actually remember.*

'It was the lark,' I replied, opting for a low Batman-esque voice, 'the herald of the morn, no nightingale. Look, love, what envious streaks lace the severing clouds of yonder east. Night's candles are burnt out, and jocund day stands tiptoe on the misty mountain tops. I must be gone and live, or stay . . . and *die*.'

Kloe giggled, and carried on with her next bit of dialogue, word-perfect. I remembered the final line, my cue – 'Therefore stay yet, thou need'st not be gone' – and replied. 'Let me be taken, let me be put to *death*. Come death, and welcome, Juliet wills it so. I'll say—'

'Nope,' she said, shaking her head. 'Wrong. You are rubbish, and fired from acting. Entertainment industry rocked as Kloe Davies wins all the Oscars.'

'Oh really?' I leaned in and kissed her. The kiss, so full of joy and joking, became a hug, and the hug brought home the stinging irony of our little exchange.

'You do know I wasn't being serious?' she said.

'About the Oscar thing?'

'No,' she said. 'The quoting the play thing. I wasn't *actually* saying my lines from *Romeo and Juliet*. And you weren't *actually* saying yours back. Because that would be so cheesy that the only option would be for me to pretend to kill myself, and then for you to actually kill yourself, and then for *me* to wake up and see that you had killed yourself, and actually kill myself, for reals.'

I stared at her as though she was speaking Swahili. 'Sorry, Romeo and who?'

'Dunno. Julian?'

'Rona and Julian?'

'Julia and Rasputin?'

'Julie Walters' respirator?'

"Bout half past ten?'

Now the laughter came, with a vengeance, and for a good minute we sat holding our sides, wet-eyed and hysterical. We were shocked into brief silence by Tara running in, still in her pyjamas, demanding to know what was going on, but as soon as Kloe and I looked at one another we started again, unable to speak, and Tara joined in. Then I remembered that we were in bed together with no clothes on and I immediately stopped laughing. 'Tara! Go back to your room! And shut the door!'

Tara rolled her eyes and shook her head. 'I'm not *stupid*, you know.' But she turned and closed the door, and I looked at Kloe again. Her expression was as horrified as mine, but within a few seconds we were laughing again.

We breakfasted together and I washed and dressed, and at about one o'clock it was time to go. Way past time, in fact. I hugged Tara tightly first, willing myself to be strong and not cry, even though her own tears stabbed me in the heart. 'You be good,' I said, 'and look after . . . Kloe. I'll be back.' *Woops. Almost said 'look after your mother'.*

'When?'

'Soon,' I said. 'Soon. Hush them tears, cowgirl.' I ruffled her hair, knowing how much it irritated her, and that got a giggle. I turned to Kloe. She wasn't crying. She didn't need to, it was all in her eyes, in the way she stood and hugged herself. I almost didn't know how to hug her, it seemed such a perfunctory way of saying goodbye. So I just did it, and held her, and kissed her, and said I'd be back soon.

'You'd better be. I don't fancy being stranded in this shack any longer than necessary.'

'Hey,' I said. 'This is an *awesome* shack.'

'It's all right. As shacks go.'

'I *will* be back,' I said. 'I promise.' I broke the embrace, and smiled like someone who knew exactly what they were doing. 'Look after each other.'

'We will,' she said. Now she was crying, although it was a dignified, mature sort of crying, and Tara was standing by her, their arms around each other, mother and daughter, blissfully ignorant. I wished I could tell them.

*You will soon.*

*This trip back to London will sort everything. And then we'll be a family.*

*How can you be so sure?*

*Because I told me.*

I headed into the forest, sniffing the damp, piny air. Chilled and fresh. I walked backwards, waving and smiling, tripped on a fallen tree branch and arse-planted spectacularly into some wet leaves, and Kloe and Tara collapsed in the doorway in a blizzard of giggles. I started trying to reclaim a bit of dignity, but then decided it was better that I looked stupid, so I made an over-the-top 'what am I *like*' face and did a silly walk until they were out of sight. I stopped and breathed deeply, calming myself, steeling myself. Off to see the wizard. 'The wonderful wizard . . .' I began to sing, but I couldn't carry on. The silence was far too complete for me to break it with my tuneless burbling.

As I walked back through the woods . . . *dark and deep, miles to go before I sleep* . . . I could feel that nagging dread in my mind. It was everywhere. The light was sickly, the decaying leaves and wet bark dripped with menace, and I was getting steadily colder, rubbing my arms to beat back the goosebumps.

*Choose your own adventure.*

*Time is a flat circle.*

*Where do I know that line from—*

'Stanly!'

It was Tara's voice. I spun on the spot. She had emerged

from behind a tree and was walking towards me, smiling. 'Tara?' I said. 'What are you doing?'

'Showing you,' she said. She stopped and stood there, incongruous in her red pyjamas and bare feet, bright, too bright, against the muddy green tones of the wood.

'What do you mean? Showing me what? And why aren't you wearing shoes or a coat, you'll get hypothermia!'

*I'm sure she was dressed when I left . . .*

She smiled again. 'I can destroy things,' she said. 'With my thoughts.' She closed her eyes and a huge explosion erupted in the distance behind her. I stumbled backwards a few steps, blinded by the flash and deafened by the boom that echoed through the trees. The force of the blast shook drips from the branches and sent birds hurrying skyward, squawking in distress.

'Tara,' I said, when I could manage words. 'What did you do . . .'

'That was the cabin,' said Tara. 'Good distance, eh? I can do better, though.'

*No . . .* 'The cabin?' I said, numbly. 'You . . . Kloe . . .'

'Don't worry,' said Tara. 'I broke her neck beforehand. She was already dead.'

'What . . .'

Tara smiled again, that innocent smile. 'You knew this would happen. They told you how powerful I am.' And then the smile was gone, and that beautiful little girl of mine looked like the most evil thing in the world. I fell to my knees, my legs gas, and Tara spoke again. 'I'm a weapon,' she said, her voice plunging a thousand octaves, filling up every available molecule of space. 'The worst.'

I looked up, looked past her. The moon was a clock as big as the sky, its hands rushing around in blinding circles. 'I'm going to destroy everything,' said Tara, 'and it's all your fault.'

'My fault . . .' Did I say that? I wasn't even sure. Couldn't feel. Couldn't understand . . .

'You're my father,' she said. 'The power comes from you. And you left me alone with Kloe, alone to kill her, snap her like nothing. Everyone is going to die. Everyone is going to bleed and drown.' Her eyes were as red as ancient suns, her skin pale, ghostly silk. Far away I could hear fire and drumming.

'Tara,' I whispered.

'You brought me here,' said Tara. 'You *made* me.'

Everything was shifting, as though the world around me were a series of pictures on top of one another; a photograph, and beneath that a watercolour, and beneath that claymation, and beneath that black and white chalk scribbles, and beneath that just crude, awful stick drawings, and someone was ripping bits of each away, exposing all the different layers, a hideous collage . . .

Someone . . .

Tara . . .

'I'll destroy it all,' said Tara. 'Everything.' She raised her hand, whatever she was, and I knew it was all over.

*Blank.*

I awoke in the dark, face down on cold damp ground, and managed to stand, looking around blindly. I was still in the woods, I could tell that much. I wiped leaves and mud from my face and tried to remember.

*Tara. Killed . . . Kloe? A weapon. What?*

'No,' I said out loud. 'No. Dream.' I must have tripped . . . banged my head or something . . . or fallen asleep . . . just a dream . . .

'Dreams sleep,' said a voice, and I froze, petrified. The voice was scratchy and spidery and seemed to come from everywhere. 'We do not sleep.'

'No need for it,' it said, as though agreeing with itself. The voice was still coming from everywhere, but from a different place . . .

*The forest is talking.*

*I'm dreaming.* 'I'm dreaming,' I said. 'This is—'

Light, as bright as a nuclear fire, and for a second I could see Kloe hanging from a tree, one foot twitching obscenely. I screamed, but it was drowned out by thunder. Dark again. I stumbled towards her, holding out my hands in the blackness, trying to find her, cut her down, but she wasn't there. *Where is she?*

'All truth,' whispered the forest.

'Your truth.'

'All the truth you can eat.'

'*Who are you?*' I screamed. '*What is–*' Another flash of lightning and there was my mother, slumped against a tree trunk, shot in the stomach. I tried to cry out but couldn't, fell backwards into the shadows again, landing hard on my back. Thunder and more lightning, and there was Eddie, on top of me, his eye sockets empty, his mouth open, fixed in a rictus howl. I rolled away, let his body slump on the floor. More thunder, war drums pounded by psychotic, spitting giants. I got to my feet and staggered, moaning, crying.

'This does not sleep,' the forest said. There was nothing in its voice, no delight or hatred or fear, no emotion, nothing human. It was just sound, like a frozen blade, dipped in acid. 'You will sleep.'

The next flash of lightning was like a streak of fire scorching my eyes, and through it I could see Connor and Sharon side-by-side against the tree, bloody and still. I was on my knees again, although I couldn't remember falling. The thunder shook me, jolting my bones, and I threw up painfully, gasping. Lightning again, and Daryl, swatted down like a fly, his last whine fading into the thunder . . .

A forest full of dead people, stripped of everything but their shapes . . .

'All the people who will die,' said the forest.

'All of them dead.'

'Because of you.'

Thorns tearing into my flesh. Nails. Drum beats spelling out deafening rage, and lightning, and howling, and when the rain came it was fire and ice pouring from a sky of blackened crimson, and there stood Tara in the middle of a burning city, buildings gutted like egg shells, people broken and scattered to winds that poured in from another, infinitely more terrible world. All the people I'd failed, friends, family, strangers . . .

And there stood Tara in her red pyjamas . . .

And there stood Tara smiling . . .

And there stood Tara, speaking in the forest's voice. 'All gone,' she said.

*No.*

'All dead,' said the forest, in Tara's voice.

'All dead,' it said, in Kloe's voice.

*All dead* in my mother's voice, in Eddie's voice, Connor's, Sharon's . . .

And there he stood in the middle of a city in flames. He had my face, my body and eyes, and my laugh as if filtered through murder and red ice. 'All dead,' he said, his grin hinting at unspeakable perversions.

'NO!' I stood up. This was beyond pain; I was willing a defeated shell to stand. Movement was like razors.

Stanly stopped smiling. Cocked his head. *My* head. 'All dead,' he repeated.

My head. *All dead.*

My head? *All* . . .

*He's inside.*

The voice of an older Stanly, almost silent, but enough for me to hear. 'Don't let it get inside your head.'

*Inside your head.*

'No,' I said. I opened my eyes a hundred times, and each time I did I healed a wound. Stanly shook his head, my head.

'No,' he said, in my voice.

'No,' I said, in his voice. *No. My* voice.

'No?'

I concentrated, and Stanly exploded. The world around him flashed and everything came apart at the seams like jigsaw fragments, the pieces whirling and glowing, all those layers, like pages being ripped from a sketchbook, and all the while that terrible drumming, so loud that my ears bled, apocalypse rhythms . . .

*Blank.*

When the light faded I was lying in the forest with no idea of how long I had been there. Everything rushed back and I rolled over and jumped to my feet with an involuntary cry. Something was lying there on the ground right where my head had been. It was vaguely human-shaped, but it was barely three feet long, its limbs spindly, its light blue skin shimmering like early-morning water. It had no face, but I could tell that it was dead.

*I killed it.*

As I watched it started to fade, and quickly there was nothing but a vague suggestion, an idea of the shape of a body, visible only to me.

*All lies.*

*A monster.*

*A . . .*

'A shimmer in the forest,' I said, and smiled shakily. 'Thanks, me.' I dropped to my knees, exhausted, and stared into space for a very long time.

The sky had frosted over when I pulled up outside Mum's house, day rapidly giving way to twilight. I glanced through the kitchen window and saw her get up from the table, her face full of relief, and the anxious heat in my stomach cooled slightly. I went in and hugged her and showered and ate, and asked if there had been any calls. 'None,' said Mum. 'But, Stanly . . . look.'

She switched on the TV and found the news. London was still reeling from the emergence of the giant dog, as well as explosions and gunfire the following night. The authorities were sticking with the animal-testing facility story, and nobody was confirming or denying that the military had been involved with the action at Freeman's place. Moreover, it was 'very possible' that there were more dangerous animals loose in London, and people were being advised to stay in their homes. The police were on high alert . . . and the *army* were backing them up.

*How did they get all this organised so quickly?*

*Maybe it was going to happen anyway . . .*

'And police are appealing for information about these five individuals,' said the newscaster.

'You've gotta be fucking kidding,' I muttered.

'It is believed that they are responsible for the release of the animal,' continued the man, indicating grainy photographs of myself, Eddie, Sharon, Connor and Skank, 'and possibly for the explosions that occurred on Monday. Authorities indicate a high probability that they plan to create further chaos. The release of the creature is being treated as an act of terror.'

*Great. The T-word.*

*Just what I need.*

'Stanly,' said Mum.

'It's bollocks,' I said. 'OK? Lies. They're covering up . . . something. Something bad. And they're blaming us.' I took out my phone and tried Sharon, then Eddie, then Connor. I even tried Freeman. None of them answered. Not a good sign. My stomach turned and I stared at my hands, trying to think straight. It didn't necessarily mean anything, did it? They might . . . *might what? Have all turned their phones off?*

*Yeah . . .*

*If they'd been caught the police wouldn't be appealing for information. They're still out there. They're fine. They have to be.*

*And I have to go back. Now.*

I went out to the porch to grab my coat. Mum ran out after me. 'What are you doing?' she said. 'You're not going back now?'

'I have to.'

'Stanly,' said Mum, 'it's getting dark. It'll take you, what, a couple of hours at least to fly home?' She paused and shook her head, as though she couldn't believe she was actually talking about flying. 'And by then it'll be *completely* dark, and you'll be exhausted, and you'll be no help to anyone.'

'But they're not answering their phones,' I said. 'Something might have happened . . .'

'And how will getting to London in the dark with no energy help them?' Her voice was so sensible and calm, the voice of reason. Voice of a mum. Amazing, considering what she was being asked to swallow.

'OK,' I said. 'But I'm going first thing tomorrow.'

There was a question on her face. *Why do you have to go back at all? Surely they can look after themselves.* I knew she wanted to say it, but she knew what my answer would be, and she knew the truth herself anyway. 'All right,' she said. 'Then have an early night, all right?'

I went upstairs, although I didn't see how I could go to bed. In fact, I felt wired, and not just in a stressed-out what-the-hell-have-I-got-myself-into way. I felt *powerful*. As though there was electricity tingling under my skin, as though I could throw trucks around as easily as breathing, tear down a building with a snap of my fingers. Right now I felt like I could take on ten of those giant dogs.

Something to do with the shimmer, perhaps? That was the only explanation that made any sense, because I *definitely* felt odd. Different.

*I should go back tonight.*

There were too many good reasons. I had no idea what would await me when I returned, how many soldiers, police or whoever else would be after me. Arriving under cover of darkness was a no-brainer. Plus, I didn't know where Sharon and the others were, where they'd been forced to hide. It felt positively indecent, staying another night in a comfortable bed, safe and familiar.

*And I need to get back into it.*

I realised that I'd been pacing around my room for nearly ten minutes. I forced myself to sit down and called Kloe. She sounded cheerful. *Too* cheerful. I could tell that the glow of our time together had already started to fade, that she was angry again, with me, with everything. Once again, all I could do was offer platitudes. Tell her I loved her. She said she loved me too, but I had a feeling that even if I did come back to her in one piece, I'd be paying for this for a while. She told me she'd spoken to her parents, that they'd been freaking out, that she'd had to lie to them. 'They saw you on TV,' said Kloe. 'Your picture, you and Eddie and the others. People are saying you're a *terrorist*.'

'I'm not,' I said, stupidly.

'Well, yeah, obviously I know that, you idiot.'

Not cool, whichever way you swing it.

*She's alive, though.*

*She'll be safe.*

*They'll both be safe.*

Eventually I hung up the phone and made to head back downstairs, but caught sight of my reflection and stopped dead. My black outfit definitely looked badass, especially the coat, but if I was going to be heading back to a heavily patrolled city whose authorities and citizens considered me public enemy number one, maybe badass-looking wasn't the way to go?

I thought my wardrobe open and started yanking out old clothes, throwing certain items into a pile on the floor, holding some up in mid-air to check sizes. Some baggy rugby jersey or other. A lumberjack shirt. Random T-shirts. Torn cargo trousers. A ludicrous-looking hat with woolly earflaps. Thick snot-green fingerless gloves. I swore that I couldn't remember ever owning half of this stuff, let alone wearing it. Ensemble assembled, I stripped to my underwear and set to the clothes with scissors and a lighter.

When I returned to the kitchen, armed with an old pair of headphones and a rucksack from my GCSE days, my mum was sitting at the table. I had a feeling she'd been waiting for me. I gave her my I-know-I'm-in-trouble smile, and she shook her head. 'Don't you try that with me.'

'Sorry.'

She clocked how I was dressed and did a pretty comical double-take. 'What . . . what on earth . . . you look like a tramp!'

'Brilliant,' I said. 'Mission accomplished. Do you still have that old overcoat of Dad's? The brown one?'

'Yes, it's in the cupboard . . .'

'Can I take it?'

'Of course you can,' she said. 'But . . .'

'Also, do you have any whisky?'

'Yes . . . why?'

I laid a load of newspaper out on the floor, put the heavy brown overcoat down and liberally applied whisky to the front, back and sleeves. 'I can't believe this,' my mum said, pacing up and down. 'I can't believe it. They said you're a terrorist. My son, a *terrorist*. It's every mother's worst nightmare.'

'At least I don't vote Tory.'

That got half a laugh. 'Thank goodness for small mercies.'

'Mum,' I said, as I dried the spilled booze with a hairdryer, 'I know this is all completely insane. And . . . it's going to get bad. You'll probably have police round . . . journalists, maybe. You have to know – you have to *believe* – that I'm doing what has to be done. I'm doing the right thing. Trying to make things better.'

'You're my son,' said Mum. 'Of course I believe you. But how can I just let you go running off to fight God knows who?'

'You're going to have to.'

'Why?'

'Because.'

She actually laughed at that. 'That's *our* line. Mine and your father's. To placate *you*. Not the other way round.'

I shrugged, donned the stinking coat and pulled the hat's earflaps down. 'A boy's gotta do what a boy's gotta do.'

'Oh shut up,' she said, and gave me a hug. It hurt. 'Silly boy.'

'I'll be careful,' I whispered.

'You'd bloody better.'

'I promise.' I stuffed my black coat into the rucksack, because at this point it felt like the kind of good luck charm that I wanted to keep with me, and secured the headphones under the hat, ready to pump noise into my ears. We went out onto the patio and hugged tightly, one more time, and I took a last look at her and my old home before kicking off and powering towards the waiting sky. It received me like an empty ocean, infinite and welcoming, washing over my body, invigorating. *Embiggening this small man.* It felt good. Right. Cromulent. And somehow even easier than before. Something was definitely different. It had to have been the shimmer, it had made me stronger. Handy, considering what unimaginable ridiculousness I was about to face.

*Rightio, then.*

*Let's get this party started, shall we?*

I made to jet off again, then remembered the one missing ingredient. These old headphones wouldn't be anywhere near as good as the ones I'd lost, but they were better than nothing. I plugged the jack into my phone and searched through my music. Something light and acoustic, maybe, or soft and ambient? Chilled-out sounds for a meditative flight, enabling me to charge my mental batteries?

Or a playlist starting with 'Hysteria' by Muse, followed by 'Song 2' by Blur, and continuing along similar lines for about thirty songs?

I smiled and pressed play, ready for a shot of pure, unfiltered *grrr*, straight to the brain.

*OK. NOW let's get this party started.*

# Chapter Thirteen

I SCREAMED THROUGH the air as fast as I could manage without the wind ripping my face clean off, hands buried in the pockets of my coat, pounding drums and end-of-the-world riffs and shrieking falsetto in my ears, assembling and dissecting possible plans in my head as I flew. While I knew it probably wouldn't be safe – or necessarily productive – to go to any of the obvious places like Sharon and Connor's or the shop, I did feel that it might be instructive so see what had gone on in my absence. Maybe there would be police or military guards. Would the places have been ransacked? The news report, with our pictures and accusations of terrorism, seemed pretty conclusive in terms of our public enemy status . . .

*And when has the news ever exaggerated anything.*

I touched down in a wooded area near the outskirts – or near the outskirts of the outskirts of the outskirts. That was one thing I had going for me: the sheer size of London meant that they couldn't be watching everywhere at once. They couldn't close every place of business, every school, every shop and every transport link, lock every family in their house, confiscate the keys from every car. They couldn't station a tank on every street.

I hoped.

*There'd be uproar if they did, surely?*

Again, I hoped. But I had a nagging feeling, based on my extended wanderings of the city, that until bullets literally started flying people would rather keep their heads down and not think about it. And if they really thought that my friends and I were terrorists, I doubted we'd be seeing any inspirational Spider-Man-style scenes in which the populace rallied behind us – or in front of us – saying that if you messed with one Londoner you messed with all Londoners. London didn't seem to be like that, at least as far as I'd seen.

*But I'll save it anyway, 'cos I'm the big damn hero.*

I went on foot for a while – or glided along at foot level, at least – keeping to the shadows, hat pulled down, smelly coat wrapped around me. One thing I did notice was that far more cars seemed to be heading away from London than into it. Made sense, and suited my purposes. If more monsters were coming, and Azathoth knew what else, then the fewer civilians around the better. I flexed my fists in my pockets, practically feeling power dancing between my fingers. I had my (metaphorical) sneaky hat on, fully prepared to stealth it up, but if push came to shove, and shove came to more shoving, and more shoving came to the application of some kind of mental attack, then so be it.

The fact that I wasn't hearing many helicopters made me feel better. Hopefully I could bank on the Angel Group underestimating my flying abilities. I could see a roadblock up ahead, with cars and a large black truck that might have been the police but smelled (metaphorically) like something else. They were stopping anyone who came through.

*Right.*

*Up, up and away.*

It was freezing, but I forced myself to go as high as I could, squinting, icy shafts of wind bypassing my clothes as though they weren't even there. I gritted my teeth and barrelled forward as fast as possible, and quickly the city started to form properly beneath me, like the endless grey pock-marked ridges and multi-coloured eyes of some bizarre beast. I had to go a bit lower to get my bearings, then shot back up, pushing the limit of my personal altitude.

First stop: Connor and Sharon's. I knew the street from high, high above, and positioned myself as exactly as I could. No way of making out any vehicles from here.

*Right. Let's do this quickly—*

I became aware of the buzzing seconds before the bullets, and instinctively motored in the opposite direction, turning my body as I moved and flying backwards so I could see behind me. Something was chasing me, a black shape, maybe as long as a car but much sleeker, and it was having no trouble gaining air on me.

*What the . . .*

*Drone?*

*Balls. So much for them underestimating my flying abilities.*

It had stopped firing when I headed away, but as soon as it had me in its sights again it was back on the attack, and I thought a bubble around myself, deflecting its projectiles, which burned bright and brief against the sky like dying fireflies. I channelled as much as I could into my flight, thinking past any idea of restriction, but the thing wasn't giving up. I tried loop-the-looping, I tried abrupt changes of direction that jarred my whole body, but each time the thing corrected its course infuriatingly rapidly and came right back at me. Even if I could defend myself against its bullets, I wasn't going to outrun the cursed thing.

*Fine.*

POP.

For some reason – possibly anxiety, or possibly the fact that it's difficult to concentrate on a sustained psychic attack when you're being chased through the sky at high speed by a drone – the blast was not super-effective, and while the drone wavered as though it had been clonked by something, it barely slowed down.

POP.

*BURST.*

*BURST BURST BURST!*

It still wasn't working, so I thought laterally.

*SNAP!*

The drone broke in half at the centre and the two halves fell away, hissing and sparking. I quickly grabbed them with my mind, not wanting them to fall on the city. We were high up, and they could do a lot of damage. I slowed down and sat in the air, staring at the broken drone and listening out for more. I was pretty sure I could hear the buzzing again, elsewhere; it was further away but definitely present. Had this one sent a message? Would more be coming? I had no way of knowing how many of the bastard things were in the sky, or if this one had been piloted towards me or flown by itself. If there was a camera attached, it was integrated too subtly into the design for me to make out, but it seemed likely that there was one, meaning that they might already know exactly what I looked like. Which would render my disguise both smelly *and* pointless. At any rate, flying was now going to be extremely difficult, if not impossible.

*Right. Time to go down.*

I could see the way back towards Connor and Sharon's, having regained my bearings. Taking a deep breath, and keeping the bits of drone safely in my wake, I angled myself towards my destination and punched it, eyes locked. This was going to require serious control. I couldn't afford to approach slowly, especially if there were more happy sky friends about. The street came rushing towards me, from a faraway toy display to a miniature film set to reality, and I adjusted my trajectory minutely, staying on target, and now I could see that there was indeed a police car parked outside the house, as well as one of those black trucks, and I kept going, kept going, kept going, *stay on target, stay on target, right a bit, left a bit, right, now slow slow slow slow SLOW DOWN—*

—and I stopped, my face millimetres away from Connor and Sharon's roof. I flattened myself against it and stayed there for a minute, listening out. No voices. Hopefully I hadn't been seen. Hovering an inch above the roof I moved silently to the edge, risking a peek into the garden. Nobody there, and no lights on in the house. I placed the bits of drone on the grass, taking care not to make a sound, and quickly and delicately opened my bedroom window, fighting to keep my heartbeat under control. Entrance secure, I flew into my room and closed the window behind me. I decided not to let my feet touch the floor, to maintain stealthiness, and levitated out of my room and into the hall like a ghost. I almost wanted to bump into someone, to see the look on their face when this tramp-like figure came hovering out of the darkness. There were no lights on downstairs either, although from the top of the stairs I could see that the front door was slightly open, the edges chipped and torn, a line of police tape across the threshold. It made me shake with anger. It wasn't our house any more.

*Their house, you mean.*

*Whatever.*

I floated into Connor and Sharon's bedroom. I'd only been in there once, and it had been immaculate, but now there were chairs overturned on the floor, and their drawers had been ripped open. My eyes fell on the painting of the geisha girl next to the bookcase. It was lovely, pale and impressionistic but unmistakably a geisha. I heard Connor's voice. *'I've got plenty of stuff saved up at home for a rainy day.'*

I carefully moved the painting away from the wall, placed it softly on the bed and regarded the safe. I wondered if he'd had time to take his rainy-day stuff with him.

*Only one way to find out. Let's hope this wasn't a wasted trip.*

It was hard to know how much of this had been lurking at the back of my mind and how much was occurring to me on the spot, but the fact that it required a combination lock that I didn't know just didn't seem like much of an obstacle. I simply stared at the lock for a long time, trying to drain away the swirl of thoughts and leave just the pure, quiet image of the device, the knob, the numbers. *I wonder . . .*

I could see the safe floating in blackness, three-dimensional, obvious. It had subtleties, but so does everything, and all subtleties are visible and understandable and breakable if you look deep enough. You just need the quiet of thinking.

*And psychic powers help too.*

Breathing regularly and softly, I managed to burrow inside the lock with my mind. I could see how it worked, every tiny detail in its machinery, what made it tick, and slowly, inexorably, I could turn things in the correct fashion to unlock it. It was like putting an invisible thread through the eye of the tiniest needle, but somehow I knew that I could do it. *Turn. Click. Back. Click. See the mechanism. Understand it. Bypass it. Just a mechanism.* I could manipulate it, see its insides and outsides and everything that made it real, that gave it a purpose. It was a means to an end. It was designed for this. You just needed to see the truth of the mechanism.

Just a mechanism.

*Just a mechanism.*

*Just a—*

Click.

*Ha. Genie. In. A. BOTTLE.*

The safe was deep and contained a few lethal-looking items: two handguns, a sawn-off shotgun and a fair wedge of corresponding ammunition. There were also holsters for the handguns and a strap for the shotgun. Not for the first time I wondered where the hell Skank got hold of this stuff . . . and why Connor had kept it.

*A rainy day.*

*Like those days when it's raining monsters and evil corpora-*
*tions and police and stuff.*

That thought made me shudder. I was *not* killing police. I
didn't even want to *hurt* any police. Angel Group soldiers were
one thing, I had to assume they knew at least something about
the company's shady dealings, but police? Guys doing jobs. In
fact, guys being *kept* from doing jobs, important jobs, probably
on the basis of mysterious orders from unaccountable people.

*Push + shove = . . .*

I attached the holsters to my belt, slid the handguns into
them, strapped the shotgun around my neck and hung it inside
my coat, quick and quiet, almost on autopilot, not totally
convinced that I was even doing what I was doing, let alone
that it was remotely a good thing. As I closed up the safe I had
a vivid flashback of myself as a child playing Duplo with my
mother, watching *Mary Poppins*, drinking apple juice, munching
biscuits, leaving colourful bricks sticky with spilled juice and
careless crumbs. I hated to think what my mother would say if
she saw me loading up on guns.

*Load up on guns, bring your friends . . .*
Find *your friends.*
*And hopefully don't shoot anybody.*

I put the ammunition in my rucksack and replaced the painting, feeling weighed down both physically and mentally. I didn't
like this.

*Create a Facebook profile and write a status, then.*
*And make like a tree, butthead.*

I exited swiftly over the fence at the bottom of the garden
and made a quick calculation. It made sense to keep low rather
than risk another stealth dive-bomb manoeuvre – I wasn't in
a hurry to encounter another drone. 110th Street was next on
my list of destinations and I used back streets, hiding behind
every wall and car, walking fast when necessary, flying close to

the ground where possible. It was strange, and not just because I wasn't used to flying at this level. It no longer felt free. I felt *strangled*, zipping behind cover at every opportunity in case I was seen, and while there were still quite a few pedestrians about, those I saw hurried with scared looks on their faces, checking behind them more times than seemed necessary, as if they knew they shouldn't be outside. Some glanced pensively towards the sky, listening out for that tell-tale buzzing, and every now and then I heard a melancholy *caw* from a dark-feathered bird. It sounded downright alien against such a deafening, oppressive hush, a violation of empty space. Even the general city noise seemed dull, and the wind had sewn up its mouth in fear rather than risk being noticed.

*Balls to this. In a big way.*

There were police cars and black trucks parked near 110th Street, so I didn't even bother exploring it, just zipped off, assumed a safe distance and tried to phone my friends again. Still nothing. At this point, there was only one place left to try.

*Time for another fly?*

*No. Too risky. If there are more things up there . . .*

There were. Definitely. I could hear them in the distance. Once or twice I was pretty sure I saw one zipping through the air. I wondered what people thought about it.

*Come on, let's get walking.*

It took a long time to get to Blue Harvest, and although there were no guards present the club was closed. Eddie would definitely have warned Hannah . . .

*They might not even know about the club, though.* Despite the nagging feeling that my friends were going to have found somewhere new to hide, somewhere that even I didn't know about, I figured I might as well try inside. Apart from anything else, I was uncomfortably aware that I was already running out of places to look, and I wanted to put that moment off for as long as possible. I thought the door unlocked and slipped in, using my phone to illuminate the walls while I found the light switches. They had dimmers, so I kept them low. Didn't want to attract too much attention, but I did quite fancy being able to see.

There was nothing that indicated any kind of struggle. No marks on the doors, and the place looked tidy. I walked slowly around the main room, tracing my finger over the smooth, cold tables, taking a moment over the pictures of those who had died in the shootings last year. The sound of bullets wasn't nearly as foreign now as it had been back then, when I'd never even heard someone fire a gun at a duck shoot, let alone try to kill each other with automatic weapons.

*And now you're carrying some.*

*Except . . . are these automatic?*

*Note to self: draft letter to NRA asking if these are automatic. Haha, you so funny.*

Hannah had recently converted the cellar into a sort of chill-out space that was open during the day, where people could drink and play pool and listen to the jukebox. It was accessible via the hall at the back of the main room, and I headed down there, already knowing there'd be no-one about. Sure enough, there was no-one about. *Crap.* I helped myself to a beer and sat on the pool table, thinking. Last time I'd been here, Kloe had been visiting. We'd come to watch a band called The Other Mother, a supremely sexy group of hyper-stylised are-they-even-humans who played weird dark cello-driven funk. It had been an amazing night.

I drank my beer and tried to work out what I should do. It was getting on now, and I'd still not had a call or anything, and while it made sense to continue searching in the dark, when it was easier to hide, my options were kind of limited. I hadn't the faintest idea where to look. I didn't even know where Nailah lived, and she wasn't answering her phone.

*Although* . . .

I checked in my wallet and grinned, because what I *did* have was the address that Nailah had given me. Lauren's. The new empowered girl.

Seemed as good a time as any to meet a new super-person.

I jogged back upstairs, stepped into the main room and froze. At the other end of the room, in the doorway, stood a boy and a dog. The boy was about my age, pale, with messy blonde-brown hair, and he wore a heavy green coat over a red hoody, jeans and trainers. The dog was, I guessed, a Doberman, and it was *big*. Not as big as the blue one, by any means, but by normal dog standards . . . big. I tried a wave. 'Um, hi,' I said.

The dog offered a bark. The boy didn't say anything. His expression was odd, slightly confrontational yet . . . sad? Reluctant? Scared? I frowned. He was freaking me out more than the dog, to be honest. 'You all right?' I tried. 'What are you doing here?'

Again, he didn't answer. His eyes were moving like those of a cornered animal, taking in the room, and his whole body was tense, ready for something . . . and then something in my brain bleeped. I recognised this kid. 'You were there the other night,' I said. 'The blue dog. You were there.'

Nothing.

'Don't worry,' I said, 'I'm not going to hurt you. I'm just—'

As I spoke, something in his expression changed. He wasn't looking at me, he was looking *past* me. Suddenly he dived to the floor and disappeared underneath a table, and with a heart-stopping snarl the Doberman launched itself towards me, razor teeth dripping with hot saliva, eyes burning with a psychotic, rabid rage where a second ago there had been placid indifference. Instinctively I flung myself up onto the ceiling and pinned my body there, just out of the creature's reach. It was going completely mental, roaring and snapping its jaws, leaping up and down and clawing at me, like some kind of low-budget Smiley Joe re-enactment.

*What do I do? What do I do?*

*Why is the quiet dog suddenly trying to eat me alive?*

*I can't kill a dog . . . not a regular one anyway . . .*

I *could* knock one out, though. I reached out with my mind, grabbed one of the tables and brought it down *crack* on the top of the animal's head, and it flopped on the floor with a whimper and lay still. Gingerly I dropped down, keeping my eye on it. It was breathing, luckily, and there was no blood, but I still felt guilty for braining it like that.

*Knock out psycho mutt with table or get ripped into shreds of warm bloody dinner by psycho mutt. Tough choice.*

I heard a scuffling and turned in time to see the mysterious boy scrambling out from under the table and sprinting out the door. 'Wait!' I chased after him, not thinking, and as soon as I emerged outside I wished I hadn't, because the boy was gone and the street was full of black-clad soldiers, weapons raised.

'Freeze!' a voice said, distorted eerily through an amplifier. 'We don't want to hurt you!'

*Yeah.*

*OK, then.*

I blasted out a circle of energy, knocking them all off their feet, then made to take off, but now I realised that there were black helicopters in the sky above, and drones beyond them, and I could see the tell-tale red of laser tracers. I banked abruptly and hurtled down the street away from the soldiers, whipping up dust and rubbish in my slipstream, maximum acceleration, feeling the heat of a bullet as it streaked past my head.

*Aah, screw this so, so much.*

I ducked to the left, down a smaller side street, and carried on flying, trying to think over the thick chug of rotor blades overhead. I'd almost completed a thought when something exploded behind me, *too close* behind me, throwing concrete and rubbish bins aside and sending a gust of smoke forward. It enveloped me, making me choke as hot acrid stink filled my throat and lungs, but I forced myself to fly faster, praying I wasn't about to go head-first into a brick wall. I managed to spot a right turn and took it; this new street opened out onto a main road, which was possibly not the greatest idea ever, but . . .

*Sod it.*

I was about ten feet from the road when two more soldiers stepped out and raised their rifles. I didn't even slow down, just grabbed them both and smashed them first against the walls of the alley and then against each other, tossing them into the air to finish. Not too high. Just high enough. I heard them land and bounce behind me as I exited the alley, and immediately spotted a truck parked up the road with more soldiers standing around it. I concentrated on their guns, ripping them away, pummelled the soldiers against the side of the vehicle until they slumped unconscious on the pavement, then focused all my energy and thoughts on the truck itself and inclined my head to the left, making it spin across the road. It smashed through a lamppost into a solid brick wall with enough force to snap the post in half and seriously dent the wall, and bricks tumbled down onto the wrecked truck. I turned sharply and flew up the road, my pulse machine-gunning hysterical rhythms. They were out for blood now. So was I.

*Where the hell can I go?*

I raged through the air, keeping close to street level, turning random corners. Here and there I passed police cars and trucks, but I was going way too fast, ducking and diving over and around them, desperately turning over options in my brain.

*Stop.*

*Think.*

*Breathe.*

I ducked down an alley and came to a clumsy stop against a wall, breathing raggedly, smoke still in my lungs. I'd sustained a large cut on the back of my hand, which was weeping blood.

'Freeze!'

*Bollocks. From hell. In a bucket of old piss.*

The voice had come from behind. A soldier. I'd let one sneak up on me. What an absolute—

'Aurghgh!' *Thump.* Silence. I turned around gingerly to see a lone soldier face down on the floor with a young woman standing behind him. She was tall and skinny and wore black, and had green eyes and a tight ponytail of auburn hair. 'Are you Stanly?' she said, taking in my grotty ensemble with a slightly raised eyebrow.

*What the hell?* 'Are you from the Angel Group?' I asked, striking a fighting stance that was probably entirely pointless.

She shook her head. 'No. My name's Lauren. Nailah told you about me?'

I frowned. 'Yeah . . . how did you know I'd be here?'

'I heard that someone with powers was fighting soldiers around here,' she said. 'I thought you might need some help.'

'Thanks,' I said. *Time to be suspicious later. Grateful first.*

Lauren nodded. 'Come on, then. Let's go. I don't really want to lead them to my house if I can help it.'

# Chapter Fourteen

LAUREN LIVED ON a respectable-looking street in a quiet residential area, and as soon as we stepped inside her house I felt comfortable and at home. We'd miraculously managed to avoid any further patrols, but I'd been on edge the whole time, ready to fight. The idea of a chair, and of downgrading from red alert to standby, felt pretty delicious.

She led me through to a small, cosy kitchen, its walls bright and alive with photographs and paintings. It reminded me a little of my kitchen back in Tref-y-Celwyn, all that was missing was a Rayburn. I stood there, feeling a bit stupid, and Lauren gave me an amused smile. 'It's all right,' she said. 'I'm not going to bite.'

'I know,' I said. 'Sorry. I'm just . . . knackered. Flew from Wales today. Plus sneaking around and fighting . . .'

'And you're cut.' She took my hand gently and appraised the wound.

'It's all right,' I said. 'If you've got some cotton wool and antiseptic or something . . .'

Lauren didn't speak. She just stared intently at my hand, and I looked as well because I could feel something strange. It wasn't pain, exactly, but something muffled and distant, as though I were feeling someone else's pain via a bad signal, and then the wound began to shrink, like time-lapse photography, the flesh repairing itself, the dark areas around it turning paler. Within thirty seconds the injury was completely gone and my hand was healed, fresh. New. I looked from the blank skin to Lauren, unable to vocalise. She smiled. 'Painful?'

'No . . . you . . .'

'Fixed it.' She turned away and set about making tea. 'I've been practising for a long time.'

I put my rucksack down and took a seat at the bar in the middle of the kitchen. 'And you can just repair it? Living tissue? Just like that?'

She nodded. I leaned forwards, fascinated. 'How . . . sorry, do you mind me asking, how old were you when your powers first started to show?'

'Eleven,' she said.

'Oh.' That was a surprise.

'You were expecting older?'

'Um . . . yeah.' *Although . . . why? Tara was younger than that when she brought me and Freeman back to life.*

'It's not the same for everybody,' she said. 'For the majority, as far as I know, it's around fifteen, sixteen. But the abilities can appear much earlier than that. Depends on your brain, your biology.'

'What happened?' I asked. 'When yours appeared?'

She had been making eye contact, standing waiting for the kettle to boil, but now her eyes dropped and she fiddled almost compulsively with her hands. 'Just . . . it was sudden.' Neither of us spoke for one of those infinite stretches of seconds, which was rendered even more awkward than normal because we didn't know each other. There was just the whistle of the kettle getting steadily louder. 'Nice outfit, by the way,' said Lauren.

'Thanks. The latest in autumn superpowered fugitive.'

'Good idea, being in disguise.'

'Yeah,' I said. 'Although I miss not looking like a shambling hobo.'

'And the guns?'

I'd actually forgotten about them. 'Oh yeah,' I said. 'Sorry. They're not mine, actually. Picked them up from a friend. Just in case.' I unhooked the weapons. 'Anywhere I can put them, maybe?'

Lauren floated the guns away from me and up onto a high shelf, pushing them well out of sight. 'Thanks,' I said. 'Really not a gun fan. So . . . how *did* you find me?'

'Nailah has a contact.'

'A contact where?' I felt like maybe I knew.

'Inside the Angel Group.' *Bingo.* 'Or in one of their sub-divisions, or something, I'm still not terribly clear how it all works. Your presence in the city was reported, anyway. That's why they sent the soldiers to intercept you.' *Damn drone must have had a camera after all.*

'So Nailah found out and told you?'

Lauren nodded.

'She told me she came to see you on Sunday. That you . . . weren't keen to get involved.'

'Well, how would you feel?' said Lauren. 'Some stranger turns up at your house, claiming to know your biggest secrets . . . I thought I'd kept myself well hidden. I was very close to leaving town after she left.'

'You changed your mind, though.'

'I decided I was overreacting,' said Lauren. 'Decided to . . . I don't know. Wait and see. And then there was all that stuff with the escaped animal, and then Nailah came back, late on Monday. She was scared. Really scared. I . . . I just suddenly felt like she was worth listening to. She told me that there were more people with powers, that she'd spoken to some, your friends. That you'd had to leave London, that bad things were happening. I still wasn't exactly *keen* to get involved, but . . .' She trailed off, made tea and handed mine over.

'Thanks. So why did you? Get involved?'

'Nailah told me a little more about what's going on,' said Lauren. 'Stuff she's heard from your friends. About the monsters, among other things. She said that everyone with powers could potentially be a target. And . . .' She paused. 'I could feel that something was different.'

'Feel?'

'In the air,' said Lauren. 'Obviously when the army and the police were suddenly everywhere, and there were drones in the sky, and that giant thing, the atmosphere changed. It couldn't *not* change. But there was something else. It's hard to put my finger on.'

'You think it's because of your powers? You're sensing something?'

'Possibly,' said Lauren. 'Let's just say that I had a very bad feeling. And I decided I'd rather make myself useful than sit at home waiting for the next catastrophe.'

I smiled. 'Well, I'm grateful. Do you have a way to get hold of Nailah?'

'Sort of,' said Lauren. 'She's . . . paranoid. And with good reason, really. She said she wants to avoid phones if at all possible, although she did give me one. Mostly we've been communicating via some . . . hidden internet site, or something. She had to write down how it works, I'm terrible with technology. She's been acting as a go-between, getting messages from her contact, helping your friends.'

'She knows where they are?'

'Yes,' said Lauren, 'but I don't, I'm afraid. I know about as much as I've told you. Nailah will get in contact, though, and when she does I'm sure she'll tell you where to find them.' She smiled. 'She's been using her blog and Twitter and things to mess around with the Angel Group.'

'How?'

'She has a number of different accounts tied to the blog,' said Lauren, 'and a few others she's involved with. They report sightings of monsters and other strange occurrences. Not the kind of thing that the authorities would usually pay attention to.'

'Until now.'

Lauren nodded. 'Until now. She's been reporting bogus sightings around the city. Trying to keep the soldiers off-balance, to keep them away from her, from me. From your friends.'

'Presumably her Angel Group contact led her to you in the first place.'

Lauren smiled again, but there was a hint of embarrassment there this time. 'No, actually,' she said. 'It was . . . I never use my powers in public. Never, ever. But I happened to be out a while back, and I saw a dog run into the road. It was about to get crushed by a bus. I didn't even think. Just moved my hand, pulled it out of reach. I wouldn't usually move my limbs when using my powers, you don't need to, do you? But I suppose . . . the panic? Instinct? It wasn't much of a movement, but . . .'

*OK, interesting.* 'Let me guess,' I said. 'Nailah was on the bus?'

'She was walking behind me,' said Lauren. 'I imagine she knew what to look for. Nobody else noticed, and I got out of there pretty quickly. But she tracked me down. Spied on me a bit, to confirm her suspicions.' She shook her head. 'Not exactly what you want to hear from a mysterious stranger . . . but a good lesson, I suppose. In being careful.'

*And a good lesson in lying.*

I decided not to let on that I'd heard a somewhat different story, or that I knew anything about Lauren's missing friend. We drank tea in silence for a little while. 'So you've lived in London for a long time?' I said. 'Did you ever try to seek out others with powers?'

She looked away. There was a lot in her head, I could see, a lot of pain and barbed memory, and I wanted to know all about it. I felt compelled to make it better somehow, to repay her for saving me, but all I'd managed to do was create another awkward silence. This was going well. 'I wanted to hide,' was all she would mutter. Then she asked if I was hungry.

'Starving,' I said.

'I'll cook something.'

'No it's fine, I can . . .'

She shook her head. 'Not allowed. Guest. And I'm a bit OCD about my kitchen anyway.' She put something classical on the CD player and began to rifle through cupboards. 'Are you a vegetarian?'

'Most definitely not.'

'Good. I have some chicken, and there's pasta . . . rice . . . something along those lines?'

'Really, you don't have to cook for me,' I said. 'Don't worry . . .'

'I'm not worried.' She sat down and things started to happen around us. The hob switched itself on, oil sloshed itself into a frying pan, and two chicken breasts emerged from the fridge and landed on a chopping board. An onion landed on a second chopping board, and two knives set about chopping the chicken and the onion into bits, striking alternately. Pots of herbs, a can of chopped tomatoes and other bits and pieces floated out of cupboards and arranged themselves on the counter, everything working in perfect synchronicity. I looked at Lauren, who was half-watching what was going on but mostly smiling at my expression. 'Powers can be fun,' she said.

'Wow,' I said. 'You can do all that at the same time? It's so . . . precise.'

'Practise,' she said. 'Plenty. Seems you're not a bad crack at it either, throwing trucks about.'

'That's different,' I said. 'Blunt. Clumsy.'

'Like I said. Practise.' She snapped her fingers and the CD skipped to a new track.

'You know you don't have to snap your fingers,' I grinned.

'Of course,' said Lauren. 'But it's fun. Surely you do it as well.'

I thought of everything I did with my mind. Every time I moved my hands for effect it seemed to be in combat. In fact, most of the time when I was using my powers these days it seemed to be in combat. It was good to see the power applied to such banal, domestic things, injecting them with magic. The onions scattered themselves in the hot oil and started to sizzle. I laughed. 'It looks really cool, to be fair.'

'I don't usually do everything like that,' said Lauren. 'I did for a while. Got *really* lazy. But you have to find a balance, otherwise you start to forget how to do things physically. I was just . . . I don't know. Showing you what can be done. And it doesn't stop there. It goes deeper.'

'What do you mean?'

'All that,' she said, pointing at the meal gradually assembling itself, 'that's just doing what you'd normally do with your hands but cutting out the physical movement. When I say deeper, I mean it should be possible to put the ingredients together with my mind and cook them just by thinking. No oven involved.'

'What, just . . . *will* it to cook?'

'Basically, yes, although it takes a degree of concentration I haven't managed to achieve yet. I did toast a piece of bread once. It took a long time and I had the worst migraine ever, but I did it. You're willing it to do something that's physically possible, using the power of your intention. Like repairing your wound, your skin would eventually repair itself anyway. I just . . . expedited the process. Theoretically you could apply it to everything.' She nodded, pouring some sauce in with the onions, and I heard the kettle begin to boil. 'You could look at a building and make it collapse. Turn someone blue. Liquify glass.' She summoned a packet of crisps to the table and split

202

them open with a thought. 'It's pretty scary, potentially.' She took a crisp and nodded for me to do the same. I took a handful, remembering how hungry I was. As I crunched them down, I wondered if this was a conversation Lauren had been waiting to have with someone, a like-minded, like-powered person. *She must miss her friend.*

'You could look at someone and kill them,' I blurted out, because of course that's the kind of thing you say in a casual conversation with a new acquaintance. 'Just like that.'

Lauren didn't seem rattled, though. She nodded. 'Yes. It makes me think that maybe the reason there are so few of us around is that the Angel Group got to them first.'

Although the kitchen was full of steam, richly infused with onion and garlic and peppers, I felt a momentary chill. 'Yeah,' I said, thinking back to my conversation with Nailah and Skank. 'That crossed our minds too. How much do you know about the Angel Group?'

'Nailah's told me a bit,' said Lauren. 'I'd never heard of them before. Very powerful. Mysterious motives. In possession of a lot of mad technology, which they're using to perform experiments.'

'Experiments with very aggressive consequences that try to eat you.'

'Yes, and that. Nailah seems to think that they're using people like us for their experiments. Either employing them, or keeping them under duress.'

'They just round us up? Put us to work?'

'To use our power.'

'Maybe,' I said. 'But . . . it doesn't make sense, does it? I mean, they've known about me and my lot for ages. Why haven't they just come and taken us?'

'I don't know,' said Lauren. 'I assume they would want your power, but . . . maybe not. Or maybe there's something more they want from you.'

*Tara*, I thought, and that made me think of Kloe. It had only been hours since I'd spoken to them but I was already anxious, despite the note from future Stanly reassuring me that they'd be fine. Worry must have been splattered across my face because Lauren asked, 'Penny for them?'

'Eh?'

'Thoughts.'

'Oh! I . . . just . . . my girlfriend. I should call and check to see if she's OK . . . but it's pretty late now. And I'm wondering if using my phone might be a bad idea.'

'There's the phone Nailah gave me,' said Lauren. 'She said . . . what's his name, is it Skunk?'

I smiled. 'Skank. Our resident stoner Q.'

'Yes, he got hold of some phones that can't be traced, or they're difficult to trace at least? Or they use an old network, or something? Like I said, I'm not brilliant with technology. I imagine it should be OK for you to use it, so long as you keep it quick. We don't want to use them very often, Nailah said. Just in case.'

I nodded. 'Thanks. I . . . I did speak to her earlier. I mean, I *saw* her just this morning. And she'll probably be asleep. So . . . I'll wait until tomorrow. Thank you, though.'

'It's fine.' Lauren walked over to the steaming, sizzling pots and pans and started to help them along with her hands. 'What's your girlfriend's name?'

'Kloe,' I said. 'Have you got a boyfriend?' *Clumsy. Blurt.* 'Or, you know. Girlfriend, anything.' Just so I had all my bases covered.

She didn't answer, just bent slightly further over the cooking. Her back looked pained, though. 'No,' she said, after a moment.

*Great. More awkward silence. Well done Stanly, congratulations on your new career as social Black Death.* Once again I tried to change the subject. 'So we pretty much know as much as each other about all this crap now, eh?'

'Yes,' she said. 'I don't know much about you, though. I assume you have a story.'

'You could say that,' I said. 'Where to begin . . .'

'I hear the beginning is good.'

We sat down to the meal, which would have tasted spectacular even if it hadn't come after an extremely tiring few hours, and I told her my story, from the second I turned sixteen and started floating above my bed, to my fighting soldiers minutes before she'd met me. I told her about Eddie and everybody, about fighting Smiley Joe, about leaving Tara and Kloe in the woods – although, as usual, I left out the familial and temporal complications. And then, for a change, we chatted about some normal things, like music and books. *Just like real life.*

We were just finishing when a phone rang. The tone sounded like something from the 1980s. 'That's the spy phone,' Lauren smiled. She hurried to the other room, and after a few seconds of muffled mumbling she returned, offering the phone to me. 'Nailah,' she said. 'She has your cousin for you.'

My heart leapt, and I took the phone. 'Eddie?'

'Stanly! Jesus. You're all right.'

'I'm fine. Are you?'

'We're all fine. Shouldn't talk for long, Skank and Freeman say these lines are secure but it's not worth taking any chances. We'll use the web thing in future, save these for emergencies.'

'The web thing?'

'Some deep web messaging system or other,' said Eddie. 'Or dark web. Dodgy web? I haven't got a clue, to be honest, but Nailah and Skank are all over it. We need to meet, anyway.'

'Yes. Tonight?'

'Probably too hot at the moment,' said Eddie. 'What with you fighting soldiers and everything.'

'Sorry,' I said. 'I was trying to be sneaky. I just . . . I wanted to find you guys.'

'I know, it's fine. Nailah's pretty certain that they don't know where you two are. So it's best if you sit tight for now and I'll try and get to you tomorrow. Just wanted to hear your voice.'

'It's good to hear yours.'

'Don't think that you're not still in trouble, though.'

'Seems like we're *all* in trouble.'

'Yeah, fair enough. How are Kloe and Tara?'

'Fine. Safe.'

'Good. I'll be in contact tomorrow. Get some rest for now.'

'Will do. Take care. Say . . . hi to everyone? I guess? Is Daryl there?'

'No, he's with Freeman, Connor and Sharon.'

'They're not with you?'

'We decided it was best to split up. Wouldn't want us all to get caught at the same time. I'll explain everything tomorrow. Tell Lauren to keep an eye on the web thing.'

'OK. Bye.'

'Bye.' Click. Lauren had left the room to give me some privacy, which I appreciated. She came back in wearing a half-decent 'I didn't hear anything, honest' smile and I handed the phone over. At least one of the weights in my stomach had lifted. 'They're fine,' I said. 'They're all fine.'

'That's good.'

'Eddie's going to try and arrange a meeting tomorrow,' I said. 'He said to keep an eye on the web thing? Sounds like he knows as much about it as you do.'

'Pretty professional group of covert rebels, eh?' Lauren smiled darkly.

'Yeah,' I said. 'Until then . . . guess I've just got to sit tight.' *This is awkward.*

'You're welcome to stay here,' said Lauren, and to her credit she made it sound as though it were completely fine, and not an obligation.

'Thanks.'

'Cup of tea?'

'Please.'

We took our tea through to the living room, which was small, friendly and full of books. There was also a shiny upright piano against one wall, its ivories so polished that I almost didn't want to touch them in case I dirtied them. There's something about a piano, though, like they're inviting you to have a play. I'd dabbled a bit, years ago. Mum had known a woman – she must have been in her nineties – who had given me some lessons, but I'd never had much aptitude. The guitar was the only instrument I'd ever been remotely good at, and I wasn't exactly good at that, certainly not by any Earth definition of the word 'good'.

'Pretty gorgeous, isn't she?' said Lauren.

'Yeah.'

'Do you play?' I shook my head and Lauren sat on the red stool and laid her long fingers on the keys. She said nothing, just started to play. I didn't recognise the piece; I could just about work out that it was classical. She was an expert, her fingers flying up and down the keys almost casually, as though she wasn't even thinking. My old teacher had played like that, even though her hands were bent and crinkled with arthritis. Hannah, Eddie's on-off girlfriend, was also a great pianist, but her style was completely different – funky, heavy, in charge, like she was showing the instrument exactly how it was done. Lauren seemed to duet with the instrument, like they were partners.

*I like both styles.*

As the music flowed from the piano I felt myself begin to

think about everything that was going on, all the feelings and craziness rising, but at that precise moment it was too much, and the music was too lovely, so I just stood and closed my eyes and shut everything else out, listening to Lauren build the piece up and up and up, adding more and more layers, until it was like a tornado of clear, melancholy notes. After a while I opened my eyes and looked at her as she played, *really* looked at her. I could practically *feel* painful memories pouring out of her, flying on the mournful wings of the piece she was playing. There was something unfathomably beautiful about it, beautiful in the way that pain can be sometimes, and I almost felt as though I should look away, like I was intruding, but no, she was sharing this with me. Or at least, it was there, and if I didn't want any part of it I could just ignore it. So I just sat down and listened, and wondered what could have happened to her. I wanted to clap when she'd finished, but it didn't quite feel appropriate, so I just said 'Wow' and she immediately looked embarrassed. *Probably not a good idea to clap, then.* I hurried to pave over it. 'Thanks, by the way. For fixing my hand.'

'Not a problem.'

'Do you have actual medical training? I figured that might help, if you did.'

'Not really,' she said. 'Basic first aid, and a bit of reading around the subject. Mostly it's in the mind. That's the bit I'm best at, power-wise. Manipulating and fixing. Not so great when it comes to fighting. Hardly any practise, for one thing.'

'You handled yourself OK earlier.'

'Thanks, I suppose. I'd prefer to avoid it, if at all possible.'

'I should give that a go,' I said, and I did kind of mean it, although I couldn't pretend that part of me didn't get a cheap thrill out of it.

*Let's try and make that not be a problem, yeah?*

Much later I lay on a blow-up mattress in Lauren's tiny spare room, comfortable in a mass of blankets but unable to sleep, everything rushing around and around, trapped in revolving doors, never reconciling, no solutions. So many questions. They bubbled and seethed and spat inside my brain, driving me nuts, scaring sleep away like rabid guard dogs. I lay on my right side, my left side, my back, my front, curled into a ball, stretched out, under the covers, on top of the covers, swapping pillows, unable to switch anything off, and even when I did manage to stop my brain from bellowing questions, I was left with Tara and Kloe's faces, and despite myself, despite knowing that I'd had to do it, I hated myself for leaving them alone.

*But I told me to.*

The last thought I had before my consciousness unravelled into sleep was that if there was any way to change the future and avoid what was going to happen so that Kloe and Tara and I could have something approaching a normal life together, I was going to do it. I didn't care what it took, if I had to burn all the power out of me, level a city, tear down the sky, I'd do it. For them.

I was standing on the burning deck, and that immediately made me laugh. I knew I was in a dream and I was glad, because it meant that I'd fallen asleep and could simply follow whatever whacked-out script my brain was improvising, the lunatic logic of limbo. The ship was a galleon, an old pirate vessel with creaking wood and whispering sails, and many fires and many spiders running from side to side as if trying to put out the fire, although they had no water. 'But we're surrounded by water,' I opined. 'For God's sake. We're in the ocean. Water, water, everywhere. Why can't we put it out?'

'Because,' replied Mr Freeman, who was trying and failing to put out one of the sails with water from a bucket that was more hole than bucket, 'fire does what it wants.'

'You're dressed like Jack Sparrow,' I pointed out. 'You look ridiculous.'

'Well, why not?' he responded, swinging his Johnny Depp hair and straightening his hat. 'It's all about fancy dress these days.'

'I don't wear a costume,' I countered.

'Maybe you should,' he rejoindered. 'Maybe lycra would suit you.'

'Wouldn't mind a cape,' I mused. I would mind a cape.

Now Tara came in, riding on Daryl's back. She was giggling, and he was energetic and puppy-like, dancing in and out of the flames. 'It's all about how you think,' pontificated a voice. It was my dad, calling down from the crow's nest. I didn't look up. I really couldn't be bothered to talk to him.

'Get lost, Dad, will you?' I riposted.

'You shouldn't talk to your father like that,' admonished Lauren, who was sitting cross-legged in mid-air cleaning her nails, nodding her head to some inaudible song.

'This is getting me nowhere,' I announced. 'I'm going overboard.'

Freeman doffed his hat and started passing round a tray of rum. 'Drink up, me hearties, yoho!' he intoned.

'Whatever,' I retorted, and dived off the ship. The water was vast, black glass, and as soon as I was in it I wished I was somewhere else. I could see shapes moving hundreds of feet below, an entire world of unnatural things with legs and eyes and tentacles where they shouldn't be, writhing in a melting pot, ready to be freed, all of them howling and roaring, desperate. I tried to turn my head away but the water was too thick, thick with memory and forlorn questions that had lost their answers, and when I finally managed to hit the surface I was standing in an empty, echoing tube station, and something was coming, I could hear it. I could *feel* it, coming down through the tunnel, still invisible at this point, and I knew it was about to scream and I couldn't listen, no, no, no. I turned around and Tara was standing there in her red pyjamas, smiling. 'It's not me you should be worrying about,' she said. 'Actually.'

And the monster roared, and I had to close my eyes and fall to the ground, because if I couldn't see it, it couldn't see me . . .

*We can, though . . .*

# Chapter Fifteen

I JERKED ABRUPTLY awake at eight. I felt profoundly unrested but couldn't get back to sleep, so I sat at the window for a while watching the blur of cold grey city lurking in the misty morning. You know when you hear about a band or person for the first time, say, or maybe you hear a word you've never heard before and then suddenly you start seeing that band or person everywhere, or hearing that word? I felt as though now that Lauren had said it, I could sense something too. Like . . . undercurrents. Layers of physical unease, unseen but definitely present, *prevalent*, pushing. Dark shapes beneath the surface. I wondered if it was because Lauren had told me about it, or if my heightened senses would have picked up on it eventually anyway. Maybe it was something to do with the shimmer, although I doubted it. I didn't feel invincible today. Quite weak, in fact. Perhaps the effects had worn off. Or perhaps I was just tired.

*Tiredness is physical. Shouldn't make a difference.*

I wish I knew how it all fitted together. What the power *was*. I knew that that whole idea of *ooh, you only use ten per cent of your brain, what if you could unlock the other ninety per cent* was bollocks, but it *had* to be my brain. Working on a higher level. That was what did it.

Why were our powers different, then? Why were Eddie and Connor super-tough, physically, and I was still a weakling? Why could Connor walk up walls and on ceilings when Eddie couldn't? How come Sharon could practically read minds and I couldn't? How come I was able to fly the way I did, but nobody else was? Connor's ability was the closest thing to flight I'd seen in anyone else, but . . .

*Maybe Sharon's right . . .*

*It's all the same thing . . .*

*Manifesting differently . . .*

A knock at the door jolted me out of this aggressive spin cycle of questions. 'Come in,' I said.

Lauren poked her head round the door. 'Morning,' she said. 'I wasn't sure how late you wanted to sleep.'

'Been up for a while,' I said. 'Just . . . thinking.'

'Coffee?'

'God yes.'

We had coffee and some toast, then I borrowed Lauren's phone to ring Kloe. She said that she and Tara were both fine, but her tone was more than a little cold. I could feel anger down the phone, and I said I was a million miles beyond sorry that they had to sit and stew on their own. I trotted out the same old lines about it being necessary and she said she knew. 'I do realise that,' she said. 'I do. Really. And I appreciate you protecting me. Us. But I still don't have to like being here. Neither of us do.'

'I know.'

'When can we go home?'

'Soon,' I said, feeling like the worst person ever. 'I love you.'

She paused before she said 'I love you too', and that preyed on my mind a lot more than it should have.

Lauren popped out to get me some spare clothes because I didn't really fancy going full method with my stinking-home-less-guy act, and had neglected to bring anything else along apart from my black coat. She came back with some T-shirts, a hoody, a pair of jeans and some underwear, which wasn't *that* awkward, just incredibly. Luckily, she then suggested that we try some power stuff while we waited for Eddie to get in contact.

*Best distraction ever.*

I'd done this a lot before but it was very different with Lauren, partly because I was already finding it much easier to do things, although we did go straight to very complex exercises. Odd ones, too. One of the first involved Lauren showing me how to play a simple tune on the piano, and when she was satisfied that I had a handle on the notes she got me to stand and play with my brain. It took a while. You'd think that not having the problem of clumsy fingers falling over each other would be a bonus, but I still kept on playing five keys when I only wanted three, or getting the chords and the melody backwards. 'Remember,' she said, 'it's nothing to do with being musical. It's precision. That's the word I always keep in my head. You're not learning to play the piano with your mind – although I think that's a pretty good party trick – you're learning to focus more directly on things. What you said yesterday got me thinking: throwing cars around really is mental strength over agility. Taking the car apart and juggling all its individual components, that's different.'

Once I'd picked it up, I started improvising. I was glad we were doing this because it meant I could keep my worries buried a little, for now. Every time Tara's face came back, or Kloe's, or the dark twisting dreamscape of monsters, or the weirdness bubbling beneath the air in London, I just concentrated harder on what I was doing. I played the tune while balancing books, pouring drinks, folding and unfolding clothes, lighting and snuffing out candles. The candles were where things really started to get interesting. I had about ten books hovering at different levels around me and was keeping them afloat and perfectly still while pouring water from a jug into a glass, and as I was moving the lighter towards the candle I was thinking *light*. A full two seconds before the lighter had even reached the candle, the wick caught fire. Just like that. Only for a second, but it definitely caught fire. Lauren let out a shocked noise and I very nearly dropped everything. *Calm.* I let everything down gently, my eyes flickering from the candle to Lauren and back again. 'Do it again,' she said. I noticed that she'd stopped saying 'try again'. I stared at the candle, my face scrunched in concentration, one fist clenched. 'Don't strain like that,' said Lauren. 'It needs to flow. Think of water.'

'I'm trying to think of burning.'

'Think of both. You've shown you can multi-task.'

'I've always been able to do that,' I said, keeping my gaze fixed on the candle. 'I used to eat, read, watch TV and chat to my dog at the same time.'

'How well did you do any of those things, though?'

'Well,' I said, staying focused, 'a lot of the food missed my mouth, I read whole chapters without taking in anything that happened, and my dog kept saying I was repeating lines of dialogue from the TV rather than carrying on our conversation.'

'Points for effort.'

'Cheers.'

Suddenly the candle lit. Making sure not to let the triumphant feeling distract me, I focused on the flame, breathing into it, in and out, as though it were coming from my lungs, from my body, my blood. It grew bigger, and then I relaxed and it stayed burning. Lauren whistled. 'That's pretty impressive. I can't do that.'

'You did toast,' I said. 'Points for toast.'

'Good idea,' said Lauren.

Within five minutes I had three pieces of hot buttered toast on a plate, never having gone near the toaster. 'That's a bit scary,' said Lauren. 'I think I might have been getting ahead of myself, there's not much I can teach you. You know it all already.'

'I just don't *know* I know it, right?'

She laughed. 'I was going to leave that bit unsaid.'

'That was probably a good shout. And anyway, I don't know if I could do what you do. The healing.'

'Practise. Different discipline.'

I nodded. Then I shook my head. 'But . . . maybe not? Maybe it's *not* different disciplines. Maybe that's the point. It's all the same power. So maybe we *can* do anything?' The enormity of that last sentence made me stop, and we stared at one another. I could tell she was feeling the tingle of fear and excitement that was rippling up and down my back, and we both giggled. Then she suggested a tea break. I was already starting to like her a lot, particularly her tea fixation.

As we sat enjoying our drinks, I tentatively asked Lauren about when she first got her powers. 'You said you were eleven?'

That expression was back. The one she always got when issues of her past came up. I knew I had no right to pry, we barely knew each other, but if you were going to tell anyone this sort of stuff . . . plus I'd told her my whole story, so it was only fair. 'Yes,' she said. 'Eleven.' She looked down at the floor, and I waited. 'My . . . my parents fought a lot,' she said, tentatively. 'All the time. Me and my brother were always hearing them shouting from upstairs. We'd hide and play. One day my brother was out and I came in from school, and my parents were screaming at each other in the kitchen, really screaming. Didn't even notice I'd come back. I ran upstairs into my room and . . . I screamed, to drown them out. And my bookshelf fell down. All the books, all over the floor.'

It was eerie how closely that echoed something I'd experienced at my house after hearing my own parents arguing. I prompted her with a sympathetic smile.

'I worked out how to do rudimentary things pretty quickly,' said Lauren. 'But it was years before I did anything as big as the bookshelf again. I didn't tell anyone, not my brother, not my friends. Definitely not my parents. For four years I kept it to myself, painstakingly practising. It was quick for a while, but then horribly slow. Agonising. I was fifteen when I finally managed to do something big, and that was after a breakup. I threw my boyfriend.'

I imagined myself hurling Ben King across the drama hall at school.

'I went to his house to talk,' she said, 'and he answered the door and we ended up fighting. One of the worst fights I've had with anyone, ever. I remember crying and thinking how much I wanted to hurt him, and then he just flew up and hit the ceiling.' She stopped to breathe. 'I didn't stay around for a second. I ran home and told my parents, straight out. I was in such a state, absolutely hysterical. I threw plates with my mind, turned over the table. I remember screaming at them and I thought my dad was about to hit me and I . . .' She stopped and I could see the glint of tears.

'Hey,' I said, 'you don't have to if you don't . . .'

'It's fine,' she said, keeping her voice under control. 'I'm fine. I . . . I held a knife to his throat. Picked it up, brought it across the kitchen, put it against his neck, all without moving a muscle. I remember it so well, there was just . . . absolute silence. The most complete, total silence I've ever heard. Or . . . not heard.' She managed a grim laugh. 'And then I dropped the knife and ran out. And I never went back.' I reached out and took her hand, wondering if that was an OK thing to do, but she didn't recoil. She actually smiled. 'Thanks.' She drew her other hand roughly over her eyes, brushing the dew drops away, and continued. 'Then I came here.' She frowned, then laughed. 'What am I talking about . . . I didn't come straight here. It just sometimes feels like I did. If that makes sense. Amazing how this city swallows up lost souls.'

'It is. Where did you go first? If you don't mind me asking . . .'

'It's fine,' said Lauren. 'I actually went to Torquay. Played the piano and waitressed at this little place called the Chinese Singing Teacher.'

'That's the actual name of an actual place?'

She smiled. 'Yes.'

'That's the best thing I've ever heard.'

'It was great. For a while. But . . . I don't know. I think I needed to not be known, if that makes sense. And everyone knew everyone there. So I decided to head to London. It was hard setting up, but eventually I earned enough doing appalling jobs to live on my own. Looks like I'll be burning through most of my remaining holiday allowance now . . . anyway. So yes, that's how I ended up here.'

'How old are you?' *Is that a rude question?*

'Twenty-six.' She suddenly looked angry. 'Fifteen years. That's how long I've had these powers. I should be . . . I should be able to . . . I . . . I don't know what the problem is.'

I didn't know what to say. I was grateful when she spoke again. 'You know, thinking about what you said . . . I think you're right. And I don't think your flying is specifically the power of flight. I think it all comes back to the mind, all of it. You think you can fly, so you do. You *think* yourself up. That's how it all works. Being able to feel people's thoughts, move things, start fires, throw . . .' She laughed. 'Throw cars around. It's all your brain.'

'So my cousin,' I said, 'his super-strength, super-toughness. He *thinks* himself tough.'

'Makes sense to me,' said Lauren. 'As far as any of this stuff makes sense. And if it's true . . . then that means it *is* limitless.'

*So I could make myself as strong as Eddie and Connor. And they could fly. And so on . . .* 'Well,' Lauren added, with a note of bitterness. 'Some of us could.'

'*You* can,' I said. 'You can. I know you can. Everyone has the same potential.'

She looked into my eyes then, and there was pain there, bright and sharp. I knew it wasn't just to do with what were talking about. 'Then I should be able to fly,' she said.

'You can,' I said, feeling a little uncomfortable because she seemed genuinely sad that she couldn't do it. 'Surely. If the theory is right.'

'Maybe,' said Lauren. 'Sorry. I'm not trying to make you feel guilty. It's amazing that you can do it. But when I first had my powers, when I was growing up in that . . . that house, I would have given anything to just fly away. Disappear into the sky.' She smiled. 'You're special, I think. You're more than all of us. And not just the flying, the way you picked things up today. It comes completely naturally to you.'

'Then why haven't the Angel Group got me already?' I'd been going over and over this in my head and it was driving me mad. 'After the whole thing at the Kulich, Pandora knew about me, and it can't have been difficult to find out where I was living. Why didn't they just come in and take me? And why send an assassin after me?'

'An assassin? That's pretty harsh.'

'Could have been worse. At least I didn't die that time.'

'Yes . . .' Lauren didn't seem to know where to look, which was understandable. I doubted she'd met many people who had died. 'Shall we carry on?' she said.

We spent another couple of hours practising and playing games, manipulating all the objects in the house, and at my request Lauren played some more on the piano. She didn't just know classical stuff, she could play the Beatles, old show tunes, the lot. She was just picking out 'Macarthur Park' when two harsh knocks sounded at the front door, making us both jump. I got up, ready to fight, but Lauren held up her hand. 'Stay here.

I'll go.' She went to the front door and returned a second later. 'Young guy,' she said. 'Blonde hair. Looks strong.'

'That's Eddie,' I said, my stomach lurching with relief. 'Definitely.'

Lauren nodded. 'OK . . . well. I'll go and let him in, I suppose.' She didn't seem happy that Eddie had arrived unannounced. *Not surprising.* I poked my head around and watched her open the door. Eddie smiled awkwardly against the darkening grey of the afternoon. 'Hi,' he said. 'Lauren, isn't it? I'm Eddie.'

'Hi.' They shook hands and Lauren ushered him in. 'Thanks,' said Eddie. 'Sorry I didn't call . . . we don't want to use the phones if we can help it. I did send a message with the web thing.'

'Oh,' said Lauren, 'sorry. I completely forgot to check that. Having trouble getting used to it.'

Eddie smiled. 'I sympathise. Anyway, I thought you guys would probably be in.'

'It's all right,' said Lauren. 'How are you?'

'I've had better weeks.' Eddie looked past her and I stepped out into the hall. It felt like we should run at each other, share a massive brotherly hug or something, but somehow I felt like I'd let him down by running away, leaving them to fight and hide. It was important, though, and I knew he'd understand. I hoped he would, at least. I grinned and offered a pretty ineffectual 'Yo.'

'Stanly,' said Eddie. He walked towards me and we did hug, tightly. When we separated I knew that he was too glad to see me to be angry. *For now.*

'All right?' I said.

'Yeah,' said Eddie. 'Safe. At the moment. You?'

'Also safe.'

'Tara?'

'Fine, and Kloe. You understand don't you? I had to get them to safety. I *had* to.'

'I understand,' said Eddie. 'It's good that you did, I think. Everything's gone ever so slightly bat's-arse, and from what Freeman's been saying it sounds like it was inevitable. A "when not if" kinda thing. So.'

I nodded. 'Did you get Hannah out of town?'

'Tried, but she wasn't having any of it,' said Eddie. 'Said the most she would do is close up for a few days and get stuck in to some reading at home.' He smiled. 'What are you gonna do? I couldn't exactly make her.'

*Hmm.* 'Cool. How are Connor and Sharon?'

'Fine.'

'Skank?'

'Yeah, he's fine.'

'And Daryl?'

'Everyone's fine, Stanly,' Eddie laughed. 'Don't worry. Daryl's with Freeman and Skank.'

'How've you found it? Talking to Freeman.'

'If I said it was really bizarre and off-putting, would that sound plausible?'

I laughed. 'Totally. He's in the same situation as us, though.'

'Yeah. And he's proving to be pretty useful. He knows a lot.'

'Good,' I said. 'How many fighters have we got all together?'

Eddie shook his head. 'Not enough. But it's better than it would have been if it was just us, I suppose.'

Lauren made some more tea and Eddie filled me in on what had happened since I'd left. Apparently Freeman had contacted him immediately after I had, and Eddie had got out of his flat minutes before the Angel Group's soldiers had arrived. He'd met up with Freeman and Daryl and later Connor and Sharon, who'd had to fight their way out of their house. Connor had got hurt pretty badly, which stabbed me with guilt, although at least he was healing fast. They'd then contacted Skank, who had immediately started mobilising 'the troops', as Eddie called them, and basically taken charge, organising safe locations for everyone to go to. 'Daryl's been calling us La Resistance,' smiled Eddie. 'It's all a bit *'Allo 'Allo*.'

The upshot was that we had a small group of people with a huge enemy to fight and not much of an idea of how to go about it. I took all this in, asked a few questions, then began my own story, about the fight with the monster dog and the battle with the Angel Group's soldiers, about going and getting Tara and taking her back to Tref-y-Celwyn, fudging and smudging the details of my future self's involvement, which was a whole different can of worms being poured into a heinously complicated kettle of fish. Then I wound my way back to London, to the kid with the green coat – 'No idea who that is, I'm afraid,' said Eddie – and then to meeting Lauren.

'And now you know as much as I do,' I said.

Eddie nodded. 'Yeah. That's . . . Christ, Stanly. I never gave you anywhere near enough credit for what you can do.'

'Doesn't matter,' I said. 'I'm here now, I'm safe, you're all safe, Tara and Kloe are safe.'

'Yeah,' said Eddie. He turned to Lauren. 'Nailah tells us you're empowered too?'

She nodded.

'Telekinesis?'

'I've never really called it that . . . but, yes, I suppose.'

'And you've been living in London for . . .'

'A long time,' said Lauren. 'But I only just met Nailah. Been keeping my head down.'

'So,' I cut in, seeing how visibly uncomfortable Lauren was talking about herself, 'anything resembling a plan?'

'It's still in the formative stages,' said Eddie. 'In fact, the stage *before* the formative stages. Possibly the stage before that, even. Freeman's brought a lot of stuff to the table.'

'Like what?'

'The Angel Group are using empowered for some grand scheme. Something that's having an adverse effect on the city.'

'The monsters.'

'Among other things.'

'Does Freeman have any idea what they're doing? Specifically?'

'Not exactly,' said Eddie. 'He says it was nothing to do with him. Not his department.'

'Morter Smith's department?'

'Yeah.' Eddie's brow creased. 'That's another thing. Whatever Smith's doing presumably requires empowered. But he took out a hit on you, rather than trying to capture you. Seem strange?'

'Does.'

'They obviously see you as a threat,' said Lauren. 'All of you. You said whatever they're doing has something to do with monsters? Like Smiley Joe and that blue dog? And it seems that it's all coming to a head now. They must be scared that you'll blow a hole in it and would rather kill you than waste time trying to capture you.'

'Makes sense,' I said. 'I just wish I knew what they were doing.'

'Nailah's working on that,' said Eddie, 'but her contact . . . who she's *very* cagey about, by the way . . . doesn't have access to everything. There are levels and levels, layers and layers within the Angel Group, according to her. Public-facing stuff, secret stuff, top secret stuff, *super* secret stuff, pain-of-death-stuff, and beyond.' He sighed. 'Hopefully we'll know more by our next meeting. Freeman's been making enquiries, so have Skank's new mates.'

'That's good,' I said. 'Eddie . . . do you trust Freeman?'

'More than I did before.'

We sat in Lauren's living room and drank more tea, discussing possibilities for plans and what the Angel Group's secret scheme might be, and Skank's new non-empowered allies, who sounded like a motley crew. Eddie stayed for dinner and eventually headed off. 'See you soon,' he said. 'Take care.'

'Always do, except when I don't. You too.'

'I'll be in touch.' He shook hands with Lauren again. 'Thanks for looking after him.'

'It's fine,' said Lauren. 'He's a good house guest.'

Eddie left and I went to the kitchen to get another drink. Lauren followed and watched me pour juice into a tall glass with my mind, concentrating on swirling the liquid around itself in a double helix. It was surprisingly easy, considering how unsettled my head was. 'Nice,' she said.

'Thanks.'

'I'm tired,' she said. 'Going to head to bed.'

'I probably will too, soon.'

'OK, well help yourself to whatever. Goodnight.'

''Night. And thanks.'

'You're welcome.'

# Chapter Sixteen

WE DIDN'T HEAR anything until the following afternoon, when Nailah sent out a message calling a meeting. Apparently there was new information. The meeting place, some random flat south of the river, was pretty far away, which meant Lauren and I finding our way across London in the dark, avoiding the military and the police. 'Great,' I said. 'I do love suicide missions.'

'At least you always know the outcome,' said Lauren.

'S'pose.'

The night was raw, nakedly cold, frost sparkling on the roofs and windows of parked cars and at the edges of the kerbs. I pulled my coat around me, breathing out hot steam, beyond glad that I'd brought it with me. Warm *and* stealthy. 'So,' said Lauren. 'How far is this place again?'

'It's a good few miles. I can fly us, but . . .'

'Risky,' said Lauren. 'There'll be patrols everywhere, and they know you're in the city. They'll probably have extra drones in the sky.'

'What about underground?' I said. 'The Tubes?' The underground system had been shut down until further notice, but as far as obstacles went, a few locked gates and empty tunnels seemed laughable.

As expected, Lauren's nearest station was closed. More importantly, there was a black truck parked near the entrance, and two armed guards. 'Arse,' I muttered.

'We could find another station,' said Lauren.

'No,' I said. 'Don't want this to take any longer than it has to.' I had a quick look around. 'Tell you what, I'll cause a distraction down the road. Hopefully they'll all come after me and that'll give you time to run into the station. Gates'll be locked, can you sort them out?'

Lauren tapped her temple and nodded.

'Cool. I'll meet you on the westbound platform. If by any chance they *don't* all follow me, you might need to do a bit of fighting.'

'I probably need the practice,' she said, sounding less than keen.

'OK,' I said, darting into the shadows. I moved past a long line of shops, feeling the suspicious eyes of window mannequins tracing my progress, and took a left past a hairdresser and a chemist. I flew low against the pavement, down the street, then circled around and peeked out from behind a large red brick building. The station was about fifty feet up the road. I looked across the street and focused on a lamppost. *Grip. Twist. Dislodge.* It took me about five seconds to uproot it, with an eye-spasming screech and a shower of sparks, and once it was fully free of the ground I swung it around and smashed two shop windows, scattering iridescent shards across the tarmac to mingle with the frost. Immediately two different alarms started to blare, piercing the eerie silence like the howls of electronic dogs, and I turned and headed back down the road, hearing the yell of soldiers and the roar of an engine behind me. I chanced a look and sure enough the truck was motoring in my direction. Both the soldiers had climbed aboard and were hanging off the foot plates at the side. *Yes.* I took a sharp right down another street, looped around several buildings and flew straight back to the station, alighting at the entrance, losing them with such ease that it was almost disappointing.

I met Lauren on the platform. She was removing two chocolate bars from the vending machine. 'Well done,' she said, handing me one.

'Cheers.' I pocketed it. 'Jump on.'

Wearing a slightly uncomfortable expression, Lauren climbed on my back. She held a torch in front of us, and I jumped into the tunnel and started to fly.

It took about half an hour to reach our intended station. Rather than face off with any guards there might have been, we broke out using a network of grimy service passages, snapping locks with our minds. We emerged on to the street and stood in the shadows for a moment, keeping out of sight in case of enemies, then continued to follow Nailah's directions. We passed a few nervous pedestrians who kept their eyes on the floor, and while there were still cars driving around, there were nowhere near as many as there should have been. *This is too strange.*

Presently we arrived at a looming, dead-faced block of flats. We'd been instructed not to ring the bell or do anything else that was likely to attract attention, so I sent Nailah the coded text we had agreed upon and Eddie emerged from the darkness a few moments later, smiling. 'Took your time.'

'Needed to tear up a lamppost and lose some soldiers,' I said. 'You know how it is.'

Eddie led us up many flights of stairs and along a corridor that smelled half of lavender and half of sweat, stopping outside a pale wooden door which he swiftly unlocked with a key that looked newer than everything in the building combined. The door gave way to a narrow hall with a banana-coloured carpet and walls covered in newspaper clippings, and Eddie took us through to a cramped living room. The place stank of cigarette smoke. *Lush.*

Connor, Sharon, Skank and Daryl were there, along with Nailah and a guy I didn't recognise. Before I could say anything,

Sharon jumped up from the lime green sofa and ran over to give me a hug. I was so pleased to see her that I didn't think about the fact that she might be cross, and it was one of the best hugs I'd ever had. When she drew back and I really looked at her there was nothing in her eyes that indicated anger or disappointment and I was so glad that it almost hurt. 'You're OK?' I said.

'Fine. You?'

'Yeah,' I said. 'Fine. Um . . . sorry.'

'Never mind,' she said. Connor stood up now, his face bruised and cut, and I held out my hand slightly gingerly.

'Hey,' I said. 'Man . . . nasty bruises.'

'You should see the other guys,' said Connor. He shook my hand and laughed quietly. Anyone who wasn't aware of what had been happening between us might not have realised anything was amiss, but I could see it in his eyes. I resolved to get him on his own at some point and try to sort things out. Skank, who was sitting next to him, nodded.

'Stanly,' he said. I might have just come in for work.

'Skank.'

Daryl came over to me and I patted him on the head. 'You all right, chief?'

'Safe and sound,' I said.

'Good. Now please don't patronise me again.'

'*Patronise?*'

'Don't say that again, either.'

I looked over at the other two. Nailah waved slightly awkwardly and I offered a sheepish smile in return. The guy I didn't recognise was wiry and bald and wore black and blue denim, and although I felt instantly suspicious, I smiled and held out my hand anyway. 'Stanly.'

'Maguire,' he said, in a gravelly Scottish accent. It was painfully obvious that our feelings were mutual.

'Nice to meet you.'

Now an adjoining door opened and Mr Freeman emerged from the kitchen with a tray bearing a large blue tea pot, a jug of milk, several mismatched cups and a tub of sugar. I blinked at this bizarre apparition, and he smiled thinly and nodded at me. 'Stanly. Glad to see you're in one piece.'

'Yeah,' I said. 'And you.' *I guess.*

'Are Tara and Kloe all right?'

*Don't mention them again, please.* 'Yeah.'

Lauren, who had been standing behind me radiating nervousness, stepped hesitantly forwards and there was another round of slightly strained introductions. We sat down, and tea was poured. 'So,' I said, breezily. 'What's the crack?'

Skank looked expectantly at Maguire, who stood up. 'Right,' he said. 'Let's cut to the meat and bone, shall we? The Angel Group. Worldwide organisation, funded up the arse and out the other end. More influence, power and technology than any other group or government. We found out recently that they've got a whole crowd of your lot under their control. Your lot being powered-up sorts.'

*Yeah, got that.*

'Now,' said Maguire. 'You've met monsters, haven't you?'

'A few,' I said.

'Freakish beasts from "somewhere else",' he continued. 'Some unspecified other place. That was all we knew for a long time. But recently, through Freeman here, we've discovered that the Angel Group is using teams of empowered, as well as the most advanced technology they can get their hands on – and that's some shiny, spanking, highly illegal kit – to break through to that other place so they can harness the power that's there. Raw energy, more potent than anything ever created on Earth. A valuable resource, to say the least.'

'And we don't know where that is?' I said. 'This other place?'

'Not even the Angel Group do,' said Mr Freeman. 'While plenty of creatures have found their way through to this side, return trips have been unsuccessful.'

'So they've been letting the monsters in?' said Lauren. 'On purpose?'

'More as a side effect,' said Maguire. 'Of their experiments, the majority of which seem to be based in London. That's why so much bizarre crap goes down in this city. The stray monsters, Smiley Joe, those living pictures you lot told us about. All products of the Angel Group trying to bust a crack in reality and suck out the juice. We've been building up intelligence on where these experiments happen. Defences, personnel, everything. And the plan is to take them out.'

'Woah,' said Eddie, 'hold on. Look, we've been discussing courses of action, survival tactics and whatnot up and down and in and out, and getting nowhere. There's ten of us here. Twelve counting your other mates . . .'

'Who are where, by the way?' I said.

'Out and about,' said Maguire. 'We decided it wasn't necessary for them to be here.'

'Oh "we" did, did we? That's reassuring.'

'If all you're going to do is flap your wee mouth . . .' growled Maguire.

'My wee mouth flaps,' I said. 'Deal with it. Look, I'm not just being confrontational for the sake of it. This is all good stuff. But put yourself in my shoes, Maguire – I don't know you from Adam.' I looked at Skank. 'Where did you find him?'

Maguire looked about ready to bust some heads, but Skank raised a hand. 'It's a fair question, Maguire,' he said, mildly. 'I'd expect you to sympathise, as someone who doesn't like surprises or strangers. Or people, generally. Stanly, you can trust Maguire. I do. I've known him for a while now.'

'How?'

'One of the guys who couldn't make it, Fitz, is an old friend,' said Skank. 'From the experimental performance poetry scene in the early Nineties.'

I blinked. 'Of course he is.'

'I caught up with him again recently via Oracle. He'd been dark for nearly a decade. I found out that he had immersed himself fully in this dodgy business. Met Maguire and Box, the other absent partner, through him.'

'Box,' I said.

'Box.'

'Right,' I said. 'So . . . may I ask why you didn't tell us about them before?'

'Because we asked Skank not to,' said Maguire.

'Why?'

'One of the first things we found out,' said Maguire, 'is that the Angel Group have spent years gathering their crew of empowered. Apparently some volunteer, although I have my doubts about how much they know before they sign up. Most don't, though, the Group gets them however they can. Blackmail, coercion, extortion, torture. As soon as Skank told us that he knew not just one empowered but four, we decided that the less you knew about us the better. That way if any of you were taken, you couldn't tell the Angel Group anything about us. And that meant we could carry on gathering information and planning.'

I nodded. It did make sense. 'Fair enough. Mercenary, but fair enough.'

'We're not *mercenaries*,' said Maguire. I wondered if he'd deliberately misunderstood me.

'No,' said Eddie, 'and to return to my original point, neither are we. Yeah, we've got some special abilities, you lot have got some heavy artillery, but that's still just a handful, a *thimble* full against the police, the army, and whatever else the Angel Group decides to chuck at us. We're not exactly the A-Team.'

'We're not exactly the B-Team,' said Nailah. 'I've already told you, I'm happy to help, but I'm not putting on any armour or firing any guns.'

'And no-one's expecting you to,' said Maguire, with an exasperated roll of his eyes. 'For Christ's sake, obviously we don't just run in with our arses hanging out. Freeman, Skank and I have a plan in the works. We won't just go stumbling in throwing cars about and hoping we get somewhere.'

'What's that supposed to mean?' I said.

'You know what it means,' said Maguire. 'I've heard your story, Mr Chosen One. Yeah, you're crammed full of that power, yeah I respect that, but your chosen strategy of running around blindly until you happen to trip over whatever you're looking for doesn't seem to have done you many favours, has it?'

'Maguire,' began Eddie, warningly.

'No,' I said. 'He's right. It hasn't done me a great deal of good. In fact it's got me nearly blown up, and then nearly shot to death, and a few other things. But I'm presuming you're going to want to utilise my power for this little crusade. And so far, you've shown me diddly fuck-all that makes me want to raise one psychic finger on your behalf. So how about keeping your comments to yourself and getting on with it.'

Maguire went red. 'You want to watch your mouth.'

'Don't think I do,' I said.

'Sorry if this is a stupid question,' said Connor, 'but did anybody, at any point, consider *not* going full vigilante and maybe taking all this information to the authorities?'

'The authorities who are definitely in the pocket of the bad guys?' said Maguire. 'No, actually, that's not an option we'd considered, 'cos I didn't really fancy having all my research shredded and then getting flushed away to some black site for the rest of my natural life.'

Connor's eye actually twitched at that. 'Now you listen to me, mate—'

'I'd rather not, to be honest—'

'Everybody be quiet,' said Sharon. She didn't say it loudly, but her voice burned with authority and presence, and it had the desired effect. Maguire shut up. I shut up. Everyone looked at Sharon, who didn't even need to stand. 'Look,' she said. 'It's all stress all the time at the moment. We don't all know each other. We don't all trust each other. But I'm having trouble seeing how getting in one another's faces and mouthing off is helping anything. Maybe it's just a testosterone issue, in which case keep it in your trousers please, boys. Eddie's right, there aren't many of us. And personally, I was banking on not doing any more fighting for at least . . . hmm . . . my whole life.' I had to look away at that. Part of me still felt like it was my fault that she and Connor and Eddie had been dragged into this, and I knew Connor thought it too. 'But,' Sharon continued, 'this is what's happening. Something bigger than us. Something bad. And unfortunately, we're the ones with the information *and* the power. So we'll get it done. And we need to work together, which means getting along, which means that if anyone has any issues or little sarky comments, keep them to yourselves, like Stanly says. That does include you too, though, Stanly. OK?'

There was a general chorus of shame-faced nodding, even from the people who hadn't been arguing. Sharon nodded. 'OK. Now. Where are we in terms of the plan?'

'It's in the early stages,' said Freeman. *Reassuring.* 'I'm still waiting for some crucial information.'

'Where from?' I said.

'I have sources.' *Again, reassuring.*

'And so do I,' said Nailah. Everyone's gazes were suddenly fixed on her and she quickly shared, in the briefest possible terms, a few details about her mysterious contact, which basically left us none the wiser. She said she'd try and get as much as she could out of them, but that she couldn't promise anything.

'The most important thing to remember,' said Freeman, 'is that we must not underestimate the Angel Group. The power, influence and resources that they have built up . . . it has taken many decades. And they are nothing if not ruthless.'

'Seems simple enough to me,' said Nailah. 'Strike at the heart, and—'

'It's *not* simple,' said Freeman, acidly. 'There is no "heart". The Angel Group is not a single entity weaving a single evil plot on a global scale. If you had any idea about how companies work, or how governments work, or how *conspiracies* work, you'd see how facile that idea is. The Angel Group is the corporate front. It occupies key positions in global finance and trade, funnelling eye-popping sums of money – entirely legally and legitimately – into any of a thousand sub-sections, sub-divisions and departments. Those who work in the shiny public-facing buildings investing and trading do not know where even one per cent of the money ends up. How stupid do you think they are? Money is secured. What other departments do with it is up to them. The right hand does not hold regular conflabs with the left. In fact, the right hand is more than likely not even aware of the left's existence.'

'What's your point, Freeman?' said Maguire. 'As fascinating as the ins and outs of the Angel Group's finances are . . .'

'My *point*,' said Freeman, 'is that while our main focus must be on the Group's most secretive, experimental department . . . unofficially referred to as Unique Initiatives, by the way, if you're interested . . . the company will not magically collapse overnight as soon as we foil this particular scheme. There's Department 9 for example, another secretive wing. Part defence contractor, part supernatural task force. You've seen the soldiers in the flash black ensembles? Those nifty drones buzzing around in the sky?'

'I have,' I said.

'Department 9,' said Freeman. 'A private army, to all intents and purposes, headed up by a team of elite advisors who in turn channel the wishes of the higher-ups. When major otherworldly events occur requiring official attention – like that blue dog, and the problem of *you*, Stanly – the UK government defers to Department 9.'

'OK,' I said. 'So, like Maguire said . . . what's your point? Or are you just trying to depress everybody to death?'

'I'm just making sure that we are all aware of the enormity of the task before us,' said Freeman. 'The Angel Group and its myriad subsidiaries are demonstrably *not* working to the benefit of mankind. I know I've not been the most trustworthy ally to you in the past, but if we are to have a chance of winning this fight, we need to be certain of two things. One, that we are united. And two, that we will go the distance.'

'Well, I for one feel very inspired,' said Maguire. 'So inspired that I might just head out to the balcony and hurl myself off it.'

'Join the queue,' I said.

That actually raised a grim smile. *Hey, maybe we'll be bestest buddies after all.* 'So,' said Maguire, 'if nobody has anything else to add, I suggest that we bugger off.'

'I would like to add one thing, actually,' said Nailah, 'which kind of follows on from what Freeman was saying. It doesn't seem realistic to try to bring the whole circus down just by fighting it with superpowers. So I'm aiming to collect as much data as possible, so that once we've accomplished our main objective we can dump it onto the internet for the world to see.'

'Yeah, sounds useful,' said Maguire, not bothering to hide the sneer in his voice.

'More useful than a bunch of wannabe Howling Commandos taking on the most powerful corporation in the world,' shot back Nailah. 'Why do you think I run the blogs? To give paranoid stoners something to whisper about? There's bad stuff happening, worse than anyone knows, and the first step towards changing that is persuading normal people to get off their asses and do something.'

'Admirable sentiments,' said Freeman. *Wow. He actually sounds sincere.*

At that point we decided that we would indeed bugger off, agreeing to stagger our exits so as not to attract attention. Sharon and Connor went first, Sharon asking me if I wanted to go back with them, but I elected to stay with Lauren. I wasn't even entirely sure why, but Sharon accepted with a smile, and Connor didn't seem bothered. I didn't try to talk about what was going on, just shook his hand. 'See you soon.'

'Hey,' said Daryl. 'You . . . could I maybe . . .'

'Yeah,' I said. 'Definitely. I mean, sorry, if you don't mind, Lauren? He's clean and well-behaved. Ish.'

'That's fine,' said Lauren. 'I was hoping to get to chat to Stanly's talking dog, actually. Wasn't quite sure what to make of it when he told me about you.'

'Been talking about me, have you?' said Daryl.

'Just saying that you're a bit fat,' I said. 'And rubbish.'

I wanted to fly back to Lauren's but it seemed like tempting fate, considering we'd managed to steer clear of trouble thusfar, so we took the tunnels again instead. When we got back to her house she excused herself and jumped in the shower, and I lingered over giving Kloe a call. She'd sounded so angry the last time. And it was dangerous . . .

I had to check they were okay, though.

'Hello? Stanly?'

'Hi, love. How . . . sorry. Pointless question alert. How's it going?'

She laughed a tired laugh. 'It's all right. Tara's in bed. We went for a little walk in the woods today. It's actually quite nice. Apart from the being trapped and scared aspect.'

We talked for as long as I felt was safe, which was definitely not as long as I would have liked. She didn't seem angry today, and I could tell that she was relieved to hear my voice, but there was a weariness in hers, and a sadness, and it stayed with me when we said goodbye, stopping me from doing anything. The meeting hadn't exactly filled me with confidence, and things were still a bit awkward between Daryl and me, and now I felt even less like catching up, let alone making up. Lauren made him up a nest in the corner of the living room – I *definitely* wasn't ready for him to be sleeping at my feet again – and eventually I made my excuses and went to bed, making sure they couldn't hear me crying.

# Chapter Seventeen

I KNEW SOMETHING was wrong as soon as I woke up. *Before* I woke up, in fact. There was a knowledge, lurking beneath the jumbled residue of stupid dreams and last night's tears, waiting for me as I forced my eyes open. The light bleeding through the window was dim and . . . *weird*, somehow . . . and I threw off the covers and scrambled across the bedroom, yanking back the curtains. 'Lauren,' I called. '*Lauren!* Daryl!'

Lauren came running in, wrapped in a dressing gown, hair tousled, followed by a galloping beagle. 'What's wrong?' she said. 'What's . . .' Her voice trailed off. Daryl rose up on his hind legs, front paws on the desk, staring out.

'Well, shiiit,' he said.

The city was covered in a layer of snow. It was definitely snow, I could tell by the way it fell, that strange thick grace . . . but it was black, like shiny dark soot. It reminded me of learning about volcanic eruptions and cities being coated in ash, but there was no volcano, no giant fire. Just a solid ceiling of deep grey cloud and streams of snow, blacker than sharks' eyes. There were a few people out in it, but they either stood, slumped, staring in disbelief, or were running their hands through their hair in despair. No happy kids with sledges, no dogs clumsy with eager confusion. I put a hand on Daryl's back, and Lauren put a hand on my shoulder. 'I think we're running out of time,' she said.

We had to assume that the whole city was covered, but

information was not forthcoming because whatever was causing the black snow – here, have three guesses – was also interfering with the radio, TV and phone signals. A couple of times we managed to get an internet connection, but it was too slow and stuttering to even attempt to call up a search engine. It was like having a particularly senile, stroppy dial-up connection. The browser that we used to access the deep web was already slow at the best of times and didn't seem to have been particularly affected, so we could at least check for messages.

'Well,' said Daryl, too brightly. 'We could go for a nice walk in the snow.' Lauren and I exchanged grim looks, and the dog sighed. 'Jeez. Just trying to lighten the mood.'

Space and time needed to be filled, so I asked Daryl some questions. He'd met Maguire's other two associates, Fitz and Box, and said that they seemed trustworthy enough. 'Fitz is pretty funny, actually,' he said. 'I managed to get Skank to tell me a little bit more about how they knew each other.'

'The performance poetry scene,' I said. 'Couldn't quite wrap my head around that.'

'The *experimental* performance poetry scene, as well,' said Daryl. 'Fitz apparently used to spit venomous, confrontational punk verse. Sort of makes sense that he'd become a heavily-armed vigilante freedom-fighter type. At least he's putting his money where his mouth is.'

'And Skank? He was a poet?'

'Not exactly,' said Daryl. 'Apparently he played theremin in some mythological sci-fi prog rock jazz funk spoken word outfit called An Armada From The Lost Moon Of Mars, or something like that. They used to get booked for all kinds of weird gigs and festivals. Usually got put on when the drugs were starting to kick in.'

I nodded. 'Right. Of course. What else would he have done?'

'I know, right?'

'And didn't he say the early Nineties?' I said. 'I thought he was like twenty-eight or something.'

'I always figured he was about thirty-five.'

'This guy's your friend, right?' said Lauren. 'And you have no idea how old he is?'

'To be honest,' said Daryl, 'if I found out that he was an ageless demi-god existing outside of linear time, I probably wouldn't be shocked.'

We managed to have a laugh about that, but conversation dried up pretty quickly and I ended up pacing around the house, trying to get a phone signal at every window. I managed a few bars once or twice, but they always faded before I could attempt a call. It was getting on for five by the time we managed to get some solid broadcasts – the radio and TV came back on, albeit laced with static, and we found a legible news channel. The snow was all over the city. Scientists and meteorological offices and authorities were all 'baffled', which wasn't surprising. People were being strongly advised to stay in their homes as a precaution, and emergency powers had been given to the army. To all intents and purposes, they – and by extension the Angel Group – were in charge of things now.

I glanced down at the phone and saw three whole shining bars of signal, and my first thought should probably have been to call Eddie, but of course it wasn't. 'I'm going to try Kloe,' I said. I moved towards the window and was about to dial her number when I caught sight of an army truck rumbling down the road. I moved swiftly aside, out of view.

'What's wrong?' said Lauren.

'Truck.'

We observed through the window, taking care to remain hidden. The truck halted a few houses down from us and sat there with its lights off. Nobody got out and the engine stayed running, the vehicle just squatting there in the dark snow. It stayed that way for what felt like a very long time. 'I don't like this,' muttered Daryl.

'Hold on,' said Lauren. 'Look.'

Two figures had emerged from the truck, familiar black-armoured soldiers, faces obscured entirely by those awful helmets. They were moving in our direction. 'Oh shit,' I said.

'Wait,' said Lauren. 'Look up the road.'

I looked in the other direction in time to see three guys, black bandanas tied around the lower halves of their faces, hurl a brick and two glass bottles at the soldiers. The brick bounced off the rear window of the truck, which was presumably bulletproof, one bottle shattered on a soldier's head and sent him stumbling, and the second smashed on the ground just in front of them. It wasn't just a bottle though, because it exploded on impact, pumping a ring of fire out across the snow. The soldier who hadn't been hit the first time was knocked onto his back.

'Have that, you Nazi bastards!' one of the guys yelled. 'This ain't a *police state!*'

A huge amplified voice responded from the truck. 'Get down on the ground now. This is your final warning.'

Each of the guys threw another bottle in response. None of these exploded, they just broke on the truck and scattered shiny, ringing shards of glass on the ground. Two more soldiers jumped out of the truck and aimed their weapons.

'*Get down on the ground!*' one of them yelled.

'They're not,' whispered Lauren.

'They are,' I said. 'We have to get out there.' I made towards the front door, but Lauren grabbed me. 'What?' I said. 'They're going to kill those guys!'

'We can't draw attention to ourselves,' said Lauren.

'She's right, kid,' said Daryl.

'Fine,' I said. 'I'll just do it from in here.' I concentrated and flipped the soldiers over, smacking them down on their backs,

241

hard. The young guys who had thrown the bottles all started laughing. 'Now get out of there,' I muttered. 'You morons, get *out* of there.'

'Not so in charge now, are you?' one of the guys was jeering.

'Get *out of there*,' I whispered.

'Yeah! You can't keep us confined! We got *rights!*'

'For God's sake,' said Lauren. 'They're getting up . . .'

I slammed the soldiers back down on the ground with my mind and finally the three guys turned and ran. 'Thank God for that,' I murmured, turning away.

'No!' said Lauren.

'What?' I looked back. The three soldiers were back on their feet, aiming, and I didn't have time to think before they fired deafening bursts, brief bright muzzle flashes in the murk. I looked up the road and saw the three young guys pitch over in the snow, face-first. None of them even screamed, they were just down. Their blood didn't show up on the snow. I slid down to the floor, my hands and face quickly shedding any fragments of feeling. Lauren was crying silently.

'Oh God,' she whispered.

'They just killed them,' I said, my voice spectral. 'They just . . .'

'We should have gone out there,' said Lauren, through a curtain of tears.

'We couldn't have expected that,' said Daryl. 'I wouldn't . . . why wouldn't they use rubber bullets?'

'To show they're serious,' I said.

'Might be their first big mistake,' said Daryl. 'London folk will put up with a lot of bullshit . . . I mean, they live here, don't they? But private armies murdering unarmed civilians? I doubt that that's going to fly.'

By now there was commotion outside, screaming. I didn't want to look. I could hear the booming voice from the truck telling everyone to return to their homes, that the situation was under control. 'People might come to the door,' said Lauren. 'Questions.'

'Then we hide,' I said.

We switched off the few lights we'd had on, drew the curtains and went up to Lauren's room, using a single candle for illumination. Nobody really spoke for well over an hour, we just half-heartedly played cards, Daryl sliding them with his paw like a seasoned card shark, each of us on edge, waiting for a knock at the door. But none came, and suddenly it was dark for real, although it had felt dark all day. 'Are you guys hungry?' said Lauren.

'No,' I said.

'Not hugely,' said Daryl.

'Me neither,' she said, but she went downstairs and started to cook something anyway. I sat in her room and looked at the pictures on the walls, many of which were cuttings from *National Geographic* magazines showing polar bears and grizzly bears and lions and foxes, all with cubs. I stared at one of a huge black bear and its cub, and something stirred in my mind.

'I watched a documentary about black bears the other day,' I said.

'Yeah?' said Daryl.

'Yeah. Apparently you should never play dead if faced with a predatory black bear 'cos it'll just maul you anyway.'

Daryl nodded slowly. 'Good advice, I guess.'

I sighed. 'God. Screw this. Hard.'

'Can I ask you a question, chief?'

'Is it "did you miss me"?'

The beagle laughed. 'No. Well, maybe after. But . . . why do you want to do this? Be a superhero?'

I raised an eyebrow. 'Why?'

'Yeah.'

'I mean, why do you ask?'

'Just wondering,' said Daryl. 'I mean . . . I've been involved with some pretty freakeh business in my time. And this whole thing, black snow, martial law, monsters, whatever you call our proposed guerrilla shenanigans . . . it's beyond the pale. It's a whiter shade of beyond the pale. It's fifty shades of grey beyond the valley of the pale—'

'OK, I get the point,' I said. 'I . . . why. Why be a superhero . . .' I stared at him, wanting to laugh, because I couldn't tell him. He waited expectantly, but after a while I just had to shrug. 'Truthfully, I have no idea,' I said. 'From the second I had my powers, I never really thought about doing anything else. Not seriously, anyway. It just . . . seemed like the thing to do.'

The dog nodded sagely. 'That's as good a reason as any in my book.' He sat there thoughtfully for a moment, then wagged his tail, something he very rarely did. 'So, *did* you miss me?'

'Why? Did you go somewhere?'

He laughed, because he knew.

Later on we finally had some communication from Eddie, a terse email saying that we all needed to meet, but somewhere else this time. Once again it was a long way, although in a different direction. 'Tubes again?' I said.

'Might not be a good idea,' said Daryl. 'I'll wager they'll suspect that we've used them, they'll be watching. Be good to have a couple of different options, so we can alternate – soon as anyone notices a pattern, we're screwed.'

'I might have an idea,' said Lauren.

It turned out that she had more than an idea – she had a plan. A fairly disgusting plan, in fact.

I'd seen it in films and on TV so many times, trooping through the sewers to stay hidden, and obviously I'd always thought 'ugh'. But trust me, nothing could prepare you. The stench was about as overpoweringly hideous as a smell seemed capable of being, as though there could never again be a worse smell than this, and it never subsided, not even momentarily. I kept the three of us levitated so we didn't actually have to touch the floors or walls, but it was still utterly rank, and slow going. The stink was almost *solid*, it pressed against your face, and then there was the perpetual drip drip drip and the clammy glistening of various unspeakable substances. After the first half an hour I was getting light-headed from holding my breath so often. Breathing through my mouth didn't help. I just got the smell translated into taste, which wasn't necessarily worse, just vile in a different way. Lauren had a torch, but it was weak so we could never see further than ten feet in front of us. Luckily she had worked it all out and written down a way through the tunnels in relation to the geography of the city above. She had a good sense of direction, so theoretically it could have been worse.

Forty-five minutes in I stopped. 'This is ridiculous, it's taking ages. We might as well fly properly, rather than floating.'

'If that means we get to spend less time in the city of lost turds, you've got all my votes,' said Daryl. 'Plus the votes of some dead people whose names I've co-opted.'

'Surely it's too cramped,' said Lauren. 'And we have to keep changing direction, we might just go slap bang into a wall.'

'No, we won't,' I said. 'It'll be OK. You just need to be on the ball with the directions.'

'Well . . . all right.' I could tell she wasn't convinced. I brought us all close together, moved us so we were in as aerodynamic a position as possible, and started to fly. It *was* cramped, horribly so, and we were sickeningly close to the endless carpet of sewage, but it was certainly faster. There were a couple of occasions when we very nearly hit a wall, but all the precision practice I'd been doing paid off handsomely and I managed to correct my flight every time. When we finally reached our destination, a manhole at the top of a very grimy ladder, Lauren said we'd probably shaved at least half an hour off the journey.

I shook my head. 'To be honest, in future, I think I'd rather take my chances with the Angel Group and cut down on the travelling time. And the mountains of crap.'

'I'd take mountains of crap over mortal combat any day,' said Lauren, from the top of the ladder, 'especially as they seem to have lost their shyness about killing people.' She pushed the manhole up with her mind and looked around. 'All clear.'

Fresh air had literally never been this gorgeous. We leaned against a wall, keeping to the shadows in case of enemies, and greedily breathed in the purity. The three of us were apocalyptically smelly, but at that moment I really didn't care, I was so grateful to be above ground that for a full minute I didn't even notice the black snow. Then the relief faded like breath on glass, and I tentatively scooped up some of the unnatural substance. It was as cold and wet in my hand as regular snow and came apart just as easily, but when I stared into it there were no patterns, no artistry. It seemed to radiate a sinister energy.

*That makes sense.*

The flat was another grotty and downmarket effort and everyone seemed on edge. Sharon still had a hug ready but stopped short of giving it to me. 'God,' she said, laughing half-chokingly. 'Sorry, but . . . you *stink*.'

'We took the sewers,' I said.

'Jesus,' said Eddie. 'Fair play.'

Daryl nodded. 'Yeah. But we had a first-class seat with Stanly Air, so it wasn't too bad.'

'And what air it was,' I said. 'Seriously, you might think we smell bad right now, but down there . . . I hope none of you ever have to experience that.'

'Not pleasant, is it?' said Sharon, one eyebrow half raised, and I immediately remembered the Worm and felt like a complete knob head. But she smiled, and so did I.

Connor was standing behind her, and I chanced a smile. 'Hey. You OK?'

'Tip top,' said Connor. 'You?'

'You know. Struggling on.' He was still off. I didn't like it.

We were joined today by Fitz and Box. Fitz was a lanky guy with dreadlocks, his neck and arms a forest of tattoos. He offered me a grin and a handshake that suggested someone you wanted to stay on the right side of. Box, meanwhile, had military-short black hair and an improbably muscled, peculiarly proportioned body that made him look like he'd been drawn by Rob Liefeld. He also looked like he could have killed me with his bare hands. He turned out to be the opposite of chatty.

Lauren, Daryl and I started proceedings, relating what had happened with the three guys and the soldiers earlier. Eddie punched a wall and Fitz cracked his knuckles. 'Bastards,' he said. 'This won't stand.'

'There'll be more where that came from,' said Maguire. 'Big mistake on their part, though. People won't put up with it.'

'No,' said Skank. 'Between the military and police presence, the lack of information, the suggestion of terrorism, the bizarre weather conditions and now this . . . I wouldn't want to be so on the nose as to say that I predict a riot, but . . .'

'I don't know,' said Fitz. 'Could be a good thing.'

'City-wide chaos?' said Connor. 'Yeah, I can see how that would be a positive development.'

'Cover for us,' said Fitz. 'Army and police are busy sorting out civil unrest, petrol bombs, all that jazz, and we can take out our targets quickly and easily in the background. They've got plenty of resources, but they ain't unlimited. Thinner they're spread, the better for us. Plus, bunch of pigs and fascists getting bricked in the head? Kinda tickles my warm bits.'

'Well, that's just lovely,' I said. 'Speaking of things that are not Fitz's warm bits, does this mean we have a plan?'

Mr Freeman laid a map of the city out on the table and addressed the room. 'We've discovered that Unique Initiatives have two primary sites where their empowered experiments are taking place.'

'I presume they're what's causing the freaky weather?'

Freeman nodded. 'Not a side-effect I'd foreseen.' He placed a very blurry photograph on the table along with the map, and although it was hard to make out what it showed at first, the realisation sent a cold collective shudder around the room. It was a human body, pale and old-looking, lying slack on a hospital bed with far too many wires and tubes poking out. The wires snaked into a large machine at the head of the bed, and I could just about make out many more in the background, disappearing into indistinct distance.

'My God,' said Sharon.

'Morter Smith's master plan,' said Freeman. 'Quite brilliant, in its own twisted way. It serves their two main purposes – subduing the threat of the empowered, while simultaneously using them as an efficient and powerful energy source. And they need a *lot* of power for what they're trying to achieve.' *Which is what? Get more power?*

*How much do you need, for God's sake.*

'Does it . . . kill them?' said Eddie.

'As far as I know,' said Freeman, 'the Group has found a way of keeping them preserved. There is no limit to the amount of power produced, it can be mined for as long as the body and mind stay even slightly alive.' He looked at our horrified faces, into my eyes. I felt sick. 'I should warn you,' he said, 'that once we release the subjects, which is how the plan currently stands, many of them will be in a disturbed, and disturbing, state. Extremely agitated, possibly violent, potentially even vegetative.'

248

'Better to be dead,' muttered Connor.

'The primary site is beneath Canary Wharf,' said Maguire. 'Secondary is upriver, beneath the East India Docks. The Shard acts as a central hub, directing their efforts.'

'The Shard?' I said, pulling myself away from the awful photograph. 'Why there?'

'Perfect cover,' said Fitz. 'As far as the public knows, it's just Middle Eastern oil barons and Russian plutocrats buying up luxury office space because they can. Those kinds of people aren't obligated to actually give any information to the citizens of the country they're squatting in, so everyone just accepts it. Ideal for the Angel Group's headquarters in London. The plan is for us to split into groups, one for each of the three sites. We take them down, and bye bye Angel Group, monsters, black snow, everything.'

Everybody looked at each other. This was starting to feel pretty damned real now . . . but I was ready. The picture of the body had been the last straw, the final nail in the coffin for the Group as far as I was concerned. I was ready to destroy them.

Freeman produced a number of diagrams, maps and photographs from a manila folder and looked around with an uncharacteristically intense expression. 'Now,' he said, 'I doubt I need to remind you all that this is going to be somewhat on the risky side, so I just want to make sure that everybody is still . . . game.'

I looked at Lauren, knowing that she had the least combat experience and had been properly thrown in at the deep end. But there was no fear in her face that I could see. She was resolved, and so was everybody else; even Connor seemed to have been galvanised by the photograph.

Surprisingly, it was Box who spoke up. 'Seems like the moment for someone to give a rousing speech,' he said, in a surprisingly high-pitched Cockney accent. 'And I can't be arsed with that bollocks. So let's just get on with it, yeah?'

Freeman smiled. 'Seconded. Now. Here it is.'

For several days we sneaked around assembling the plan, working out who would be where at what time and what they would need to do. Those of us with telekinesis practised fiercely with one another, taking it in turns to play as unstoppable forces and immovable objects, and between them Skank, Maguire, Fitz and Box gave us a kind of Wikipedia version of paramilitary strategy to observe. And all the while, black snow continued to fall, thickly.

There was nothing on the news about the murders of the men on Lauren's road, but we were starting to notice more and more people out in the streets when they weren't supposed to be, which made it both easier to traverse the city and much more tense, because if anyone had recognised us as terrorist suspects we'd have been screwed. I phoned Kloe whenever I could find a signal, reassuring her that it was nearly over, constantly going over what my future self had told me, that within a week and a half of leaving them in the woods everything would be over, everything would be fine. It was what allowed me, eventually, to sleep at night, to put up a lead screen between my inner eyes and the mental projection of Kloe and Tara's scared faces, or the rows upon rows of sleeping prisoners, their power sucked from them against their will, or the imagined face of Morter Smith, whose name and phantom image I was starting to hate more than I'd ever hated anyone or anything. I couldn't wait to come face to face with him, to hold him down as I tore his horrific work down around his ears, to rub his face in his failure.

By the end of the meeting on Sunday everyone was ready, and we were set to strike the following night. First Maguire, then Fitz and Box, then Nailah and Skank, then Connor and

Sharon left our latest shabby meeting place, but I hung back and went through to the kitchen, where Eddie was staring out of the window, smoking a cigarette. 'Yo,' I said. 'Can I have one?'

'Nope.'

'Thanks.' I sat on the counter. 'Ready for this?'

'Not even remotely. Why, are you?'

'Haven't got the foggiest.'

Eddie laughed grimly.

'Eddie?'

'Stanly.'

'Remember back before I came to London? When you just rang up out of the blue?'

'Dimly.'

'Why did you? You never really told me.'

'Why did I call?'

'Yeah.'

Eddie shrugged. 'I . . . I just had a feeling. That's all. Turned out I was right.'

I nodded. 'Yeah.' A *feeling*.

*There's always more to these powers than you think.*

My cousin laughed again, but ruefully this time. 'Pretty good job I did of protecting you from all this stuff, eh? We're not even on the same team tomorrow.'

'Makes sense to split the superpowers equally,' I said. 'Although I do enjoy watching you laying smackdowns, so I'll be sorry to miss that. And as for protecting me . . . you didn't have to take that responsibility quite so literally.'

Another rueful chuckle. 'I suppose not.' Eddie looked at me. 'You know, you're a pain in the arse,' he said. 'In *everyone's* arse. In fact, you're such a pain in the arse that you remind me very much of me at fourteen.'

'I'm eighteen.'

'Like I said, me at fourteen.' Eddie's eyes flashed with mischief, a look that I wished I saw on his face more often. 'But you're pretty impressive too.'

'Gee, thanks cuz,' I said. 'Best pep talk ever.'

'You're welcome, squirt.'

'Admit it,' I said. *Please do. Please admit it.* 'A part of you, even a tiny part, ever since you've had powers, has wanted to do something like this. Crazy mission taking on the bad guys, all righteous and outnumbered.'

Eddie took a last drag on his cigarette and flicked the butt out into the night. Then he winked at me. 'Don't tell anyone. It'll spoil my image.'

'The image of a perpetually worried, nagging old woman?'

Those mischievous eyes again. 'Best secret identity ever.'

I grinned, and we exchanged an incredibly manly hug, and I left.

I got to sleep surprisingly quickly that night, what with the merry-go-round of new information and worries twirling in my brain, and at some point my eyes opened and I was standing in the garden of the first house I'd ever lived in. The garden was long and tangled and wild, a jungle for a small child. My dad hated gardening.

Mum stood behind the kitchen window, looking out at me. I waved and she half-waved back, distracted. My dad was leaning against the fence, smoking. 'You've been gone a long time,' he said.

'So have you.' The sky was changing so fast, blue to silvery mirror to twilight, burning sunset to night, back to blue.

'How does it feel? Having to do things yourself? Look after yourself?'

'You threw me in at the deep end a bit.'

'You taught yourself to swim.' He exhaled smoke and it

curled into different shapes, dancers and guards and animals, shimmering.

'Never been much of a swimmer.' I ran my finger along the grip of the gun. 'More into my flying.'

'I never really did either,' said Frank. He looked towards the kitchen. Mum was making tea or something behind a window made of things they never said to each other.

'I'm sorry I turned out wrong,' I said.

He shrugged. 'Can't have been all your fault.'

'But this isn't how it's meant to work,' I said. The gun was a comfort. 'I'm not grown yet. I'm supposed to call you when things get scary. You're supposed to come and sort it all out. That's what parents do.'

'You're supposed to be a superhero,' said Frank. 'Batman never rang his parents when the going got tough. Superman didn't.'

'Their parents died before they assumed superheroic status.'

'Kind of the point. A bit.' Frank sounded sort of like Daryl now. 'We're not dead. But we can't help you.'

'You should be doing this for me.' The gun, trembling in my hand. The barrel, pressed against the head of the man. The man, kneeling in the grass. His face, shifting like the sky, too rapid to be anyone real. 'I shouldn't be killing. What would Mum say?'

'She certainly wouldn't be happy,' said Frank.

I raised the gun to the sky. 'Just one thing, before I go.'

'Mm?'

'This is not a daddy-issues thing.'

'I never said it was.'

I laughed a gallows laugh and pulled the trigger, and even though the BANG was written on a piece of comedy paper that fluttered to the ground, even though I didn't even point it at the man with the shifting face, he still keeled over, dead. I sighed, a sigh that made the whole town shake, and tossed the gun to Frank. 'Do me a favour and empty it.'

'What did your last slave die of?'

'Insubordination.' I looked back towards the kitchen.

Mum had turned away.

# Chapter Eighteen

LAUREN AND I spent most of Monday going over and over the plan, ad nauseum. I kept wanting to call Kloe, and when I eventually worked up the courage I didn't even hint that there was something going down. She was OK again, tired but bright. She said that she and Tara were thick as thieves now, sharing secrets left right and centre. This was so achingly wonderful and warming to hear that I found myself laughing much louder than I should have.

*Probably a good clue that everything's very much not OK.*

Six o'clock rolled around after another full day of coal black snow and fear, and as I watched real darkness overtake the peculiar not-quite-darkness of the day, I almost felt ready. Lauren was strangely calm, although I knew how apprehensive she was about fighting. I'd given her as much advice about combat as I could based on my limited experience, testing her reflexes by throwing things that she had to deflect. She was stronger and more adept than she would give herself credit for. I knew she'd be fine.

I *hoped* she'd be fine.

We went out into the city wrapped in our coats, keeping to the shadows. There were no patrols in the vicinity at the moment and we quickly reached the point where we needed to split up. 'You be careful,' I said.

She smiled. 'You too.'

'*Please*. Be careful.'

'I will. Don't worry.' She patted my shoulder as if she wasn't sure what to do or say. 'See you later.'

'Yeah. Good luck.'

She disappeared into the thick, overbearing night, armed with the weapons I had taken from Connor and Sharon's safe, to meet Eddie, Box and Nailah at their rendezvous near the Shard. Their part of the plan involved storming the place, creating a healthy amount of havoc, finding Nailah's contact and stealing as much data as possible. It almost sounded fun.

I had a feeling that mine was going to be less fun.

I glided through the night, low against the black carpet. Although my group's target, the inspiringly-named Research Site One, was positioned beneath Canary Wharf, the actual entrance was almost a mile away, and it would take some high-level hacking – something that, unsurprisingly, Skank was taking care of – before we could even think about getting in there and raising the requisite level of hell. I kept turning the plan over in my head as I flew, thinking about how much violence my role was going to require.

*Seems to be what I do these days.*

I reached the Tube station and hid across the road behind a car. Once again there was one truck at the entrance, and three guards that I could see, leaning against the vehicle talking.

*Speaking of violence . . .*

All the colours were weird, the orange street lamps and black snow distorting everything, giving the street an unpleasant drunken quality. I blinked to re-focus, narrowed my eyes, concentrated. The truck spun away from the entrance and came to rest about twenty feet down the road, knocking two of the guards to the ground, the other sent stumbling off-balance. I took advantage of the confusion and flew full-pelt towards the Tube station. Without slowing down I lashed out mentally, knocking the third guy into the other two, shot straight past them and carried on flying, down the steps, tearing open doors and gates like they were nothing, gliding over ticket barriers and down the still, silent escalators. The lights were off and I held my torch in front of me as I flew down into the bowels of the station. I took a right, alighted on the platform and breathed. The silence was complete down here, no voices or distant clanking and rattling, not even the murmur of wind. It seemed more unsettling today.

*Ain't everything?*

The leftward tunnel would take me where I needed to go. I took one more deep, not-particularly-calming breath and stepped towards the edge . . .

The noise that suddenly erupted from the darkness fused all the hairs on my body and my spine iced over. It was an impossibly deep roar, something huge and very, *very* alive, and it was coming from the other tunnel. Eastbound. It reverberated around the platform for an agonisingly long time before dying away and I tried to remember how to move my limbs.

OK.

*What. The HELL. Was that.*

The word *monster* suggested itself to me. I wished that it hadn't, or at least that it wasn't such a plausible suggestion.

It wasn't close, which was a slight comfort, but it definitely wasn't as far away as I would have liked it to be. Ideally, I wanted it so far away that there was no physical way that I could hear even a suggestion that it existed. I stood for a second, waiting. *Should probably move. Guards will be down here soon.* The familiar silence after the roar was both comforting and worrying, because it wasn't peace, it was just a gap between terrors. Five seconds, ten . . . and then it came again, distant and enormous and unknowably furious. It made the giant blue dog's roar seem like the yelp of a Chihuahua.

Something strange was coming over me. Alongside the utter paralysing fear, there was . . .

Curiosity?

*No way. I'm not going to search for the source of the monstrous noise.*

*Come on! How bad could it be?*

*Really bad. Quite seriously, terrifyingly, 'sob for Mum and collapse in a pool of whining bad' bad.*

*Wimp.*

*I'm not a wimp. Most definitely a not-wimp. And anyway, seasoned not-wimps would probably balk at this.*

*Plus, mission to do.*

With this conflict still rolling around in my head like a pair of battling tomcats, I stood up and walked gingerly to the edge of the platform. The roar didn't come.

*Maybe it's gone away.*

As if on cue, it came again. I shivered. Being hot and shivery is a very strange feeling.

*You were saying?*

*Shut up. I said 'maybe', didn't I?*

*Definitely one of the worst sounds I've ever heard.*

*Yeah? What was worse?*

*The worst sound, then.*

This whole debate was putting me further on edge so I looked defiantly away from the roar and took off into the darkness. This was easy now, especially compared with the sewers. No trains, no stinking human waste, just the smell of dust and ageing metal, and me, and my light. All I had to do was follow it.

The journey took about twenty minutes and I used it to go over the plan yet again, as well as my last short conversation with Sharon.

'Love you,' she whispered.

'You too,' I said, willing my voice not to shake. 'Take care of yourself. See you afterwards.'

Connor had said nothing. Not even 'good luck'.

My last conversation with Kloe kept coming back to me as well, but this I forced myself to ignore. It wouldn't do me any good. Purpose turned the air around me to ice and I emerged from the tunnel with the plan carved into my mind, like an incantation into living rock. I could visualise the words, every step. I was ready. I flew up through the station with my coat flapping in that strange processed breeze, and Skank and Maguire met me at the entrance, dressed in the black uniforms of Department 9 soldiers. I didn't ask how they'd disposed of the suits' owners. Daryl was there too, dressed as himself, which threatened to make their disguises slightly redundant, but I didn't have the heart to say so. They led us to the truck they'd commandeered and Skank drove us towards our destination, or as close as we could get to it at any rate.

'Right,' said Maguire. 'We don't move until we have confirmation that the others are in place. Now let's go over it again.'

'Really?' said Daryl. 'I think if anyone needs it repeated at this point, we should probably call the whole thing off. Actually, that's not a bad plan . . .'

'Let's go over it again,' repeated Maguire, slowly and with more of a growl in his voice. Daryl made a face at him behind his back, and I tried not to giggle.

'No problemo,' I said, as chirpily as possible. 'Concealed entrance down to Site One. You guys can get past the computers, but because of the high alert there's also a big patrol and a bunch of soldiers. I create a distraction while you two do your lock-picking thing with the laptop, then I follow you down and we go in and do some smashing.'

'Well done,' said Maguire.

'I learn fast,' I said. 'Especially when I go over plans every five minutes for what feels like years.'

Maguire looked ready to say something snippy, then thought better of it. We sat in silence for a while, waiting, and Skank smoked several cigarettes. Finally I decided to try breaking the ice. 'What's your origin story then, Maguire?'

'Eh?'

'Your history. Maguire's Tale. How'd you come to be General Custer-ing this little assault?'

'Not sure it's your business.'

'It isn't. I'm just interested.'

'Why?'

'I want to see you as a rounded human being rather than an irritable Scot with a master plan.'

'I warned you about that lip . . .'

'How long have you lived in London?'

Maguire looked exasperated, but shook his head in resignation. 'Twelve years.'

'What did you do before this?'

'If you must know, I dealt cocaine and heroin. Mostly heroin.'

That stopped me. 'Really?'

He nodded. 'Yep. I was one of the city's biggest suppliers of illegal narcotics. That's how I met Box, he used to be my . . . right-hand man, I suppose.' My expression must have betrayed me because Maguire shook his head as though I were unbearably naïve. 'Look,' he said, 'don't start judging me or whatever you're doing with that face. Yeah it's a scummy disgusting vile drug and nowadays I'd lamp anyone who tried to shoot it in front of me. But it's what I did. Box persuaded me to get out, in the end. We got clean together, then Box told me about these rumours he'd heard. Showed me enough to make me want to get involved.'

'But why? Why did you want to get involved? Why fight them?'

Maguire frowned, but it wasn't an irritated frown. It was more like he was trying very hard to find the right words. 'I . . . to begin with, to be honest, it was just the idea of saying a big *fuck you* to . . . to some embodiment of "the man". You can imagine what an enticing prospect it was for an angry, directionless guy with skills. A huge conspiracy, an evil corporation, corrupt government figures. And the more we learned about them, the more I realised that this world's not ours any more. It hasn't been for a long time.'

'Ours?' said Daryl.

'People's,' said Maguire. 'Ordinary people. It belongs to the Angel Groups now, to the big conglomerates, big pharma and big oil and the military-industrial complex. Profit and secrets. The revolving door of corruption, politicians and lobbyists crawling in and out of one another's pockets, selling anyone and everyone up the river. Not one of them ever met a principle they couldn't abandon, a scruple they couldn't look past. And the more I learned about this mass of unaccountable scumbags, the more I wanted to smash 'em to bits. To see what happens next.' He laughed grimly. 'Probably going to be absolute mayhem. But you know. Phoenixes, ashes, blah blah blah. Be interesting to see what emerges from the anarchy. Funnily enough, when we brought Fitz on board, Box recruited him from a gang of self-styled anarchists. And did those pathetic wee bastards want to help us lay down some *real* anarchy? Proper honest-to-God smash the system stuff? Did they bollocks.' He shook his head, looking like he wanted to spit on the floor to emphasise his point. 'Anyway. So eventually we found Skank, and then you bunch of weirdos. No-one else wanted to know. No-one gives a rat's arse about what these bastards do, so long as it doesn't get in the way of them doing exactly what they want to do when they want to do it. People just want a quiet life.'

'I sympathise,' said Daryl, darkly.

'Not saying I'm on the side of the angels, by any means,' said Maguire. 'Don't want to paint myself as a crusader for democracy and transparency and truth or whatever. I'm not a particularly moral guy, although seeing what the Angel Group's been doing to those empowered certainly turns my stomach . . . but what I have got coming out of my arse is conviction. Which is in pretty short supply these days. So it seems as though I might as well make use of it.' He looked at me, and I felt like there was actual respect there, maybe for the first time. 'I think you've got it,' he said.

'Hope so.'

Maguire smiled a smile that you wouldn't want to encounter down a dark alley – or a brightly lit one, to be fair – and glanced at Daryl. 'And I'd like to read your tell-all biography sometime.'

'Not much to tell,' said Daryl.

'Oh, I'm sure there isn't,' said Maguire. 'Talking beagle fighting an evil corporation. Nothing juicy there.'

Daryl offered a polite laugh, but it was painfully obvious that this was not a subject he wanted to talk about. Maguire shrugged. 'Fair enough, if you don't want to get into it. I'm not one to pry, generally. One question, though?'

'Shoot.'

'Why do you want to fight them? The Angel Group?'

Daryl's eyes flickered to his paws very briefly, then back up to the Scotsman. 'Reasons,' he said.

'Fair enough.' Maguire suddenly put a hand to his ear. 'Fitz?'

'What's going on?' I said.

'Earpiece,' said Skank. 'Woops.' He handed me a small piece of plastic and showed me how to insert it in my ear.

'Feels weird, doesn't it?' said Daryl.

'I'll say. Where'd you get these?'

'All the guns and equipment come from acquaintances of

myself and Maguire,' said Skank. 'Not all people you'd necessar-ily want to associate with. Maguire's got his reputation, which is how he can get so much stuff. And I've got wads of cash. The two go together quite nicely.'

'So I'll be able to hear everyone else?' I said. 'Eddie and stuff?'

'No,' said Skank. 'Sorry. We decided that having everybody tuned to everybody would be far too confusing, far too noisy. Worse than multiplayer *Call of Duty*. We can talk to everyone within our own groups, and the group leaders can hear each other too.'

*Group leaders.*

*Don't remember voting for them.*

*Ha ha.*

'Right,' said Maguire. 'Go time.'

'Distraction o'clock?' I said.

'Yeah,' said Maguire. 'And . . . well. I had an idea about that, if you're up for it . . .'


*OK, maybe I was wrong about this not being fun.*

If you'd not known that they were guarding something, it would have looked like a load of army types hanging about a bleak industrial ground doing not much of anything. They'd set up a huge perimeter fence around the area and there were three trucks and roughly twenty soldiers, and what looked like some kind of mobile command centre next to a large tent. The soldiers were a mixture of regular army and the Angel Group's black-clad Department 9 special forces types. I couldn't help but wonder how much the regular army ones knew about the others, or if it was just a case of 'shut up and follow orders'.

As for me, I was standing some way away from the main gate, next to a car that I'd quietly brought with me.

*A tall fence. Oh dear. However will I bypass this fiendish security device.*

I jumped into the air and pulled the car up underneath me, rising about thirty feet off the ground. Then, standing on its roof and striking an appropriately stylish pose, I sent both of us hurtling through the air and over the gate. I heard yelling, heard the first bullets, and ducked down, the wind whipping harshly at my skin. Keeping a bubble around myself to deflect the bullets, I surfed the car through the air, tense, ready, three seconds, two seconds, one second . . .

NOW!

I relaxed control of the car and stepped off its roof, staying in the air, and the vehicle kept on going, right towards the centre of the three parked trucks. Soldiers scattered, and I gave one slower one a psychic helping hand so he wouldn't be crushed. The car bashed right into the side of one truck and they bounced away from one another, spinning and shedding broken glass and pieces of warped metal all over the black snow. Beyond the confusion, I saw a pair of soldiers and a galloping white blur disappear into the tent by the mobile command centre. 'We're going in,' crackled Maguire's voice in my earpiece. His was the only voice I could hear. *Kind of wish I knew what was going on with the others. AAARGHSHITGUNS—*

Soldiers were firing at me. I kept my bubble around myself and started to fly this way and that, up and down, dipping and diving as fast as I could, twirling, serpentine. This was a risky strategy, as complicated flight took a lot of concentration and at any moment I could potentially let a bullet slip through my psychic shield, but I just kept thinking *focus focus focus come on now the practice pays off* WOAH AHHH GRAB THAT GUY THROW HIM OVER THERE OK *focus focus come on* AAH DODGE GO OVER THERE NOW OVER HERE UP THERE PICK UP ALL THAT

WRECKAGE THROW IT OVER THERE OK *focus*
*focus . . .*

Maguire's voice in my ear: 'We're in!'

*Oh thank Christ. This is really stressful.* 'OK!' I said. *Right.
Onward.* I swooped down towards the ground, as low as I could
get, then abruptly pulled up and hammered it towards the big
tent, bullets zipping past me. I threw as many mental punches
as I could, knocking soldiers off their feet and skirting battered
vehicles. Into the tent, over three unconscious soldiers and *down*
through the concealed entrance, a circle in the floor giving way
to a spiral staircase. I could hear soldiers pursuing me, running,
shouting, shooting, but as I disappeared through the hole the
hatch slammed shut behind me.

Skank, Maguire and Daryl were at the bottom of the staircase, in a very long corridor that lead further downward. 'Well,'
said Daryl. 'That was . . . incredibly dangerous.'

'You can handle yourself pretty well, for a beagle,' said
Maguire. He was standing over two more unconscious soldiers,
and Skank was staring intently at his laptop screen.

'I've locked the entrance,' Skank said, 'although I'm not sure
how long it will hold. Nice work by the way, Stanly.'

'Thanks.' *I think my heart might explode.*

'Yeah,' said Maguire. 'Well done. Come on, we need to go
*now.*' Skank slid his laptop into its bag and we started to jog
down the corridor. I could hear the chaos above, muffled by
metal and rock but still highly off-putting. Two soldiers appeared from around the corner, weapons aimed, and without
breaking stride Maguire fired twice, getting both men in the
kneecaps. They collapsed, yelling hoarsely in pain, and we
hurried past them.

'Jesus!' I said.

'That seemed unnecessary,' said Skank.

'Kneecaps are fine,' said Maguire. 'They won't bleed out.' He raised a hand to his ear. 'Box says they've successfully penetrat-ed the Shard. They're well on their way up already.'

'And they're all right?' I said.

'Lauren and your cousin are fine,' said Maguire, tersely.

*They'd better be.* 'And the others?'

Maguire tapped his ear. 'Freeman? You in?' He listened for a few seconds and I kept my fingers crossed, thinking about Connor and Sharon. To be honest, in my head Freeman was kind of expendable, but the other members of his group most definitely were not. Maguire nodded. 'They're fine. They're in.'

We encountered four more soldiers before we reached the end of the corridor and I made sure to take them down before Maguire could repeat his special move. *Better a minor con-cussion than never being able to walk again.* We stopped at a wall-sized silver door with a big red number 1 printed on it and a small computer pad to one side. 'Right,' said Skank, pulling off his helmet. He knelt down by the computer and connected up his laptop. 'Let's open the pod bay doors.' Maguire, Daryl and I stood facing away from him, waiting for reinforcements.

*Surely this was too easy.*

We stood that way for two unbearable minutes, nobody speaking, Skank working quietly and methodically on the laptop. I was just about to vocalise an anxious thought when Maguire jumped, causing Daryl and me to jump too. 'Box?' said Maguire. 'Box!'

'What's wrong?' said Daryl.

'Box,' said Maguire. 'He said . . . ambush. Empowered . . . I think . . .' He looked at us, disbelief and fear filling his eyes and voice. 'I think someone shot him.'

'What?' I said. 'What about Lauren and Eddie? Nailah?'

'I . . . what? Freeman? What the hell's . . . taking fire where? Well, get out–' Maguire was cut short by the huge door chugging open and a bullet hitting him square in the back of the head. He pitched over, blood spattering on the spotless white floor of the corridor.

The door revealed a huge cargo area with two piles of metal crates stacked floor-to-ceiling and another identical door at the other end. There were also about ten soldiers. Skank had ducked to the side and was laying down covering fire and Daryl was crouched by him, eyes darting, looking for an opening.

*How about we make one.*

I launched myself in, feeling the heat as bullets burned the atoms in the air around me. I made straight for the ceiling and started picking up soldiers and hurling them around, mental tentacles flailing everywhere, thinking bullets away. I lashed out at the stacks of crates and they overbalanced violently, clattering, some splitting open as they struck the floor and spilling weapons and electronic equipment everywhere. One crate impacted against a soldier's head, cracking his helmet. He went down hard and I swooped back down and flew towards the last two, cold with purpose, psychically disarming them and extending both my arms to the height of their chests. I had sufficient velocity, coupled with a bit of help from my brain, to clothesline, lifting them clean off the ground, and they sprawled through the air. I stopped dead, mentally gifting them with some added speed, and they hit the opposite wall. It sounded like at least a couple of bones cracked.

I landed and looked back at Skank. He was speaking into his earpiece while Daryl made the rounds in the room, pinpointing any soldiers who were still conscious and taking them out with swift, brutal body blows. 'Hello?' said Skank. '*Hello*, is anyone there? What the hell's going on? Lauren? Eddie? Nailah?'

'Are they all right?' I said.

'No answer.'

'Oh God . . .'

'This mission is over,' said Skank. 'We are getting out of here.'

'Oh no we're not,' I said. 'We came to do a job, we're going to get it done.' I turned and flew to the other door. 'Can you open this?' I called.

'No,' said Skank. He was standing up now. 'Well . . . probably, but I'm not going to. How long do you think we're going to last, three of us against whoever's beyond there?'

'Probably about as long as four of us would have lasted,' I said. 'And to be honest, I don't care. I'm going to destroy that place. If you don't fancy it, you can open the door for me and then get out. I don't mind. But I'm taking that torture chamber down.'

'Stanly,' began Daryl, but before he could continue the other door opened of its own accord. I tensed my body, ready for more fighting, but I wasn't ready enough. Something came through the door and struck me in the face. I tumbled sideways through the air, hit the wall and fell to the floor, forcing myself to get up before I could register the pain properly.

I turned and faced my attacker and my stomach knotted, my skin rippling with disgust.

It was about the size of a bull, and a sickly yellow colour, with six chunky legs and a mass of tentacles writhing on its arched back. It must have been one of those that hit me because my face stung like it had been whipped. The tentacles were disgusting, but it was the face that made my blood ice over. It was massive and flat, its wide mouth crazy with teeth, and covered with what seemed like *thousands* of eyes, all different colours, all blinking out of sync with one another. The combined sound of all those eyes blinking was sloppy and wet, and when you added that to the rustling made by the tentacles, it added up to about the vilest thing I'd seen since . . .

*Smiley Joe.*

I'd just started to wonder why the thing wasn't coming at me when someone walked out from behind it: a tall, heavy-set man in a brown suit, with cropped hair and a mean green-eyed face. Beyond him, in the corner of an identical staging area, was the kid I'd seen at Blue Harvest, slumped unconscious, still wearing his green coat. 'Hello, Stanly,' said the man. 'My name is Morter Smith.' He offered a thin, vampiric smile. 'Get him,' he said.

'Daryl, Skank, RUN!' I yelled.

The beast leapt towards me and lunged with its tentacles, but I curved around it and positioned a crate between the two of us for protection. The thing was quick though, it spun around and thundered back towards me, extending tentacles to grip my crate and fling it aside. Skank was firing with his gun but either he kept missing or this thing wasn't worried about bullets. Daryl ran towards it but it batted him away with a tentacle and I winced as he struck the wall. 'I said *run*!' I yelled.

'We're not leaving you with that!' said Skank.

'Bloody right!' said Daryl, getting back to his feet. His hackles rose and he bared his teeth, preparing to rejoin the melee.

'No!' I yelled. 'Get out of here! Help the others! They're in trouble! I can handle this!'

'I—'

'HELP THE OTHERS!' Adrenaline flooded my body and I lashed out with my mind, lifting Skank and Daryl up and depositing them firmly on the other side of the big door. I yanked it closed a split second before Daryl could jump back through, and allowed myself a micro-sigh of relief before another tentacle came snaking towards me. I dodged and flew up to the ceiling, momentarily out of reach of the revolting thing, and tried to concentrate on it, to grip it and throw it or bash it against the wall, but it was too quick and forced me to dodge again, this time by going down. I ducked, only just missing its mouth, rolled underneath and rocketed between its many legs, picking up crates and lobbing them at it from every side. The creature deflected them almost playfully with those bastard tentacles. I flew as fast as I could to the other end of the room, spun and dropped down onto my feet so I could have a quick break from flying and concentrate. *Breathe. Breathe.* I stared at the advancing monster, focused and hurled it at the wall.

At least, that was my intention. But the beast didn't move. It just shrieked and kept coming.

*What the hell . . .*

*Telekinesis didn't work on Smiley Joe, remember?*

*No. NO! No way no way no way this is not FAIR . . .*

*It worked on the monster dog though! You got its eyes!*

*And Sharon . . . the Worm . . .*

*You just need to concentrate . . .*

Unfortunately it was pretty difficult to concentrate properly with this pile of hellspawn coming at me, tentacles writhing, teeth snapping. I dodged again, picked up another crate and hit the thing in the face. It screamed its awful scream but it didn't stop, it just came at me with a renewed vengeance, and the whole time Smith was just standing, watching, not even laughing, just watching.

*This was a trap . . .*

*This thing is going to kill you.*

Nothing I did worked. Any projectiles were knocked aside with embarrassing ease and I wasn't able to stay still long enough to get a proper psychic grip. After another failed attack I flew back to the far wall, turned and waited . . . but this time the beast stopped as well, staring at me, tentacles moving like long slimy sea plants. The eyes were definitely the worst part, every one of them horrible, alien, staring, like the eyes of a Martian shark.

It was giving me time.

Why was it giving me time?

Was it giving me a *chance*?

*This is ridiculous. I can throw a truck but I can't throw this piece of crap?*

*Damn it, Stanly,* CONCENTRATE.

I stared, letting all of the energy buzz and spark and spit inside my brain, thinking of bottles of fizzy drink that had been shaken too much, thinking of overloading electricity sub-stations, of solar flares, thought and thought and *thought* until it felt as though my eyes were going to burst in their sockets, and I reached out with my powers, with everything that made them *mine*, that made me *me*, and wrapped my mind around the body of the beast.

*I have it!*

YES!

Wrenching a roar from the pit of my stomach I sent the creature sprawling into the wall so hard that it made a pretty impressive dent. It howled again but recovered instantly and came at me, still shrieking. I moved to dodge but this time I was too slow and a tentacle caught me on the side of my head. I slammed into the floor, face down, and warm blood spurted from my nose. It hurt. A lot. Then another tentacle came, like a steel boot in my side, and I felt myself flop through the air and thud against the wall. I hit the floor again, completely winded, and those godawful tentacles wrapped me up and started bouncing me around the room, against the ceiling, the floor, the wall, the ceiling, the floor, the wall, the floor. Then it flung me at the far wall and let me fall to the ground. I spat a huge spray of bitter blood, my body so overwhelmed with pain that I could barely see, but I made myself, *forced* myself to get to my feet, staggering drunkenly. I picked up a crate with my brain – *because physical pain is physical pain it's nothing to do with your mind your mind is fine your mind is fine yeah maybe half blind with agony but otherwise fine* – and threw it, but my aim was off. I was seeing triple. *Six Krustys,* my brain burbled uselessly as the crate sailed past the creature and broke open against the wall. I stumbled and fell to my knees and realised that I wasn't totally sure how to get up.

'Hmm,' said Smith. 'That didn't go very well, did it? Bring him here.'

Almost tenderly, the creature scooped me up with its tentacles and took me over to Smith, holding me up so that we were face to face. A pathetic trophy. I was too bruised and beaten to resist, I just hung limply, very aware that I'd never bled this much before, not even when I'd been shot that time. I tried to focus on the multiple Smiths staring into my eyes. 'Stanly Bird,' he said.

I gurgled something.

'You know,' said Smith, 'considering all the trouble you've given our soldiers, I'm quite seriously disappointed to finally meet you.' His voice was harsh, chalky, cold. 'Everything you knew is over,' he said, his translucent green eyes flashing but empty. 'You might as well try to accept that.' The last thing I saw before everything bled away was a face with a thousand eyes, every one blinking at me . . . and then there was nothing.

# PART TWO

## ?????????

My head hurts.

?????????????????????

What happened?

???????????????????????????????????????????????????

*Kloe . . .*

# Chapter Nineteen

PAIN IS LESS . . .
   I feel like I can open my eyes.
   I open my eyes and get shakily to my feet.
   *Where . . .*
   I'm in a white room, featureless, a perfect cube. Maybe fifteen by fifteen feet, no visible way in or out. There is a sound, a heavy humming, like a distant generator. It seems to come from above, although disorientated isn't a disorientated enough word for how disorientated I am, so it could be coming from anywhere. I could be imagining it. No smell . . . almost an *anti*-smell, the place is so clean and sterile that there's just an absence of odour, save my own sweat and the rusty tink of old blood.
   I look down at myself. I'm barefoot, and my clothes have been replaced by light blue hospital pyjamas. My legs suddenly feel as though they're about to give way and I have to steady myself against a wall.
   *A thousand different-coloured eyes watching . . .* and then an impact, and the echo of a cold voice . . .
   *Why didn't I fly?*
   Too weak to fly.
   I remember thinking that.
   *Too weak to do anything.*
   *Too weak to fight.*
   I'm weak now, and aching all over, my limbs full of fresh, rapidly drying cement. I must be malnourished . . . I have no

idea how long I've been here. Time doesn't seem to be on my side at the moment. Mouth is dry. Brain seems to be functioning as well as can be expected, but I'm buggered if it can actually make sense of what's going on. I run my hands through my hair, over my chin. Several days' worth of stubble. I remember the last time I shaved, it wasn't that much stubble ago. That must mean I've been here since about yesterday? A day and a half at the most? Is that reassuring?

I have no idea.

I move slowly and unsteadily around the room, feeling my way along the walls, searching for anything that could be a hidden exit, weak points, but there is nothing. I remember the last time I was in a similar situation. Smiley Joe was on his way. *At least I had company, though . . .*

*Use your powers, you idiot.*

I look up. Can't reach the ceiling. I turn to the nearest wall and concentrate, fashion a ball of psychic energy, feel it expanding until my vision clouds slightly, and then let it fly invisibly towards the wall. No impact, no sound. It should have dented it at least, surely? Nothing. *Bollocks.* I look up again. Maybe something in the ceiling, ventilation of some kind? I close my eyes for a second, trying to regain some strength, kick off from the floor, head straight up . . .

Except I don't. I jump about a foot, then drop down again. My legs abruptly give way and I'm on my back, coughing, groaning.

*I can't fly.*

*I can't fly.*

*What the . . .*

It must be exhaustion. That telekinesis really took it out of me. Just exhaustion. If I rest for a while and try again . . .

I already know I'm kidding myself. I can't fly.

It's gone.

Does that mean the telekinesis is gone too? Maybe the wall's just too tough, that's why there wasn't a dent or anything, and the flying thing is just exhaustion? I think it but not one part of me believes it. It's all the same. If one thing isn't working . . . but I felt it in my head, I *felt* the energy build up, I felt myself release it and . . .

Did I?

I don't know . . .

I look desperately around the room again for something, anything to move. Not even a speck of dust. I pull off the hospital shirt and throw it on the floor, wincing as I take in the pile of bruises and cuts that my upper body has become. I look down at the shirt, pathetic and crumpled on the ground, and concentrate as hard as is humanly possible. Filter out the echoing words, my own internal rantings, everything, until my mind is completely clear, an open snowy plain as empty as this room. I lift with my brain . . . and the shirt stays where it is. I try again. Nothing. Over and over again I try to move the shirt, make it rustle, even a tiny bit, but there's nothing, no effect, not a goddamn thing. *Damn it, damn it, DAMN IT.* Fear and confusion react like two combustible chemicals and rage bellows through me, fiery and energising. I run at the wall and pound on it with my fists, shouting. '*Smith*! Smith, where are you? What the hell have you done to me? Where am I? Smith! *SMITH!*'

Silence, apart from my own ragged breathing. As quickly as it came the rage is gone and I'm exhausted, totally spent, and hurting. I collapse and crawl over to the shirt, pull it back on, sit cross-legged. I'm out of ideas, out of options. All I can do is wait for something to happen, for someone to come. Can't plan a surprise attack. My powers are gone and I'm not physically strong, I never have been. Can't even make myself strong . . .

I close my eyes and think back to the beginning of all this, searching through the blurry, fragmented mush, vainly trying to make sense of it all, to find something that I missed, something that can help, a tiny shred of comfort. Something to suggest that this whole thing hasn't been the most gigantic balls-up ever imagined.

All I can manage is *we were stupid.*

In fact, stupid is the understatement of pretty much forever. We walked merrily into a trap, and now Maguire is dead, and probably Box, and who knows what's happened to the others?

I remember the fight, feel the echo of savage blows on my body, and I force myself to my feet and try to fly again, jumping and concentrating with everything I've got, which admittedly isn't much. Once again I fall back to the floor, flightless, powerless, useless.

I lean against the wall and try to assemble some thoughts. The beast battered me, that much is certain, but it looks like my captors have patched me up. I've been here about a day, I think. I haven't actually got a clue, but that's my guess and I'm sticking with it.

What do they want with me?

*They've taken away your powers. Isn't it obvious? They want you out of the game.*

*Then surely they'd have killed me?*

'What do you want?' I yell. 'Smith! What do you want with me?' I didn't really expect anything to happen, but shouting makes me feel a little better.

This is a lie.

I hug my knees to my chest. At least I know Kloe and Tara are safe . . . or are they? Now I think about it, if the whole assault on the Angel Group was a trap, couldn't that have been a trap too? Get me well and truly out of the way so they could go after Kloe and Tara? Names and faces and possibilities tangle around one another in my damaged brain, ideas igniting and burning out too fast to consider properly. There was nothing in the note from future me about this, nothing. Why wouldn't he . . . I . . . have mentioned this? Why would I let myself trundle into a trap like this?

*Maybe I need to be here. Maybe this is* supposed *to happen? That must be it.*

I have to stay calm, think in the here and now. I have to assume that Kloe and Tara are OK because right now there is nothing I can do for them. When – *if* – I escape I can go to them, but for now I have to bury the faces of possible traitors, the nagging suspicion that Maguire or Box might have been stringing us along. Or Nailah? Lauren, even? Now that I think about it, it could have been anyone, if it *was* anyone . . .

*Is Daryl in on it?*

*No. No he isn't.*

*I know he isn't.*

I ignore myself and stand up again, but even as my eyes dart around the poker-faced walls of my cell, I know it's pointless. I'm not getting anything done until someone opens a door. If this place even *has* a door. Maybe they assembled it around me while I was unconscious.

Maybe this is my tomb.

This is not a comforting thought, and I have not-comforting thoughts to spare, so I bag it up with the suspicion and paranoia and throw it out to be collected later. There must be something I can do . . .

A piercing whine of static cuts through the sterile air. I press my hands to my ears, wincing at the intensity of the sound, and now there's a voice, sexless, amplified so that it echoes around the room like the malevolent ghost of a dead sound wave. 'Close your eyes.'

'Why?' I yell.

It repeats itself. Identical, no intonation. 'Close your eyes.'

'Why—'

It doesn't ask again, and then I understand. The room fills with light, so bright that my retinas are scorched, electrified. I fall to my knees, clutching my face, blinded. I can feel myself turning upside-down. Colours and fragments of myself and the featureless room kaleidoscope in my head, it seems to—

# Chapter Twenty

WHEN I WAKE up again I'm attached to the wall, upright, with black metal straps around my wrists and ankles. There is a man standing in front of me. Brown suit, arms folded, staring me straight in the face. I know him. His shape, the narrow green laser orbs in his eye sockets.

'Smith,' I say.

He doesn't nod or smile, doesn't speak. He just regards me with those eyes. They're nasty eyes, full of bad deeds and worse intentions, and I'm scared, but I don't show it. I can't. *Stay nonchalant.* He's got me by the balls, so to speak, but I'm not giving him any more satisfaction than he's already got. As far as I'm concerned this happens on a regular basis, and it doesn't worry me. In fact, being strapped to the wall in some surreal *Prisoner*-esque jail cube is a refreshing change of pace. I hold his gaze and smile brightly. 'How's it going?'

He says nothing.

'Where's your mate?'

Nothing.

'The tentacled flat-face eyeball cow thing?' I offer. 'Not around any more? Rental period expire? You have to take him back to Pets At Home? Hope they don't mind him coming back with a few—'

'Stop talking,' says Smith. 'I'm not here for banter.' So. He obviously has no patience for my particular brand of sparkling wit. Hopefully that'll come in handy because it's about the only weapon I have at the moment.

I smile apologetically. 'Oh. Sorry. I must have got the wrong end of the stick, I thought that was why I was here. Obviously someone ballsed up the booking. How embarrassing. I can get going if you want—'

'You don't understand, do you?' he says. 'I can do anything to you that I want. Anything. And not "within reason". I'm not governed by any kind of procedural law. I am not a policeman, nor am I a government agent. I don't report to anyone. I can take you apart piece by piece until you tell me what I want to know, and nobody is going to come in here and tell me to stop. There is no-one behind a two-way mirror with one eye on your vital signs and the other on a list of dos and don'ts. This place, to all intents and purposes, does not exist.'

He's telling the truth, I know he is, and now I'm really scared. I hear Freeman's words echoing in head. *In all my time with the Group, few ever worried me. Smith frightened me. He is a ruthless, back-stabbing, self-serving psychopath.* I look down at myself. I feel so much skinnier than usual in these ill-fitting pyjamas. Completely helpless. No powers. No friends.

*No hope.*

'Where is Tara?' he says, and a hot flush of relief steams through the fear. *They're safe.*

*He doesn't know where she is.*

*They don't have her.*

I want to grin, cackle with laughter, spit in his face, but I don't. Instead, I make a decision. I've read about torture. I've seen it on TV and in films, and it's obviously going to be exactly the same in real life, hopefully, I think. I know that even the most hard-ass Navy SEAL has been known to give up everything to make it stop. Thinking about the fights I've been in, with Pandora and with Smith's pet monster, I think – *I hope* – that I have a relatively high pain threshold . . . although that's pretty much definitely because of my powers . . .

And now they're gone . . .

Either way, I have no idea what this guy is going to dish out. All I know is that he's going to use everything at his disposal to get the information out of me. And I can't give it to him. Whatever he chucks at me, I'm not going to tell him where Tara is. I'm never going to tell him. Never.

I tell myself that, but I know I can't be sure, and for a second I entertain a plan B. I remember Scott Masters, remember his sudden amnesia. Maybe I can do the same if I feel myself giving up, I can just wipe my own mind somehow . . .

Except, no. Because my powers are gone.

*Well. This is a pretty shitty state of affairs, eh old boy?*

'Sorry,' I say. '"Tara"? Doesn't ring a bell, I'm afraid. Have you tried Directory Enquiries? You'll probably need a surname, though.'

Smith doesn't bat an eyelid. He hits me in the stomach, driving all the breath out of me, and I choke on nothing, heaving. When I get my breath back I look up at him and smile. 'So,' I manage to say. 'While we're chatting . . . this is one of those black sites I've heard so much about, presumably? Experimental torture techniques? Gitmo reimagined by Lovecraft?'

'Lovewho?' says Smith.

'Jesus. Philistine.'

'I don't get much time to watch films.'

'He was an author, you jeb end.'

Smith frowns. '"Jeb end"?'

'Something they say back home. I haven't got a clue what it means.'

'Oh.' Smith hits me again. He follows it up with a sigh, as if he's not entirely sure he can be bothered to spend the rest of his day doing this. I sympathise. 'In answer to your question,' he says, 'no, this is not one of those black sites you've heard about. This is the White Room.'

I frown. '"The White Room"? Like in *Angel?*'

'*Angel?*'

'*Buffy* spinoff? Set in LA? Best series finale ever? I guess you don't watch much TV either.'

As expected, he hits me again. 'Those sites are just rumours. Rumours we allow to spread.'

'Rumours you *allow* to spread?' I spit on the floor. 'Why?'

'To scare any conspiracy-minded idiots who might think of investigating,' says Smith. 'And to further discredit said conspiracy-minded idiots in the eyes of anybody else who may come across their horseshit online.' He leans in. 'Trust me – White Rooms are much worse than anything you might have heard about.'

'Oh, goody.'

'Where is Tara?'

'Where are my friends?'

'I'll find her eventually, you know. So you might as well tell me.'

'I'll find my friends eventually, so *you* might as well tell *me*.'

'Your friends.' Smith snorts. 'Your cohorts in the century's most pathetic terrorist attack. I'm afraid they won't be bursting in here to rescue you. Thomas Maguire is dead, as you know. David Silver should be by now, he was certainly shot enough times.'

'David who?'

'I believe you know him as "Box".' Smith doesn't seem impressed by the nickname. My stomach sinks.

*No. No time for grief.* 'Where are the others?' I ask. 'Lauren?'

'The pretty ginger one?' This time there is amusement in his smile, but it's a twisted amusement, like thorns that have learned to laugh. Dread drops through me like an anvil, all the way to the bottom of my stomach.

'What did you do to her?' I say. 'Did you kill her?'

'Of course not,' he says. 'Far too valuable. We hooked her up to one of our machines. She's proving to be a great boost to the power supply.'

I lose it for a minute, thrashing against my straps and shouting with rage, spitting the foulest profanities that I can muster. Smith just watches me, utterly unimpressed. 'As for your spy,' he says, 'your mole . . .'

*Who?*

*Nailah's contact?*

Smith looks interested now. 'Did you even know him?'

I don't answer.

'Did you even know his *name*?'

Again I say nothing, staring defiantly at him. Smith laughs. It's the sort of laugh whose owner you'd kick out of your house if they tried it at a dinner party. 'Well, if you're interested, his name was Stephen Lee. And your friend Nailah, along with your extremely impressive cousin Edward, did manage to reach him, even after "Box" took the aforementioned bullets. They found Mr Lee just in time for one of our soldiers to shoot him in the back of the head.'

I close my eyes.

'Did you really think we wouldn't see this coming?' asks Smith. 'You think someone can betray our organisation, passing on secrets and information, without our knowledge? And what did you think the punishment would be? Suspension? Docked wages? We're fighting for the *world*.'

'So are we.'

He snorts. 'You have no idea what's happening. And you're lucky we caught you and your pathetic crew before you could do any real damage.'

*Whatever mate.*

'All this,' says Smith, 'all this risk, to yourselves, to the world, and for what? To steal some data? Rescue a single empowered?

An empowered who is here by *choice*, might I add. A willing participant.'

*Who is he on about?* 'Willing? Yeah, pull the other one, it's got—'

'Shut up,' he says, irritably. 'Let me state this very clearly – your incessant quipping is in no way charming. It does not disarm me. In fact, it actually makes me want to hurt you more.'

'Oh,' I say. 'OK. Would you prefer it if I was the gritty reboot version of myself?' I adopt an over-the-top frown and a strained Christian Bale growl. 'Willing? Yeah, pull the other one, it's not wearing hockey pads.' I blow a raspberry, and although Smith responds with a particularly hefty punch, I like to think that I won that exchange.

'I will admit,' Smith continues, 'that some needed to be coerced. It's a shame, but it's a necessary evil. The one you came here to rescue, however? Sally Daniels? One hundred per cent willing. Terrified of her power. Your friend Nailah was convinced otherwise.'

*Sally Daniels? Who . . .*

*Nailah . . .*

*Lauren's friend? Is that who . . .*

A whole shower of pennies drop, although I take great pains not to show it.

He doesn't know why we were really here.

*He doesn't know we know.*

I decide to play along by saying nothing. 'She must be special,' says Smith, 'to go to all this trouble.'

'Yeah,' I say. 'Love Sally. She's great.'

'Well, she won't be going anywhere any time soon,' says Smith. 'Neither will Lauren. And neither will you. And the rest of your allies will suffer. Just wait and see what we do to that traitor Freeman.' He smiles that ghastly smile again. 'I'm a big believer in zero-tolerance policies.'

*You have never met a liar like Smith. That's what Freeman said. Don't trust a word he says, not a single word.*

I'm actually thinking quite fondly of Freeman at this point.

*Wow. Things must be bad.*

I say nothing. I have to take this. Absorb it, file it away. Not think about Lauren hooked up to one of those awful machines, not think about Nailah watching her friend die.

I just have to think that *some of them made it out.* They must have. Eddie, Nailah, Daryl, Sharon . . . they must have escaped, because if they hadn't he would be telling me about it. He'd enjoy crushing me with it.

Smith must think that that's enough for now, because he nods to some invisible eye and there is that flash again, that retina-slashing blast. I don't know whether I black out or what, my brain is too scrambled, but when my vision returns Smith is standing in the corner of the room and the floor in front of me is covered with spiders. All different types: fat hairy-legged sods, translucent spindly buggers, the sneaky sly bastards that like to appear without warning from underneath sofas, beds and piles of paper when you're not expecting them, all moving towards me, little aliens.

*Oh God.*

My skin is erupting in goosebumps, crawling. Words cannot express how much I hate spiders. I always have. They're the single most freakish thing ever to evolve on this planet. Give me a giant blue hellhound any day.

*God. No.*

'Where is she?' Smith asks again.

*This isn't pain.*

What he's giving me isn't pain.

*This is fear.*

It's psychological.

All in the brain.

And I'm *king* of my brain.

They're harmless.

*Apart from the poisonous ones.*

But surely he wouldn't be introducing poison this early? He doesn't want me dead. He wants Tara's location, he's going to keep me alive for as long as humanly possible. Ergo, none of these spiders are poisonous.

*But that's not the point, is it?*

The first ones are at my feet. 'Where is Tara?' he asks again.

I look at him, and say nothing. 'I can get rid of them easily,' says Smith.

'I adore the natural world,' I say. 'And all of God's beautiful creatures.'

*Close your eyes, Stanly.*

*Close your eyes and think of Kloe.*

I keep my outer eyes closed, and my inner eyes fixed on Tara and Kloe's faces, happily playing a game in the cabin, eating together. I picture taking Tara to the fair, to the cinema, something normal. Buying her popcorn. I try to feel Kloe's touch on my skin, rather than . . .

*Rather than nothing, all right? There is literally nothing to feel right now.*

I can hear Smith's voice still, somewhere far away. 'Where is Tara?'

That's a good question. Where *is* Tara? Let's see, shall we? I picture the three of us, out walking by the dams about twenty miles from Tref-y-Celwyn, on the most impossibly perfect sunny day, drinking in the lushness, the breathtaking views. I see Tara skimming stones. I kiss Kloe's neck and she nestles against me as we watch our daughter.

'Where *is* she, Stanly?'

His voice is really muffled, for some reason.

Why?

*Because of the water. Lovely water from the dams, cascading. Really loud.*

*Definitely not because I'm screaming.*

Surely he's got to realise that this isn't working. It isn't working. It isn't.

*It isn't.*

The flash comes again and I am hanging from the wall. Smith is standing front of me. There is a brief pain in my head; it lasts for about ten seconds before subsiding, but I'm pretty sure it wasn't there before. How many times can they keep blasting me unconscious?

Never mind that.

*They're gone.*

*Everything is awesome!*

*Everything is cool when you're not covered in spiders!*

'Right,' says Smith. 'Well. Worth a try.' He stares at me. 'Trust me, though, that's not half as bad as it gets.'

My voice is shaky when I speak, but I manage to level it out. 'Can I have a sandwich?'

His eyebrows twitch. 'Hmm,' he says. 'Well, fear obviously isn't working. Fear on its own, anyway. I imagine you've seen quite a lot that frightened you. It's not enough.'

'Do you know what *would* be enough? A sandwich. Like . . . a fresh white baguette, bit crusty, real Welsh salted butter . . .'

'What about pain?' says Smith. 'Good old-fashioned blunt pain?'

'Nah,' I say, 'that'd be crap in a sandwich. Good old-fashioned Welsh salted butter, and fresh iceberg lettuce, and then crispy bacon and chicken breast with a hint of garlic. Don't worry if you haven't got any actual garlic, though. Garlic salt is fine. Or garlic butter, even. Maybe instead of the real butter . . . actually no, that'd be weird . . .'

Smith puts his head on one side, reaches into his jacket and pulls out a revolver, keeping his eyes locked on mine. 'Where is the girl?' he asks, yet again.

'Why did you send that assassin after me?'

'I didn't send an assassin after you.'

*Liar.* 'What about the blue dog?'

'I had nothing to do with that.'

*Liar liar PANTS ON FIRE.* 'Oh? Really? Never mind, then. I'll be heading off . . .'

The smile is gone and he is pressing the barrel of the gun against my right kneecap. *Oh God, no. Please . . .*

*Is this karma?*

*I didn't even shoot anyone in any knees . . .*

'Where is the girl?'

I look him straight in the face, unblinking, and he shrugs. 'Fair enough.'

BLAM!

This time I lose consciousness all by myself.

There is more. More pain, more of the same question. Smith thoughtfully bandages up my knee, and I try to think about getting my powers back. I'll be able to repair it just like that. It'll be easy. Or after I rescue Lauren, maybe she can do it for me. Then I can slowly break all of Smith's bones. Maybe even remove some.

Yeah, that'll be nice.

Smith seems to decide that I deserve a brief break, so he leaves me for a bit. I want to pass out again but can't.

*This is really very unpleasant indeed.*

A memory flickers through the red, a forgotten afternoon. Falling down a hill when I was thirteen, seriously hurting my arm and jarring my back. Nothing broken, but it hurt so much to move that I didn't think I was going to be able to get up and walk home. Me being me, I'd forced myself to get up by constantly repeating *I am Federal Agent Jack Bauer and this is the longest day of my life* in my head, and walked all the way home in severe pain with those words echoing through my mind. It was a technique I adopted for such situations for a while afterwards, whether it was an injury, bullying or whatever, and it worked surprisingly well.

I wonder if it will work today. Somehow I doubt it, but it's worth a try.

*What would Kiefer Sutherland do if he were in my position?*

*Probably be in a lot of pain. He isn't really Jack Bauer, you know.*

*Lies. Lies. I have detected your lies.*

This banter with myself is almost helping to avoid the pain.

*It really isn't.*

*Close your eyes and think of Kiefer Sutherland.*

*I bet he's just as tough as Jack Bauer. If not tougher. I mean, have you seen that video where he jumps on the Christmas tree? What a nutter.*

*Yeah,* says Daryl's voice. *Proper mentalist.*

*Ah. Missed you, pal.*

*Don't think of Lauren. Don't think of your friends. Don't think of Kl- I SAID DON'T THINK OF HER THAT MEANS HER NAME AS WELL, OK?*

Smith is back, regarding me clinically. 'You've been shot before, haven't you?'

I speak through gritted teeth. 'Yep. Turns out it's more fun the second time. Who knew?'

He allows me another one of those quarter smiles. 'Well you're in luck. We've taken your powers, but they leave a . . . residue. An extra toughness, better pain resistance. This is good for me, because it means I can shoot you at least twice more if you don't tell me what I want to know. And then I'm going to move on to some slightly less humane methods.'

'What, send Morrissey in to give me a lecture on vegetarianism?' I'm slurring a bit. 'You *monster*.'

That actually seems to inspire a genuine smile. It's kind of worse than his other smile. 'The funny thing is,' Smith says, 'that I could probably have him here within an hour. But then I'd have to kill him to keep him quiet.'

'Do us all a favour. Bring Bono as well. We'll have ourselves a party.' Smith swims briefly in my vision, and I blink hard to focus. 'Do you do a lot of this?' I ask. 'Torturing people? Is it a hobby? Or are you just one of those really committed ends-means-justified types?'

'I do what is necessary.'

'That's pretty much what I expected you to say.'

'Don't presume to judge me,' says Smith. 'You have no idea what I've seen in my time with the Angel Group. What I've had to do. What has been *necessary*.'

'Is *this* . . .' I look down at my bandaged knee, '*really* necessary?'

'Was it necessary for you to burst into our top secret facilities?' says Smith. 'You think that because you have some special abilities, normal rules no longer apply to you? That you are suddenly the highest authority, answerable to no-one, above the law?'

'Um, as the kettle in this situation, might I remind you, the pot, that you're currently torturing me in some off-the-books black site, rather than arresting me and letting me speak to a solicitor? You want to talk "above the law" . . .' Shame I couldn't properly work 'black site' into the kettle-pot analogy, but I forgive myself on account of all the torture. It doesn't matter anyway, Smith's smile is gone and the barrel of his gun is against my left thigh. 'You're going to tell me where the girl is.'

'Has this ever even *worked*?' I ask. 'Torture? Has it ever yielded positive results?'

His eyes flicker. 'It has in the past.'

'Oh. Well. That's OK then.'

'Where is the girl?'

'Last I heard,' I say, 'she was sitting on a beach, earning twenty per cent.'

BLAM.

The same routine. Pain. Bandage. Some kind of injection. 'Why do you keep patching me up?'

'Because I don't want you to bleed to death,' says Smith, as though I'm stupid. 'Yet. You're tough, I'll give you that, but not that tough.' He stands back. 'I can make you a deal.'

'Really? That's very nice of you.'

'Tell me where the girl is,' he says, 'and I'll kill you.'

'Not the most enticing deal I've ever heard, if I'm honest.'

'If you *don't* tell me where she is, you're going to suffer the same fate as your friend Lauren. I'll plug you into our machine. Living death.'

'You're going to do that anyway,' I say, my vision clouding and unclouding.

He smiles because he definitely is going to do that anyway. 'Correct.'

'Why do you want her so much, anyway? I mean, she's *great* company and all, but . . . she's just a little one.' *Does he want her for her power? Are they going to plug her in?*

*No.*

*They're not.*

*Not ever.*

*So grit your teeth, kiddo.*

*Do it for her.*

Smith doesn't answer my last query, he just motions to an unseen individual. 'Give him one hundred volts.'

We try electricity for a bit, which is a whole new, exciting world of not fun. Through the pain, insofar as I can form proper thoughts, I'm actually kind of impressed with myself. I imagine Miss Stevenson from school pinning a medal to my chest, a gold star for being the world's bravest drama student.

*Why Miss Stevenson?*

*Why not? Have you ever been tortured?*

*Well, yeah. I'm being tortured right now.*

*Well, exactly. So you should know that logical thought processes are not necessarily forthcoming.*

*Fair enough.*

*Who am I even talking to . . .*

*Me. Yourself.*

*But if you're me, and I'm yourself, then WHO WAS PHONE. It's coming from INSIDE THE STANLY.*

*Haha.*

*Ha.*

*I'm so screwed.*

'Where is the girl?' asks Smith.

'The Dragon Tattoo Parlour,' I say. 'Mos Eisley. Kentucky Fried Chicken. Old Trafford. Get knotted, you anus.'

*Haha.*

*I said 'anus'.*

More electricity, and I black out again. When I wake up Smith is nodding. 'I'm impressed,' he says. 'I really am. I never would have thought that someone your age could stand this. But it's finished, Stanly. Tell me where she is.'

'Noooope.'

'Tell me. I can offer you some relief.'

I snigger. '*Phrasing.*'

Smith grimaces, reins himself in, then speaks again, calm and thoughtful, as if working out how to approach a tricky piece of DIY. 'You're right-handed, aren't you?'

Coincidentally, this is the moment that I realise he's holding a chainsaw.

'Woah,' I say, lapsing into a kind of squashed Texan accent. 'Woah, woah. Hold on there, sport. You want to be careful with power tools, they can be kinda tricksy, y'know, could have someone's eye out . . .' *At which point it stops being funny.*

'Where is the girl?'

'She . . . is . . . somewhere. In the world . . . place. Probs.'

He revs it. The noise is rusty, eager, like a Rottweiler desperate to be let loose. 'Where is the girl, Stanly?'

'Are you sure you don't want to know anything else?' I ask. Inside I'm panicking, but my mouth can only manage a kind of detached, lethargic drawl, which I guess works with the whole nonchalant angle, although it's probably not going to inspire Smith to put away his chainsaw, and oh my good Christ he's actually going to use a chainsaw on me. This is what I get for leaving Wales. 'I could tell you where some other girls are, maybe,' I say. 'I know where . . . dunno . . . at least three *completely* different girls . . . might be. Locations. Yeah?'

He revs it again and gets it going properly, chugging, growling. 'Where is she? This is the last time.'

I look at him, trying to focus. 'Last orders,' I mumble. 'Mine's a JD and Coke on the rocks. Hold the rocks. And the JD. And probably the Co—'

He brings it down.

It feels weird.

There's a redness that reminds me of the Black Knight in *Monty Python*.

Someone, possibly me, is telling me to *not look down* . . .

Someone else, probably Smith, is asking me where a girl is, some girl or other.

A girl?

Like I've got time to know where any girls are right now.

What a berk. What a silly man Smith is. He really is.

I wish I could talk.

I'd say all the words I knew that described him.

I'd tell him about all the things I've heard about his mother.

I'd . . .

I'm . . .

I'm standing in the corner.

I blink. There I am, in the corner of the room, fully-dressed, smiling. I'm flickering like bad reception, but I can see myself. And I'm fine. It's . . .

*It's the pain.*

*But* . . . no. I recognise the smile. I can see it in my memory, through the crimson blur of blood and bullets. I can . . . it's . . .

Stanly.

Stanly smiling . . . with my mouth . . . with my face . . .

Smith's voice. Shouting now. 'I'm losing patience! *Where is my daughter?*'

Stanly smiling with my smile.

And . . .

What does he mean? *My daughter* . . .

I can speak.

'She's *mine*,' I say.

The other me . . . can he speak?

'I'm afraid she isn't, Stanly.'

She . . . I . . .

Why am I looking at myself?

Smith: 'Wait a minute . . . no. No! He can see it!'

I can speak with Stanly's voice. Through the horror, I can speak. 'No,' I whisper.

'For Christ's sake, you're supposed to *keep the damn thing under control!*'

'No.' Louder. 'No.'

'You—'

'She's MINE!' I bellow, in Stanly's voice. My brain expands. The Stanly in the corner explodes, flying apart like broken glass, glowing fragments filling the room, a blinding flash. Morter Smith flies backwards, hitting the wall, and I can feel the pain wriggling back inside my body like worms escaping into the dirt, burrowing underground, spilled blood returning to ruptured veins and arteries. I flex the fingers of my right hand. Still attached. I move my leg. No pain in the knee.

*All in my head.*

I'm lying on my back. This isn't the White Room. This is somewhere else.

*All in my head . . .*

I sit up, broken straps falling away from my wrists and ankles.

*Right.*

*Now I'm CROSS.*

# Chapter Twenty-One

AN ALARM SQUEALS, cutting my head in half. I blink. *Reality? Is that you?*

*No-one's listening.*

*Hahaha.*

*Hmm. Don't like the sound of that laugh.*

I look around. I'm on a low metal table in the centre of another square room, although it's smaller and grubbier than the White Room. The floor and ceiling are dark grey, as are all but one of the walls; the other is transparent, with a door at one end, and I can see what looks like a control room beyond, with banks of computers and monitors and some white-suited technicians scrambling to their feet. Morter Smith is there, slumped against the wall, unmoving.

*OK.*

I slide off the table and my eye catches something, a flicker at the edge of my vision. Lying on the floor by the head of the table is a shimmer. It's twitching. I don't think it's dead . . . it's not vanishing like the other one . . .

*That's all it was.*

*A shimmer . . .*

I look down at myself, at my hands. I can feel the echoes of the pain, the spiders, but there are no scars. I seem to be whole, mostly.

I look at the door and think *open*.

It doesn't open.

'No,' I say. I try again, but it doesn't budge. 'No!' I look at the table and think *overturn*. It ignores me, just sits there, a useless object. *Like me.*

*No no no no NO.*

A voice comes over some hidden intercom: 'Stand down.' I ignore it and stare at the table, concentrating. Why isn't it moving?

*Did they really take my powers?*

No. They didn't. They couldn't have. Morter Smith didn't break my restraints for me, did he? He didn't hurl himself against the wall. It was all an illusion. Psychic wool pulled over all my eyes, inner and outer, the lies of the shimmer. I'm just not concentrating hard enough, my brain still thinks that the lie is real. Got to *break it. Focus. Hawk stare. Laser-guided missile. Hyper-aware mega-badass ESP targeting module. Focus. Concentrate.*

CONCENTRATE.

The table doesn't move.

'*FUCK YOU, YOU STUPID TABLE!*' I yell.

The table flies towards the transparent wall and smashes through it, showering the terrified technicians and Smith with glass. The sound of cascading fragments is almost nice, like a slightly de-tuned xylophone falling down a hole. I smile. 'There we go.'

Two security guards burst into the control room and raise their guns in my direction. I barely even need to think, the table just flies back into the air and pummels both of them to the ground, and I rise and float through into the control room, holding the technicians and the guards down. Several more guards arrive but the barrels of their guns are already bending, creaking, tying around themselves in knots, and the guards themselves are leaving the ground, flying into walls and ceilings, held there, struggling, yelling, helpless. *See how y'all like it.* I kneel down in front of Smith. He's alive, but definitely unconscious. I can still hear his words in my head. *My daughter.*

*I'm afraid she isn't, Stanly.*

'I'm not done with you yet,' I whisper. Then I stand up and take another look around. There is someone else there, cowering in the corner by a big buzzing console. A boy, maybe my age, in a heavy green coat . . . I stare at him, my dazed brain turning over and over. 'You,' I say. 'From Blue Harvest, and . . .' I frown. 'They got you too?'

He doesn't answer, just looks at me. Frightened . . . but . . . not? *He's not tied up. He's just . . . there.* 'You're . . . you're with them?' I say. He doesn't speak. 'Who are you?' Still no answer. 'Do you realise who these people are? Did you see what they just did to me?'

Still he says nothing, and I shake my head, fresh out of patience. 'Fine, whatever.' Another set of guards arrive, guns and truncheons drawn.

Guns bent.

Truncheons snapped.

Some legs broken, possibly.

'Not very nice, is it?' I say, shooting a quick, disgusted look at the boy, and then at the technicians. 'Pain? Fear? Profoundly un-fun, wouldn't you say? Decidedly not *bendigedig.*'

The technicians look mystified, and I roll my eyes. 'It's Welsh for "brilliant".' I beckon for effect and one of the technicians rises up from the floor, whimpering. I hold him in the air a few centimetres from my face. 'Right,' I say. 'You're going to tell me where the empowered are kept.'

'H-he,' stammers the trembling technician. 'I . . . I can't . . .' He's too scared to make sense, gibbering nonsensically.

'Fine,' I say. 'I'll find them myself.' I drop him and leave the room, emerging in a long, bare, white corridor with doors at either end. I close the door behind me, thinking *lock.* Gratifyingly, it makes a locking noise. I look to my left, then to my right, the insistent mewling of the alarm filling my brain, disrupting my thoughts, grinding, *whining*.

*WherethehelldoIgo* . . .

Despite the horrific time I've just had . . . or that I thought I had . . . I feel pumped. Buzzing. Like I did the other day. It has to be the shimmer, the after-effect. I feel like Popeye after a six-pack of spinach.

*Fun fun fun.*

*Now, left or ri—*

Some guards burst through one of the doors, making the decision for me. I think a shield, bending their bullets around me, and shove them all back through the door in a flailing pile before sprinting in the other direction. The floor is cool beneath my bare feet and I tear the next door open with my mind before I get there, barrelling straight through and colliding with a guard. We both sprawl on the floor, struggling. I feel a savage rage bubbling in my veins and headbutt him repeatedly, his face momentarily becoming Smith's sneering green-eyed death mask, but then I register his bellows of pain, not Smith's voice, and the rage is gone, and I keep running. Only one way to go. Through another door. Electronically locked or not, they all slide apart without me even needing to concentrate.

Another corridor. Everywhere looks identical.

*I don't even know where I am.*

*I could be underwater.*

*I could be in bloody* space.

*I'm probably not in bloody space.*

It's hard to believe that this is a real place. I feel like I'm in a computer game, with endless corridors and enemies to fight. More guards are closing on me from behind, and as I pass through more and more doors I instantly slam them shut behind me, my feet and heart pounding. A group of guards emerge through the door in front of me and I part them psychically, diving through, rolling, back on my feet, closing the door, *now a left turn and—*

BANG.

AAAAHASHIIIIIIIIIIITBOLLOCKSAAAAAARGHTHEY-SHOTME! The thought manifests itself as a strangled, yelping roar and I take the first door on my left, stumbling into an empty conference room, clutching my shoulder. There is only one entrance, the one I just came through, and I look at it and think *lock.* There is an encouraging series of metallic clicks and I collapse against the wall, panting. The room is dominated by a big mahogany table and I think that over to the door for luck, then look down at my wound, which is pumping blood. One stray bullet. Just one. That's all it took. Real pain now, very real, and *really* extremely incredibly bloody horrible, high and bright, disrupting my vision. I've been shot before, a long time ago, although that didn't last very long, but this is worse.

*Right, what do I do . . .*

*Tear up my shirt?*

*I've got hardly any clothes as it is.*

*Got to keep pressure on it, though . . .*

*Could use the burning trick? Like with the toast? What's the word . . . cauterise it?* I look down at the wound and try to think of fire, of burning, but I can't, I don't think I'm allowing myself, I know it'll hurt too much. Got to think of something else . . .

*Unless . . .*

I remember the safe at Connor and Sharon's. A mechanism, yes, and not alive, but I managed to get inside it with my mind and work my will. I've been opening and locking doors with ludicrous ease. And Lauren fixed my cut before. I seem to remember her saying she's done more than that, so it's obviously possible . . .

*After everything else I've done?*

*It's beneath me.*

I sit up a bit, biting my lip, and loosen my grip on my shoulder. My hand looks like it's been dunked in blood-coloured paint. *Or, alternatively, like it's been gripping a bullet wound, possibly?*

HAHA.

Focusing on not passing out, I pull down the sleeve of my papery blue shirt so I can get a proper look at the wound. It leers at me, red and black and dark and wet. If it had a voice it would be the voice of a fat, greedy man.

*That's not a helpful thought.*

*Concentrate.*

*Pain is nothing. Disgust is nothing. Just concentrate.*

*It's all about the concentration.*

I stare at the hole, moving beyond the superficiality of it, the blood and the torn flesh. I let everything else, the situation, the sound of the alarms and the guards banging on the door, fade to an indistinct background buzz, and slowly, almost lazily, I let myself fall into the wound, maintaining as much psychic pressure as possible to stem the blood flow. Won't be much use repairing myself if I've already bled out, that's science that is, biology mate . . .

*I can see the bullet.*

*Lodged . . . but not too far . . .*

*Tiny and glistening. So small. How can it cause so much damage?*

*Because it's very solid and gets fired into you at an incredibly high speed, and also flesh is weak.*

*Oh, thanks. Is that science too?*

*Grip it.*

*Like you would with tweezers.*

*Careful, careful.*

*Got it.*

*It hurts . . .*

*Ignore it.*

*Pull. Gently . . .*

I'm biting my lip so hard that I can taste copper. *Concentrate.* I have a grip on the bullet, but the pain is intense and I'm feeling decidedly woozy.

*No. This is not a good idea.*

I decide to leave the bullet. It'll just mean more bleeding, and I'll probably pass out from the pain. I learned that from films, I think.

*So . . . straight to surgery . . .*

*The easy bit!*

I giggle, not a little hysterically, and look back into the wound. *Concentrate again.* I have to see into the microscopic fibres and molecules and tiny twisting creepers of matter that make up my flesh, my skin, and I have to bend them, shape them. At first nothing happens. *Damn it. Focus. Concentrate.* See into myself. See what I'm made of. I try not to concentrate on the sound of the enemy, surely they'll be through the door any minute . . .

CONCENTRATE. The damn word will be on my tombstone.

I can see the fibres, I can *feel* them. I close my eyes and will them to grow. My wound is starting to feel itchy, weird on top of the pain. I open my eyes and it's just like when Lauren was fixing my cut, like watching the wound happen in reverse, it slowly gets smaller, paler and paler, the blood flow lessening, thinning out, and suddenly it's gone and there's just new bare flesh, and I feel light-headed but also elated.

*Like I said. Beneath me.*

It still hurts like hell, though.

*Probably 'cos there's a bullet in there, still.*

*Oh well. Never mind, eh?*

I'm back in the conference room, back in reality. Voices and batterings against the door. Surely they should have unlocked it by now? Maybe my mental lock is too strong. That's encouraging. Seems like they're not interested in taking me alive anymore, which suits me fine, but just me against every single soldier in this base, as well as whatever monsters they might have at their disposal? I don't particularly love my chances.

*Or do I?*

*Shut up. First order of business is to find out where I am.* This room doesn't seem likely to give up any clues, there isn't even a computer; aside from the table and chairs there's just a projector and a flat white screen. I look up. There is a silver grille up there that presumably gives way to a ventilation shaft. I wonder . . . it might be a possibility . . .

New sounds from outside. Screams. Shouting.

'What the hell?'

'What are you doing?'

'You're not—'

Then the sound of heavy blows, painful impacts, bodies hitting walls, a few gunshots . . . and silence. I wish I could see through doors. I stand motionless, trying to decide what to do. It could be a trap . . . but it didn't sound like it. It doesn't *feel* like it. Too sudden, too brutal. Maybe I've got an ally? Another escapee? Or . . .

*Eddie? Maybe Eddie's come to help me?*

I decide to open the door, but I'm ready. The second anything tries to attack me, I'll strike. I manage an approximation of a martial arts stance, just because it makes me feel more threatening, push the table aside and I think *unlock* and *open*. Click, click, and a metallic purr as the door slides open and I nearly have a heart attack. The multi-tentacled yellow monster that recently battered me senseless is standing just outside the door, watching me, rustling and glistening disgustingly. I shudder, but for some reason I'm not as afraid as I feel I should be. Maybe because it's not doing anything, it's just standing still. Maybe because of all the unconscious guards scattered around it. Is it . . . it can't be *helping* me?

*Blatantly it's escaped, turned on its captors . . .*

I don't care. I owe this thing some pain. For some reason my lips decide to smile, and I raise my arms. 'Come on, then, if you think yer 'ard enough.'

It doesn't do anything. It doesn't even try to get through the door, it just regards me with all its horrible eyes for a few more seconds before walking backwards down the corridor. I stand like an uncertain lemon for a moment then gingerly walk after it, stepping over the many sleeping soldiers and quickly thinking multiple *locks* so no-one can burst into the corridor. I'd rather deal with this weird beast right now than get shot again. *What is it doing?* It just stands silently . . . and I notice that it's carrying something on its back among all the constantly-shifting tentacles. I squint to get a better look and see a familiar green coat. The kid. The thing has him. I'm not particularly keen on this guy because he seems to be one of the enemy, but I'm not about to let this piece of Lovecraftian livestock eat him, so I beckon. 'Come on! Let's 'ave it!'

The creature starts to walk towards me and all the adrenaline in my body ignites, ready for the inevitable violence, but it doesn't attack, it simply lifts the boy in the coat from its back with its tentacles, deposits him gently on the ground next to me and trots into the conference room I've just vacated, as calm as a well-trained pet. It goes and sits in the corner and stares at me again. I'm thoroughly confused at this point. I close and lock the door and look down at the boy. He opens his eyes and at the same time I hear the beast start to jump and thrash around in the other room, knocking over furniture, going completely berserk, whining all the time in its skin-crawling alien falsetto. I look from the door to the boy. 'Should I let you stand up?' I say.

308

'I'm not working with them.' His voice and accent are as neutral as his expression.

'Prove it.'

'I did some damage back there,' he says. 'Broke some stuff. Think the intercom's off.'

'Oh you did, did you? Pull the other one.'

'They made me use that thing to attack you before,' he says, sitting up and rubbing his eyes. 'I took it over again just now, but I knew that as soon as I gave up control it would attack. So I put it in there.'

'You . . .' I frown. 'You were . . . *controlling* that?'

The boy nods. 'Yes. Animals are my . . . it's what I do.'

'That *thing*'s not an animal.'

'Yes it is. Are you going to let me stand up?'

'I don't know. Why should I? You were controlling it when it beat the living crap out of me. To all intents and purposes, *you* beat the living crap out of me. So I don't see why I shouldn't beat the living crap out of *you* in return.'

'I didn't know all the facts when I did that. I thought you were the bad guy.'

'Well, I'm not.'

'Neither am I.'

*I'm still not letting you up.* 'What's your name?' I ask.

'Alex. You're Stanly.'

'Yeah, I know. Smith told you I was the enemy, I presume?'

'Yes,' says Alex. 'He was pretty convincing. And all I've really seen of you so far is chucking stuff about and fighting people. Seemed legit.'

'We'll see about that.' I think for a second. 'Why were you at Blue Harvest the other day?'

'I was with the patrol. Smith said he wanted me to see the effect that you and your friends were having on the city . . . the soldiers thought that I might be able to take you by surprise, better than they could. Said you'd be expecting soldiers, not me. So they let me into the club.'

'You were controlling that dog too?' I remember him diving out of sight, the dog's behaviour suddenly changing from docile quiet to snarling fury.

'I thought you were going to kill me,' says Alex.

'Fair,' I say. Soldiers are hammering at the doors at either end of the corridor. 'And you were there the other day, when the blue dog appeared.'

'Practice,' says Alex. 'I can . . . I can sort of sense when monsters are going to appear. I feel it. Felt that one coming, thought I might try taking it over. But then you were there, fighting it . . . I sort of forgot.'

'You *forgot?*'

'I was watching you fight,' said Alex. 'Got . . . distracted.'

'Great. Would have been handy if you *had* taken it over. Thing nearly ate me.' *Also, hmm, guess maybe Smith didn't send the Blue Meanie afer me. Gee, I owe that guy an apology.*

'Sorry. I've never seen someone who can fly.'

I shrug. 'So you don't know anything about the Group's bigger plan? Why they want the girl?' That suddenly brings me rocketing back to Smith's words, words that had briefly faded in the chaotic supernova of what-the-fuckery exploding in my mind. *Where is my daughter? My daughter,* he'd said.

*She can't be his.*

'Sorry,' said Alex. 'I don't know anything—'

'Why did Smith say she's his daughter?' I say. 'That's impossible. She's *mine.*'

'I *told* you I don't know anything about it. I don't even know who you're talking about.'

I shake my head. 'It's impossible.' *Leave it for now. Worry about escape.*

'Sorry,' says Alex again. He doesn't sound sorry.

'You don't know what's going on.' I shake my head again. 'I don't believe you, I'm afraid. This couldn't be more of a trap.' I mentally lift him off the ground and hold him against the wall, staring straight into his eyes.

'Let me down!' he says. There's something in his eyes, beneath his quiet demeanour. Something almost feral. He's dangerous.

*Makes two of us.*

'No,' I say. 'The Group really thinks I'm that bone-headed? That I'm going to make instant friends with someone who's been present at most of my most recent beatings, just 'cos he happens to say he's not working with them any more? What proof have I got? None.'

'I swear,' says Alex. 'I'm not with them. Not now. Not after . . .'

'After watching them torture me? Turned your stomach? Diddums.' I slam him against the wall, harder perhaps than I intended, or perhaps not, because I'm very angry. 'Maybe they were right, telling you I'm the enemy. These people have consistently dumped industrial skips full of shit on me and my friends. Tried to kill us. Now they definitely *have* killed at least two. So I'm not particularly inclined to trust anyone right now. I'm sure you understand.'

'I understand,' says Alex. 'I swear. But you need to believe me. You've got barely any allies. I've got *no* allies. We need each other.'

'I've been getting on just fine without possessing animals, thanks.'

'I took out all these guards!' Alex gestures at the unconscious bodies filling the corridor.

That almost approaches a good point. I relax my hold and he drops to his feet, looking like he really wants to hit me. I kind of want him to try. He doesn't, though, he just stands there, and

I grin. 'Go ahead,' I say. 'Smack me if it makes you feel better.'
*Yeah, that'll help matters.*

*Kind of past caring.*

'They lied to me,' says Alex. 'OK? They told me that you and your friends were out to destroy the city. That your powers were out of control. Smith said that if I helped them, they'd do something for me in return.'

'What?'

His eyes drop to the floor. 'None of your business.'

'Business my arse. What did they offer you?'

'I said none of your *business*, all right?' There's a new blaze behind his eyes. 'Just . . . believe me. It was something I really want. Wanted. And just now, after you left . . . Smith woke up. He was furious. And he told me I was useless and that the deal was off. And that I was lucky he didn't have me killed.' Against my better judgment, I'm starting to believe him. 'So I found that monster and took it over and came to find you. I get that you don't trust me. I wouldn't if I was you. And just because I trust you more than I trust them doesn't mean I actually trust you. We just . . . we both need to get over it.'

I take a moment to think about that. *Could still be a trap.*

*If he tries anything he's easily taken down. Look at him, he's barely taller than you are.*

*And he's got that animal thing . . .*

*He might come in useful.*

*Plus, when he mentioned what the Angel Group offered him . . . that look in his eyes . . .*

*I've gone on looks in people's eyes before. Often it means sod all.*

Grudgingly I nod and offer my hand. We shake gingerly. 'OK,' I say. 'Now where the hell are we?'

'Underground somewhere, near their secondary research site.'

This is music to my ears and immediately my brain begins to whirl a very basic plan into shape. 'Good.'

'Why?'

'Where are the empowered kept? Which direction?'

Alex points down the corridor. 'That way. It's pretty far, but . . .'

'Get your monster under control,' I say. 'We're going to set them free and destroy that place.'

His eyes widen. 'Destroy the drawing area? Why?'

*The drawing area . . . name makes sense, I suppose.* 'Do you even know what they're doing in there?' I ask.

'Not exactly . . . just that they're drawing power from the test subjects . . .'

'And using it to bust a hole in reality,' I say. 'A bloody great big one that's most likely going to destroy the world. And they're not *test subjects,* by the way, they're people who have been kidnapped and tortured.' *Except for the ones who might have chosen to be there?*

*Oh yeah, those ones. The ones* Smith *told you about. Don't be an idiot.*

'Now you see why we wanted to destroy the sites in the first place,' I say. 'Why I was captured. I don't know if any of my friends are even still alive, but the least I can do is finish what we started. Get the beast, now.'

Alex nods slowly. 'OK. Look . . . when I take over an animal, my body just lies there. Still alive but . . . no mind. No consciousness.'

That makes me shiver. 'That must be weird.'

He shrugs. 'It's dangerous. For my body. Can you try and make sure I don't get shot while I'm controlling it?'

'Yeah. What happens if your body dies while you're in the thing? Do you know?'

For a nanosecond there is a dark flash across his face, a look that reminds me of the one Lauren wore when I asked her about her past. The poison of memories too painful to bury, grief and fury. It doesn't last long but it answers my question. 'Sorry,' I say. 'Didn't . . .'

'Forget it.' He closes his eyes and instantly his body folds, becoming slack and lifeless. He breathes, but barely. It feels like it should be more unsettling than it is, but I'm too preoccupied to register it properly. I can still feel spiders' legs scuttling across my skin, raising shiversome bumps, and I keep glancing at my hand and flexing it, just to make sure it's there.

The monster has ceased its thrashing and wailing. I think *unlock* and *open* and it squeezes its bulky but oddly flexible mass through the doorway. It – *he?* – picks up the unconscious boy on the floor and wraps him up in several tentacles, laying him on its back, and I think an extra shield around him, a shield whose maintenance I assign to a tiny molecule of my mind. Enough to keep it up, not enough to be a distraction. I nod at the beast. 'Um. Lead the way, then.' Trying not to think about the weirdness of all this, I follow the monster down the corridor towards the sounds of yelling and banging.

*Here we go.*

I tell the door to open and it does. I think *blast* and the crowd behind it scatters like leaves. The monster rushes forwards and starts hammering security guards and soldiers into the walls and ceiling, cracking helmets and, I'm pretty sure, breaking a few limbs. They don't even have time to get any shots off and I'm suddenly extremely relieved to have this disgusting thing as an ally. I walk through the doorway and follow it past our disabled enemies, most of them knocked unconscious, some groaning in pain. I wonder if any are dead.

I feel less bothered about that than before.

# Chapter Twenty-Two

T HIS PLACE HAS too many damn corridors. We fight
our way through more than I can count, all of them identical and full of security, and after a while I start to feel numb,
my thought attacks damn near unconscious, instinctive. I can
almost see them, bright blue tendrils glowing from within,
wrapping around limbs and hitting stomachs and backs and
faces. The word *concentration* doesn't feel like it means much
now. Doors seem to open of their own accord, anticipating
my thoughts, and eventually we reach a new hallway, a square
silver one accessed via a much more obstinate door, and I know
we're nearly there. I can feel something nearby. Something very
powerful. There is another door at the end, with a thumbprint
scanner, and I imagine a blank clay thumb pushing into it,
moulding around the green light, creating the correct print. The
door opens and I can't resist a smile. *Could have a pretty decent
career as a bank robber when this is all over.*

The door gives way to a big hexagonal control room, the
whole far wall of which is made of glass. The place hums,
hot with technology and stress, readouts flashing on big
wall-mounted monitors, levels of something green rising and
falling, and five people spin to face us as we enter. Four of them
are white-coated technicians whose faces go dim with fear. The
fifth is someone I know very well. 'Hi Pandora,' I say.

Pandora, red-suited and shiny-haired, doesn't look as frightened as the technicians, but she seems far from pleased to see
me. 'Stanly . . .'

'Don't say a word,' I say, 'or you're dead. That goes for everyone in this room. I'm talking exploding heads.' I turn to the Alex beast. 'Hold on for a second.' I think the door closed, lock it and address the technicians. 'Seal off all entrances and exits to the drawing area. Nobody gets in. And I want all communications turned off.' One of the technicians looks at Pandora, who seems uncertain, and I feel a flash of temper, pick up an empty chair with my mind and smash it to pieces against the wall. '*Now, please.*' Pandora nods, and the trembling technician inputs something into a computer. 'Good,' I say. 'Now. Pandora. I'm shutting this place down and you're not stopping me.'

'I—'

'*Quiet.*' Another bubble of anger bursts, white hot, and she shrinks back a little. 'Sorry,' I say. 'Not in the best mood. Apart from anything else, there's a bullet in my shoulder. Now, is that the drawing area down there?' I point through the window and she nods. 'Good. Take me to it. And while we're at it, you've got some explaining to do.'

Pandora walks over to a door at the far side of the room, shaking and sweating, and inputs a code. The red light above the door turns green and it slides open. I turn to the Alex thing. 'Stay here until I call for you. Keep them in check.' I gesture for Pandora to continue and follow her through to a semicircular balcony. I walk to the guard rail and have to grab it to hold myself steady.

*Woah.*

The room is vast, as long as a football pitch, and most of the floor is covered by rows upon rows of people on high-tech hospital beds, still and colourless as corpses, covered in winking, ghostly lights. Each has a blue sheet stretching from just below their necks to their ankles, and they are all hooked up to monitors with multiple drips feeding them a variety of fluids, some clear, some dark. At the head of each bed is a bigger computer hooked up to the subjects' temples and various areas on their limbs and chests. I nudge Pandora with a thought. 'Keep walking.'

We follow a spiral stairway to the floor and take in the sleeping people, some of them young and fairly healthy-looking, some fading and decrepit, their veins clearly visible. I keep scanning across them, men and women, young and old, black, white, bearded, bald, and notice something else. Around each head, *hugging* them, are what seem to be bubbles, soft transparent hazes that ripple slightly every now and then.

'Shimmers,' I say. 'How . . . what are they doing?'

'They . . . they feed on psychic energy,' she says, managing to keep her voice pretty level. 'It's the essence of the power we use. The shimmer processes the power, and it's transferred through them into the machinery.' She nods upwards and I follow her eyes. What I thought were just big circular ceiling lights are actually rotating slowly, their light pulsating, throbbing. That feeling I was getting outside, the suggestion of power, the air in here is *thick* with it. It's intoxicating, a constant subtle headrush. 'They, in turn, focus the energy to break through to the other world.'

'The other world . . . the shimmer world? Is that where you got the shimmers? Did you abduct them?'

'They've been coming through for years,' says Pandora. 'Driven by curiosity.'

'And the people . . . how are they alive?'

'The shimmers. As well as feeding on thought, they produce it. Visions, dreams, nightmares, anything. They tap into your memory, your fears, your desires, feeding you a constant river of information. The brain is constantly digesting the information, so there is always energy, always power for the shimmer to withdraw and transfer. Perpetual motion.'

I feel sick. 'So they're all just dreaming. Forever.'

'Essentially,' said Pandora. 'It also creates a kind of stasis for the body, slowing down all functions, metabolism . . . effectively, they are in comas, regulated by our systems, chemicals and the natural abilities of the shimmers.' She looks at me. 'Stanly—'

'Shut. Up.' It's taking most of my concentration to stay still, to not double over and puke acid on the floor. I want to destroy it all, this whole place. I manage to compose myself, breathing deeply, and turn to Pandora, fists clenched. 'What happens if they wake up?'

'Most of these subjects have been here for at least two years,' says Pandora. 'Studies and experiments suggest that there would be . . . problems.'

'What kind of problems?'

'A sudden release of power . . . they would be extremely confused, both mentally and physically. In worst case scenarios, they could be left as vegetables . . . or insane.'

*Just like Freeman said.*

I don't know what to do. I have to let them all go, I *have* to . . . but it might kill them.

*Or worse.*

I round on Pandora. 'Why do this? Why torture us?'

'I'm sure you wouldn't believe me if I told you that many of these people were volunteers,' says Pandora.

*What?* 'Smith said that,' I say. 'I figured he was lying.'

'He tells many lies,' says Pandora. 'That wasn't one of them.'

I don't want to believe her . . . but part of me does. 'Who the hell would volunteer for this?'

'The precise nature of the experiment was left . . . vague,' says Pandora. 'But you'd be surprised what lost, hopeless people will sign up to. I'm sure it's not a stretch for you to believe that many who manifest powers end up alone, drifting, afraid to make connections. We made it our business to track them down. Many came willingly.'

'And the others?'

She shrugs. 'Not so willingly.'

I shake my head, trying to keep my anger under control, wanting to bounce her around the room. 'But *why*? Why do it? The world is falling apart. Monsters, black snow, and . . . why? For power? Bloody *power*? Explain it to me. Please.'

Pandora is quiet for a few seconds, then speaks slowly. 'The monsters . . . the atmospheric disturbances . . . unavoidable side effects.' She shakes her head. 'What I told you when we first met was true. Saving the world has always been the priority. Once we *have* the power, imagine how things will change! Think of how strong you are. Imagine what could be done with that strength on a global scale. It could be the beginning of the future. A *better* future. And if London has to suffer some climatic disruption and a few extra monsters which are easily taken down by either an empowered or simply a few people with big enough guns, then so be it.'

'So be it,' I repeat. 'I thought as much.'

'Stanly—'

'Tell the technicians to turn then off.'

'I can't—'

'You're going to do it.' I think *rise* and *grip* and Pandora floats several feet off the ground, clutching at her throat. 'Tell them,' I say. 'I know you want to survive. I know you'd rather survive and fail than die for your cause. I *know* you. Tell the technicians to turn off the machines.'

'I . . .' she gurgles. 'I can only switch off these machines, there's still the primary—'

'My next stop. Do it.' She doesn't speak, and I feel the volcano inside me erupt again. '*TELL THEM!*'

'All right! All right . . . let me go!'

I do and she drops to her knees, rubbing her neck. Then she looks up towards the control room and calls out in a strangled voice. 'Turn off the drawing machines! That is an order!'

I can see the technicians. They all look terrified, confused, but they start pressing buttons. Across the room bright blues and greens start to become red or wink out altogether, like a sea of dying Christmas lights. The all-pervading buzz and hum of machinery grinds down to silence, stillness, and the great circular devices on the ceiling stop rotating, although they continue to glow. 'It's done,' Pandora whispers.

'Right.'

*Now for these shimmers.*

I don't know how I know what I'm doing. I don't even know *what* I'm doing. I look out at this living cemetery, spectral faces frozen in projected dreams, and I feel like I should be sobbing and pounding my chest, but I'm not. I just close my eyes and think *wake up* and suddenly I'm not in my head any more, I'm like vapour, and my thoughts are coruscating silver threads moving in and out of the aisles of beds, through the hearts of the shimmering parasites and into the deepest chasms inside the empowered, their sleeping souls.

A woman's voice. *'Throw me the ball again!'*

A man's. *'This is my favourite.'*

The smell of incense, the touch of sensual skin, loving whispers in the shade of night . . .

Clinking two wine glasses together . . .

Bare toes burrowing into hot, glittering sand . . .

*'Where are we now?'*

Immense buildings, bent and twisted, organic, green and blue, with great unblinking eyes that shift their focus and expel the shadows of unknowable entities . . .

The voice of something not human. Barely even a voice, more like something pretending to be a voice. *'We need them.'*

320

A different voice, identical. '*We need sustenance.*'

'*Please.*'

A little girl's voice. '*Mummy? Are we going in the aeroplane today?*'

The taste of spaghetti and meatballs. Bitter wine. Hanging upside-down from monkey bars. Skating across wisps of cloud. A hug the size of the universe. Slowly falling asleep in the folds of a black hole.

'*We need them.*'

Stanly's voice. '*Please let them go.*'

'*We need them.*'

'*They need to be free.*'

'*We need them.*'

'*Please. I'm asking. Leave of your own accord.*'

'*We need them.*'

'*You were put here by the Angel Group. You don't belong here.*'

'*We belong.*'

'*We need them.*'

'*They're innocent! Leave them be!*'

'*They are innocent.*'

'*We are innocent.*'

'*I won't ask again.*'

'*We need them.*'

The strands of moonlight that carry me start to tingle. '*Let. Them. Go.*'

I feel anger leaking into the voice, that weird neutral collective drone. They're getting ready to fight me. Around the edges of my vision I see the tell-tale silhouettes of my nightmares, of madness rising.

*Not this time. I warned you.*

The moonlight reddens, blood rushing into it, igniting, and Stanly's voice fills the space, fills everything, as huge and furious as the God of Gods. '*LET THEM GO!*'

The volcano erupts.

A flash of thought and pain bright enough to—

Stanly slides back inside himself, flies—

—backwards—

—I hit the wall and open my eyes, dropping to my knees, my whole body trembling. The shimmers are writhing, falling off their host heads, not shimmering now, *flashing,* in pain, and for a second, a stomach-churning second, I think I've killed them, killed them all with my thoughts . . . but I haven't. One by one they retreat to the edges, as far away from me as possible, using their arms and their legs, a weird lolloping gait. Alive. Terrified of me, but alive, and I look back at the empowered and feel a barrage of physical jolts as hundreds of eyes flash open, and then there is a wave of energy so dense, so full, so intense that my mind can barely take it, and I realise that it's their power, all that power being released. They've no way of controlling it. Beds start to lift into the air, life-support machines pop in Catherine wheels of acrid sparks, and many of the empowered themselves begin to levitate, limbs flailing. Pandora is rooted to the spot, staring, horrified and fascinated. I manage to drag myself to my feet and move towards them. One of the people closest to her, a bald man, has gone into a spasm. He rolls off his bed, out from under his blanket, and his naked body hits the floor. He coughs. Splutters. Turns his head, and even from over here I can see there is nothing in his eyes, no understanding. He doesn't try to speak because he doesn't know he can. All over the room similar things are happening, empowered crying and rolling off their beds, some too weak to get up, some managing to stand, looking around in utter, abject confusion. I stand there, helpless. What can I do? I spin around to look at Pandora. 'What do I do? What do I *do*?'

'Nothing,' she says, as I knew she would, as I hoped so hard that she wouldn't. I walk forwards a few steps then stop. I can't bring myself to get closer to them. I can't look them in their eyes. I can't. I can't. I . . .

*There must be something.*

There must be. This power, this new power, I can feel it, I'm *different* now. There must be something I can do, otherwise why do I have all this in me? What's the *point* of it? To fight people? To smash things? Is that what I am now?

Lauren's voice in my head. *We can do anything.*

*Anything.*

*If you want to do it, you can do it.*

*Don't think.*

DON'T THINK.

I don't. Trying not to choke on the air, so thick with expelled energy, I let my mind fade back into itself, past common sense and knowledge, past experimentation, into the deepest recesses, the core of myself, where the bright white spark lives, spinning at a billion miles per hour, screaming out possibility. Empowered start to rise and fall, finding their way back to their beds, which in turn touch gently back down on the ground. The empowered turn over, every one of them, confused and terrified, and I lay them all down on their beds and I think *sleep*. I think *peace*. I think *beautiful dreams*. Eyes start to close, almost lazily. Moans and screams and cries and tears subside. Within a minute there is silence once again. They sleep, and when they wake up hopefully things will be better, even slightly better will do. The shimmers are lined up along the shadowy edges of the room, no longer flashing, just quietly glowing, observing, and I wonder if they have the faintest idea what's happening. Something tells me they don't.

Pandora is staring at the empowered, her own face a painting of incomprehension. 'You . . .'

'Shut up.' I look up at the lights in the ceiling, the power collectors, and I think *destroy*. Each one dims instantly and the room is drenched in the bloody glow of emergency lights. Only now am I aware of the alarm again. 'One down,' I say, then look towards the control room. 'Come on!' Alex, inside the beast, carrying himself on its back, runs out and down the stairs and to my side. 'We're going,' I tell him.

'What are you going to do with me?' asks Pandora.

'I don't have time for you,' I say. 'You get off easy. For now.' I wonder where Smith is. *Probably too afraid to face me.*

*He should be.*

'Tell Smith I'll be back for him,' I say. 'Tell him I promise.' And I turn and walk towards a big rectangular door in the wall, hoping there'll be a way out in this direction. I think *open* and we go through the door and there are guards again, and guns, and it's so typical and *boring*, we go through them like bowling balls crushing pins, they're not even people, not even obstacles, we just push them apart and move along. Alex takes the lead. *Good. He'll get us out.*

As we traverse more and more corridors I start to see signs of damage. This must be where Connor, Sharon, Freeman and Fitz fought their way in. I wonder where they are. I wonder what state the city will be in. Eventually we run out of guards and we're walking up a sloping corridor just like the one at Site One. There's a complicated door that takes a stream of sideways thinking to open, and an elevator whose code I have to unscramble from nothing, and then we ride up, up, up, me squashed against the monster, which I'm starting to notice smells strangely fishy. A clang as the elevator stops, and I think the doors open. Another corridor, another door . . .

And, finally, we're out.

# Chapter Twenty-Three

THE SKY IS gone, obscured by the thickest, darkest clouds that I've ever seen. They shift and stretch like great animals as jagged loops of lightning coil and spit between them, thunder reverberating close by . . . or distantly? I actually can't tell. I look around at the barren docklands in which we've emerged, at the beleaguered buildings that seem to be half sinking into the river, at the snow, which has started to melt. It's more like oil now, warm and sticky. In fact, everything is warm, what should be bruising November cold smothered by an otherworldly humidity. The air is as thick as it was in the drawing area, and it's not just weird heat, the pressure of a corrupted atmosphere, there's something else, a taste, an essence that I recognise. It's something I've been aware of for a while but could never quite quantify, those undercurrents, pure *dread*, like radiation from a box that should have been kept locked and far away. I remember it bleeding from Smiley Joe's horrible empty eyes, from those living pictures at the Kulich Gallery, from the giant blue dog, and the tentacled beast that Alex is controlling. That energy, the stuff from somewhere else, like the energy given off by our power, it's like that, only *deeper*, older, primal. It's bleeding through, mixing with the nitrogen and oxygen and air, adding its own hues.

I notice that the monster has lifted Alex from its back with one tentacle. It seems to be handing him to me. I take the slack boy and hold him up, and look at the monster. It stares back, inscrutably. 'What do you want?' I ask. It can't answer me.

*Doesn't need to.*

*He wants to leave it.*

I nod and turn around. The door from which we emerged is camouflaged, you'd never know it was there. I think *lock*, then turn back to the monster and think *lift*. It rises into the air until it's just high enough to be harmless. It's not difficult, not like manipulating monsters usually is, and I wonder if I've broken through that particular barrier. *God, I hope so. What a tedious handicap that was.* I leave the creature there and Alex jerks abruptly back into consciousness. He stumbles and nearly falls to the sopping, oily ground, but I catch him. Above us, the monster immediately starts to writhe and wail. STAY STILL AND SHUT UP, I think, with a ferocity I wasn't quite expecting. The creature obeys. *Wow. OK then.* 'You all right?' I say.

Alex nods, breathing deeply. 'Yeah.'

'How was it in there?'

He shakes his head. 'Strange. Really strange.'

'Nice going back there. You were . . . you did well. And that site is out of action now. We need to get to the other one. I can fly us there.' *I can . . . but I almost don't want to.* Even though I should be entirely focused on taking out the primary drawing area, I need to see what the city has become, at street level. There are blatantly people who'll need help. Could well be monsters about. *Things are getting worse, though. Don't want to take too long destroying the other area, or it'll be too late.* 'We should walk for a bit first,' I say. 'See if anybody needs help.'

Alex is obviously far from convinced, but he doesn't object. He just nods.

'You can stay out of the monster for a bit if you want,' I say. 'Until we reach trouble or something. But you will need to get back in it.'

'Fine.'

'OK. I'll keep it with us.'

Just then, a bright orange explosion erupts on the horizon, over the river somewhere. Both of us jump. 'Damn,' I say.

'What do you think it was?'

'Not sure. Hold on, we're going up.' I fly the three of us to the edge, up and over the water, depositing us on the other side, and we walk in the direction of the explosion, the monster suspended in the air above us. The closer we get, the more we can hear. Sirens. Smaller explosions. A fog of voices, muted by distance. I'm not feeling any less unsettled, so I decide to break the silence. 'So. How old are you?'

'Nineteen.'

'Ah. I'm eighteen.' He doesn't respond, but I'm undaunted. 'How old were you when you first got your powers?'

'What d'you mean?'

'Your animal-control thing. How old were you when you first realised you could do it? I've never heard of anyone with that power.'

'It's not . . . I dunno. I was fifteen when I first did it, but I used herbs at first. Incense. It didn't just come naturally.'

'Really?' This is new and interesting. 'What did you do?'

'Just burned them. Hot-boxed my bedroom until it was basically all I was breathing, and then . . .'

'What happened?'

'I don't really want to—'

'I don't really care.' It comes out harsher than I'd intended. 'What happens when you do it?'

He's constantly looking at the ground as he walks. 'I . . . it's changed as I've got better at it. At first I just kind of . . . I left my body. Floated around. Like . . . my essence or something. And I'd just fly around until I found something I liked, and I'd go inside it, and then I'd be . . . it. Still me, but . . . not as much.'

'Not as much?'

'Just . . . I'd know things. Know who I was. The animal never

327

took over. But I could feel everything that that made it . . . *it*.
If you see what I mean.'

'I do a bit.'

'But then I . . .' He stops for a few too many seconds, and
I think that's all I'm getting, but then he presses on. 'I worked
out that I didn't need the herbs. That I could do it by thinking.
It took a long time, but now I can do it just by looking at an
animal for a second.'

'Fairish.'

He shrugs. We walk for another minute before I decide to
keep hacking away at the ol' ice. 'You're from London, then?'

'Yeah.'

'Which part?'

'I don't live here anymore. Used to live south. I've been away
for a while.'

'Why did you come back?'

'None of your business.'

'Where'd you go?'

'Also none of your business.'

'Whatev—'

'Seriously, I said it's none of your fucking business.'

'Fine. Jeez.' I decide not to attempt any more conversation
starters. I don't know how long we walk for. I can still feel those
spiders' legs on my skin, and checking my hand is still attached
has almost become a nervous reflex.

A fox runs across the road just ahead of us, looking almost
cartoonish. I laugh and look at Alex, but he doesn't even smile,
just stares at the animal until it vanishes into a peninsula of
shadows. His expression has shifted oddly. I can see the pain
from before, the anger. His fists are clenched. 'You all right?'

'Fine.' I don't press him.

We pass a park and I remember meeting Kloe at St. James
Park last year, the surprise of my life. Well, one of the many,

many surprises. Definitely the best, at any rate. That threatens to send me down a dangerous tangent so I bury the thought. Something else I'm getting surprisingly good at.

A car zooms past, packed with people and luggage. The orange light from the lampposts seems fatigued, there are brighter red and blue flashes coming from far away, and another explosion kicks fiery shards into the sky. I can hear smashing glass and yelling, sounds like it's coming from the next street. 'You ready to get back in that thing?' I gesture towards the hovering monster. Alex nods and I set the beast down on the pavement. He stares at it briefly and then collapses. This time I think I can feel the swapping of essences, a strange velvety breeze beneath the air that makes me shiver. The creature wraps Alex's body up in its tentacles and lifts him onto its back. 'Stay here for a minute,' I say. 'I'll check it out first.'

I jog down the road and around the corner. Up ahead is a big electronics shop, its front window smashed. A boy and a girl, neither of whom can be much older than me, are climbing out on to the pavement, one hefting a massive television, the other with armloads of random audio equipment. I find it slightly unbelievable and . . . *infuriating*. A time like this, and they're *looting*? It makes me so angry that I stride towards them. 'What the hell are you muppets doing?'

Both of them stop dead, rooted to the spot, staring at me. The boy looks me up and down, obviously deciding that a skinny barefooted kid in hospital pyjamas isn't any kind of threat, and manages some sneering bluster. 'None of your fucking business, *mate*.' *Everyone seems to want me to mind my own effing business.*

*Maybe I should give that a go.*

All the items that they're carrying fly out of their hands and across the street, shattering as they hit concrete, sparks and glass and plastic flying. The boy and the girl gasp and clutch each other, and I walk slowly towards them, rising about three feet off the ground for effect. 'Everything. Is going. To *hell*.' I gesture around, just in case they haven't noticed. 'And that's not a metaphor, you knob heads. The city is literally dying around us. And you're stealing TVs? *Why the hell am I trying to save you useless people?*' My furious thoughts yank several more televisions, a hi-fi and some speakers through the obliterated window of the shop and they land like a ring of bombs around the girl and boy, who scream and grab at one another more desperately.

*OK, Stanly, stop.*

*They're terrified.*

I realise that I'm shaking and drop clumsily to the ground, ashamed. 'I'm sorry,' I say. 'I . . . yeah. Just . . . do what you want.'

I turn and start walking away, and the girl pipes up behind me, 'We weren't hurting anyone!'

'Go and help some people,' I say, not looking back. 'Or just . . . get out of the city.' I hear them run and shake my head. 'You wouldn't even be able to pick up any TV channels. Cretins.'

I return to the corner and motion for Alex to come. The creature walks towards me and I make some momentary calculations. I can see the Shard from here. I definitely have plans to hit there, but my number-one priority has to be the primary research site. We walk on, passing several cars obviously desperate to get out of London. I wonder how long I was in that prison and wish I'd thought to ask Alex. It would be nice to know what kind of timeframe I'm dealing with . . . although I suppose it's academic. Things have deteriorated massively, however long it's been.

We take a left turn and I stop dead, as does Alex, because there is a monster up the road. It's at least nine feet tall and a burnt red colour, its three legs ending in cloven hooves - yeah, literally - and it has long powerful-looking arms and an elongated triangular head. Even from here I can see light glistening off the razors that line its mouth. It's standing over a young man, and for a moment I think he's dead and that it's preparing to chow down but then I see that he's trying vainly to crawl away, shaking with silent, terrified tears. The monster's not in a hurry. It's *playing* with him. It raises one clawed hand almost lazily, ready to swipe at him, but I think *stop*, halting its attack. It feels what I've done, snaps to attention and emits a low angry buzzing sound. I'm about to drag it in for a beating when Alex leaps straight over my head like a show-jumping horse, drops his unconscious body next to me and barrels towards the demon, shrieking with his host's weird siren. The monster lunges to attack but Alex ducks under the slicing swing of its claws, grabs both its arms with his tentacles and snaps them back against themselves with a sickening crunch of bone. The red monster is howling a nails-on-a-blackboard combination of high-frequency scream and grating buzz, but it's helpless as Alex brutally takes out both its legs with his tentacles. Then, gripping it around its waist, he does a sort of sideways body slam, crushing it against the road with every ounce of his solid bulk. The thing lies there, spasming, its droning buzz gradually fading. Alex lets go and trots back towards me in the manner of a dog that's just pulled off a clever trick for its master. The young man has been watching the fight, transfixed, and I yell, 'Hey! You! *Run away now!*' He jerks in fright, scrambles hurriedly to his feet and sprints away. Just as well because now an army truck emerges from round the corner further up the road, accompanied by four soldiers on foot and . . .

A *tank?*

*Sigh.*

I mentally lasso the Alex beast and his helpless human body and pull them both out of the way as the soldiers let rip with their machine guns. I think the bullets off-course, keeping my eye on the tank. Bullets I can handle, but the tank is massive and probably extremely heavy . . .

*Which means nothing, remember?*

*Soldiers, tanks, it's all just stuff.*

Up go the four soldiers, flipping upside down and flying in different directions, bouncing against walls and lampposts. Over goes the truck, onto its back, wheels spinning indignantly like a helpless insect. I turn to the tank, which has swung its gun barrel around, bringing it to bear on Alex and me, and think *miss* just as it erupts. The fiery projectile zooms past us and hits a building further up the road, letting loose a thunderous explosion. I think *open* and the hatch on top obeys me, and I feel three people inside and think *out*. One by one they're pulled through the hatch, yelling and swearing, arms and legs flailing, and I toss them aside like toys and think *bend*. With a wrenching grind, the tank's gun barrel twists around itself, rendered useless.

Most of the soldiers are back on their feet now but Alex is already on them, bashing away with his lethal tentacles. 'Leave one conscious!' I yell, just in time. He stops short of smashing the last soldier against the floor, coils a tentacle around his waist and lifts him up. Dragging Alex's human body in the air behind me, I run down the road and quickly deprive the soldier of his helmet. He's quite young, maybe late twenties, with brown curly hair. It's weird seeing a soldier with a face. 'You know what I can do,' I say.

He nods.

'Tell me what's going on.'

He answers reluctantly. 'We've been trying to keep order . . . there's been rioting. People started attacking patrols and police across the city. Lots of people just ran, trying to get as far away from London as possible, what with the snow and the sky. And the . . . creatures.'

'But the Angel Group don't want anyone getting out?'

'All exits were blocked off a few hours ago. London has to stay sealed.'

'So they can contain the chaos.'

'Yes.'

'Are there lots more monsters?'

'Sightings have increased massively in the last hour.'

'Right,' I say. 'Well I want you to get on the blower to the other armed forces and tell them that *this* monster,' I nod in Alex's direction, 'is not an enemy. And neither am I. We're trying to help. *We're* trying to sort out the Angel Group's rather epic balls-up.'

'We're trying to—'

'Help? It's nice that you think so. Get on it.'

'Tell everyone to leave him alone? You've got to be joking. You just attacked—'

'Fine.' I'm all set to clonk him one on the head, but an alternative idea occurs. I think *sleep* as an experiment, visualising the command as a blanket of thought, waves of suggestion enveloping the soldier. If *bend* works on a gun, why shouldn't this work on him? Sure enough, his eyes close, his head droops. *Wow. Must explore that one further.* As I place him on the ground I catch sight of my bare feet again. I'd forgotten. I check the soldiers' footwear but their military-issue boots are too big for me, so we press on through the shadowed city. All its angles seem odd, the buildings out of proportion, and stranger things are happening; at one point we pass a parked car that seems to be in the process of melting into the floor, the bottoms of its wheels distorted, almost square. Further ahead, I see patches of a weird red fungus on the walls of buildings, rustling in the not-quite-breeze, and every now and then we pass another group of panicked people. No army vehicles, luckily. I tell people to find shelter, that it'll be over soon. I don't think my appearance fills them with confidence. Then another explosion tears up the black sky somewhere ahead, and a muffled cheer echoes. *Cheering?*

*Rioters.*

*Great.*

'Stop here,' I say. 'I'm going to go up and have a look.' I fly straight up through the bubbly air until I can get a decent view. About a mile ahead there is a line of army vehicles and police, and beyond that a huge crowd of screaming civilians, many of them brandishing what look like flaming torches. An amplified voice is telling them that this is their last warning. A Molotov cocktail scythes through the air in response and explodes on a police car, blowing out all its glass and licking the air with fiery spirals, and the army lets loose a retaliatory rain of gas grenades that burst among the rioters. More screaming, plumes of smoke rising, panicked people stumbling, clutching their eyes. Some simply rush through the curtain of gas, blindly wielding whatever weapons they have.

*What can I do?*

*Something.*

I think *part* and to an extent it works. The majority of the fighters fly backwards and sprawl on the floor but they just get up again and launch themselves back into it, like nothing happened. I can't very well stay up here and part them all night until they get bored . . .

So I go in, flying across the chaotic scene, thinking my way around everybody who isn't in some kind of uniform, gathering them up in a psychic net and pulling them along with me, out of the melee, out of the violence. I fly down the nearest street, ignoring the furious shouts and frightened screams, even deflecting some projectiles, because of course they're throwing things at me. 'I'm trying to help, you dicks!' I yell. 'You need to stop!' I chance a look behind me. The police and army don't seem to be pursuing, luckily. 'You're going to get yourselves arrested, or killed! Get to safety!' Some people seem appropriately taken aback by the appearance of a flying boy, but mostly they tell me to get knotted, shove it up my arse and – once again – mind my own effing business.

*Y'know . . .*

I let go, not particularly inclined to cushion anyone's fall, and stop and turn in the air. Some of them waste no time getting to their feet and running right back the way we came. Some stare up at me, gobsmacked. But the majority, gratifyingly, take the opportunity to run for safer pastures. Or at least, safer than home-made bombs, gas grenades and pissed-off special forces types.

*Possibly.*

I loop around a building, fly back and drop down next to Alex and the monster. 'Streets are crazy. We're going up.' I think *stay close to me* and launch back up into the air, high up, further than guns or rockets can reach, gripping Alex and the monster he inhabits with my thoughts. The ceiling of monstrous clouds looks far too close, as does the prowling lightning, and I think a shield around us, hoping it'll work against such vicious sky electricity. I assume the reason there are no drones is that they've all been destroyed by said electricity, and I'd like to avoid that if possible.

I can see much more of the city from up here and it looks terrible. So much fire, so many terrified crowds, and many of the roads and bridges are entirely choked with cars trying to escape. I can just about spot the area where the Jonathan Kulich gallery is and wonder idly how the paintings are looking right about now. We pass back over the river and I glance down, and I'm pretty sure I can see shapes below the surface. That really chills me, and although I feel like I should investigate I really don't want to. I remember the awful roar from the Tube station and hope I can stop this madness before the owner emerges.

*If it hasn't already.*

We touch down on a residential street about ten minutes from Canary Wharf and I spot two elderly people hurrying away from us, a man and a woman, loaded with bags. They remind me of Oliver and Jacqueline and I feel a pang, hoping that they're all right . . . although my mind lingers uncomfortably over Morter Smith's words. *Where is my daughter.*

*What if it's true?*

*Why would they lie to me?*

*No time. Definitely no time.* I call after the couple. 'Hey! Where are you going?'

Their heads both turn in my direction, terror in their eyes. 'The . . . that's a . . .' the man splutters, pointing at Alex.

'Don't worry,' I say. 'It's . . . it's not a bad one. I promise. Please, tell me where you're going?'

'We need to get out of the city!'

'All the exits are blocked,' I say, wishing I didn't have to tell them. 'There's . . . there's no getting out.'

'But we *have* to get out!' moans the woman. 'It . . .'

'You're safer in your home at the moment,' I say. 'Trust me. Please, just go back. And . . . don't worry. I'm going to fix everything.' *Everything?*

'How?' asks the man. 'You're just a boy.'

'I know,' I say. 'But . . . trust me.'

They look at one another. The woman seems convinced. *Wow, she must be desperate.* 'If he's telling the truth . . . we probably *are* safer at the flat, Ronnie.'

'Isobel—'

'Let's go back.'

'I'll take you,' I say. 'Do you live nearby?'

'Yes.'

'OK. I . . .' Suddenly something occurs to me, and I turn to Alex. 'Look . . . if we're going to be attacking, your body . . . your human body . . . it's going to be seriously at risk.' I look at the old man, who is entirely bewildered by this, of course. 'OK,' I say. 'To cut a long and extremely bizarre story a bit shorter . . . but no less bizarre . . . my friend is controlling this monster with his mind.'

The patterns of confusion sewn into their faces pop a few stitches as they try to comprehend what I'm telling them. 'I . . .' says the man. 'But how on earth . . .'

'Don't ask,' I say. 'Basically, his mind leaves his human body and goes inside the monster so he can tell it what to do. But it leaves his body empty and defenceless. If his body dies then his mind is stuck in the monster. Are you following?'

They just stare at me. 'I'll take that as a yes,' I say. 'Now, we're going to be getting into some serious violence, and having to protect an unconscious human body is going to be a massive pain in my arse. So I was wondering if I could leave my friend with you? At your house?'

Ronnie looks less than enthusiastic. 'Oh . . . oh I'm not sure . . .'

His wife seems equally reluctant. 'We couldn't protect him if anything happened . . .'

'I'm not asking you to,' I say. 'Just . . . hide him in a cupboard until either I come back or he wakes up. Please.'

They exchange concerned expressions and helpless shrugs, but Isobel nods slowly. 'All right then. I suppose . . . if it's that important.'

'It really is.' I turn back to the Alex beast. 'Pass me your body if you understand everything that was just said.'

Even through the fog of alien thought processes I can sense that Alex is not keen to leave his body with two pensioners we've only just met, but after a few seconds three tentacles deposit the empty nineteen-year-old in my arms. 'Well done,' I say, thinking myself stronger to carry him. 'Stay hidden. I'll be back.'

Isobel, Ronnie and I walk in silence. After about five minutes I spot a group of guys and girls up ahead, ranging from about fourteen to quite a bit older than me. They're talking furiously, and many of them have weapons. They see us coming and one of them, a big guy with a shaved head, steps to the front wielding a cricket bat. 'Who are you?' he says.

'No-one,' I say. 'I'm just escorting these people home.'

He looks at the old man and woman, and then at the unconscious boy in my arms. 'And who the fuck are *they*?'

'None of your business, that's who they are.' *Yeah, how about my business is none of someone else's business for a change.*

The big guy steps forwards. 'You what?'

I don't even bother negotiating. I just think, and the group flies apart like toys. 'Come on,' I say to Isobel and Ronnie, and we hurry through them. 'Stay down until I'm gone if you know what's good for you,' I yell back. Amazingly, no-one follows us.

We get to their house and Ronnie leads me upstairs. The house smells comfortingly of clean laundry and baked bread. He shows me an airing cupboard wide enough to lay Alex down comfortably, and then we go back downstairs where Isobel is standing, hugging herself and looking worried. 'Lock all your windows and barricade your doors,' I say. 'Board up the windows if you can. If you have weapons keep them to hand, just in case. Designate the safest room in the house and *stay there*.'

'Thank you,' says Ronnie. We shake hands. 'And good luck.' He puts his arm around his wife.

'Cheers.' I leave and they close and lock the door behind me. I head down the path and back towards the group of people who are all on their feet and looking furious – but also confused.

The shaven-headed guy steps forwards again. *Surprise surprise.* 'How'd you do that before? You one of those freaks?'

'Yeah,' I say. 'Very much so. Now what the hell are you doing, starting on defenceless elderly people? Everything's going to shit, why don't you just get out of the city?'

He shakes his head. 'Nah. We're staying. It's *our* city. Anything that happens, we're going to stay and fight.'

I kind of admire him, although he seems more like a thug who wants to hit stuff than a selfless protector of the city. 'Fair enough,' I say. 'That probably works out well since all the exits are blocked anyway.'

'Fuck off,' squeaks one of the smaller ones behind him.

'See for yourself,' I say. 'But I've got to go. Excuse me.'

The shaved dude swings his bat from side to side in front of his legs. 'I should give you a beating, to be honest.' He says it as though it's an obligation, a chore he doesn't mind doing but doesn't feel massively enthusiastic about either.

'You wouldn't get one hit in,' I say. 'Don't let the bare feet and pyjamas fool you, I'm a proper hooligan. Actual lethal weapon. Honestly, I'm *insane*.' I must not sound as mean as I feel because a few members of the gang laugh, and one of the girls says, 'Hit him Dav!'

'Dav,' I say, 'if you swing that bat, I will put you down. Seriously. I could turn all your brains into rice pudding just by thinking.' *I probably could, couldn't I?* 'I don't want to, though. Now . . . you don't seem like a bad lad.' *Wow, you don't sound like you're lying at all.* 'Why don't you . . . I don't know. Go and help some people? You seem like you want to do something useful. You could try and break up some riots? Or . . . fight monsters?'

*You're basically telling them to either become good Samaritans or face certain death,* says Daryl's voice in my brain. *I doubt they're keen for either.*

They're all laughing, which suggests Daryl's voice is correct. Dav looks like the sort who'd rather cave an old person's head in than lend them change for the bus, let alone fight the good fight, but I stare at him anyway. 'Please,' I say. 'You can see what's happening. Everything's going to hell in a shopping trolley. Rather than just hanging around accosting people—'

'Why don't you piss off!' yells one of the others, lobbing a beer bottle. I don't even flinch. I just stop it in mid-air and they let out a collective gasp. I focus on the bottle and motion with my hand as I shatter the glass, just to screw with them a bit more. The pieces stay in the air and I twirl them around one another, like a diagram of the solar system and its various orbits. The gang are lost for words, some of the dumber ones following the floating shards with their heads like dogs. I snap my fingers and all the bits fall to the ground.

'I can do a lot more than that,' I say. 'So don't try anything, yeah?'

Dav looks like there's a very real conflict going on in his head. I've seen practically carbon copies of every single member of this gang all through my life, from the corridors of my school to the streets of London, from the little nasty ratty ones who follow at the back, to the sneering-faced girls who stand like charity shop molls behind their men with their arms folded, to the big ones, the arrogant, ignorant thugs who simply delight in wallowing in their own testosterone, in causing pain, asserting their superiority. So many like them. Doesn't matter where they come from, rich or poor, stupid or intelligent, they've all got that same cruelty, that disregard for everyone else's feelings, everyone else's lives. Waves and waves of identikit parasites. And now here's Dav, a prime specimen, and I can actually see the marbles of his dilemma rolling around inside his skull, bouncing off one another, and I chance a smile. Maybe this one's different. 'Come on Dav,' I say. 'Do the right thing for once. Be the one we need.'

Dav shrugs. 'Might do. But I still don't like you.' He lunges at me with the bat and I effortlessly pluck it away and spin it around. I fully intend to break his nose with it, and come within a millimetre of doing so . . . but then I stop the bat, just in time.

No.

*Not the way I do things.*

*He might be a dick . . . but I'm the powerful one.*

*I'm not the bully.*

The result is the same anyway, he jerks backwards in shock, loses his balance and falls on his arse, hard. I bring the bat into my hand, thinking towards the rest of the gang, holding them down so they don't try anything stupid, and advance slowly on Dav, who actually starts trying to crawl away. I stand over him and swing the bat like a pendulum, making some severe eye contact, hoping it communicates just how disappointed I am. I'm about to tell him to hoof it sharpish when I notice his blue and yellow skate shoes, the style that I like wearing, even though I've never skated. 'What shoe size are you?'

'What?' he asks.

'Your. Shoe. Size.' I emphasise each word by knocking the bat against the floor.

'Eight.'

*Small feet for a troll.* I smile what I hope is an utterly un-hinged smile. 'That'll do.'

# Chapter Twenty-Four

SEVERAL ARMY VEHICLES rush past as I head back in Alex's direction, and I keep my head down. They don't notice me. I run through oil-slickened streets, tangerine light reflecting off clammy puddles and dancing in the gutters, staying as surreptitious as possible, and find the monster squeezed into an alley . . . with a body in the dark behind him. 'Did . . .' I stop myself. I was about to ask if he was responsible. *Of course not.* I crouch down to get a better look. It's a man, middle-aged, with a grimy tangle of beard obscuring the lower half of his face. One of his arms is bent the wrong way, and there is blood matted into his hair and beard and clothes. He must have died pretty recently. I know that he's dead, I don't even need to check for a pulse. There's no life coming from him, he's just meat and bone and fabric.

This might not be the first body we've passed. But it's the first one I've really noticed. I want to cry. I want to puke. Surely I can't just leave him here?

What do I do?

I look at the Alex beast. 'What shall I do?' It doesn't shrug, but it might as well have. I run to the mouth of the alley, look out, see that there are a couple of abandoned cars. Maybe if he's in a more obvious place someone will find him? Maybe? Is that the right thing to do? That's better than just leaving him in an alley, isn't it?

I think towards the man's body, pick him up, pull him through the air towards me. I think the nearest car's passenger door open and start to float him towards it . . . but this means I'll have to move him into a sitting position. That doesn't seem right. Like I'm some weird puppet master, messing with dead limbs . . .

*Oh God. What is this?*

I settle for laying him down on the back seat, making sure I close his eyes. Then I shut the car door and turn back to Alex, who is watching me almost quizzically with his hundreds of eyes. I take a deep breath. 'Right. Come on. Site's less than ten minutes away. Let's . . . *urgh* . . .' I clutch my stomach and double over, overtaken by a dizzying wave of nausea. My vision clouds, my body fills with acidic hurricanes, my bones warp. It feels as though milk is bleeding from my teeth. Everything seems to go upside-down, I feel my knees hit the floor but the floor is the ceiling . . . and then, almost instantly, it passes. I'm shaking and feel weak, but things are at least the right way up. I get unsteadily to my feet, possible explanations beginning to sprout in my mind. I haven't eaten for God knows how long, or even had a drink. I've been going non-stop, hurling torrents of power. I got shot. *Haha, I actually managed to forget that I still have a bullet in my shoulder.* I suppose it's not unreasonable for my body to require a bit of a recharge. At any rate, I can't mount any kind of attack in this state. I tell Alex to wait there, and head back down the street to a small darkened supermarket. The door poses no problem and I help myself to water, fruit, cold meat and bread, all of which taste utterly orgasmic. I mix and match a few vitamin tablets as well, remembering something my mum used to say. *Like giving chicken soup to a dead person. Can't hurt.*

Having just seen a dead person, the thought isn't as comforting as it might have been.

I return to Alex and wish he could speak because addressing this thing is not getting any less strange. I feel better for having eaten, but I'm still not ready to burst into the drawing area.

Security has undoubtedly been doubled now, too. But I can't afford to wait.

*Time for a plan B, methinks.*

I hate seeing the soldiers' faces. It reminds me that they're real people doing jobs, that someone needs to pick them up after I've hurled them about, that they'll need to visit hospitals, be visited. Seems almost unfair to put them in such dehumanising helmets – obviously they protect them, but they also make them much easier to attack. This one is far too young to be fighting: he has curly blonde hair and childish cheeks and as I remove his uniform I keep repeating to myself that I'm doing what must be done. I've been left no alternatives. I drag the black combat gear on, fumbling with the fastenings on the boots and helmet, then pick up the young soldier, take him to an abandoned car and deposit him on the back seat. I sling his gun over my shoulder, take a deep breath and kind of wish I hadn't, because the helmet stinks of sweat and possibly halitosis.

There are more vehicles and soldiers milling around the entrance to Site One than before. It's going to be tough sneaking in. People are walking about, yelling into walkie talkies, but I manage to pass most of them unnoticed. As I head towards the tent that conceals the entrance I spy a pair of guards on sentry duty. Actually, I spot their big machine guns first, and then the attached grenade launchers, and then the guards. *Balls.*

*Oh God.*

*This was the stupidest idea ever.*

*I've got no ID.*

*I've got nothing.*

*Come on, Alex . . .*

I keep walking, trying to look like I'm supposed to be here, but also not wanting to get to the entrance before Alex does his thing . . .

Then it comes, that high, whining, shuddersome shriek, and something smashes, probably a car. Some of the soldiers run to investigate, and yeah, so sue me, it's pretty much the same plan as before – *good job that other soldier didn't send that message around like I asked him, I guess* – and I glance over my shoulder, making it look like I'm considering going after the other soldiers, before carrying on towards the entrance. *I'm supposed to be here. I am. I am. I am. I . . .*

A thought occurs. I remember that soldier back in the city. Telling him to *sleep*.

*Maybe . . .*

*I'm not the droid you're looking for.*

*You don't need to see my identification.*

I keep walking, trying to look like I'm supposed to be here, but now rather than just thinking *I'm supposed to be here*, I'm *supposed to be here* inside my own head, I try to push the thought outward, out of my brain, like radiation, a cloud of suggestive smoke around me, my own personal chameleon circuit, subtler than an invisibility cloak. I reach the guards. I nod. They nod, and let me past.

*Was that me?*

*Or them?*

*Whatever.*

I head down, joining some more black-clad soldiers, one of whom nods at me. *Lots of nodding down here.* He tells me that they're requesting more guards in the main area and I nod, obviously, and follow them down my millionth blank corridor of the day, to the door where Maguire was shot. They've already mopped up the blood, and when we go through the cargo area where I fought Alex I notice that all the crates I knocked down have been replaced. It all looks immaculate. *How did they find time to clean up while the world was ending?*

More halls and more stairs, deeper and deeper. I keep thinking *I'm supposed to be here*, keep moving with confidence, a slight swagger, keep trying not to think about the last abysmal catastrophe of an attack, about Lauren strapped to one of those nightmare beds, having her soul sucked out and regurgitated back into her mind by those creatures. I try not to think about Maguire, about Box, all those bullets Smith was talking about. I try not to think about what might have happened to my cousin, to my friends. Most of all, I try not to think about my family, alone in the woods.

A silver corridor, just like the one at the other base. The drawing area must be on the other side. I've been trying to keep my pulse and heart rate as slow and steady as possible, to stay calm and focused because I don't need another collapsing episode, but my blood is suddenly thundering around inside me and it's all I can do not to shake. *Come on. Cover it up. Swagger. Purpose. Nearly there. Nearly finished.* I can't believe it. I'm finally going in. This is it. The big climax. One more fight and the world will be saved.

I feel as though the fact that I'm about to bring another legion of empowered into that horrific wakefulness, into utter bewilderment and pain, should bother me. And it does . . . but it also doesn't. They have to be released. I just hope that the shimmers don't put up a fight. I don't want to hurt them. I already killed one, in the woods, even though I didn't mean to. That one seemed aggressive, it attacked me, I was defending myself . . . as far as I can tell, the ones in the drawing areas aren't even aware of what it is that they're doing.

*I will fight them, though, if necessary.*

*Need to rescue the empowered.*

*Rescue Lauren.*

She's been there a couple of days at the most. She'll still be Lauren. She'll know what's happening.

*God, I hope so.*

The final door slides open and we step through. This drawing area is at least as big as the other one, maybe bigger, and the noise of the great machines is like a distant jet engine, something impossibly volatile and complex pumping raw power in and out, round and round. I can feel the energy, as before, but it doesn't hit me as hard. Perhaps you acclimatise?

*Never mind that. Look who it is.*

Morter Smith is standing in front of the first row of beds with about eight soldiers, all armed with noticeably bigger guns than the average grunts. I want to reach out and choke the life from him right here, but I restrain myself, gripping my stolen gun so hard that my hands hurt.

Smith steps forward. 'Research Site Two has been completely disabled,' he says, 'as a result of the incursion by the terrorist empowered. The project is in serious jeopardy. Stanly Bird is most likely on his way here, and rest assured, he intends to finish what he and his allies have started. You have only been informed in the vaguest of terms what the consequences will be if these terrorists succeed, and I apologise for that.' His voice takes on a different tone now, and it's one that seems utterly foreign coming out of his mouth. He sounds like a leader. 'You have all been hand-picked because of your skills, your loyalty and your willingness to see the bigger picture, and you have served with distinction. We are beyond such petty distractions as nation states and regime changes. We are not fighting for religious freedom, for the purity of one country or one ideology. We are fighting for the human race, and the planet on which we live. No goal can be more important.' Now his voice hardens again, and I get the familiar chill. *Fair dos, Freeman said he was a good liar.* 'So suffice it to say that if Bird succeeds in his endeavour, the effects will be catastrophic in ways that none of us can begin to imagine. If he does manage to get down here, I don't want any hesitations. Shoot to kill.'

347

*Wow.*

I line up with some other soldiers and try to compose myself, keeping that one thought in my head, round and round. *I'm supposed to be here.* I sneak a glance at the hexagonal control room jutting out of the wall above and see another familiar face behind the glass, scrutinising everything happening below. *Lucius.* Immaculate suit, immaculate hair, slight and sinister. The true believer of the two I met at the Kulich Gallery, utterly convinced that he is on a mission from God. I wonder if it comforts him. I wonder how many of the soldiers I've fought believe the same thing, whether in their own heads they are righteous defenders. I wonder how many of the empowered they've enslaved believe in the same God, whether those who volunteered had even an inkling of what they were being asked to do, or if they were simply so desperate to shut out the pain, the noise in their brains, that they'd sign anything. Anything for a bit of peace. I stand there, hating the Angel Group, hating Morter Smith, hating so hard that I can barely think straight. Smith's bare-faced *lies*, telling these men that they're protecting the world.

*Keep it together, kid.*

*Not long now.*

Morter Smith's phone rings and I notice that Lucius has pulled out his own. Smith answers. 'Lucius?' I see Lucius speaking urgently, and Smith turns his back on us, and I smile behind my black face plate. *Now.* I think *part* and the soldiers fly in different directions, weapons escaping from their hands. There are many yells of surprise and hard thuds and groans of pain. I think *spin* and whirl Smith around to face me, I think *drop* and his phone hits the floor, I think *up* and his arms are raised above his head, I think *freeze* and he is immobile. I think *off* and my helmet is off my head, on the floor, and I'm pointing my gun at him. 'You should probably re-think your door policy,' I say. 'They're letting in any old riff-raff these days.'

Smith smiles and I barely have a second to wonder what it means before something launches itself down from the metal balcony above us. My gun is no longer in my hand, it's whirling through the air, and I'm rising off the ground, a foot, two feet, against my will, my limbs completely paralysed. I can't speak, I can only move my head, and even that takes a huge effort. Smith is no longer under my control and stands there watching me, dusting off the lapels of his suit for effect. *Arsehole.* Now someone lands behind him and stares at me with terrifying, empty eyes, and my stomach sinks way, way down. I know him. Tall, paler than pale, spiky black hair, his black suit and white tie blending perfectly with the black and white of his hair and skin, like a possessed portrait.

*Leon.*

*But Eddie killed you . . .*

He's added some accessories to his outfit, a samurai sword in a scabbard on his back and a pair of handguns visible inside his jacket. Really completes the human anime character look. I struggle, physically and mentally, but nothing happens, all I can do is blink furiously. It's a horrible feeling, panic rising inside, bubbling, popping, a horrendous vertigo. I think *release* and *no* and *out* but nothing happens. My limbs don't even tremble. I just hang in the air like a puppet on invisible strings with Leon watching me, unsmiling, un-anything. One by one the soldiers are getting up and running over, weapons raised, but Smith raises his hand. 'Hold your fire.'

*Well, that's a relief, I guess.*

His smile cracks and I see the hate that drove him while he tortured me, and he hits me in the face, hard.

*Ow. Maybe not such a relief.*

I can't make a sound, can't express pain in any way. He hits me again, in the stomach, but I can't bend over and all my air is gone and I can barely even choke. Smith shakes his head. 'Do you have any idea what you've done? The slightest clue?'

I can't answer him.

'You know,' he says, 'when you ran amuck and destroyed the other drawing area, I thought you'd gone mad, or that it was some kind of revenge against me for what happened in the White Room. But it was never about rescuing one empowered, was it? You wanted to destroy the drawing areas all along. Why?' He stares into my eyes as though he's never seen anything so confusing or ugly before, and I see a flash of understanding in his. 'You didn't know, did you? What they're really for? What we're trying to do? You just swallowed whatever crap you were fed, hook line and sinker. Well, let me lay it out for you in terms that you will hopefully understand. You may have *doomed* this city. We barely have enough power flowing into the machines to keep the tears closed. Monsters are appearing everywhere. If we can't milk every last drop of energy from our empowered here, pulling off some kind of minor miracle in the process, that is *it*. No containment. Bigger holes than *anyone* will be able to plug. Monsters will flood in, and God only knows what else. The world will drown.'

*That's not possible.*

*He's lying.*

'It was Freeman, wasn't it?' says Smith. 'He served you and your crew of retards a steaming plate of pure horseshit, didn't he? Told you we were trying to rip *through* to the other world.' He shakes his head, like he can't believe someone could be this stupid. 'I don't know what his agenda is, beyond apparently having gone insane, but it is *over*. When my people find him they're going to kill him. When we find your other friends we're going to plug them in, just as I'm going to do to you shortly. You've got power to spare. You might just be the key to stopping this. You can undo some of the damage you've done.'

*Damage I've done?*

*But I thought . . .gun*

'The girl will have to wait for now,' says Smith. 'I was foolish before. I let her cloud my judgment, let her get in the way, because I thought I had you over a barrel. I didn't realise how dangerous you really were. I should have hooked you straight up to the machines, maybe none of this would have happened.' He breathes deeply. 'It doesn't matter now, though. You'll go to sleep, and no longer represent any kind of threat, and I will find my daughter - *my daughter* - without you.'

*Tara . . .*

*No. He can't. No.*

*She's mine.*

'How dare you?' says Smith. The composure that he has just about regained slips and he hits me again. Some of the soldiers look at each other. Uncomfortable looks? It's hard to say. It's hard to think. It's hard to care. 'How *dare you* keep my daughter from me?' Smith practically snarls. 'You and Freeman and whoever else is in this with you? How *dare you?*' Another punch. Leon allows me to go slack when they hit, which is very charitable of him, but I can't seem to feel them any more anyway. I feel like a ghost. Another punch. Nothing.

*I'll have to let him plug me in.*

*It's the only way.*

*If he's telling the truth . . .*

'Lying.' I manage to squeeze it out; the words are strangled, barely human.

'Lying? Really?' Smith moves closer. 'Look into my eyes.' His face is right up close to mine. I can smell his breath. I can see his eyes. I can see truth.

'Didn't . . . know . . .'

'I believe you,' he says, 'but it doesn't matter. I'm going to put you on a bed next to your friend Lauren. You can keep each other company.'

A crash sounds out. It came from pretty far away but that's clearly still too close for Smith, who snaps around. 'What the hell was that?' His phone rings and he answers immediately. 'What? There's . . . *what*? I . . . well kill it then! It's that little turd Alexander! Under no circumstances can he be allowed down here with that thing! *Kill him!*'

*Alex . . .*

*No . . .*

Smith hangs up his phone and rounds on me again. 'So you've got him helping you. I should have plugged him in when we first found him, useless whinging little prick. As soon as his miniscule brain managed to comprehend that maybe I *don't* actually have the power of fucking resurrection, he turns on me.' He draws a gun, cocks it. He's sweating like anything. 'I don't know how you managed to convince him to destroy the machine. He's known since he signed on what we're trying to do. He's either stupider than I thought or he's simply got a hard-on for the end of the world. Either way, he's dead.' He turns to Leon. 'Take him to a bed.'

I start moving through the air, Leon walking impassively alongside me. I can't move my head but my eyes flash around desperately, looking for something. Anything. I can see that Pandora has joined Lucius up in the control room. They speak briefly, then she leaves and appears on the balcony. She hurries down the stairs and walks towards Smith. 'You're going to—'

Smith doesn't speak to interrupt her, he just raises his gun and shoots her in the thigh. The venom in his expression suggests that he's been wanting to do it for a long time. Pandora doesn't make a sound at first, she's too shocked, collapsing to the floor, shaking and clutching at the wound. A dark scarlet puddle is already forming on the pristine floor. It takes a few seconds for her to scream, but when she does it's piercing, terrible. Smith points his gun at her. 'Shut up.'

She doesn't at first, so Smith fires at the floor just next to her. That silences her. The guards all seem really uncomfortable now, it's obvious from their body language, the way they're looking at one another, even if their faces are obscured. Smith seems to notice, and if anything it makes him even more pissed off because he starts yelling at them. 'This isn't a bloody seminar! We might have a dangerous monster heading down here in a moment, with a psychologically disturbed teenager in the driving seat. Assume positions and get ready to blast the bloody thing! NOW!' The guards mobilise, running towards the door while Smith turns back to Pandora, shaking his head, his gun hand trembling with fury. 'Of all people,' he said, 'I never expected *you* to side with Freeman. I thought you were committed. One of us. Obviously not. What is it about destroying *everything* that so turns you on, Pandora?'

*She lied too.* It makes sense. Perfect, horrible, obvious sense. She was in on the whole thing, from the beginning. My mind, which barely feels attached to my body, drifts back to the Kulich, when I beat her and rescued Tara. It was Pandora who told me that the little girl was my daughter.

*Freeman and Pandora . . .*

*How could I have been so stupid?*

She can't speak, she's in too much pain, her head wobbling from side to side. Smith brandishes his gun. 'You knew *all along* where she was! You knew! You *knew* I had a daughter, you knew before I did, and you *hid* her from me, you gave her away, gave her to this cretinous wannabe superhero. You hid my *child* from me! How *dare you?*' He loses it, fires twice, and Pandora snaps backwards, her head hitting the ground. She doesn't even

353

twitch. Dead. Leon has stopped to observe, but his expression is still entirely unreadable. The grim pool beneath Pandora's body spreads. More worried looks between the remaining soldiers. Smith is panting heavily, and now Lucius emerges onto the balcony.

'What are you *doing?*' he bellows, running his hands through his hair.

'She's a traitor!' Smith yells. 'She betrayed us all! She might have ended *everything!*'

'There are procedures, Morter! We have *rules!* You should have done things by the book! Just as you should have with *him!*' Lucius gestures towards me.

'Don't lecture me about procedures, you sanctimonious tosser! Pandora conspired against us! And as for *this* one—'

'*You should have done things by the book!*' Lucius yells again.

For a second I wonder if Smith might shoot Lucius as well, but he forcibly reins himself in. 'When this is over,' he says, doing a passable impression of a reasonable human being, 'I will answer for what I've done. You have my word on that, Lucius. But right now, as far as procedures, guidelines and rules go, *it doesn't bloody matter*, all right? *Nothing* matters apart from sealing us off from the other world. Are we agreed?'

'Nothing matters?' repeats Lucius. 'Nothing? Did I imagine all the time that you have wasted searching for the child, then?'

'Don't push me,' says Smith. 'Not now. Not today.'

Lucius wants to keep blustering, I can tell, but he seems to think better of it. Maybe he had the same thought as me. Better not to resist. Better to give up. 'Fine,' he says. 'Just . . . get on with it.' He returns to the control room and Smith turns to Leon.

'Get him on the bed *now!*' he yells.

Leon continues to float me towards the rows of slumbering ghosts, and I see an empty bed, all the various tubes and electrodes ready to be allocated, a shimmer sitting placidly in a glass box at the head of the bed. A lady in a white coat scurries over and picks up the box, and I am turned over in the air and lain down gently on the bed. It's grotesque.

*No.*

*No.*

I look to my left and there is Lauren, and I think *no* so hard that it momentarily breaks Leon's mental grip. I feel him struggle to maintain it, but I'm not fighting to escape, just staring, and I'm quickly under his control again. Lauren looks so peaceful. I wonder if her shimmer is giving her good dreams. I hope it is. I hope they're good memories. God, I hope it's not like what I've had. I look at the creature and will it to be kind. I remember the one in the forest whispering to me, as did the others at the other drawing area. They think. They're alive. *Be kind to her*, I think. I think it so hard, trying to filter every ounce and shred of power I have into it. It makes no indication that it's heard me.

*I have to let them hook me up.*

*If it'll save the world.*

*It's the only way.*

Another crash, much closer. 'Leon!' yells Smith. 'Sort him out *now*, I need you to go and help those useless bastard soldiers!'

*There's nothing I can do.*

*They'll kill Alex.*

Except it won't be him, just the creature. He'll be back in his body. He'll go free.

*Did he really know what would happen?*

*Did he really want to destroy the world?*

Electrodes are fitted to my temples and chest and I feel my last drops of fight trickling away. I failed. I practically dived into the trap that Freeman and Pandora laid for me and nearly ruined everything. Tara's not mine. She never was. My future self never left me that note. It must have been Freeman. He had the cabin in the woods built. All him. A trap just big enough for me to fall into, covered with the bare minimum of leaves. The perfect story. I . . .

*He knows where Tara and Kloe are.*

Freeman knows. He must do. It was his plan. Get them to the middle of nowhere where I couldn't protect them.

*He didn't give them to the Angel Group . . .*

That must mean he wants them for something else.

Something worse.

I have to go and get them. I have to.

*If I go . . . the world may end.*

What do I do?

What *can* I do?

The distorted slam of a heavy body against metal, and the big door bends towards us. He's here. Another crash and it bends again, and now there is a slight opening and I see tentacles snake through, gaining purchase, trying to force the door apart. A howl of rending metal and Alex leaps almost gracefully through the gash in the door, and Smith and the soldiers fire at him and draw blood but he doesn't slow down, tentacles snapping like whips, pummelling, brutal. A soldier's back visibly breaks, others are pounded into the floor and up towards the ceiling, and Smith is hit hard in the head and sprawls across the room . . .

And I'm free. I sit up on the bed and watch Leon run towards Alex, forgetting all about me. Alex leaps at the silent empowered, wailing, wrapping him around and around with tentacles and hammer-throwing him through the air towards Morter Smith. I jump up onto my bed and yell, '*Alex! Stop!*'

He actually stops. Turns. Looks at me. 'Alex,' I say, holding up my hands. 'You have to stop this. It'll destroy everything! It'll destroy the city! People will die!' As always, it's so hard to tell whether he really understands me. He is watching, and he could even be thinking, but how the hell do I know? 'You have to stop,' I say. I get off the bed and walk towards him, keeping my hands up, trying to keep my voice calm, reassuring. 'It's over. We have to—'

His tentacles move almost faster than I can see, one to my stomach and one to my face, and as I fly away from him I think *stop*, but nothing happens. Leon must still be blocking my powers. 'No!' I yell. 'STOP!' Alex ignores me, grabs one of the beds and bats Leon away with another tentacle. The empowered and the shimmer lying on the bed roll off onto the ground and Alex chucks the bed straight at the one of the massive power collectors on the ceiling. The bed lodges there with a splintering crash and blue flames spit from within the shattered light, spraying plastic and glass. A shockwave passes through the other lights, bursting them, and they belch flame and debris. All the readings on the computers bleed to red, an alarm screams, and a wall of expelled energy knocks me to the floor as fire rushes across the ceiling, the smell of smoke and electricity burning my nostrils. I see Leon leap towards Alex, the sword rising from its scabbard seemingly of its own accord, but the monster doesn't even try to fight back. He just sits down heavily, all of his tentacles becoming instantly inert, and Leon lands on his back and plunges the sword into the back of his head. The beast slumps, dead, the sword finds it way back to its sheath, and its silent owner turns to Morter Smith like an animal quietly awaiting instructions. Smith, for his part, is holding his temples and shaking his head in disbelief. 'No,' he says. 'No, no, no, *no*, NO!'

*Good point, well made.*

A deep, primal rumble shakes the place. The control room's

357

glass windows shatter, sparks fly from computers and machinery, alarms howl, and I just sit, numb to it. Blue light cuts a blinding swathe through the air as though a great claw has gouged a tear in reality itself, and something drops out onto the floor of the drawing area, something twisted and black and slimy, with far too many arms. Leon immediately leaps to engage it. Smith is still standing there.

I can't seem to move.

Leon makes short work of the new arrival, and Smith turns to me. 'LOOK WHAT YOU'VE DONE!' He reloads his gun and comes towards me, raising the weapon, aiming directly at my head.

'You need me.' My voice sounds weirdly neutral.

'What?' He doesn't lower the gun.

I look up at him and our eyes meet. 'You need me now. You can't afford to kill me.'

'You *deserve* to die for what you've done.' He is vibrating with rage, but I can tell that he knows I'm right.

'Maybe. But if I die now then this city is definitely one hundred per cent screwed. And most likely the world shortly after that.'

He wants to kill me. He's desperate. I understand. But he doesn't do it. His arm drops to his side. 'Fine,' he says, his voice low and curdled with hate. 'What . . .'

'I'm assuming there's no way of fixing that.' I point at the ruined discs on the ceiling.

'Are you having a f—'

'A "no" would have been fine. So we need to go up, into the city. Help the soldiers, the army.'

'I—'

'Tell Lucius's lapdog to get his . . . brain off me.'

'You must be—'

'Tell *him*,' I say. 'I'm less than useless without my powers.'

358

'Fine.' Smith nods at Leon, who doesn't visibly register the order, but I feel lead lifting from my bones. I look at the empowered. They're still sleeping, which is almost hilarious. I sweep across them with my mind, scattering unfriendly bits of hot glass and plastic onto the floor, and walk over to Lauren. 'Will she be all right?'

'She's been plugged in for less than forty-eight hours,' says Smith. 'She'll be disorientated but unharmed.'

'Lucky you.' I pick up an unconscious soldier, think *off* and relieve him of his uniform, then concentrate on Lauren's shimmer, the warped watery blob of living dreams around her head, entering whatever passes for its mind with my own. *Release her*, I think.

*No.*

*I won't ask again.* I think RELEASE and the shimmer howls inaudibly inside my mind, but I don't kill it, just force it off, and it falls from Lauren's head to the ground and retreats into the shadows. Lauren's eyes open and she sits up gasping, panicking, crying out. I grab her shoulders. 'Lauren,' I say. 'Lauren! It's me! Calm down! Calm down, it's me, it's all right! You're all right!'

It takes her a little while to stop hyperventilating, and when she does she stares at me in terror and confusion, her eyes huge and bright and painful. 'I . . . Stanly?'

'Yeah.' I smile, which seems both the most and least appropriate thing that anyone could do right now.

'What—'

'Lauren,' I say, 'I'm so sorry, but we don't have any time. Things are unravelling, the monsters are pouring in. I need you fighting.'

'Pouring in? How?'

'Freeman lied,' I say. 'It was all a lie. The Angel Group were trying to keep the monsters *out*. He tricked us, we . . . it's . . .

anyway. Why and how doesn't matter. Not now. We need to be out there, helping people.'

'But . . .'

'Lauren.' I hug her to me, fiercely. It feels like the thing to do. She hugs me back, at any rate, albeit hesitantly. 'I'm so sorry for what you've been through. I'm so sorry you have to wake up to this. But there just isn't time. Can you deal with it?'

I think she understands. She nods slowly, anyway. 'I . . . I wanted to look for Sally . . .'

*So that was her friend.* 'How did you know she was here?'

'I . . . Nailah told me. I always thought she'd just run away, that she'd left town. She was so scared of her powers . . . then when we got to the Shard, Nailah told me she was here.'

*Well that was great timing.* 'I wanted to come and find her,' says Lauren, 'but I . . . I knew we had to finish what we were doing first. I promised, though, I promised I'd come and look for her . . .'

'Sorry to interrupt,' says Smith, 'but there's a slight *end of the world* happening outside, so could we hurry this along?'

'Shut up,' I growl.

'It's OK,' says Lauren. 'Just . . . wait a second. Please.' She pulls on the uniform I've given her, then starts running through the rows of empowered, looking at faces. I'm surprised at how methodical she seems to be, how focused, considering what's happened. 'Here!' she calls. 'Here she is! She's here!'

I run over. Sally is about Lauren's age, with long black hair. She's sleeping peacefully. 'I want to wake her,' says Lauren.

'Don't!' says Smith. 'She has been here for over a year. She will be confused, disorientated, possibly dangerous. The best thing that you can do is leave her to sleep with the rest. And if by some miracle we manage to sort out this unholy mess, you can come back for her then.'

'He's right, Lauren,' I say.

'I will leave a squad behind to protect them from any . . . unwanted arrivals,' Smith adds.

*Wow. That's . . . half decent of him.*

Lauren doesn't say anything, she just stares at Sally's sleeping face, her own face full of such familiar pain. I've seen it all before, in her eyes, in her piano playing. I feel as though she's going to come with us, and I know I need to hurry her along, but I just can't. I want to give her a second, just a second. I feel as though I'm intruding. I turn back to Smith and see Lucius hurrying towards him. He is dishevelled, his suit torn, a huge purple bruise bulging on his head. 'The explosion knocked me out,' he says. 'What . . . why are they free?'

'We're helping,' I say.

Lucius nods helplessly. 'Fine. I . . . the machine is useless. Tears are opening all over the city. The army is mobilising. We have some tanks . . . it . . . I don't know if it will be enough.'

'What about fighter planes?' asks Smith.

'The atmospheric disturbances are too dangerous. It's affecting communications as well, we can use radio within a certain distance, but there's no way of transmitting anything outside the city.'

Smith nods. 'Well, I don't particularly want to be having long involved conversations with overseas shareholders at this point. So we'd better get out there and use what resources we have available.'

'You have us as well,' I say. 'And my friends are still out there somewhere.' *I hope.*

'We could do with about a thousand more of you,' says Lucius, sounding almost accusatory.

'Maybe if you hadn't been so keen to turn us all into *batteries*,' I shoot back, 'that wouldn't be an issue.'

'Shut up,' says Smith, 'both of you. We are going.' He walks away, Leon and Lucius in tow, and I turn back to Lauren.

'Lauren,' I say. 'Please. We need you. Sally will be safer here than she will be with us.'

'I know,' she whispers. She leans down and kisses Sally's lips so lightly, so tenderly, and for a second my brain threatens to break and flood with images of Kloe, feelings that I really don't need right now, feelings that could get me killed. I bottle them. *You've messed up, kid.*

*You don't get to indulge yourself.*

*Not now.*

*Harden up.*

Lauren stands up. 'I'm ready.'

'OK,' I say. 'Let's go.' I take her hand, grateful for something that's not brutal and hateful, and we follow Smith towards the exit. I look briefly at the dead Alex beast as we pass, wondering if he's woken up elsewhere, what the hell he was thinking, what I should do to him when I find him, and we leave the room with the empowered still slumbering.

Corridor. Cargo areas. Unconscious bodies. More corridors, all bathed in bloody emergency lighting. Alex really did a number on the soldiers, most of whom look like they won't be awake for weeks. Up some stairs. Bent limbs and shattered helmets. We pick up a few who have regained consciousness; they're shaken up but they're also well trained and armed . . . and all we've got. A couple who are capable of fighting but injured enough to slow us down are sent to watch over the sleeping empowered. I'm suddenly regretting injuring so many soldiers, we're probably down a significant number of possible helpers. *One more screw-up to add to the list.* No-one asks about me or Lauren. Another storage room, and another tremor that knocks us all off balance and sends an avalanche of heavy crates toppling down with a noise like fifty drum kits being blown up. I glance at Leon, still utterly expressionless, and wonder what goes on in his head.

'Nearly there,' says Lucius, clutching the machine gun he appropriated from a disabled guard. He doesn't look comfortable with it.

I try to imagine what we're going to find above.

I *can* imagine it . . .

But I can't.

# Chapter Twenty-Five

THE HATCH HAS been left open. Smith goes first, the others behind him, and I bring up the rear, keeping my breathing level, flexing my fingers, trying to be ready, as though anyone could ever be ready for this. Sounds that were muffled before are now terribly clear, screaming and howling and roaring, explosions and thunder, the crackling of other-worldly electricity. I'm expecting footfalls, the stomping of huge intruders, but as of now there are none. *Small mercies. Large mercies? Some kind of mercy.*

A soldier is standing at the entrance to the tent with his gun raised, the barrel shaking. 'What's the situation?' asks Smith.

'It's . . .' the soldier's descriptive acumen fails.

'How are we doing for manpower?'

'Not well. Reinforcements are coming in from outside the city, but . . .'

'All right,' says Smith. 'Come on.'

We leave the tent. It's still dark outside – although I suddenly realise I haven't the faintest clue what time it is, or even what date it is – but the air is lit by sporadic blue flashes, wounds ripped in the skin of the world, and there is an all-pervading flicker of orange and red from numerous fires. The site is strewn with bodies and the wreckage of vehicles, and as I breathe in the air my vision clouds and I feel suddenly faint. I stumble, and I notice Lauren and even Leon do the same, and I know why, because that feeling from downstairs, that feeling of raw undiluted *power*, has increased tenfold up here. Lauren moans and clutches her temples and I move to catch her as she staggers, but I recoil, because I can *hear* her. I hear her voice, as clearly as if she'd spoken out loud. *It's too much,* she thinks, *too much, oh God . . .*

*She's right. Too much.*

Lauren jumps. 'You . . . you heard me?'

'What the hell is wrong with all of you?' asks Smith, with all the sensitivity of someone with no sensitivity whatsoever.

'It's the energy,' I say. 'From the other world. It's so strong, like vertigo . . . nausea . . . we can hear . . .'

*I knew these freaks would be a bloody liability,* Smith thinks, and I move towards him but Lauren stops me. 'Don't.'

'Keep your thoughts to yourself,' I say to Smith.

His eyes widen. 'You *heard* . . .'

'Shut up,' I say. 'We'll be fine.' I look at Leon. He has closed his eyes and is standing very still. I realise that I can't hear anything coming from him, although I can hear a blur of thoughts from the rest of the soldiers. Terror. Fury. Distrust - of us, mainly.

*I can't go on with all this noise in my brain. It's not—*

'You'd better be fine,' snaps Smith, 'because we need to get a bloody move on.'

'Just give us a second,' I say. 'We . . .' *What? What can we do?*

Lauren takes my hand and looks right into my eyes. 'We can shut it out,' she says. 'OK? We can shut it all out. We can.'

'How, though . . .'

'Just *do it,*' she says, not harshly, but firmly, and I know what she means. It's like anything else we try to do with our powers. We just don't allow it to happen. We impose *our* will. I'm about to close my eyes when a line of blue appears in the air in front of me and something launches itself through, a wolf-like humanoid, pure white, its purple eyes glowing like lava lamps, feet and hands lethal with curved claws, and I immediately think *punch*. I mean to give it a hefty whack, but what I actually do is blast it straight up into the sky, fifty feet, a hundred feet, more.

'Oops,' I say. 'Didn't mean to do that.' Presently the creature comes back down, impacting a little way away with an impressively gruesome *splat*, totally pancaked. Lauren actually chuckles. '"Pancaked",' she says. 'Good word.'

'This is all very bloody *cute*,' says Smith, 'but–' He's interrupted by gunfire as the soldiers take aim at something swooping down towards us, a leathery brown bat-like creature that hisses as bullets tear holes in its wings. Leon is still silent, eyes closed, but his sword rises from its scabbard, spins up and bisects the creature. The two dead, twitching halves spiral to the ground but the sword remains in the air. *Pretty neat trick.*

'Hmm,' says Lauren.

'We need to *go*,' says Smith.

'Carry on without us,' says Lauren. 'We'll catch up. We're no use to you if we can't get our powers under control.'

'Fine,' says Smith. 'Leon, are you ready?'

Leon opens his eyes and offers the barest nod.

'Good,' says Smith. 'At least someone round here is vaguely reliable.'

'Where are you heading?' I ask.

*What does it matter*, he thinks, *we're all fucked anyway.* 'No we're not,' I say, more to contradict him than because I disagree with what he's thinking. Smith's mouth twists. He really doesn't like me reading his thoughts.

'You'd better get that under control,' he says. 'I don't want you wandering around inside my head.'

'I have no desire to be anywhere *near* the inside of your head, you arse—'

'Stanly,' says Lauren. 'Don't. Where are you heading, Smith?'

Smith turns to Lucius. 'What do you think? The Shard?'

'I haven't got the faintest idea,' says Lucius. 'It seems academic at this point.'

'Then why don't you sit down and wait patiently to be eaten,' snaps Smith, which seems unfair, considering the thought that just went through his head. He fingers the grip of his gun, as if deriving some perverse comfort from it. *Maybe not so perverse, actually.* 'We'll head for the Shard,' he says, finally. 'Try to secure it.'

'We'll catch up with you,' says Lauren.

They head off, weapons at the ready, and Lauren leads me back into the tent and sits us down in the corner. I feel like I'm going to throw up everything I ate earlier on. I'm trying not to hear Lauren's thoughts, trying so hard that my eyes are watering, and it might be working, they're already becoming muffled . . . although maybe that's because she's got her own brain under control . . . but it's not just her thoughts, and it's not just the oppressive weight, the weird humidity, it's the other sounds, the myriad *wrong* noises in the distance, the calls of whatever horrors are waiting out there for us, the high ululating siren trills and deep bass roars and grating bleats, like the awful ambient noise from some hellish alien zoo, and over that the sporadic boom and crash of explosions, and screaming, human screaming, and this is *our fault*, it's *our*—

'Shh,' says Lauren. 'You need to calm down.'

The idea of calming down when the world is literally ending is so ridiculous that I have to laugh, a sound I was half convinced I'd never make again.

'Well,' says Lauren. 'Sometimes you have to laugh, don't you? Now close your eyes.' I do as she says. 'We're fine, OK?' she continues, her voice perfectly level. 'Our minds are our own. Our powers are our own. We don't have to let anything in, or out, if we don't want to.' Her voice is so soothing. And what's more, I *believe* what's she saying. I believe it. In my head, and in my chest, and . . . and *deeper*. I don't just believe it, I *know* it. Whether because I already know it or because she's putting that knowledge inside me, I don't know – *doesn't matter* – and she keeps talking, variations on a theme of 'we're OK, we're in charge', and I don't know how much time passes, I'm sure it can't be long, but when she stops I open my eyes and she smiles, and I can't hear anything coming from inside her head.

'Can you hear my thoughts?' I ask.

She shakes her head and smiles, and we get to our feet and step back out into the world, or whatever it's turning into. The reports of heavy guns rumble, far away but not, and then there's another sound, a piercing TSEEEW as an arrow of lightning streaks from the sky and tears right through a concrete wall, expelling dust and flame. Fire climbs behind the nearest row of buildings and something howls. A light, warm rain has started to fall. It feels incongruously pleasant. I turn to Lauren. 'Shall we?'

She nods.

'I'll fly us.'

'Are you sure?' I don't have to read her mind to know what she's thinking – she doesn't want me to lose control and launch us both into space or something – but I take her hand. 'It's all right,' I say. 'I can do it. Trust me. And . . . I don't know. Might be good to get a bird's-eye view. See what we're dealing with.'

She's not convinced, but she nods, and I think *just gonna fly, fly like normal, fly like this isn't even a thang*, and up we go, and it *is* different, it's usually effortless but this is like . . . if there was something more effortless than effortless, this would be it. It's like I'm not even doing it myself, it's just happening, and I have to lock on to myself, overthrow it, re-assert control, force myself to be in charge, even though it feels *good* for it to be so easy, subconscious, autopilot. Up we go, and I ask

Lauren to think a shield around us in case of *aaah things like that!* Something swoops towards us, a four-winged shadow, but it glances off the bubble that Lauren has created and I think a snapping motion and *crunch*, there go two of its wings, bye bye, haha this is easy – *no no no not easy don't get cocky* – and I realise that I'm not in charge, definitely not. *Need to get under control.* I thought I was, I thought I had it, but – *stop panicking stop panicking stop panicking* – no, I *do* have it. I do. I bring us to a halt in the air, gripping my inner panicking self and forcing his head into some cold water – *yeah shut up shut up shut up useless boy* – and we survey London, our city, bathed in bright violence. 'My God,' whispers Lauren. 'Look at that.' Less than a mile away we can see a beast bigger than a giraffe, with many-jointed arms and a single huge red eye, swinging at a group of soldiers, knocking them aside like skittles. It opens its mouth to roar but then takes the full force of a tank projectile in the head and topples over. Another rumble shakes the ground and the front of an old Victorian building half crumbles into the road.

And then I look to my left, and I can see the neighbourhood where I left Alex, and I have to find him. I *have* to. 'Detour.'

'What? Stanly—'

I pick up a lot of speed very quickly, flying full pelt in the direction of Ronnie and Isobel's house. 'Stanly!' Lauren yells. 'What are you doing? Where are we going?'

'Need to find Alex!'

'Who?'

'Another empowered! He did this!' I bank sharply, dodging some lightning. I'm starting to realise that I can feel when it's about to come, the air takes on a different quality, a subtle acridity, like a smell but . . . kind of *beneath* a smell, something that I pick up in some unspecified area of my brain. It means I can swing to the side as it snakes viciously towards the ground. In

369

less than thirty seconds I land us on the street and start jogging up the road towards the old couple's house.

'Stanly!' Lauren calls.

'Wait there! I won't be long.'

*Shouldn't be doing this.*

*No time.*

*I have to, though.*

Several houses and cars are ablaze and people are running around, hysterical and panicked. Ronnie and Isobel's house, mercifully, isn't burning, its front door is closed, windows boarded up . . . and Alex is standing in the garden, looking up at the fiery sky. He looks completely lost, like a child in a supermarket who can't find his mother. I bellow his name but he doesn't seem to notice me, even when I'm right in front of him, grabbing his shoulders, shaking him. 'Alex! What did you *do?*'

He doesn't look at me. 'I'm . . . I . . .'

'You *knew* this would happen!'

Now he looks at me with those empty eyes, and barely nods. 'Why?' I ask. 'Why did you lie to me? Why would you want *this?*' The ground shivers again, and the roof of a burning house collapses inward.

'I'm sorry,' says Alex, although he doesn't sound sorry or upset or angry or happy or anything. His voice, his eyes, his whole body, they're empty. Like he checked out and only left a little bit of himself behind.

'Why?' I ask again.

'I lost her,' he says. 'She . . . I lost her, and they said they'd get her back for me. He said they would . . . but they didn't. They can't. And now I'll never have her back.' There are tears now, his voice a low cracked drone, and I take my hands from his shoulders as he speaks. 'What's the point of a world where everything just ends?' he asks. 'Where everyone lies? Where everyone's cruel? What's the point? Why is this world worth saving?'

'Because it is,' I say.

He just shakes his head, and I snap. I thought I was angry before but now something erupts, a rage that makes my fist hot, and I punch Alex in the face as hard as I can, as hard as I've ever punched anything or anyone, so hard that his head snaps around and he stumbles backwards, and it hurts my fist but I don't care. 'So you'd destroy it?' I yell. 'The whole world? *Everything*? All the other lovers who are lucky enough to be alive, you'd have them die, terrified and screaming? Because of *your* pain? Because your pain is so *fucking* important?' I hit him again and he doesn't resist, he doesn't answer, he doesn't even look me in the eye. I can hear Lauren shouting my name but I don't care. Everything I did, I always *thought* I was doing the right thing, I thought I was helping, even though this world and its people make me feel sick sometimes, but Alex, this guy, this *thing* . . . he knew, and I hate him, and I hit him again and again, screaming. 'I *didn't know*! You did! Look what you've done!' He's still not fighting back and something is trying to drag me away from him, someone with power. I spin around, ready to attack whoever it is, but it's Lauren, pulling me away, and her expression is like a bucket of cold water.

'Stanly,' she says. 'You have to stop. You can't do this. You can't fall apart.'

'But he—'

'Look at him.'

'Lauren—'

'*Look*.'

I look, and as quickly as the rage came it subsides, because I'm not just looking, I'm *seeing* him, bleeding and pitiful, crying silently, on his knees. How can I hate this thing? What even *is* he any more? 'Alex,' I say.

He looks up at me. 'What about the girl I love?' I ask. 'She doesn't matter? Because you lost yours?'

He just stares.

'You've condemned her. You've condemned everyone. Every*thing*. To die.'

'It was dying anyway,' he whispers. He isn't looking at me now, he's staring past me, at the chaos, the crumbling city. 'Look at the world, Stanly. The way it is, the way things work. The way people are. It was dying anyway.' He can't even kneel now, he falls back, slumped against Ronnie and Isobel's front door. 'I just helped it along.'

There's no reasoning with him. He's gone. Useless. No fight in him whatsoever. He might as well be dead. 'Fine,' I say. 'If that's how you feel. I have to try and *save* it.'

'Why?' He really doesn't know.

'Because,' I say. 'Because . . . I do.' I turn back to Lauren, ready to leave, to stop indulging myself and get on with what I always say I'm supposed to be doing . . . but something stops me. 'What was her name?'

'What?' asks Alex.

'What was her name?'

When he answers, it's almost too quiet for me to hear. 'Leila.'

I nod. 'Lovely name.' I crouch down in front of him. 'I'm sorry you lost her. I really am. The girl I love is called Kloe, by the way. And if anything happens to her, I'll be back for you. And you'd better hope you've been eaten by a monster.'

He just stares at me, and I grab Lauren with my mind and fly us both away.

*Rightio.*

*Time to try that hero thing, I suppose.*

'I'm sorry,' I say, as we fly. Lauren doesn't answer. I'm glad I can't hear her thoughts.

We catch up with Smith and the others quickly. They're

making their way along by the river, presumably heading for the nearest bridge. 'You took your time,' says Smith, with typical grace.

'Whatever,' I say. 'Where are we heading?'

'Tower Bridge.'

'Bit of a way. I'll fly us.'

'Why on earth didn't you suggest that before?' snaps Lucius.

'I don't *have* to take you.' He shuts up, and I extend my mind around our party and lift us all into the air, to a comparatively safe height, up and over the river. We're barely halfway across when something breaks the surface and bites its way towards us, three triangular jaws snapping, teeth as crooked as arthritic fingers, two serpentine tongues moving around one another. Smith fires into the mouth until his gun is empty and the creature curves away, hissing furiously, re-entering the water with a splash.

*They're getting bigger.*

We cross the river and I decide to keep us in the air, continuing towards the Shard and keeping an eye out for—

*(Stanly . . .)*

I jerk with surprise and almost drop my passengers, and Smith showers me with colourful insults.

*(Stanly . . .)*

It's Sharon's voice. It *is*. It is, I know it is. But . . . she's in my head. Kind of? No . . . not in my head exactly, I can *hear* her in my head, but her voice is everywhere, in the air, like I'm just tuning into it. Obviously she would be picking up on the same power that Lauren and I picked up on, and she's using it. Boosting the signal.

*She's looking for me.*

*She's alive.*

I can't believe it. Maybe they're all OK. *God, please can they all be OK.* 'I have to take us down!' I call. We land, taking cover in the shadow of some buildings, and I sit down and close my eyes and think. *Sharon,* I think. *Can you hear me?* I imagine my mouth as a huge amplifier, my ears as satellite dishes, my brain a great pulsating mass pumping waves of thought out through the city, blanketing it in Sharon's name. *Can you hear me?*

(*Yes.*)

I can't believe it. I actually laugh out loud. 'What the hell are you laughing at?' says Smith.

I ignore him and think. *Where are you? Are you OK? Are you all together?*

It takes a few seconds for her to reply. Her voice is faint, but definitely there. (*We're OK. I'm with Connor, Eddie and Skank. Fitz bolted.*)

*Things get a bit too anarchic for him?*

Sharon laughs. It manifests as a sort of tickle in my head. *What about Nailah?*

(*We did catch up with her but she went off again. She said she was going back to the Shard.*)

Well that's a coincidence and a half. *What? Why?*

(*She said she wants to finish what she started. Get as much information as possible, show the world what the Angel Group has done.*)

*She doesn't think the world will notice the force-10 monster apocalypse? Christ's sake. Where are you guys?*

(*Eddie's place. Eddie wants to come and find you. So do I.*)

I bet Connor doesn't. *Can you try to make your way to the Shard too? That's where I'm heading.*

(*It's a bit of a way . . . lots of monsters . . .*)

*Take my mum's car. It's still at Eddie's. Unless something's eaten it.*

(*OK. See you soon, I hope.*)

*You will. Take care.*

(*You too.*)

374

I open my eyes and stand up. The sounds of Armageddon rush back into my ears, and Smith looks at me, radiating distrust. 'I was talking to my friends,' I say.

'What?'

I tap my temple. 'Psychic radio.'

Lucius looks intrigued. 'Fascinating!'

'Where are they?' asks Smith.

'Good few miles away.'

'I've never heard of empowered being able to communicate over that kind of distance.'

'Things are different now,' I say, somewhat inadequately. 'Ready to fly again?'

'To be honest,' says Smith, 'I think I'd rather go on foot.' There's a general chorus of nodding and agreeable noises from the soldiers, and I shrug.

'Suit yourselves.' I reach out, levitate the wreck of a car and bring it towards me, rotating it slowly over my head. Smith raises an eyebrow. 'Weapon,' I say, and we press on. The rain has intensified. It's refreshing. More importantly, my powers feel like mine again. *Guess you get used to it.* Considering the rage I felt when we found Alex, considering *everything* for that matter, I now feel strangely calm. Seems like there should be adrenaline. I should be pumped. Maybe I should be cracking wise. I'm a super-person, after all – the *hero* suffix doesn't really feel appropriate now – and apocalypses are what we do.

*Less of the plural. Let's try to get this singular one out of the way.*

I'm surprised that there aren't more people around, but grateful too, especially when we emerge on the soggy black expanse of Southwark Park and see a giant striding across it. It's at least twenty feet tall, legs like redwoods, its top half an obscene bundle of limbs and mouths, like a scrunched up drawing of a monster, and when it sees us – or notices us, or whatever it does, because I don't spy any eyes – it lets loose a siren scream and a jet of some stinking pink gas that fouls its way skyward. It starts to stomp in our direction and the soldiers let rip with their guns and I rise up off the ground and hurl my car. The bullets don't seem to cause it much bother but the blunt trauma of the vehicle visibly shakes it and it lashes out with one long knotty arm, catching one of the soldiers and slamming her into the ground. The giant keeps coming . . . and then it's not coming. It screams and thrashes its tangle of limbs and I look behind me to see Lauren and Leon staring at it, Lauren's face a mask of furious concentration, Leon's eyes slightly narrowed, which for him is downright emotional. *They're keeping it at bay.*

I look back at the beast and throw the vehicle again, once, twice, thrice, four times, the dead chassis shedding more and more burned bits of itself with each impact, and finally the creature falls, coming to earth with a crash that makes the ground vibrate. The soldier it knocked down is nursing a bleeding head wound, and she empties a clip into the fallen monster with extreme prejudice. 'Save your ammunition,' snaps Smith, and we head on through the park. My eyes are adjusting to the dark much easier than they might normally and I notice that the trees look weird. Their trunks are warped, like parts of them have melted, the branches sag and there's a rusty red film over the leaves. They smell weird too, like burnt treacle. Another fun side effect of whatever the literal hell is going on.

I'm grateful when we reach the streets again. Urban destruction I feel like I can handle, but the trees made me feel funny in my stomach. We can spy the Shard now, rearing up a few streets away, muzzle flashes lighting up the sky around it; looks like soldiers have already thought to reinforce their position. 'Hey!' Lucius calls, pointing. 'Look!'

A woman is running in our direction, dragging a small child by the hand, with something in pursuit . . . no, two . . . no, *three* things . . . *not things, oh God* . . . and for a second I think I know them and my whole body goes cold – *no no no black multi-legged no SMILEY JOES NO* – but as they pass through a patch of light I see that they're actually dogs, black six-legged red-eyed hounds letting loose horrible strangled barks as they scuttle along. They're still fairly horrendous-looking . . .

*But at least they're not Smiley Joes.*

*Just dogs.*

*There are scarier things than these.*

*These are* nothing.

Lauren psychically drags the mother and child towards us as Smith and the soldiers lay down covering fire. Leon sends his sword whipping towards the dogs, slicing away the legs of one – *nice* – and I pound the other two with relish, basically flattening my car – and them - with the force of the blows. Now there are just silent stains where once there were monsters, and I toss the dead car aside. *Goodbye old friend*, someone in my head thinks, and I actually have to stifle a giggle.

It's the first time I've seriously considered that maybe I've gone a bit mad.

The dog that Leon de-legged is still alive, howling and thrashing around but basically helpless. The sword returns to its sheath and the two guns emerge from inside his jacket and float over. They position themselves above the creature and fire, and it stops thrashing, and the weapons whip back into Leon's jacket, lightning quick. 'Show off,' I say.

Leon glances at me, as blank as ever. 'Come on,' says Lucius. 'Let's press on.' The soldiers move in protectively around the woman and her child, telling them everything's fine and to come with us, and we continue towards our destination. Trucks and tanks have formed a perimeter – *yay, I love a good perimeter, me* - around the Shard, interspersed with soldiers and gun platforms, but Smith doesn't even have to show his ID, they just part and let us through, although I'm not exactly oblivious to the looks I get from some of the soldiers. *Sod you. Here to help.*

We head into the typically boring corporate lobby, all anonymous décor and rubber plants. Smith goes to talk to some men in suits while the woman and her son are handed over to another soldier. 'It's all right, madam,' he says, pulling off his helmet and smiling as though we're dealing with an earthquake or a flood rather than this Book of Revelations bollocks. 'We have an area downstairs for civilians, come with me.'

I turn to Lauren. 'Apparently Nailah's on her way here. She's dead set on completing her mission, whatever she thinks that is. They'll kill her if she makes trouble. Can you keep a look out?'

'Yes.'

'Are you all right?'

'I think so,' she says. 'Are you?'

'Yeah. Sorry about before. I'm all business now.'

She nods and pats me on the shoulder. Every little gesture helps. 'OK,' I say. 'Um . . . right. I'm going to try and work out what the hell to-' I'm cut off by another tremor, a massive one. Multiple windows shatter and people stumble around, flailing, falling to the ground.

'Leon!' yells Lucius. 'Stanly! Lauren! Many more like that and we'll be in trouble. Be ready to use your powers to stabilise this building, we don't want it falling down around our ears.'

I'm about to say that that's a good idea when an awfully familiar noise, a thousand times louder than anything else we've been hearing, swamps everything, drowning the sounds of gunfire outside, wiping out the lightning. It seems to be coming from everywhere. It's the roar that I heard in the Tube station, the worst of all the cries of those furious rampaging entities, full of the promise of pain, the whimpering of the dying, the burning of worlds. Seeing the face of whatever could make a sound like that . . . surely that really *would* drive you mad. I look through one of the glassless windows. Somewhere north, a series of fireballs whoosh upwards into the infernal sky.

*It's out.*

*It's here.*

# Chapter Twenty-Six

'WHAT THE HELL was that?' yells a voice. It's familiar, although I'm sure it's not someone I've met, and I look to the source. One of the suited men standing with Smith.

*Well bloody 'eck.*

It's the Lord Mayor of London himself. Derek something. Derek Brook? Brooks? I think it's Brooks. Short and portly, balding, posh. Smith is on a walkie talkie, barking questions. I run over. 'Any idea what that was?' I ask, even though I really don't want to know.

Smith holds up the walkie talkie. Through the static we can hear a cacophonous crashing, and beneath that a terrified voice. Most of what they're saying is obscured by stabs of interference, the reports of guns and that infernal thumping and banging, but I manage to make out the word 'big'.

And the word 'tentacles'.

Then the radio is silent.

'Well,' says Smith. 'Shit.'

'Shit indeed!' Brooks yells. 'And may I ask why the hell this terrorist isn't rotting in a cell somewhere?'

*Hold on a second there, pal, are you referring to me?*

'Change of plan,' says Smith. 'Now, we—'

'*Not good enough!*' the mayor blusters. 'The prime minister entrusted *you* with this, Smith! You assured us that the infestation was under control, and that everything would be back to normal! I'd call this pretty bloody far from normal! And *why is this terrorist not—*'

'I'm not a terrorist, *sir*,' I say. 'I'm here to help.'

'Oh, you are, are you?' The mayor rounds on me. 'Here to help, are you? So it wasn't you and your band of *terrorist friends* who caused this in the first place, was it? Who destroyed our defences and allowed these unholy abominations to broach our city, to destroy this, the cradle of English civilisation, culture, finance? To defile this great symbol of democracy?' Smith rolls his eyes and moves away, talking into his walkie talkie, obviously pleased that someone has distracted the mayor, and I'm just about to open a six-pack of verbal whoop-ass on the Right Honourable Mr Brooks when something catches my eye. The wall behind him is *sweating*. Clear droplets of liquid are running down it, and it starts rippling. I step back without thinking and the wall expands outwards, becoming a great black mouth . . . and swallows the mayor whole, mid-sentence. Just like that, he disappears, sucked into a blobby distended mass the same colour as the wall. I can hear what sounds like chomping going on within. There is a chorus of screams, of things being dropped, of people saying *oh my God* and *what was that* and *the mayor*, and a bunch of soldiers open fire, but as quickly as it appeared the thing has vanished, becoming flat and dry, a wall again. My skin crawls. It could be anywhere. I look around, up at the ceiling, at the floors, at the other walls. We cannot have this thing on the loose. Smith is talking at me, other people are talking at him, shouting, demanding, but I shut them out and try to *listen* for it with my mind, reach out, sense it.

Something tickles the back of my brain and I spin on the spot and think STOP just as it lurches down from the ceiling towards me. I grab it with a thought, stop it in its tracks, grip it, keep it gripped as it snaps its not-exactly-jaws, a shifting amorphous grey thing, strong – *but not as strong as* me – and I feel where it ends and the ceiling begins and I *yank*, pulling it out of its home and holding it in the air in front of me. It's struggling

381

for dear life, snapping its not-quite-mouth, trying to make the shapes of fists and blades and tentacles, like sludgy liquid metal desperately searching for a form, and I yell at everyone to *fire* at it. Happily, they obey. Bullets fly from all sides, tearing into it, and I can feel that they're hurting it, it doesn't make a sound but I know it's in pain, the thrashing becomes more violent, more spasmodic, and the soldiers keep emptying their weapons, and I can feel it giving up, feel it weakening. It's nearly gone. Nearly . . . nearly . . . dead. Just a mass. A nothingness. I toss it to the floor.

'Well,' says Smith. 'It appears that we're going to need a new mayor.'

'For goodness' sake, Morter!' says Lucius, crossing himself. He sounds as though he's aged about four decades in one evening. I *sympathise*. 'Have some respect!'

'Don't get pious with me, Lucius,' snaps Smith. 'You hated the blathering, ineffectual Etonian prick as much as I did.'

'But . . . respect for the dead . . .'

'Respect my arse. If you really think we've got time for respect right now, I'd love to know exactly which apocalypse *you've* been witnessing.' Smith turns away and strides towards the front door. 'Right, now. Let's go and find out what this latest minion of Hell is, shall we?'

'Smith,' I say.

'What?' He clearly doesn't want to speak to me. *Tough.* 'Did you have a plan B?' I ask.

'What the hell do you mean?'

'If the drawing areas didn't work,' I say. 'If that . . . for what-ever reason . . . didn't do the job. Did you have another plan?'

Smith frowns, and in that frown I sense a *yes*, so I cheat. I read his mind. Just enough to know that I was right, that it was a yes, and he must see it in my eyes because his hand goes to his weapon. 'Stay out of my head,' he says, 'or so help me God I will *shoot* you—'

'What was it? The plan B? What is it?'

He makes a massive effort not to lamp me one, and motions towards a quiet corner. I follow him. 'Those creatures,' he says. 'The shimmers. They're the reason that the monsters are coming through. They all come from some . . . some other dimension. We barely know anything about it. Just that the laws of physics, of biology, of *everything*, are very different from here. With a few exceptions.'

'Like the power.'

'Yes,' says Smith. 'Whatever it is in the brain chemistry of empowered people that allows them to do what they do, that . . . essence, energy, power, whatever you want to call it, it exists as a . . . an element, for want of a better word, in the other dimension. The shimmers have a bizarre relationship with it, we've barely been able to understand it, but as far as we can tell they both feed on it *and* produce it. And somehow, they found a way through from their world to our world, and they like the power that we have over here. Maybe it's a different bloody flavour or something. Who knows. But the point is that they want more of it. And their dimension and ours . . . they're not meant to interact. As you can see.'

'So? Plan B?'

'Freeman,' says Smith, contempt dripping from his tongue as he says the name. 'He theorised that it might be possible to close the tears from the *other* side. From the shimmer world. He had a whole strategy, but it relied on us finding a way through to their world. Something that nobody has been able to do. Our best scientists couldn't even begin to think of a way.'

'Couldn't they just do what you were doing at the drawing areas, but . . . in reverse?'

'Oh,' says Smith, slapping a hand to his head. 'Brilliant! Do

383

you have a degree in advanced interdimensional physics? Such a shame you didn't come on board years ago! Because nobody else in the Angel Group thought of that!'

'All right, Sammy Sarcasm. You could have just said yes, and that it didn't work.'

'The point I'm making,' says Smith, 'is that effectively there is *no* plan B. Unless we can miraculously find a way through to the shimmers' dimension. If you think of a way, please feel free to book a one-way ticket. Now if you'll excuse me.' He stalks away and I flip my middle finger at his retreating back. *Great. No plan B.*

*So more monster fighting, then.*

Lauren is just heading outside as well. I follow after her and am about to call her name when I hear another familiar voice through the din. It's Nailah. 'Let me in!' she yells. 'Let me *through,* I *have* to—'

'Lauren!' I say. 'Get her! Make sure she doesn't get shot!'

Lauren pushes her way through the perimeter of soldiers, reappearing a minute later with Nailah in tow. Her clothes are filthy and several vivid bruises stand out on her face. She's clutching a baseball bat, which is dripping with various shades of goop. *Monster blood.* 'Wow,' I say. 'You fought your way here with that?'

Now she sees me, and her eyes widen. 'Stanly! You're all right! Yeah, I decided to *Resident Evil* my way here. It's fucking mental out there.' In the distance there is another earth-shaking, sanity-curdling roar.

'Yeah,' I say, trying a smile to see how it feels. 'Shit got real.'

We bring her in and sit her down on a sofa in the corner of the lobby. 'After it all went tits up, we ran,' says Nailah. 'Me and Eddie . . . Lauren, I'm so sorry, we didn't want to leave you, but—'

'It's all right.' Lauren smiles reassuringly.

'I got separated from the others,' said Nailah. 'Ran . . . hid. Tried to track down some of my contacts, Oracle and Weird, Sister types, but they'd all skipped town. Pussies.' She smiled darkly. 'So I went looking for Eddie and co again. Found 'em. More hiding. For ages, just hiding and waiting . . . then everything started going to hell. Properly.'

'We were misled,' I say. 'The machines . . . they were keeping the monsters out. Not letting them in.'

Nailah shakes her head. 'Well . . . damn. So the evil corporation wasn't so evil after all.'

'There are degrees of evil,' says Lauren.

'Yeah,' says Nailah. 'That's why I'm here, actually. Decided I might as well try and get what I came for in the first place . . . should have realised I wouldn't be able to just shout my way in. Stupid plan, really. It's just that it's all . . . it's all got a bit hectic.' Her eyes are glassy, but I see her steel herself inside, see her suck the tears in. Lock 'em in a box. *Tough broad.*

'I'm sorry about Stephen,' I say. 'Your friend at the Angel Group. I heard that they . . .' It seems slightly distasteful to come out and say 'that they executed him', even though that's what happened, even though that's exactly the thought I'm putting into her head.

*Couldn't possibly come out and actually say it, though.*

*Always something to be cowardly about.*

'Thank you.' She shakes her head fondly. 'Stephen. Such an idiot.'

'Do you have family in London?'

'No.'

'Good. And look . . . your big data dump idea? Just forget about it. At least for now. It was a good plan, but now . . . now we just need to focus on stopping what's happening. Somehow.' As if to illustrate my point, the new faraway arrival roars again, jellifying my spine.

'What the hell *was* that?' whispers Nailah.

'You don't want to know.' *I certainly don't.*

'God,' says Nailah. 'This is too much . . . what the hell . . .' She closes her eyes and brings her breathing under control. 'Lauren,' she says. 'This isn't . . . this probably isn't the time. But we might, you know, die. Horribly. So there's something . . . I wanted to tell you before, but . . . it's my fault. That your friend Sally's in that place. It's my fault.'

Lauren frowns, confused. 'What do you mean?'

'I saw her,' says Nailah. 'About a year ago. Using her powers. Completely by accident, but . . . then I followed her. And I saw her doing it again. And I took a picture, and I put it on the blog, and then she disappeared, and I realised . . . it had to be me, it was my fault, the Angel Group must have seen the picture . . . I'm so sorry . . .'

'So . . . you knew about me? Before you came?'

'Yes.'

'But the dog I saved? You didn't see me?'

Nailah shakes her head. 'I was bluffing. Just said I'd seen you using your powers, hoping you'd fill in the blanks. And then you did. Lauren, I'm so, *so* sorry, after she disappeared I swore I'd never scoop anyone else like that, but—'

Lauren puts her arm around her shoulder. 'It's fine. It's all right. It wasn't your fault.'

'But—'

'She volunteered. Sally volunteered.'

Now it's Nailah's turn to look confused. 'She *volunteered*? But how . . .'

'I don't know,' says Lauren. 'I haven't had a chance to talk to her . . . but she did. She volunteered. And I managed to get her out. It's all right.'

A soldier hurries over to me. 'Stanly Bird?'

'Yeah?'

'Mr Smith wants to see you.'

The soldier leads me outside. Smith is there with Lucius and a group of soldiers, some regular army, some Angel Group special forces. 'What's going on?' I ask.

'That noise,' says Smith. 'The new arrival. It's in Regent's Park. Looks as though it tore its way up from under the ground. It's by far the biggest one we've seen so far. I'm mobilising as much force as we can, heading out to destroy it. Some empowered backup wouldn't go amiss.'

I nod. 'Fine. I'll—'

(*Stanly!*)

I jump. 'Woah!'

'What the hell's the matter with you?' asks Smith.

'Sorry,' I say. 'My friend Sharon. She's talking to me . . . wait a second.' I walk a little way away and think a reply. *Sharon? Are you OK?*

(*We're about half a mile from the Shard. We had to stop and help some people. Are you there? Can you come and help us?*)

*I'll be right there. Hang on.*

I turn back to Smith. 'I need to go and help them.'

'But—'

'If I get them,' I say, 'that's three more empowered to help out with this thing. We'll meet you at Regent's Park. All right?'

'Fine.'

I think towards Lauren. *Lauren, the others are nearby. I'm going to help them. Smith is heading to tackle that big bugger we just heard.*

(*Stanly? Hello? Can you hear me?*)

*Yes, you're doing it right!*

(*OK. This is strange. Stanly . . . I don't think I can. Whatever it is . . . I don't think I can face fighting it.*)

*That's OK. You and Nailah stay here, help out. And I'll be back. Be careful.*

(*I will. You too.*)

I kick off and fly, bringing up my internal map. I know where Eddie's place is in relation to here, so I know which direction to go. My ears are full of chaos, a horrifying abstract noise choir of wailing car alarms, explosions, thunder and monstrous, unintelligible war cries, and I can see more monsters: small ones scurrying down alleys, bigger ones climbing up the sides of buildings, blobs and claws and tentacles. Some of the buildings themselves are . . . they're *distorting*, some covered in that weird rusty stuff, some bending or collapsing in on themselves . . .

*It's going to get worse.*

*Shut up.*

*No time for thoughts like that.*

*Moment to moment.*

*That's the only way.*

A flurry of activity catches my eye and I slow my flight to look down. The road below is lined with expensive-looking town houses, and something is lumbering along it. Another monster. It reminds me of those fish that you see in nature documentaries, the ones that live at the very bottom of the sea; its body is a fleshy, transparent pyramid, its internal organs glowing psychedelic colours, every inner process surreally highlighted, it has six giant insect legs and its front is a mess of feelers and eyes. A crowd of people are rushing it with makeshift weapons, and in amongst them, oh God, yes, *yes*, my heart bursts, because in amongst them I can clearly see Connor and Skank side-by-side, Connor with a pair of handguns and Skank with a shotgun, firing and firing. Skank is keeping a safe distance but Connor runs forwards, plants his feet on the side of a house and runs nimbly up, positioning himself halfway up the second storey so he can get a better angle. Standing secure on the vertical wall as though it's still pavement, face set, he continues to pump bullets into the monster. It makes a low rumbling noise and lashes out with one of its feelers, sending a guy flying – *woops let me yelp ya there* – and I psychically catch him before he can brain himself on a car . . .

*My mum's car!*

It's parked just down the road and Eddie, yes *Eddie* is next to it, wrestling with something that looks like a mish-mash of horse, dragon and overweight woman. He lands a hard kick in its gut and batters it about the face with his fists, and it whinnies in pain but immediately hits him back, a serious *wham* that looks like it should have taken my cousin's head off. He stands his ground, though, shrugs it off, spits some blood on the floor and dives in, walloping the thing to the ground. He keeps on hitting it until it's not moving any more, and I'm about to shout a warning because something else is coming at him, another ghastly misshapen catastrophe of glued-together bits, but Sharon – *yes that's definitely Sharon's voice yes yes YES* – beats me to it, telling him to '*Get down*', and I want to whoop with joy. Eddie ducks, just as his deformed opponent gets the business end of an uprooted lamppost straight through its distended belly, impaling it against a tree, and Sharon walks into shot, grim-faced, streaked with dirt and multi-coloured blood, a second lamppost rotating above her head. She jerks her head and psychically yanks the other makeshift spear from the dead beast with a noise that makes me think, inexplicably, of a cow being yanked through a gap that's much too small. 'Nice shot!' I yell.

They all look up and Sharon cries, '*Stanly!*'

I look around. There are no cars on this street, apart from my mum's, and for one ridiculous second I think *can't smash it, I'll get in trouble.*

*Did that thought really just cross my mind?*

*It's been a strange day.*

I reach out, pick the car up and lift it off the ground. 'Get away from that thing!' I yell. Sharon and Eddie pass on the instruction and the crowd gratefully disperses, and I wrap my mum's car up with my brain and hurl it with as much force as I can muster . . . and in it goes, splitting the beast's side, penetrating its belly or whichever essential bit of it I've ruptured. Luminous multicoloured fluids start spurting out, decorating the street, and the creature bellows in agony and tries to crawl away, but it can't, it's too badly hurt. Connor and Skank resume firing at it and the crowd set upon it with their own weapons while I land bumpily and run over to Sharon and Eddie. They both wrap me up in a steel embrace that crushes my breathing, but I don't care, relief washes over me: *something* might at least momentarily be all right.

'*You're safe,*' Eddie whispers.

'Fine,' I choke. 'You?'

'Yeah. You know you made me admit that I secretly wanted to do all this superhero-y ass-kicking business? Is it all right if I take it all back?'

'Yes.'

The embrace breaks and he looks me up and down. 'What happened to you?'

'They captured me.' I don't really want to go into specifics. 'But I escaped.'

'And the, uh, uniform?'

'Ah,' I said. 'Um . . . yeah. I tried to break in again. Didn't go that well.'

'It really doesn't suit you.'

'Yeah,' I say. 'Little short for a stormtrooper, eh?' I smile weakly, and he shakes his head and offers the distant evolutionary precursor of a smile in return. 'What about you guys?' I ask.

'We've been hiding out,' says Eddie. 'We thought we might go and try again, destroy the machines, but . . .'

'We were wrong,' I say. 'The Angel Group weren't trying to open a doorway. They were trying to close it.'

'What?' Eddie's face is a portrait of disbelief and shock.

'We screwed up,' I say. 'I screwed up.' Saying it makes it sink in in a way it hadn't before. In the midst of this maelstrom of bloody, impossible mayhem, I feel the full weight of what I've done. Laying into Alex before made it feel almost better, like I wasn't responsible, but now . . . 'We should go,' I say. 'There's stuff to do . . . people to help.' Eddie nods. 'Where's Daryl?' I ask.

Eddie and Sharon exchange looks. 'I'm not sure,' says Sharon. 'When everything went wrong at the second site, Connor and I got separated from Freeman . . . then when Skank and Daryl found us and told us what happened, Daryl said he was going to find him. Find Freeman, I mean. Find a way of getting you out . . . we haven't seen either of them since.'

*Oh God.*

*Daryl . . .*

'He'll be fine,' I say. 'He . . . he'll be all right. He can handle monsters.'

*Please can he be all right.*

*Unless he was in on . . .*

*NO.*

No. He wasn't in on this. There's no way.

*He's betrayed you before—*

*NO. SHUT UP BRAIN.*

Connor and Skank hurry over. 'Stanly,' says Skank. 'You all right?'

'Same as always.'

'That bad, huh?'

I smile. 'You?'

'Five by five.'

'Connor,' I say. 'You OK?'

'Honestly,' says Connor, reloading his guns, 'I have been better.'

'I know the feeling.' I tell them about the beast in Regent's Park. No-one looks particularly keen, understandably. 'I don't know how we actually fix this,' I say. 'Smith said there was a plan B at one point, but it doesn't seem . . . anyway. For the moment, I think we're just going to have to try and kill as many monsters as possible.'

Eddie and Sharon nod. Connor shrugs, which is as good as a nod. Skank cocks his shotgun, which I take as a yes. 'Cool,' I say. 'Hold on.' I think *grab*, I think *steady*, and I fly. Up into the fiery sky, over the dying buildings. Even now the sensation of flying gives me a molecule of comfort, and I hold on to that. I don't wallow, I don't indulge, I don't overdo it, I don't try to convince myself that things really are going to be OK. But like Lauren's pat on the shoulder before, every little helps.

Except it doesn't really. Because now we pass over a building and see Regent's Park . . . or the place formerly known as Regent's Park . . . and I stop us dead in the air.

*Oh.*

Enormous isn't big enough. Gigantic isn't big enough. This thing must be nearly a quarter of a mile in diameter, a bulbous, pulsating green dome ringed by a hundred tentacles as thick as ancient trees, and at the centre is a huge round mouth, a chasm full of chainsaw teeth, each one as long as two people. It's trying to haul itself out of the massive crater it's lying in - *oh God there's more of it, this is just the head*. It roars again and I feel like I might spontaneously combust because that would be preferable to sharing a universe with this thing. A line of tanks is converging, looking comically tiny. We hang in the air and I look over at Eddie. 'Um. So. What d'ya reckon?'

'If I said I haven't got the faintest inkling of a clue and would kind of like to curl up in a ball and cry, would you hold it against me?'

'Not at all.'

'What the hell do we attack?' says Connor. 'It's . . . it's so . . .'

BLAM! BLAM! BLAM! BLAM! A barrage of fiery tiger coughs as the tanks launch their first rounds. The projectiles hit the beast's great green bulk and it bellows and shakes, causing another tremor that reduces several nearby buildings to piles of dust and ruined concrete. As the smoke clears I see that the monster's flesh is blackened but unbroken and it lashes out with a retaliatory tentacle, swatting a tank and propelling it spinning through the air like a little toy. It crashes down in a car park, demolishing several cars. Sharon narrows her eyes, concentrates and sends both of her lampposts towards the beast like orange-tipped javelins; one impacts against it and bounces off, the other goes straight into its mouth and is effortlessly ground into powder by the monster's teeth. The tanks fire again, uselessly.

'Stanly!'

I look down. An open-top army truck has pulled up and a number of soldiers jump out . . . along with Lauren. 'Thought you weren't coming?' I call.

'I changed my mind!' she yells. 'And now . . . I kind of wish I hadn't!'

'I'm bringing you up!' I think towards her and lift her up to meet us, and there is a bizarre exchange of nods. *Oh yeah, hi, how are you, how've you been, nice to see you, oh, monsters, yeah, totally, yeah apocalypse, yeah, well bye then . . .*

*What are we going to do?*

*What. The. HELL. Are—*

'Take us over the top of it,' says Skank, suddenly. 'Over its mouth.'

'You're *joking!*' says Connor. '*Over that mouth?*'

'Only weak point as far as I can see. If Stanly is absolutely certain he won't accidentally drop any of us into the jaws of hideous doom, I think it might be a workable strategy.'

'I'm certain,' I say. *I have to be.*

'Oh God,' says Sharon. She closes her eyes for a second, then opens them and nods decisively. 'OK then. Fine.' She brings her one remaining lamppost back above her head.

'Worth a try,' says Eddie, doing an admirable job of keeping his voice level. 'I guess.' He reaches into his jacket and pulls out the sawn-off shotgun I took from Connor and Sharon's safe about fifty years ago.

'Lauren?' I ask.

She nods her head and speaks inside mine. (*Please don't drop us.*)

I try a reassuring smile and nod. It feels a bit silly.

OK.

*Up we go.*

I take us higher and fly us towards the monstrosity, trying to ignore the webs of lightning above our heads. The rain is really heavy now, hot rather than warm, and more angry blasts rend the air as the tanks fire again, arcs of light curving gracefully over the forest of flapping tentacles and exploding around the mouth. It shudders and roars and everything shakes. I lift us up again as a tentacle whirls past, too close for comfort, then fly above the whirlpool of blades, allowing Skank, Eddie and Connor to aim their guns and let rip. Bullets ricochet off monstrous teeth, shedding sparks, some find their way through and strike flesh and it screams again, letting loose gusts of wet, stinking breath. I just concentrate on keeping us all in the air. Lauren is summoning everything she can from the ground around the monster and launching it into its hellish maw, bits of twisted metal and concrete blocks and burning wreckage, and Sharon javelins her lamppost in. It disappears briefly, then the monster burps it back up and it slices towards us. Sharon catches it with her mind and sends it down again, and Lauren drops a whole car – *ah, car-throwin' buddy* – but the monster obliterates it. 'This isn't working!' yells Eddie.

*It really isn't.*

The tanks fire again. Pointless. Completely pointless. Why can't they just . . .

*Aha.*

'I'm sending you all down to the ground,' I say.

'What?' asks Eddie. 'But—'

'Trust me.' I think *go*, ignoring their various protestations, and fly them back and away from the mouth, safely down through the tentacles. Then I turn my focus to one of the tanks, beckoning the vehicle. It obediently leaves the floor and comes towards me, and I hope the occupants understand the plan I'm formulating and don't try to blow me out of the air. I bring the tank right up next to me then tilt it downwards so the gun is pointing directly into the monster's mouth. I sneak a glance at my friends and see they're keeping the tentacles occupied with bullets and improvised projectiles. 'FIRE!' I yell, amplifying my voice with my powers and hoping it reaches the soldiers inside the tank. 'BLOODY FIRE, NOW!'

BLAM! A fireball launches straight into the mouth, blowing apart hundreds of teeth and exploding deep within. The monster belches a pillar of fire and I feel myself and the tank hurtling away from it, through the air, propelled by a hot shockwave. I'm spinning over and over, I can't tell what's up and what's down, all I can hear are explosions and roaring, all I can do is try and slow myself down and hope for the best. 'Oof.' I hit the ground and bounce and hit it again and roll, and somehow end up in a sitting position on a carpet of broken glass, staring at the monster as it writhes and roars in agony. Its tentacles are going berserk and I see another tank flying up, and another, but I'm not doing it . . . Lauren? Sharon? *Yes!* The two of them are standing a way away from me, looking up, and tanks are firing and firing into the monster's infinite belly, hollowing it out. Now Leon appears out of the darkness and raises a tank of his own, blasting and blasting, and the creature is dying, I can see it, I can hear it, I can smell it, I can *feel* it. It's nearly finished. Another blast and a new roaring scream, desperate now rather than angry, and Eddie turns towards me, grinning. 'Well, looks like I didn't kill Leon after—'

THUMP. A spasming tentacle hits him with the force of a speeding truck and he flies away from me, far away, too far for me to see. 'Eddie!' I yell. 'EDDIE!' I jump to my feet, run and take off, closely followed by Connor, who is sprinting as fast as I can fly towards the husk of a gutted building where I think Eddie must have fallen. I drop to my feet and run over crunching rubble, and I can see him now, I can see his arm, yes, *yes*—

—*no*—

I stop, as does Connor. Eddie is lying on the ground, eyes closed, his face a mess of blood, his arms and legs at the wrong angles. I stumble over to him, the screams of the defeated beast fading away, absorbed into useless frequencies, fall to my knees next to my cousin and reach out to take his hand. Limp, completely limp. I think *open your eyes* but he doesn't obey. I look at his chest but there is no breath, and I think *breathe*, but he doesn't obey. I think *open your eyes, breathe, breathe, BREATHE*, I'm thinking the words and screaming them, although I can hardly hear myself, and I can hear that Connor is talking to me but I can't hear what he's saying, unimportant words of some kind, I'm too busy to listen, busy thinking, because I think things and they happen, that's how all this works, I think them and that makes them true, so when I think *live, bloody live Eddie, LIVE you bastard, breathe, breathe, breathe, open your eyes*, and when I scream for him to *OPEN HIS FUCKING EYES RIGHT NOW*, he should, he should do what I say. But he doesn't. Why won't he do what I *tell* him? I'm sobbing into his neck, shaking him, my tears pouring into his blood, crystal and crimson making a mosaic on his skin, but he won't breathe.. He won't open his eyes. He just lies there like an old doll. Like he's forgotten himself. He's forgotten how to live. How? How can anyone forget how to live? I don't understand.

'Come back.' I'm whispering. I can hear my whisper above my screaming. My screaming? Is it mine? Or am I just whispering? Whose name is that? Stanly? 'Stanly.' Connor's voice. 'Stanly, he's gone.'

NO.

'He's dead, Stanly.' Connor might also be crying. I'm not sure. It's hard to discern individual sounds. A million miles away there might be one more roar, and then multiple reverberations as all those lifeless tentacles come crashing down. That might be what's happening. I think I can hear Sharon's voice too. I think she might be there. I think she might be crying too. I think . . .

I don't know what I'm thinking.

I'm thinking *he's dead*.

I'm thinking *he's really dead*.

And if I think it . . .

That means it's true.

# Chapter Twenty-Seven

S OMEONE SPEAKS, AN unfamiliar voice, clear and cold, cutting right through the deafening silence. 'We must continue.'

Somehow I'm standing up again. My body turns itself around and I look where everyone is looking, at the source of the voice. Leon. He regards me, face inscrutable, hands behind his back, sword in its sheath. 'What?' I feel myself ask.

'We must continue.' I think he might be French. 'More to kill.'

'You don't tell us what to do.' Connor's voice is a low growl.

'It does not matter,' Leon said. 'Friends, enemies. Does not matter now. There are more to kill.'

'I'm not just going to leave him here.' It's me speaking again. My own voice is strangled, guttural, but childish in comparison to Connor's. I'm not sure why I'm comparing them. I . . .

'Stanly . . .' Sharon's voice?

'You must.' Leon.

'No.' I lunge at him and feel him try to stop me, freeze me in the air as he did before, but I'm not going to let him, not now. I send a mental punch in his direction that knocks him backwards but he doesn't look at all rattled, he just comes at me with a kick that I barely dodge, feeling the wind across the side of my head. I try to bring my leg around to trip him up but the manoeuvre is far too clumsy and his foot slams into the back of my head with such force that my vision fragments and I nearly topple over. I don't let myself, though, instinct kicks in and I fly up over his next two attacks, landing behind him and visualising twin chains of glowing thought that wrap around his arms, pinning them to his sides. His sword rises from its scabbard but I think *snap*, shattering the blade like glass, then I think *over* and he's down, pinned to the floor. I hold him there and suddenly, as though abruptly tuning to a new station, I register all the other voices. Sharon crying *no*, Connor yelling for me to stop, Skank saying *this isn't helping, for God's sake*. Lauren is there too, but she's not speaking. Just looking at me, at Eddie, her face so full of sorrow, grief, grief for *me*, because I've lost . . . no, no, no, NO.

*No.*

I look down at Leon and I can feel emotion, real emotion. He's angry. It comes off him like red steam. 'So you do feel.' I really don't sound like myself. Connor moves to pull me away, Sharon is trying to use her powers, but I'm blocking them all. Nobody's getting near me if I don't want them to.

'Yes,' says Leon. 'But I do not let emotions control me. You do. You will not survive this.'

'I'm not leaving Eddie.'

'You have to.'

'No I *don't*.' I tighten my grip on him. 'Maybe I'll kill you, huh? Balance it out a bit? Kill you like Eddie should have?' I start to constrict his breathing, and he gags.

'Stanly, STOP!' cries Sharon.

'You . . . must . . .' chokes Leon. 'The city is—'

'Doomed,' I say.

'No,' says Connor. More lightning strikes nearby, bathing us in crackling heat. Somewhere, something explodes. Something's always exploding. That's the way things are now.

'There's nothing we can do,' I say.

'We took that thing down.' Sharon's voice shakes, her face is wet with tears, but she points firmly towards the dead giant. 'We killed it. We can—'

'They'll keep coming,' I say. 'Millions of them. Never stopping. Never ever. And there'll be worse ones that that. So much worse.' As if to hammer home my point, another tremor comes, shaking the abused earth with malignant joy. Leon struggles but I keep him flat and helpless with my wrath. 'We can't just keep fighting them. It's pointless. They'll wear us down and then kill us. Like . . .' I look at Eddie and my vision blurs, and I find that I can't say his name.

'You can't give up.' Lauren's voice. 'You can't.' Now she speaks in my head. (*You're the hero.*)

'I'm not,' I say. 'This is all my fault.'

'We don't have time for this, Stanly,' says Connor. 'We need you strong. We can get through this if we—'

My mind is starting to drift. Something is dawning, truly dawning. *This is the end. It's the end. And I should be with Kloe. There's nothing I can do.*

*But I have to fight . . .*

*Fight what?*

*It's just going to keep coming.*

Something else explodes, as though shown on TV far away. Screaming isn't really screaming now. Gunfire? A distant, half-hearted drumbeat. And now I hear the sound of mighty footfalls, something new. I look out across the city towards the source. The air is clogged with smoke and flame and rain, but through it I can see an enormous shape moving, bigger than Big Ben. 'There's nothing I can do,' I say. 'I'm going to Kloe and Tara.'

'You can't,' says Connor.

'I'm sorry.' I let go of Leon and start to walk away, just as a curtain of white and blue is drawn across the air in front of me. A monster steps out, tall and spindly with pincers and a long tail. I immediately think *break* and it bends unnaturally and moans like a pig with a mouth full of cotton wool, then I think *down* and it falls, and I keep walking but Connor grabs me, whirls me around. His face is furious, stained with tears, blood, dirt.

'Oh, no!' he yells. 'You are *not* just going to leave us. You can't!'

'This is *it*! IT! *The end*! I'm going to find Kloe and spend it with her. I'm—'

'What would Eddie say?' Connor is bellowing, angrier than I've ever seen him. 'If he saw you giving up now? Walking away from this mess? Away from us? Is that any way to honour him?'

'It doesn't *matter*.'

He loses it. Throws a punch. I stop it . . . except no, I don't. I was going to let it come, but someone else stops it. I look past him. It's Lauren. She's stopping him. I look back at Connor. 'I'm sorry.'

'Say it again,' he says. 'Say it doesn't matter. Say Eddie doesn't *matter*. Say the rest of us don't *matter*. *You* dragged us into it. You were so desperate to be the superhero, to fight the bad guys, to use these powers. Well, here we are. The big fight. We're in this because of *you*. Don't you dare walk away.'

*He's right.*

'I'm sorry,' I say, because I am going to go, even though I know he's right.

*No.*

*You have to stay.*

*Can't go.*

I *am* going to—

(*Stanly.*)

I jump. Connor frowns. 'What?'

'Freeman,' I say. 'He's talking to me. In my head.' I turn around, as though he's going to be there, and I think and shout at the same time. 'Where the hell are you, you son of a bitch? I'll *kill* you—'

(*You'll do no such thing. You can stop what's happening. The world was never meant to end, not properly. Come to the Kulich Gallery. Remember the pictures. I'll be waiting for you.*) And he's gone. I know that he's gone. I look around, at Connor, at Lauren, at Sharon, at Skank, at Eddie. The broken soldier. My brother.

'Stanly,' says Sharon. 'What—'

'I have to go,' I say.

'Oh,' says Connor, 'so you *are* going. Running—'

'I'm not running away,' I say. 'I'm going to find Freeman. He says that this, all this, it can be stopped. He was the one who had the plan B in the first place.'

'Plan B?' asks Skank.

'I don't know what it is,' I say, 'but it's the only . . . I can't think of anything else. I'll go. And if I can stop it, I'll stop it. And then I'll kill him.'

'He lied to us,' says Connor, 'this whole time, he was lying. Everything he's ever said, to any of us. How do you know—'

'I don't. But if there's a chance that I can stop what's happening, I have to go.'

'Then we're coming with you,' says Sharon.

'No,' I say. 'You all stay here. Help people. Try and contain the monsters as much as you can. You're all as capable as me. I'll go and see what . . . I'll come back when it's done.'

'What if you don't?' says Lauren.

'I will.' I look at Connor. 'I'm sorry.' He doesn't answer. I look at everyone, and I say it again, and the words mean nothing. Or maybe they do. I don't know. They just seem like what I should say. I look at Leon. 'Kill as many as you can.' He nods. Sharon moves towards me, like she's going to try and hug me, but I can't do it. I step back, shake my head. 'Sorry. I . . . I'm sorry. I can't. I'll . . . I'll be back.'

And before she can say anything I fly up into the acid sky,

over the crumbling buildings, set on what I have to do. A black pterodactyl-like apparition swoops towards me, clacking wickedly sharp mandibles, and I think my cousin's name at it, spelled out in fire, tearing a wing clean off. Down it goes. Ahead, a tall flat-faced ogre lumbers down a street, kicking cars aside, bearing down on a small group of people. They're boxed in by the wreck of a lorry, cowering, screaming. I slow, think that name again, think a net made of it, *Eddie*, and I throw it around the monster's head and yank it hard to the left, straight into the side of a building. Glass explodes, masonry crumbles and the monster lets loose a low, almost plaintive roar. It's the kind of noise that something sentient might make, something that feels. Feels *pain*.

*You shouldn't be here, then.*

By the time I've finished bashing its head against the building, said head is barely a head any more, and said building looks like it's had an encounter with several bazookas. I let the dead giant topple, then flick the lorry aside so the people can run, and on I fly.

'Stanly!'

*Leave me alone, brain. Stop messing.*

'STANLY!'

*Wait . . . what . . .*

I look to my right, because there *is* a voice, a real voice, one that I recognise. Racing across the rooftops parallel to me is a blur of feet and white fur, calling my name. 'All right kid?' Daryl yells. 'How about a lift? My feet are killing me!'

*Poor choice of words.*

*But by Christ I'm glad to see you.*

I reach out with my mind and scoop him up. Just in time, too, because there's a gap between buildings up ahead and I'm not sure even this dog could jump it. I bring him in, not slowing down, and keep him in the air beside me. 'Fancy meeting you here,' Daryl says. 'Of all the bits of sky in all the apocalypses in all the world . . .'

'Yeah.'

'It's all a bit much, really, isn't it?'

I nod.

'And there I was, two days from retirement . . .' The dog seems to notice me properly for the first time, and his tone changes. 'What's wrong? Apart from everything?'

'Eddie's dead.'

The beagle closes his eyes. 'God. Shit. Oh, man. I'm so sorry.'

*Can't talk about this now.* 'Where have you been?'

'Looking for Freeman. Then for you.'

'He played us all,' I say. 'The Angel Group were—'

'Trying to close the gaps,' says Daryl. 'Yeah. I had a hunch that might be the case. And I was all like, "well done, hunch, maybe you could have made yourself known *before* everything skipped the handcart and went straight to hell".'

'Yeah. Well. It's done.' A gash opens in the sky ahead of us and something falls out, but it has no wings and it just keeps falling, splatting against the pavement below. It's almost funny.

'So where are you heading?' asks Daryl.

'Going after Freeman. Isn't that where you're going?'

The beagle shakes his head. 'Nope. Was trying to find you. Only just managed to pick up your scent. Fair few distracting odours around, as I'm sure you can imagine. Like trying to pick out the scent of one human hair from a mountain of Satanic potpourri.'

I want to laugh at that, but I can't. 'Freeman said there might be a way of stopping what's happening.'

'Really? How?'

'You don't know?'

Daryl frowns. 'No. Why would I?'

'You worked with him for years. You were passing him information the whole time I knew you.' This seems as good a time as any for this conversation, flying through a sky racked by a supernatural storm above a burning city.

'I *swear*,' says Daryl, 'he never told me his plans. I didn't have the faintest inkling. You really think I'd have let all this happen? *Really?*'

'No . . . but . . .'

'But what? Jesus, when I met up with you that night – after *saving* you from that dog I might add – I hadn't spoken to the bastard for over a year! I thought he was dead!'

'Sorry,' I say. 'But back home. In Tref-y-Celwyn. Didn't he send you to spy on me?'

'No! I told you what happened. I told you the truth. I ran away from the Angel Group, lived with a boring old man for ages, and then found you. Made friends. Then your powers appeared.'

'And you knew what they were.'

'Yeah.'

'And you didn't tell me.'

'I couldn't! I . . .' Daryl shakes his head. 'When I was with the Angel Group, I helped Freeman find people with powers. I can sense it in humans.'

'You *what?*' My head spins. 'So . . . the empowered they plugged into the machines. You found them? You tracked them down?'

'I helped, yes. I didn't know that was where they were going, but . . . yeah.'

A memory shines in my head with unusual clarity, considering how numb I've felt since . . . since lately. Maguire asking Daryl why he wanted to fight the Angel Group. *Reasons*, the beagle had said. 'You wanted to rescue them,' I say. 'That's why you were on board with Maguire's plan.'

'That's one reason,' says Daryl. 'Like I said, I had no idea about the machines when I was with the Group, I didn't know what was happening. I thought we were helping them. Taking them to safe places, giving them counselling . . . and yeah, you don't need to say the word *naïve*. Sometimes we believe what we want to believe. We go with what information we have.' His voice is heavy with guilt. It's not a shade I've known him wear very often. It's odd. 'I knew what the power was when you got it, but I ignored it,' he says, 'because you were my friend, and because I wanted . . . normality. For both of us. Then *bam*. You're developing faster than anyone I'd ever encountered. Freaked me out. So I contacted Freeman for advice, because he was the only person I knew.'

'You trusted him.' I can't keep the contempt from my voice, contempt that he doesn't deserve, that I have no right to feel.

'Yes,' says Daryl, more firmly than I'm expecting. 'Stanly . . . it's hard to explain. Maybe some time we can sit down and I can tell you about working with him, but . . . we were partners for a long time. And in all that time, he never screwed me over. Not once. He had my back. He saved my life several times. He screwed *other* people over, sure - trust me, the dude did plenty that scared me. But he was always on the level with me. And maybe that makes me naïve, but . . . I don't know. I guess I just assumed he was one of those people you want as a friend, but definitely not as an enemy. So who else was I going to go to for advice?'

I don't answer. I want to chew him out for being so stupid, for being naïve, for letting the scumbag get in his head.

*Might be more than a touch hypocritical.*

'At first I didn't give him any specifics,' says the beagle, 'and he just gave me advice. Tips to help you develop smoothly. I've seen people's powers mess them up in a big way and I didn't want that to happen to you . . . look, the majority of empowered that I met before you, their abilities took years to develop to even half your strength. There were the odd few who were different, but mostly . . . anyway. Suddenly, in less than a few months, you had them down. Not exactly super-duper powerful, but your level of control was beyond anything I'd seen. So I contacted Freeman again and he managed to wheedle details out of me. And then . . . then we came to London, where he was based, and . . . well, you can guess.' He looks straight at me. 'I never betrayed you like you thought I did. I swear. I never knew what Freeman was really like. And I have no idea what his plan is. When Pandora killed him, I thought that was that. I ran away. Then suddenly there he is, out of the blue, alive.'

I nod. 'I believe you.'

'Thanks. I . . . I wanted that straight. Between us. In case . . .'

*In case we die.* 'Yeah.' I feel like I should smile at him, but I doubt my face is going to be into that. 'Pandora was working with him,' I say. 'This whole plan to release the monsters, she was in on it.'

'That doesn't surprise me. I never trusted that woman.'

'She's dead now.'

'Oh.' A pause. 'Can't say I'll be losing much sleep over that.'

'We might be sleeping for a very long time if we don't stop this.'

'Thanks for that.'

'You literally just brought up the possibility of us dying.'

'Yeah, as a subtle hint that I left hanging in the air.'

'OK. Sorry. Hard to be positive about all this, though.' I gesture at the city formerly known as London. We're nearing the Kulich, and I can see something wrapped around Big Ben, a great leathery red octopus-looking creature. It seems to have punched its way through the clock face and is hugging the spire with its tentacles. I think towards it, yank it from its perch, send it wriggling towards the river, trailing shards of shattered clock.

407

'Point taken,' says Daryl. He's looking down at the streets, where war is blazing. Soldiers and civilians and so many monsters, misshapen, furious. Lightning strikes the ground, tearing through the concrete, and as we fly over the river I see the Millennium Bridge crack in half and tumble into the water, fire and smoke rising. Nearby, on Southwark Bridge, two massive monsters stand on a carpet of ruined cars. One is red and black with five legs and a head like a lion drawn by a psychopath, the other is bipedal, hunched and asymmetrical, with wrecking balls for fists, and they're smacking the hell out of one another, causing the whole bridge to buckle. 'They're fighting each other!' I say.

'Jesus,' says Daryl. 'That's . . . good. I suppose. Is it?'

'I guess *woah*—'

Something comes screeching out of the water and arcs right over the bridge. It's the triangular mouth thing from before, only now I can see that the mouth is attached to a long, thick, sinuous yellow body. It grabs the ball-fisted monster in its jaws and drags it over the other side of the bridge, disappearing back into the river with a huge splash. The red and black creature bawls like a demonic gorilla and jumps over the edge of the bridge in pursuit, as if angry that its opponent has been stolen. 'Well fuck me sideways,' says Daryl.

'Quite.' We clear the river and keep flying. Almost there. 'Oh,' I say. 'One other thing . . . you know I said Tara was my daughter?'

'Yeah, still reeling from that—'

'Well, I don't think she is, actually.'

'Oh?'

'Yeah. I think she might be Smith's.'

'*Morter* Smith?'

There's a part of my brain that wants to be sarcastic and say *no, the other Smith we've been talking about lots lately*, but it's like a different language, one I don't know how to use any more, so I just say, 'Yeah'.

'Blimey,' says Daryl.

'Yeah.'

We lapse into silence, and minutes later I see it. The Jonathan Kulich Gallery. A big white cube of a building with only a few very small windows, surrounded by what looks like an electrified fence, although a good portion of it has been ripped away. There are so many signs bearing variations on the words NO ENTRY that about half of them seem redundant. No soldiers, though. I take us over the fence and we land and look up at the building. Its face gives nothing away. 'He said to meet here?' asks Daryl.

I nod. I can't help but feel wary of the place. After all, the last time I was inside I was beaten up and killed. That would be enough to put anyone off, and I wasn't keen on this particular building even before it became the scene of my death . . . and now I'm here to meet the mastermind of the end of all things. Eddie's lifeless face momentarily flickers in my mind and my chest burns, molten with grief. I blink hard, trying to quell it. It won't do anyone any good.

'Hey!' We both turn and see a girl of about fifteen running towards us. She has a crowbar in one hand and a young child hanging off the other. His face is wet with tears and snot, she is filthy and determined-looking.

'Are you all right?' I ask.

'OK,' she says. 'We . . . our house was destroyed. Our parents are . . . I don't know where they are.'

I glance at Daryl. 'I . . . um. I don't know what to . . . can I help you?'

'You were flying,' she says.

'No, I . . .' *Why lie?* 'Yes I was.'

'You're the one who was in that video.'

'Yeah.'

'And you were on TV.'

'Was I?'

'They said you're a terrorist.'

That actually makes me laugh, although the laugh is cracked and cynical and uncomfortable in my mouth. 'I'm not a terrorist. Check out my uniform.'

She shrugs. 'I figured it was stolen. But I'm not really worried about terrorists now, anyway, what with the monsters and all. What are you doing?'

'I'm trying to help,' I say. 'Honestly.'

'How come you can fly?'

'I don't know,' I say. 'It just kind of . . . happened.'

'Can we come with you?' she asks. 'I haven't got a clue what to do. My brother . . .'

'I'm sorry,' I say. 'You can't. I can't . . . I have . . . I'm going in there to try and stop what's happening.' *She might even believe me if I sound half convincing.*

'What are we supposed to do then?' The child lets out a snotty snob, and the girl kneels down and hugs him to her.

'Hide somewhere,' I say. 'Hide until it's over. That's all I can offer you.'

'Can we hide in there?' She nods towards the gallery.

*Should have thought of that.* 'Yeah. Come on.' I walk towards the Kulich with Daryl by my side and the girl and her little brother scrambling after us. The entrance slides open at my command and we enter the darkened, familiar lobby. The architecture is entirely minimalist, white walls and uncomfortable-looking furniture. 'Hide under the front desk,' I say. 'If anything comes in here, just . . . don't make a sound.'

'Thanks.' The girl goes to the desk with her brother and ducks under it. The little boy buries his face in her neck and she strokes his hair and offers me something resembling a smile. 'Good luck.'

'Thank you.'

Amazingly, the lift is still working. Daryl and I ride it up, and a bland, tinny approximation of 'Come Fly With Me' plays. 'They've changed their tune,' says Daryl. 'Actually kind of appropriate.'

*Hmm.*

We stop, get out and walk. Another long corridor. I'm sick to the back teeth of these. For several minutes we walk silently, past small rooms full of identical furniture and the same old random art, and then we enter another hallway, one I remember. I remember the way it made me feel the last time I walked along it, because I'm getting a diluted echo of that feeling now. There's the stainless steel door; the potted plants that used to stand sentry on either side have vanished. I think *open* and through we go, into the big room, the room where Freeman died the first time. All the furniture is gone, there are just the photographs on the wall . . . except they're not photographs, just big bronze frames surrounding what looks like calm grey water. They ripple every now and then but show nothing. I move towards one and can feel energy emanating from it, dizzying power. 'So . . . where is he?' asks Daryl.

'The other world. Wherever the monsters and the shimmers come from. That's where Smith said things could be fixed.' As I speak, something I've been trying not to think about finally overrules me, pushing its way to the front of my thoughts. It's been nice having company, and it kind of had to be Daryl . . .

*But he can't come with me.*

'So the paintings lead to the monster world?'

'Must do,' I say. 'Dunno, maybe with everything that's happened they've like . . . mutated, or something. They were pretty random before, I think they showed what they wanted . . . but now they must be portals.' I walk forwards. *He can't come. Tell him he can't come.*

*Wait.*

*I want to try something.*

I stare into the grey mass within the painting and think *show me Kloe*, and after a few seconds the greyness begins to change, to take on form and colour. It shifts into a perfect image of the shack in the forest, bathed in green-tinged sunlight. It makes me squint. I'd pretty much forgotten what daylight looks like. 'I have to know,' I say. 'If they're all right . . .'

*If they're all right then screw going after Freeman. I'm going to them.*

*No I'm not.*

*And if anything has happened to them, I'm definitely going after him.*

*Who are you kidding, dickhead?*

*You're going after him whatever happens.*

Now I see Kloe's face at the window and I feel like my blood has turned to sunlight. It shines from my eyes, from my skin, pouring out. Tara appears next to her and for a millisecond that could be a billion years, everything is all right. There are no such things as monsters, they belong under the bed in your dreams. Death, pain, violence, betrayal, endless night, black snow, none of it is real. None of it exists. There is just me and my family. Morter Smith is forgotten. Tara may be his daughter, but she's *mine*. I stare at my beautiful Kloe as she and Tara wash up their plates and chatter, smiling and laughing, and I want to sob with joy . . . except I can't. There's no time. 'Are you going to say goodbye?' says Daryl.

'I couldn't,' I say. 'If I go in there, I won't come back.' I take one last look at them, at my family, the other two thirds of my soul, and I blow them a kiss, and I think *stop* and try to ignore the horror in my chest as the picture fades to grey.

'Right,' says Daryl. 'So . . . how does this work?'

'Search me.' I focus on the painting, and I concentrate.

I think *show me the monster world.*

I think *let me in.*

The grey lake trapped in the frame shifts as though blown by a gentle wind and begins to change colour. Dull grey becomes vibrant silver, cerulean blue, white . . . then black begins to bleed into the white like oil into milk, and the oil becomes blood, and then it is still, and I'm looking into another world. There are no monsters that I can see, just a cave of rusty red rocks and scarlet stalactites and stalagmites. An acidic smell wafts from within the painting. 'Guess that must be it,' says Daryl. 'Right . . .' He takes a deep breath. 'Lead the way, kid. Methinks that shit's about to get cray cray.'

'Yeah,' I say. 'You're not going.'

'You what?'

'You're not coming with me,' I say. 'You're staying here.'

'Come again?'

'You heard me.'

'Yeah, and, um, *no.*'

'Daryl—'

'Who killed Big Blue?' the dog demands. 'Out of the two of us? Who took down the *elephant-sized killer dog?* Who?'

'You, but—'

'Yeah, exactly! Me! It's not like I'm the hired help, you're not dragging Mrs Overall around with you. I've got *mad* skills, mate!'

'Not the issue,' I say. 'Not even remotely. I need you here in case . . . in case I don't come out. If I manage to do whatever I'm supposed to do in there but I don't escape for whatever reason . . . I need you to find Kloe and tell her what happened. Tell Tara. Tell my parents. Tell everyone. I don't . . . I want them all to know. That I love them. And that . . . that any

413

promises I might be breaking, it's because I'm trying to fix things.'

'You stand a much better chance of coming back if I go with you,' says Daryl.

'Maybe,' I say. 'But think about it. Freeman's been orchestrating this for . . . I don't even know how long. Years, at least. He knows I'm going to be about as pissed off as a human being is capable of being. He wouldn't ask me to meet him if he thought there was any way I could get one over on him.'

'Stanly, *please* . . .'

'I'm asking you,' I say. 'As my best friend. Do this for me. Please.'

He hangs his head. 'Fine. But you'd better come back. Or else.'

I pat him on the head, hopefully not in a condescending way. I don't really know what to say, so I say nothing.

And I step through.

# Chapter Twenty-Eight

THE ACIDIC, SMOKY smell is far stronger in here than out there and the humidity is much higher, like I'd imagine the atmosphere in a rainforest to be. I take a couple of exploratory breaths. Definitely oxygen. *S'pose Freeman would have warned me if I wasn't going to be able to breathe.*

*Unless he just wanted to kill me.*

*Which would actually have been a pretty good plan.*

Marvelling at how easily I would have marched into that theoretical trap, I look behind me. No portal, just a blank crimson wall with the vague impression of a room and a dog, like it was scratched in with a piece of stone thousands of years ago. It gives me a shiver, and I turn my back on it and start to walk. I can hear strange noises far away, bleeps and whirrs and the calls of bizarre birds, and something like wind but not. Like waves of thought, psychic tides. This cave goes on for several minutes, barren, just dust and rock, and I'm beginning to wonder if this is it when I spy an opening in the wall ahead. It's pretty small, just big enough for me to squeeze through. I'm rapidly heating up in my soldier uniform so I take it off, apart from the boots. Back in my Angel Group hospital pyjamas. I slip through the opening into a narrow, constricted tunnel with a metallic odour to it and crawl along for a little while, occasionally catching myself on sharp outcrops, but pain seems to bounce off me now, like rain.

The tunnel ends very suddenly and I tumble out, rolling head over heels and landing on my arse on what feels like grass. It's blue, though, and rustles in the lack of breeze like sea vegetation. I stand up. This new plain is massive. In the distance loom purple mountains tipped with snow, with indistinct swirls of rainbow colour beyond. It's hard to know what colour the sky is, obscured as it is by a ceiling of peach-coloured clouds through which many-winged birds swoop and glide. I feel weirdly calm and slip my boots off, just because it feels like the thing to do. The grass feels nice between my toes and I'm about to set off when I hear thunderous footfalls. My stomach lurches, although not as much as I feel it should, because the beast coming towards me is a giant, bigger than the one we took down with the tanks, bigger perhaps than whatever I saw through the smog back in London. *Wherever that is.* It's humanoid and covered in brown armour, its two enormous legs ending in great clawed feet and leading up to a bulbous pock-marked body, with two hefty arms that swing slowly as it walks. I can barely even make out its head – I can just about see that it's sort of triangular. The thing is so tall that I'm utterly, comically dwarfed, and I get ready to fly and defend myself . . . but it doesn't attack. It doesn't even seem to notice me. It just stomps straight past and continues on its way. I stand there for a moment, dumbfounded. *Lucky.*

*Oh well. Onwards.* The air is still very warm but the grass is cool and damp and kisses my toes. I almost feel bad walking on it with such dirty stinking feet. I proceed for about five minutes and don't spy any more giants, but then the carpet of grass abruptly gives way to a sheer cliff that I'm sure wasn't there before. There is another cliff hundreds of feet beyond, but they're separated by a huge yawning gulf. I can just about see water far, far below, dark green, and even the vague impression of things swimming in it. I think I should probably put my boots back on but I realise that I left them back there where I exited the cave. *Haha. Silly.*

*Wait, what?*

'Silly'?

*What the hell is wrong with me?*

It's the air here, the *feel* of this place. It's like being stoned. I slap myself hard, again, *again*, and make myself remember why I'm here. I'm here because London is being trashed by monsters. I'm here because I need to save it, and the world. Because people have died, and more will die.

Because Eddie *is* dead.

*There it is. Good old pain.*

*Sharp.*

*Focus.*

I take a deep breath, jump out into the nothingness and fly . . . except I don't. I fall, turning over and over, *water sky cliff water sky cliff water sky cliff*. *What? No!* I think *fly* over and over again and suddenly stop falling, jarring my body and winding myself. I'm not even halfway to the water below. I sit panting in the air for a moment, getting my breath back, keeping my mind on staying there, then fly up and across the gap between the cliffs, touching down on more blue grass. Another brown giant strides past in front of me, and again it doesn't even seem to notice I'm there. I frown. Surely I should have seen it coming. How could something so huge have surprised me like that?

*This place . . .*

I fly low over the grass, the springy blue tips tickling my chin, towards a collection of big sandy-coloured rocks about half a mile away. When I get there, I see that the biggest one has a doorway in it. I don't know how I know where I'm going. I just have a feeling . . .

*Can I trust it?*

I close my eyes and think Freeman's name. I think *where are you, you son of a bitch.* I think it with everything I have. And after about thirty seconds . . .

(Here. Waiting.)

That's all I need. I close my mind again, fall to my knees and crawl through the hole in the rock, into pitch darkness. I barely have time to get used to the dark before the floor gives way and I'm rolling down a steep incline, grazing myself repeatedly on sharp little stones, making a hollow rattling noise as I roll. The tunnel is cramped but I manage to sort of re-position myself so I'm sliding rather than tumbling. I can see light now, white light at the end, and I slide out of the tunnel into water. It's warm, ankle-deep and a translucent pink, and I can see thousands of tiny gold wasp-like fish buzzing around the sand on the bottom. I'm in another cave, except this one is bright purple and its irregular walls are covered with shining silver specks . . . and there's something up ahead, coming towards me. It scuttles into a shaft of light that doesn't visibly come from anywhere, and I stop breathing for a second. Black. Fat. Too many legs. Smiley Joe.

*No . . . oh God, no . . .*

*Wait . . .*

It looks different. Its mouths are small, gummy-looking slits, rather than horrible toothy lamprey maws, and it moves slowly, almost shyly, making an odd low bleating sound. It stops a little way away, giving no sign of having even noticed my presence . . . *like the big brown thing . . .* then kneels, a pretty stupid-looking movement considering the shape of its body, and starts trying to dunk bits of itself in the water, to reach the little fish with its mouths, splashing madly. I watch it, bemused, but it still doesn't acknowledge me, it just keeps fishing, so I step past it and continue through the watery cave.

*This place is . . .*

I'm not even sure how to finish the thought. The cave ends at a stone staircase leading further downwards and and I follow it into the black, treading carefully. It's rough and sharp under my bare feet, and I curse my stupid stoned self for leaving my stupid boots back at that stupid cave. I can hear invisible things flapping about in the dark . . . they sound like they're *giggling* . . . and there is a damp, cold smell. I descend for a long time until light finally appears: a bright green glow above me. A gap of some kind. I fly towards it, feeling tiny things brushing past me, and float through the window into . . . *a forest?*

A sort of forest, anyway. The browns and greens look right and there is grass and bracken and trees, but it's all distorted as though through frosted glass and fish-eye lenses. Trees growing sideways out of gaps in the air, ropes of grass dangling from a ceiling I can't see. Everything is filtered through different shades of green and my nose fills with a scent like rotten apples. There is something dangling from a twisted branch in front of me, a red ribbon gently flapping, and I take it because it reminds me of Tara. Gripping the ribbon hard and gritting my teeth, I start to run through this strange upside-down forest. Once or twice I try to look left or right but the clashing of perspectives and dimensions makes me feel dizzy and sick so I keep my eyes fixed straight ahead. I'm sure there are big things flying above me, or maybe walking or sitting on the impossible ceiling, but I don't look. I *mustn't* look. I'm not sure how I know that, but I do.

Then suddenly it all stops, like I blinked and someone changed the reel, and I'm standing at the edge of another huge cliff. Seems like I should have seen this coming. There is no cliff on the other side, though, just a wall of mist with the suggestion of immense things moving beyond, strange shadows bigger again than anything I've seen so far, and the rumble of voices, the murmuring of ancient, unknowable alien gods. I glance down at my hand, looking for the ribbon, for comfort, but it's not there. I dropped it . . . or never had it. I peer over the edge of the cliff. No water below, just red rock. *I'll take my chances down there.* I jump, remembering to think *fly* this time, and dive down, down, down, flipping over at the bottom and landing neatly. The ground down here vibrates with the echoes of monstrous strides, and the indistinct shapes beyond the mist fill me with a new fear, even though I've so far been left alone by everything I've met.

I look around. To my left and right are endless stretches of red rock, forward is an army of unseen giants. I really don't want them to become visible giants, but the thought that they might shortly be stomping around my city spurs me on and I start to run towards them. This is the way anyway, I know it is, somehow. I run, face set, tensing myself, ready to do battle with whatever lies within. Glowing with readiness, I jump forwards and break through—

And I'm falling again, falling falling falling through mist, past random splatters of colour, the grumbling beasts obviously much further away than I thought, if they're even there at all. I want to think about flying but for some reason it doesn't feel right. I'm not falling normally, my descent is slow, lazy. It's quite refreshing. I land gently after several minutes and open my eyes, despite not being able to remember closing them, and find myself standing on a path of black rocks about a metre wide, leading across a bubbling green lake. It's boiling hot down here and stinks, myriad new ghastly smells that I've never sniffed before. The air is hazy and there are definitely things swimming in the green water, although nothing breaks the surface, and at the other end of the path I can see a doorway in a lime green wall. I start walking gingerly towards it, then my brain kicks itself. *Fly, idiot.* I fly, making sure I stay right above the path, and enter the doorway in the wall. Another cramped tunnel to fly through, then out and into another cave, at least I think it's a cave . . . everything's suddenly topsy-turvy again . . . I'm standing on solid ground . . . but I'm

half upside-down? There is definitely a path in front of me
. . . but it's both behind and beside me as well, and snakes
back on itself . . . although it continues in a straight line . . .
*aaaaah* . . .

*Focus.*

FOCUS, BOY.

I close my eyes and try to unscramble my thoughts. When
I open them again I find that things have changed, but not for
the better. I'm in a distorted chamber of purples and blacks
and greens, and there's water, and things moving, and I'm sure
there's an exit not very far away so I start to run towards
it. Only I'm going backwards. And straight up. But no . . .
down . . .

*Focus.*

*Stop thinking.*

I squeeze my eyes shut and keep running through this new
cold place. I don't feel like I'm going anywhere, it's like being
on a treadmill. I clench both fists and remember the ribbon,
remember the sight of it, the feel, even if the actuality of it
isn't there, was never there, and my feet touch the ground,
no, not ground, air, nothing but air, and I fly forwards and
feel myself transferred from cool back to warmth. I open my
eyes in semi-darkness, which is a relief. Everything seems
the right way up in here, also a relief, and I walk through an
oily-smelling corridor of metallic rock, wiping sweat from my
face with my sleeve. Beyond this corridor I can see golden
sand and I start to run, I start to run, I start to run, I start
to – *yes I'm running OK that's what's happening* – so desperately
grateful for something normal, like running. Out and onto the
sand . . .

I take everything in very fast. I'm standing on a beach in a
cave of crimson rock, a cave vast enough to fit ten cathedrals.
Where the sand ends there is pure, glittering blue water that

stretches out to the edges of the cave, and standing at the water's edge with his back to me is a man in a grey suit. I can't see his face but I know exactly who it is, of course.

*Freeman.*

*I would have words with thee.*

# Chapter Twenty-Nine

FREEMAN TURNS. CLOCKS me. Smiles broadly, like he's pleased to see me. Like this is some kind of *reunion*. 'Stanly! Glad you made it, I—'

*Choke*. His words are cut off, squeezed into a splutter of saliva as his throat constricts. *Up*. He levitates, a foot off the ground, two feet, clutching at his throat. I walk towards him, maintaining my mental grip on his windpipe, my hands shaking because they'd really rather it was them doing the gripping. It's taking a lot of willpower not to just tear him in half now, see what would happen if I thought *eviscerate*, or just *die*. 'You're going to show me how to fix what's happening,' I say, 'or I'm going to end you. Right here. And I'll make sure you don't come back this time.'

Freeman's eyes bulge, his face shifting from red to purple, his body twitching. I know for a fact that he can't breathe. But he keeps smiling, and says something I can just about make out. *'That's not how this is going to work.'*

Something grabs me from behind, wrapping around my waist. I try to struggle but it holds my head and limbs in place. I manage to look down and recoil at what look like thin, sinuous black creepers restraining me. They're *alive*. I try to look behind me to see what's doing this but I can't, which I think might actually be a good thing. Whatever it is, it lifts me off the ground and holds me in mid air. Freeman drops down on to the sand and rubs his throat, coughing. He takes out a handkerchief, wipes his eyes, replaces it, shakes his head. 'Stanly,' he says.

'Stanly, Stanly. Did you think that that was going to be it? You really can be disastrously dense sometimes.'

I think *punch* and his head jolts back. Blood trickles from one nostril and finally that smile vanishes. He scowls at me, taking out his handkerchief again and wiping the red from his face. 'Now, now,' he says. 'Less of that, if you please.' He doesn't make any kind of movement but I feel something change between us, and when I think *punch* again my attack comes up against a crackling wall of opposing thought.

'You're empowered,' I say.

He nods. 'Somewhat.'

*I shouldn't be surprised.*

*He shouldn't surprise me any more.*

'I would have thought you'd have worked that out,' says Freeman. 'I mean, I have spoken to you telepathically *twice* in the last hour.'

*I didn't even make the connection.*

*Too much in my head . . .*

*Missing important things . . .*

I try thinking *sleep* at him like I did at the soldier earlier, but it does nothing, and he shakes his head again, a disappointed teacher admonishing a favourite pupil. 'See above, re: dense.' He turns away from me, walks to the water and kneels down. 'Shimmers,' he says. 'Fascinating beings. Truly. Like nothing we've ever seen in our world. Little living dream factories feeding on pure, concentrated power.' He turns back to me, grinning like we're on safari and he's just spotted something particularly cool. 'This whole lake is made of them you know. This is their home. Where they originate. They sit together, pumping out energy, dreams, nightmares. Monsters.'

'They . . . *make* them?' I've given up struggling physically, but I can't even do it psychically now. I can feel him blocking me, like Leon did before. This feeling, this impotence, is unbearable. It fills me with rage – and I'm glad, because I can feel fear in there as well, the threat of absolute terror at whatever fresh abomination has me in its grip. I'd rather rage than fear.

Freeman nods. 'Dreams made flesh by the raw energy that fills this world.'

'None of them attacked me, though. Why . . .'

'Here they are benign entities.' Freeman stands and looks around, appraising the cave like he's considering buying it. 'It is only when they emerge in our world that they become blood-thirsty. I use the terms *dreams* and *nightmares* for your benefit, you must understand that here they are meaningless. There is no human concept of evil, no idea of terror. A nightmare to you, here is just . . . an object, an entity, a neutral presence. They are harmless apparitions, projections from the minds of the shimmers. They simply exist.' He walks back towards me and smiles, and there is a curl at the edge of his lip, a sneer. Such contempt. 'It's our world that turns them into monsters.'

'What's holding me, then? Doesn't feel very benign.'

'It is under my control,' says Freeman. He laughs. 'Did you think that little oik Alexander was the only person to work out how to control animals? He can't even stay conscious while doing it. Honestly, Stanly.'

'Well, Jesus,' I say. 'Sorry. But I've had rather a lot on my mind of late. Things like being tortured and beaten up, my cousin *dying*—'

At that, Freeman has the gall to stop smiling and affect an expression of sympathy, which makes me want to rip out his lungs. 'Edward? Oh, I'm terribly s—'

'I don't know if you have any respect for me,' I say, 'but if you do, if you have a single *shred* of it, don't say you're sorry. Don't you dare. You have no right.'

He nods. 'Fair enough. You were saying, about having things on your mind?'

425

'Oh yeah. Well, the biggest one was probably *the world ending.*'

'It hasn't ended yet,' says Freeman. 'That's the point. Did you really think I wanted to destroy the whole world?'

'Well, I wasn't party to the intimate details of your psychotic megalomaniacal breakdown,' I say. 'So . . .' He opens his mouth, but I interrupt him again. 'But that was *not* your cue to explain the whole thing to me in excruciating detail. Every second that you chat bollocks, more people in London are dying. So why don't you just skip to the end and tell me how I stop it? What's plan B?'

Freeman laughs. 'To be honest, a little bit more devastation up there will suit my purposes nicely. There are some fairly high-ranking Angel Group personnel still in London and it'll be very handy if they're all crushed into a paste by monsters before I return. It'll make the clean-up that much easier. Although I wouldn't mind killing Morter Smith myself, to be honest.' He's actually beaming. 'And surely you want to know how you've ended up in this position? I'm sure the curiosity is gnawing away at you.'

'There's no time.'

'But this is the big climax!' he grins. 'The hero and the villain, facing off! The plot revealed! Surely you won't deny me my big monologue, I thought you *loved* this sort of thing? You certainly seemed to enjoy it last time, at the Kulich.'

'There's no *time!*' I yell. 'Just *stop it!*' The last two words explode from inside me, manifesting as concentric rings of thought that break through Freeman's barriers and cause him to stumble. The thoughts carry on past him, into the living lake, and for one vertigo-inducing second I can see infinity, a cavern deeper than the universe and filled with memory, and then we're not underground any more, we're standing in white space, and Freeman is smiling again and speaking, although it sounds like it's taking more effort than it should.

'Interesting trick,' he says, breathing heavily. 'Trying to get inside my head, are you? That's a new one . . . you'd make a pretty good shimmer yourself.'

*I didn't even mean to,* I say. Except I don't say it. It's just a thought. I try to say *I don't want to be in your head,* but again I don't say it. I don't understand what's happening. I can still feel the grip of the black creepers around me, still sense the presence of something monstrous, but right now I don't seem to be an actual mass. I'm just essence, floating . . . although Freeman seems to be able to see me. *What's going on,* I think.

'What's going on,' says Freeman, 'is that I really, *really* want to tell you the whole story. And not just the *once upon a time there was a boy named Stanly* bit. I want you to see the whole picture. And maybe doing it this way will make it a bit more exciting, a bit more interactive. Give it a bit of *pizzazz.* Plus it will also make it more difficult for you to use those pesky powers against me.'

*At least let me talk, then.*

He nods and I try an experimental word. 'OK.' OK. 'So,' I say. 'We're really going to do this.'

'We are.' Freeman smiles gleefully. 'Go on. Ask me anything.'

'All right. Why do you want to destroy the Angel Group?'

'I don't,' he says. 'I want to unite it. And I want to control it. You see, Stanly, the *core* of the Angel Group, when you strip away the corporate façade, the sub-committees, the private military arm . . . the part of it that makes the really important decisions, the part that authorised the imprisonment of the empowered and so on, has been dividing and dividing for years, ever since its inception in the late nineteenth century as a private interest group dedicated to the study of supernatural phenomena. And in recent years it has been getting worse. On the one hand we have the traditionalists, the religious fanatics who want it all to come back to God and worship and divine destiny and all that rubbish. They may be less in number than they were even fifty years ago, but trust me, they hold on to their ludicrous and outdated beliefs with a psychotic, iron grip.' He rolls his eyes, 'cos we're two buddies in the pub, putting the world to rights. 'And on the other hand, we have the likes of Morter Smith. Vicious, pragmatic, devoted to saving the world by whatever means necessary, and well past the point of giving a rat's posterior about the Biblical side of things. I joined years ago and originally I was on the latter side.'

Everything flashes and we're back by the lake. Freeman looks down at it, a pane of gently wobbling living glass, and breathes deeply. 'Then I started to realise that both sides were wrong. We had the knowledge, the power, the money, the influence and the capability to *run* this world, to effect real change rather than saving it from behind the scenes, paying lip service to democratic checks and balances. But like most of the bloated, corrupt institutions on this planet, we were drowning in dogma, in bureaucracy, in pathetic self-interest and short-termism. Utterly moronic decisions were being made all the time. It's amazing the organisation didn't just collapse in on itself.' He clears his throat. 'One thing on which both sides could agree was that the empowered were a liability, an awful risk. So as soon as their numbers started to swell – in tandem with the appearance of monsters and shimmers in various spots around the world, interestingly enough – we started snapping them up, probing them, locking them away. Smith's final solution was greeted with roars of applause from all sides, a way to stem the flow of monsters *and* keep the empowered out of the way. His side were worried about them rising up and taking over, the religious side still couldn't suppress the fear that they were agents of *Satan*, bless their little ignorant socks.' He smiles. 'Whatever your feelings about Morter Smith, you have to admire the ruthless bastard.'

'Get a room.'

Freeman laughs. 'Well, anyway.' He closes his eyes and there is another blue flash, and we're still in the red underground cave with the golden beach, only I'm absent again, and so is Freeman . . .

*No he's not . . .*

There is a man there, kneeling at the water's edge, a man in a suit, and I know it's Freeman even before my vision whirls around to see his face, but it's a younger face, a face full of fascination, even wonder. His smile in this time is real. I still want to reach out and strangle him, but unfortunately we seem to be doing that weird non-corporeal brain film thing again.

Now I hear his older voice again. 'I discovered this place, you know. I spent years studying the shimmers behind the Group's back, working out a way to close the gaps between here and our world without enslaving the empowered. I always thought the empowered could be so much more useful than the Group was willing to admit. I never told them that *I* was empowered, of course.' A laugh echoes across the years. 'I thought our kind could be essential. We could use my method of sealing off our world from the shimmer realm, and then use our ludicrous level of influence over the governments of the world, plus our private army, plus *another* army of superpowered soldiers, to bring *order* to the place. Actual, genuine order. Not the pathetic, unstable, trembling excuse for structure we have at the moment, always thirty seconds away from collapsing into anarchy.'

We're somewhere else now, a big grey room with a long grey table behind which sit many distinguished-looking men and women in grey suits. Younger Freeman stands addressing them silently, his lips moving but no sound coming out. The voice I hear is older and comes from everywhere. 'Obviously my idea was laughed out of the room, because traditionally having a shred of imagination is frowned upon within the Angel Group. Smith's was unanimously approved. I pretended to forget about it. But it kept preying on my mind, and then one day Pandora approached me about a meeting.' I see Pandora, who looks barely a week younger than she did the last time I saw her, talking quietly with younger Freeman over a drink. 'She said she was extremely interested in my idea, and that she was prepared to use her authority to lay the groundwork for its implementation. By now the majority of the empowered that we'd discovered had been plugged into Smith's machines, but there were a few that I'd discovered during my tenure and . . . "neglected" to inform the Group about . . . and I set about meeting them, one by one, and setting them little tests.'

'Tests?' *Ooh look, I can speak again.* I see flashes, a younger Sharon, her hair a dirty-blonde dye job, a younger Eddie, his hair a dark mop much like mine at sixteen, Connor, already chiselled and handsome. I see each of them speaking with Freeman, their eyes all nervous and distrustful, and God the déjà vu . . . there are others too, a few I don't recognise. 'You sent them to fight monsters,' I say. 'Confused teenagers!'

'The ones who survived deserved to,' says Freeman. We're back in what I think is reality, him standing with his hands folded behind his back, staring out at the lake, me hanging in the air, a captive audience. 'The ones who didn't . . . didn't. I approved a very select few, and Pandora managed to hold Smith and his dogs off from capturing them, for various unspecified reasons. Very handy that she outranked him, she could tell him to jump and he'd have no choice but to ask how high.' He smiles. 'She really has excelled herself. All to be part of my new order. Quite a partnership.'

'Oh, she's actually dead now, by the way.' Pandora's corpse flickers momentarily on the beach and Freeman glances down at it, although he appears unmoved.

'Oh?' he says. 'Shame. She was really quite excited about ruling the world.'

'Where do I come into this?'

'Ah,' Freeman grins. 'Now the meat of it!' He's *loving* this. Every second of it, his villain monologue, telling me exactly how much of a Machiavellian shitbag he is, while my world burns. 'When you came on the scene, I couldn't believe my luck. The most gifted empowered we'd seen since recruiting that dead-eyed sociopath Leon, and you were right under my nose. The cousin of one of my other projects, no less.'

'Don't you dare talk about—'

'Edward? I'm sorry to hear about his death, I really am. But he was always too stubborn, too untrusting. He would never have made the team. You, however . . . what a find. Impression-able, scared, in dire need of a mysterious mentor figure.'

'You fu—'

'*Shh.*' He draws a finger to his lips. 'Daryl told me everything I needed to know about you. Entirely innocently, of course, he really did love to talk about you. You've made quite an im-pression on that beagle.' He smiles, as if to say *how sweet*. It makes me want to puke, although at the same time, thinking of Daryl does make me feel a little better. It gives me some strength. 'Stanly Bird,' says Freeman. 'Loner, outsider, a media child in love with heroism and stories and pure, basic, simple good versus evil, despite the cynical façade he likes to put up. A superhero in the making.'

'Don't tell me,' I say. 'We're not so different, you and I. We're two sides of the same coin.'

'Not at all,' says Freeman. He sounds amused by the idea. 'We're very, very different. You're an idealistic child who's not as bright as he thinks he is. I'm a ruthlessly pragmatic genius who is probably even brighter than he thinks he is.'

'You're a *maniac*. You're . . .'

'The bad guy?' he says. 'If that helps you to make sense of this whole thing, then yes I am. I'm the villain, you're the hero. And you'd be amazed how easy a hero is to manipulate.' He looks at me, locking eyes with a sudden, fierce intensity. 'Or maybe you wouldn't.' I can see myself now, in a series of rhythmic flashes. Early flight in the woods, slamming my bedroom door and knocking things over with angry, involuntary thoughts. Things he couldn't have seen, but it's like he's drawing them out of my head, projecting them for us, my very own 'previously' montage. Now I see London, our first meeting, and we're actually standing there, side-by-side, as we were, and he is looking at me and speaking, although the words are not the words he used at the time. 'I told you enough about the Angel Group to make *them* the bad guys. Enough that there was no way you'd ever change your mind, even if someone gave you some evidence. That's why I sent that assassin Masters after you, with Smith's name in his head of course.'

'You . . .'

'Yes,' says Freeman. 'I sent him. And as soon as he gave you the necessary information, it triggered the memory wipe that I implanted. It's a neat trick. I'd say you should learn it, but . . . anyway. It was all a matter of timing. Introduce the Angel Group, a potential threat. Give you more time to develop your powers, to think that the Group was going to leave you alone . . . then *bang*. Introduce a very real threat, give it a name and send you on your way.'

*Jesus.*

'Of course,' he says, 'Smith nearly put paid to the whole thing, as is his prerogative, being an Olympic-level pain in the backside. He was desperate to bring you and your friends in, terrified at the idea of rogue elements running around when his precious plan was so close to fruition, so he went over Pandora's head and dreamed up that "terrorist" rubbish. Shutting down the city and everything . . . he always did have rather a penchant for desperate measures.'

'You're one to talk.' We're standing in space, buffeted by winds of time, and Freeman's voice is multiplied by a hundred, his laughter by a thousand.

'Very funny,' he says. 'Anyway. I had to work pretty fast at this point. I'd been anonymously drip-feeding information to those imbeciles Maguire and Silver for a while, leading them in the wrong direction, channelling them towards Skank, predicting that through him they'd eventually team up with you. It was all falling into place and then Smith blundered in. Lucky that you happened to show up at my flat that evening, I hadn't planned that.' We're in the little living room of Freeman's poky flat, the explosion that tore away the wall frozen, fire and smoke hanging as if painted in three dimensions. 'But it worked out pretty well. I convince you that they're after me, gaining your trust, you *distrust* Smith even more, he tries to frame you as terrorists. You already thought he'd tried to have you killed. *Voila!* An arch nemesis is born.'

'It might interest you to know,' I say, 'that Smith and I have become best buddies since he tortured me.'

He's looking at me almost fondly. 'Lovely. But academic now, really. May I continue the story?'

'Do you have to? No offence, but it's been going on for bloody ever. Couldn't you just whack the rest on an Extended Edition DVD and I'll get to it after I save the world?'

'But you *love* stories,' says Freeman, and now something else drips into his voice. Just a tiny edge of mockery. I actually prefer it, it's better than the unctuous, fatherly tone he's been adopting up until now. 'That's the whole point. And this is actually one of my favourite bits, because again, I didn't even plan it. Imagine my surprise when I found out that Smiley Joe had kidnapped not just you but *Tara*, a little girl we already knew about. How much more perfect could that have been? I'd love to know whether it was a coincidence, or whether your power somehow drew you to that alleyway.'

'Drew me there?' *Like it drew me to the park, when I found Kloe . . .*

'We still know so little about how it all works,' says Freeman. 'Prophetic dreams, feelings, sudden knowledge, even subconscious knowledge that we should go a certain way . . . it's fascinating. But however it happened, the important thing is that it *happened*. An instant protective bond. Some quick thinking and last-minute scrambling on my part, and presto. Pandora kidnaps Tara to draw you into a confrontation with the Group. Daryl hit the nail on the head when he said there was something suspect about that meeting, that it was right up your street. Of course it was. We designed it that way.' He smiles, triumphant but somehow regretful. It's a weird combination to wear on one face. 'I think that was the last straw for the poor beagle. The guilt must have been appalling. And he had absolutely no inkling of my grand scheme.'

*Tara . . .*

I need to know, but I don't want to give him the satisfaction of showing I care, so I ask a different question. 'Why did Pandora shoot you?' We're in the top room at the Kulich now. Phantom Pandora nods her head, bullets fly with the volume turned right down, Freeman's body jerks and he falls . . . but then he gets up, looks at me, smiles, speaks, even as his wounds continue to bleed in front of me.

'Well, by now I was definitely out of the Group. They didn't trust me one iota. So Pandora made it look like she'd killed me to stop Lucius becoming suspicious.'

'You faked your own death.'

'In a manner of speaking,' he smiles. 'I was going to use my own power to heal myself but before I could . . . I just healed. Like *that*.' He snaps his pale fingers and we're back in the cave of shimmers.

'How?'

'You! When you brought yourself back from the dead, you brought me back as well. And Leon, as a matter of fact. There was no way he would have survived the beating your cousin gave him otherwise.'

'I didn't bring myself back,' I say. '*Tara* did.'

'So you assumed,' says Freeman. 'In actual fact, Tara has no abilities. She's just a normal little girl.'

I *brought* myself *back from the dead*.

*And Leon . . .*

*And Freeman . . .*

I feel sick again, deep down, like my soul itself is going to throw up.

*I could have saved Eddie.*

Freeman smiles a little sadly. 'Heard that, did you?' I say. 'So I could have saved him, then?'

'Let's not dwell on such things,' says Freeman. 'Let's talk about Tara. There was never anything special about her, at least not in the way we led you to believe. But once you'd come back from the dead and we'd implemented our little dearest daughter gambit, we knew you'd carry on protecting her. All to keep the Group as the bad guy . . . and to keep her from Smith, of course.'

'So she is Smith's.' I can't help it. I need to know. And like Freeman says, hell, might as well not dwell on the fact that I could have brought my cousin back to life. *Live and learn, eh? Better luck next time, Stanly.*

*What is the POINT of you?*

'She is indeed Smith's,' says Freeman. 'Her mother was a

low-ranking Angel Group employee who made the mistake of getting involved with him. He was married at that point, by the way.'

'Why the hell would I care—'

'The devil is in the detail.' Freeman smiles. 'Anyway. Knowing what a thundering arsehole Smith is, and seeing that the mother was utterly unable to cope, Pandora made arrangements to have her transferred, and for the baby to be quietly adopted by a kindly, childless couple. Smith never even knew there *was* a child. The synchronicity of you running into her was quite beautiful – who better to protect her than our friendly neighbourhood superhero Stanly?'

'Smith knows about her now, though.'

'Yes,' says Freeman. 'Someone . . . can't imagine who . . . arranged to have some sensitive files delivered to him just a few days ago.'

'*You?* Why?'

'You already hated him,' says Freeman. 'I thought he would benefit from a good reason to hate you in return. Plus, if I'm absolutely honest, I quite enjoy making his life unpleasant. I genuinely can't stand the man.'

*And I genuinely can't stand you.* 'What about Mr and Mrs Rogers? Did you pay them off or something?'

'They were rewarded handsomely for looking after the girl, yes.' An almost subliminal image of Pandora handing a cheque to a younger Oliver Rogers. 'And for keeping up the charade that she was yours from the future, of course. That took some threatening as well, as I'm sure you can imagine. But as I've probably communicated, as well as being rather good at forward planning, I'm also a gifted improviser.'

I feel like a donkey with the word GULLIBLE painted on it. With shit. 'You wrote the note. And built the place in the woods.'

'I had it built, yes.'

'And the shimmer that was there?' A flash of the woods, and a man in a dark suit opening a crate and releasing something. It's barely visible, like liquid air, and disappears quickly. The man turns towards me and morphs into Freeman.

He nods. 'Yes, I had it left there. After shimmers link with empowered, there's often an interesting side effect. The subject's abilities get a sort of . . . shot in the arm. It's one of the reasons that Smith's infernal machines are so dangerous. If any empowered were to wake up their power levels would be enormous, but without the necessary control.' I think of the release of energy when I woke the empowered at the secondary site, and they appear around us, spasming and freaking out as they're jerked back into reality. Freeman continues speaking. 'Leaving that shimmer for you served a few purposes. For one, it would give you a bit of a head start and you'd know what you were dealing with when the time came. Secondly, it would ramp up your power levels, which I knew would come in handy. And it was a nice extra detail in the story, to thicken the plot.'

I look at my hand to make sure it's still there. Spiders' legs run all over my body. I hear Smith's voice, hear him yelling. '*You're supposed to keep the damn thing under control!*'

A *shimmer*.

*Alex.*

He *was controlling the shimmer Smith used.*

HE *tortured me.*

I wish I'd hit him more when I saw him earlier.

'My intentions when I made you leave Kloe and Tara in the woods were honourable,' says Freeman. We're back in the cavern, the *real* cavern, in real life, or whatever I have that passes for a real life, and I grab the opportunity for another attack, but Freeman moves to catch it, twisting it around and sending it right back at me. It racks my whole body, disorientating but not exactly painful. 'Nice try,' he smiles, rubbing his temples. 'Pandora wanted the girl to stay safe,' he continues. 'She was never quite as enamoured with the idea of adding Tara to the plan as I. And I knew you'd work better if the love of your life was safely hidden away. I never wanted any harm to come to either of them.'

'This still doesn't explain why you wanted to release the monsters,' I say. 'I thought you wanted to bring order to the world. It's not order up there, it's bloody *chaos*. It's Armageddon, you tit, people are *dying*! You made me a murderer!'

Freeman shakes his head. 'No, no, no. I've made you a *saviour*!'

'What?'

'It quickly dawned on me that I wasn't going to be executing any sort of regime change using political strings alone,' says Freeman. 'I needed Smith's plan to go quite spectacularly wrong. What better way than for his machine to be destroyed and hundreds of monsters released into the capital city? Smith is disgraced, I step in with my solution, *et voila*! Within a year I'm running things, and the world as you knew it – chaotic, unstable, dangerous – ceases to exist.'

'Not going to happen,' I say. 'Smith knows it was you. He—'

'Will not survive the night,' says Freeman. 'Even if he's lucky enough not to get his head bitten off by a monster, there are . . . other methods by which he might meet a sticky end. And most importantly, there is no material proof. Just the word of a few people based in a city that's currently being devoured by an apocalyptic rain of otherworldly abominations. I have plenty of allies outside the blast radius. And when the smoke clears, nobody is going to care who did what. What they will care about is what they've *seen*. What they're now aware of. Great striding beasts, beyond comprehension. Humans love the ritual of othering – it's one of the best ways of bringing them together, uniting them against a common enemy. And now they've seen the other to end all others. Who knows? I might even have accidentally achieved world peace.'

'This plan,' I say. 'Did you copy it from Alan Moore?'

'I beg your pardon?'

'It's all a bit *Watchmen*, isn't it?'

'I've never read it.'

'Philistine.'

'Charming,' said Freeman. 'But as I was saying . . . the world will be scarred, of course. In need of reassurance, structure . . . and who better to provide that than me? A man with a soothing voice and a master plan.' He laughs again, such a normal laugh, hiding a demented psychopath. All this information is spinning in my head and I try to clear it, focus, come up with some kind of solution.

But all I can think is *I've lost*. He has me. His plan has gone off without a hitch, all because I'm the world's thickest, most easily-led superhero. In fact, the irony of the word *superhero* is so vile to me that I never want to hear it again. If I want to save the world then it means him winning. Fury and shame and guilt rise inside me, hot, acidic, burning and twisting and wrenching, but there's nothing I can do about it. My head hangs, defeated.

'So where do I come in?'

'Ah,' says Freeman. 'Of course. To business.' That laugh again, making me shiver. 'We realised that the shimmers were causing the cracks in reality, trying to come through to our world, to discover the source of the energy that they could sense, and letting the monsters out in the process. Quite accidentally, I might add. Shimmers are no more vindictive than a thunderstorm. I theorised that if we gave them a big enough source of power to feed on, they would close the gaps. We experimented on much smaller scales and my hypothesis was proved right. One of the reasons the Group first turned down my idea was that we simply didn't have anyone strong enough. Leon is one of the best, but Lucius vetoed us using him. *Profoundly* un-Christian, wouldn't you say? And obviously I wasn't going to volunteer. I'm not powerful enough anyway. But then you came along. After you brought Leon, yourself and I back to life at the Kulich, *that* was when I knew it had to be you. My own personal Chosen One.'

'You're not powerful enough?' I ask. 'You're the one who's got me at your mercy.'

'Only because you're letting me,' smiles Freeman. 'Poor Stanly. Still living the story. You could have me on my knees right now. You could be hurling me around this cavern, and there wouldn't be a thing I could do. But this is the climax, and I am the villain, and in *your* head that means that I am more powerful. That it will take some kind of miracle, or an outside agent, to help you stop me. Untrue. You are more powerful than me. You just don't—'

'*Don't say it,*' I say. 'The villain-explains-it-all shtick? Sick of it. Several stops past sick of it, in fact. No more. Let's just get this over with.'

'As you wish.'

'So how does this work? You throw me to the shimmers and they stop what's happening?'

'That's the long and short of it.'

'What about when I die? They won't be able to feed off me any more.'

'They can keep you alive indefinitely,' says Freeman. 'So that's not a problem. As I said, absolutely remarkable creatures. It's almost a shame to permanently close their world off from ours, and most of them have already quietly found their way back here so there'll be few if any left for us to study.'

Realisation, like choking on clarity. I'm finished. This is it. There is no alternative . . .

*Unless I give them Freeman.*

*He's got to be lying.*

*He's got to be as strong as me.*

*Maybe . . .*

*Worth a try . . .*

'What makes you think you're going to get out of this cavern alive?' I ask. 'To go back and fulfil the rest of your plan? I mean, if you're telling the truth, and I *am* more powerful than you, I could just kill you and *then* give myself to the shimmers. That seems like a pretty good compromise to me.'

Freeman's hand flies to his mouth. 'Oh, goodness gracious me. I didn't think of that.'

I roll my eyes. 'Spare me. Come on then. What insanely clever idea did you come up with to stop it from happening?'

'Not especially clever,' says Freeman. 'A touch clichéd, in fact. But no doubt effective. If I don't send a series of messages at a certain time, Kloe and Tara will die.'

'You son of a—'

'Grow up,' he snaps, his face suddenly a cold, ruthless mask. 'Did you honestly think that I sent your twin Achilles heels to an isolated spot in the forest purely out of the goodness of my heart? To keep up the charade? Yes, I wanted to keep them safe, but that doesn't mean they weren't going to come in handy at some point. If I don't leave this world, they will never leave that forest.'

*Bastard.*

*You bastard.*

'You said your intentions were honourable.' My voice has gone small again.

'Sometimes one must be economical with the truth,' says Freeman. 'And what does it matter anyway? Truth, lies . . . what does it matter?'

441

I hang my head. I'm almost prepared to let him see tears. 'Why would you do this?'

The voice that responds is suddenly, weirdly, different. Sad. 'Why would I do this,' he says. 'Why, indeed. Maybe I didn't. Maybe it's all just another story.'

I look up, and the smile he wears seems so sad, so kindly, so genuine, that I want to tear it from his face. It's *real*. He really feels it. And he has no right to. 'But as I said, it doesn't matter,' he says. 'The result is the same. What matters is the position you are in now, and whether you can afford to pick and choose which parts of my story to believe.'

I desperately try to think of something, grasping at straws, picking at the logic, even though I know that it's pointless, that he has me. 'But the empowered,' I say. 'They're all damaged beyond repair, vegetables or insane or worse! So much for your army of superpowered people!'

'Not beyond repair,' says Freeman. 'I can help them. People can almost always be fixed.'

'It'll take time, though! Can your new world order afford to wait that long? And I took apart half the Angel Group's soldiers, even before the monsters started coming!'

He shrugs. 'They'll live. And broken bones can be fixed with a thought.'

'But if I could take them all down by myself—'

'Why do you think they keep spectacularly failing to kill you?' asks Freeman, as though I'm an irretrievable dunce. 'Pandora and I started recruiting a long time ago.'

I keep struggling, but whatever monster Freeman's controlling keeps my body maddeningly in place, and the grand puppet master keeps my powers at bay. He shakes his head. 'Honestly, Stanly. Resistance is quite literally futile. You want to save the world, this is the price you pay. It's a shame but . . . that's the way this particular story goes.' There might be sympathy behind the self-satisfaction, it's hard to tell. 'You don't belong in that world anyway,' he says. 'Not in the *real* world. A young man with the powers of a god? How could you ever . . .' In a flash, his smug expression is blown apart, and the fragments re-shape to form anger and disbelief. '*You!*' he cries.

I can feel things happening behind me, fighting, snapping. My unseen captor lets go of me and I'm flung forwards, knocking right into Freeman. The two of us sprawl on the sand and I roll over onto my back and look up, and up, and up, and *up*. My skin frosts over. 'Holy spider,' I whisper.

# Chapter Thirty

I THOUGHT THAT I'd got pretty used to big and horrible in the last few hours, but the monster standing in front of me now, looming over the doorway through which I entered the cave . . . well, it's not the biggest, but in terms of horrible, it makes the green tentacled blob look downright huggable. Its eight huge legs are jet black, its bloated red body dripping with slime, and it has twenty glassy hubcap-sized eyes and shining metallic pincers in front of a horrendous dribbling mouth. It's roughly the size of the blue dog, and it makes me want to shit my soul out of my body. The black creeper things that were holding me are like thin tentacles snaking out from the sides of its fat, awful head, and they're writhing around trying to fend off someone who I've never been more glad to see. 'Daryl!' I cry. 'You fucking legend!'

The great spider is fully occupied trying to attack Daryl as he rushes in and out of its many legs, biting at its soft spots every chance he gets. 'Freeman!' he yells, between bites. 'How long have you been empowered, you lying shit heel? And how come I didn't pick up on it?'

'I've been planning this for years,' sneers Freeman. 'It's my *masterwork*. I wasn't about to let myself get rumbled by a beagle. There are ways of hiding—'

'*Shut up*,' I say, flying to my feet. Freeman jumps up too, his thin face stretched and grim, and we face each other and attack simultaneously. Neither of us moves but our minds erupt, spitting fury. I visualise lightning and fire and bullets and arrows, bright flashes of psychic violence, deadly fireworks, and Freeman counters, teeth gritted, filling my head with pain. I don't let it stop me, though, I turn it around, throw it back at him, his own imaginary sword clashing against his shield and causing blue and red sparks to fly. I can sense what's happening behind me, Daryl running rings around the spider, and out of the corner of my eye I see him rip into one of its legs. It staggers, not making any noise apart from the constant frenzied *clickclickclickclick* of its pincers, and I think of a nuclear mushroom cloud and launch it in Freeman's direction, fire hotter than the very centre of the angriest sun. I think of asteroids, an express train, an anvil plunging from the sky towards some hapless cartoon, and draw it all together into a hurricane of colour and light, hundreds of flaming multicoloured spirals, the jaws of an immense, god-like wolf, the bite and venom of the world serpent, and I send it hurtling, bellowing at Freeman, everything I've endured over the last few days, the pain and the rage and the violence, Eddie, *Eddie*, I see him, a spectral warrior manifestation of my cousin, like a Patronus, and my attack hits home and Freeman staggers, his nose and ears letting loose little sprays of blood. I grip him and think *lift*, taking him up into the air, and I think PAIN and he screams, clutching at himself, at the thousands of imaginary tortures I'm visiting on him, plunging down every artery, lighting up every nerve ending. He screams from the very depths of his soul, or whatever he has in place of one, and as I watch him writhe around in agony I conjure more, thinking of all the deaths he's caused, everything I've done because of him, thinking of Tara and Kloe alone in the dark of the woods, of his threat to kill them, of Lauren plugged into that goddamn machine, of Eddie lying dead in the rubble, the city falling to pieces. I gather every last shard of pain that has been visited upon me and the ones I love and I give it right back to Mr Freeman in kind. I know I can't kill him, I can't risk it, but by

445

God I owe him this before I let him go, this is the *least* that I owe him. He's turning scarlet, screeching at a blood-chilling pitch, only my blood isn't cold, it's hot, hot with delight, basking in revenge. I can hear Daryl yelling for me to stop but I don't care, he's busy with the spider anyway, and suddenly I realise that I'm not actually scared of it, I don't care about the spider, I'll kill it with my bare hands if Daryl can't finish the job, I'll kill it and then I'll kill a hundred more, I don't care about *any* monsters in fact, there's nothing to be scared of, not death, not beasts, and especially not this puppet-mastering motherf—

'STANLY!' yells Daryl. It makes me shake and I stop and look at him. He's killed the spider, it's slumped in a great stinking heap of broken legs, and Daryl is standing in front of it, shaking his head. 'Don't.'

'Do you know what they did to me?' I ask. 'They tortured me. Got inside my head. I thought I'd been shot. I thought I'd had my hand cut off. I hung there powerless while Smith did what he wanted. All because of Freeman. Look at what he's done! Everyone he's killed! He deserves to *hurt.*'

'He does,' says Daryl. 'But you're not a murderer. Let him go. He'll answer for what he's done.'

'I wasn't going to kill him. Trust me. Just some fun torture.'

'Stanly. Please. It's not you. It's not who you are.'

'You don't know that,' I say. 'I don't even know that. Not any more.' And I mean it. I don't have the faintest clue who I am at this point. I'm shaking, my breaths big and painful. I let Freeman drop to his knees on the sand and he moans in pain . . . then he mutters something.

'Tick tock, Stanly. The world is still ending.' He looks up at me, his eyes weakened but still defiant. 'The shimmers demand a sacrifice.'

'Then they'll have one.' To hell with letting him go. I'll

feed him to the shimmers, and then I will fly to the forest and rescue Tara and Kloe and kill anyone who tries to come near them. I will fill their brains with insanity and snap their necks before they can get within a hundred feet of my family. I'm not playing his games. His ultimatums, his traps, his Rube Goldberg schemes, he can *shove them up his arse* because *I am not playing*. I pick him up again, twirl him, hold his face about an inch from the blue lake and close my eyes, letting the fury subside, letting my mind drift. Almost instantly I can feel them, thousands of strange minds clustered together, barely aware of what's been happening, the meaning of the power that's been unleashed. They *feel* the power, yes. But they haven't the faintest inkling of what it signifies.

*Take him*, I think. *He has power. Take him. Take him and leave my world. Please.*

Ripples of thought, of . . . is it discussion? I can't tell. Then a response. *No.* Not the word, more like the *idea* of the word . . . and not just that . . . the reason is there too.

*He was telling the truth.*

*He's not powerful enough.*

*What about me then*, I think, without pausing, because to pause would be to comprehend what's going to happen, and I'm not sure I want to do that. *Will I do? Take me, everything in me, all my power. Keep me here forever. But leave my world alone. Seal yourselves off.*

More of those abstract waves of cognition, cool and blue inside my head . . . and then they say *yes* and my heart drops to the very pit of my stomach. *Thank you*, I think, and I bring myself back to my body. I turn to Daryl. Somehow, he knows. 'It has to be me,' I say.

'What?' The disbelief in his voice makes my guts lurch. 'No. That can't be—'

'Daryl,' I say. 'It's the only way.' I drag Freeman back from

447

the water and throw him across the beach. He lands on his back by the cave exit, next to the corpse of the massive spider, and sits there, rubbing his eyes. 'Looks like you were right,' I say. 'I'm the only one who can do it.'

Freeman stands up, straightens his tie and nods. 'I'm sorry, Stanly.'

'Yeah,' I say.

'I want you to know that it was never personal,' says Freeman. 'I never hated you. You truly are a fine young man, possibly the only individual I've ever met worthy of the word *hero*. I salute your bravery. And I swear that Kloe and Tara—'

Daryl moves so fast that I don't even have time to think about stopping him. Neither does Freeman. The dog is just a blur of white flying straight at him, and with one snarling movement he rips the man's throat out, spraying both their faces with blood. Freeman's eyes bulge, his face clouds over in disbelief, then he gurgles up a flood of dark red and collapses to the ground, twitching. Daryl stands over him, panting, and spits out bloody flesh. 'Daryl!' I yell. 'No! No!'

'What? What's—'

'Kloe and Tara!' I drop to my knees next to Freeman and roll him over. 'He said someone's going to kill them! If he doesn't get out of here . . .'

'Oh God . . . Stanly, I . . .'

'Shh. Be quiet, please.' I stare at Freeman. The life is leaving him, I can see it, I can feel it, and I can't let it. I can't let him die. I can't lose Kloe and Tara too, I'm weak and not a hero and I need them to be alive even if I can never see them again, no matter the cost. I concentrate on the blood, the torn flesh, the ruptured veins. I let my brain find its way in, see the mechanisms, how everything should work, how it's been damaged, how it can work again . . . *got to do it, do it fast, do it now, no time, NO TIME . . .*

And, hating myself, I bring him back to life. Again. He sits up, gasping, clutching his repaired throat, looking wildly from me to Daryl. 'He . . . I . . .'

'Shut up,' I say. 'Shut your mouth. And *listen*. I'm going to stay here. I'm going to give myself to the shimmers. And you're going back to London.'

'I—'

'I said *shut up*,' I say. 'This is the deal. Tara and Kloe will not be harmed. My friends will not be harmed. If they are, I will know. I knew to find Kloe in the park that time, and I knew to go to that alleyway to meet Smiley Joe, to save Tara. I knew, without knowing. And if you hurt the people I love, I'll know that too. Even in here, asleep, I will *know*. And I will tear my way back through, and I will rain a fresh apocalypse down on you. Whatever new world you think you're going to build, I will burn it down. It will *burn*. And so will you. Do you understand?'

He nods.

'Now get out,' I say. 'Get the hell out and don't say *one word* to me.'

Freeman nods again, scrambles to his feet and leaves the cave. Daryl watches him go, looking away from me, staring. 'Daryl,' I say. He doesn't answer. 'Daryl, look at me.'

He turns slowly. 'It's OK,' I say.

The dog shakes his head. 'No it's not,' he says, his voice catching in his throat. 'No it's not! I should have . . . I came to save you.'

'You did,' I say. 'You saved me from . . . having to do this alone. You're with me. That's the best thing.'

'It's not fair, though.' He's crying. 'It's not *fair*!'

I shrug. 'Did you expect it to be?'

He can't answer that. He just shakes his head. 'It's not fair.' I kneel down and he comes to me and I hug his bloodstained white body to mine.

'Thank you,' I say. 'You're my best friend.'

'I never had a better one,' he whispers.

'Please,' I say. 'I need to get this done, so listen. I have things . . . things you need to do. Freeman might leave you guys alone. After all, none of us has any proof of what he's done. So he might not see us as that much of a threat. But you need to keep an eye on him. I don't know what kind of world he's planning on creating . . . you need to watch. You need to look after everybody.'

'I will.'

'And Kloe,' I say. 'You need to find her, and Tara.' I think the forest into his brain. 'Tell Kloe that I love her, and that I'm so, so sorry. Sorry for not keeping my promise. Explain why. Help her understand.'

'I will.'

'Tell them all.' My parents' faces appear in my mind, first like a mirage and then clear as day, Mum and Dad leading me around the garden, little chubby child me, barely stable on brand new legs.

'I will,' Daryl says, again. 'I promise.'

The embrace is broken. I stand up, look at the cave wall and think *show me the real world*, and the rock seems to melt, forming an indistinct impression of the Kulich gallery beyond. 'Go,' I say. 'Before there's no way back. Go *now*.'

Daryl runs to the window I've created. He looks back briefly and smiles through tears, human tears from canine eyes. 'Here's looking at you, kid.'

I actually manage a laugh, and then he is gone, and so is the exit. I turn back to the vast lake, silent but deafening with thought, and I walk towards it, into it, letting the water that isn't water cover me over, trying not to think about how goddamn weird this is. *It's just water. Just pretend it's water.* I can, almost, and it's so cool, so comfortable, so refreshing. Such relief.

*Please give me good dreams.*

Their reply is like whale song and xylophones. No words, just an alien melody and a meaning behind it that I feel in a place beyond my consciousness, beyond my heart. It fills me to the brim with hope and joy and I close my eyes. Journey's end. I've run the miles, and now I can sleep.

I think *thank you.*

Smile.

Float away . . .

???????????????????????????????????????????????????

The sun shines on, bright as new life, bright as love. I smile, marvelling at the pathetic fallacy, the poetry that drips from the sky as I stand on the bank of the lake, my bare feet enveloped in cool damp grass. I watch little colourful birds hop and skip across the surface, pecking at wily, unseen fish. I watch the sunlight create patterns in the water, a benevolent breeze massaging the thick green leaves in the trees. I feel an arm slip around my waist and don't look at her for a second because I want the moment when my eyes fall on her to be perfect, I want the anticipation to build. It doesn't last long. I can't help myself. I look into her eyes and they are sparkling and gorgeous, she stands there in a flowing white and red summer dress, her hair blowing out behind her like music, her lips rosy, smiling. She kisses me and it's like coming back to life, and I take her in my arms and let her magic warm me up. *I love you*, I think.

*I love you*, she replies.

And another arm around my waist, my little girl, giggling and delighted, her blonde hair in curls. I scoop her up and hold her even though she's heavy, and she kisses me on the cheek and beams. 'Love you, Daddy.'

'Love you too, little 'un,' I grin.

'Can we fly today?'

'I expect that can be arranged.'

'You said you'd teach me too,' says Kloe.

'Seems as good a time as any.' I put Tara down and grab her and Kloe's hands tight. 'Just follow my lead. It's easy.'

'Show-off,' says Kloe, a teasing smile playing across her lips.

'He is *such* a show-off,' says Tara.

'I honestly don't know why we put up with it.'

'Me neither.'

'If you guys are quite finished?' I say.

They giggle and nod.

'Good,' I say, unable to resist a laugh of my own. 'Then let's go.'

And we take off together and fly towards infinity, and the sun shines on, and everything is as it should be.

THE END